Praise for the
of Susan Meissner

A Fall of Marigolds

"Hits all of the right emotional notes." —*Booklist*

"Like the golden threads of a scarf sprinkled with marigolds, Susan Meissner weaves two unspeakable New York tragedies—the Triangle Shirtwaist Fire and 9/11—into a shimmering novel of love and acceptance. Meissner's heroines, Clara and Taryn, live a century apart, but their stories are connected not just by a bright scrap of fabric but by love lost. A compelling novel, *A Fall of Marigolds* turns fate into a triumph of spirit."
—Sandra Dallas, *New York Times* bestselling author of *Fallen Women*

"Meissner has crafted a thoughtful story about lost loves and times past, illustrating how quickly disaster can take away what we hold most dear, and how ultimately we must move forward with hope in our hearts."
—Margaret Dilloway, bestselling author of
The Care and Handling of Roses with Thorns

"A transportive, heartwarming, and fascinating novel that will reso-nate with readers in search of emotionally satisfying stories connect-ing past and present, and demonstrating the healing power of love."
—Erika Robuck, bestselling author of
Hemingway's Girl and *Fallen Beauty*

"Weaves a compelling tapestry of past and present, of love and loss and learning to love again, of two women connected through time in a rich and unique way."
—Lisa Wingate, bestselling author of *Wildwood Creek* and *Tending Roses*

"Susan Meissner knits the past and the present with the seamless skill of a master storyteller. A beautifully written, moving novel that had me gripped from the first page."
—Kate Kerrigan, *New York Times* bestselling author of *Land of Dreams*

"Deftly weaves a story of love and loss . . . an inspiring story of hope and the belief that with tomorrow comes a new day full of promise." —Lorie Conway, author/producer of *Forgotten Ellis Island*

continued . . .

"My eyes welled up more than once! And I thought it especially fitting that, having already shown us the shape of mercy in a previous novel, Susan Meissner is now showing us the many shapes of love. *A Sound Among the Trees* is a hauntingly lyrical book that will make you believe a house can indeed have a memory . . . and maybe a heart. A beautiful story of love, loss, and sacrifice, and of the bonds that connect us through time."

—*New York Times* bestselling author Susanna Kearsley

"Meissner delivers a delightful page-turner that will surely enthrall readers from beginning to end. The antebellum details, lively characters, and overlapping dramas particularly will excite history buffs and romance fans." —*Publishers Weekly*

Lady in Waiting

"Both the history and the modern tale are enticing, with Meissner doing a masterful job blending the two." —*Publishers Weekly*

"Meissner has an ability to mesh a present-day story with a parallel one in the past, creating a fascinating look at two lives where each tale is enhanced by the other. Intricately detailed characters make for a truly delightful novel." —*Romantic Times*

The Shape of Mercy

"Meissner's prose is exquisite, and she is a stunning storyteller. This is a novel to be shared with friends." —*Publishers Weekly*

"Meissner has a gift for intriguing, meaningful stories, and this novel is no exception. Lauren's present-day life is mirrored in elderly Abigail's and again in the diary of Mercy Hayworth, who lived in the seventeenth century. . . . The insights into perception and prejudice are stunning." —*Romantic Times*

OTHER NOVELS BY SUSAN MEISSNER

A Fall of Marigolds

The Girl in the Glass

A Sound Among the Trees

Lady in Waiting

White Picket Fences

The Shape of Mercy

SECRETS

of a

CHARMED LIFE

SUSAN MEISSNER

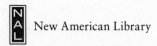

New American Library

New American Library
Published by the Penguin Group
Penguin Group (USA) LLC, 375 Hudson Street,
New York, New York 10014

USA | Canada | UK | Ireland | Australia | New Zealand | India | South Africa | China
penguin.com
A Penguin Random House Company

First published by New American Library,
a division of Penguin Group (USA) LLC

First Printing, February 2015

 REGISTERED TRADEMARK—MARCA REGISTRADA

LIBRARY OF CONGRESS CATALOGING-IN-PUBLICATION DATA:

Meissner, Susan, 1961–
Secrets of a charmed life / Susan Meissner.
pages; cm
ISBN 978-0-451-41992-7 (softcover)
1. Sisters—Fiction. 2. World War, 1939–1945—England—London—Fiction.
I. Title.
PS3613.E435S435 2015
813'.6—dc23   2014027190

Printed in the United States of America
10   9

Set in Sabon
Designed by Spring Hoteling

For my Umbrella Girls—
Stephanie, Bree, and Chelsey

"Our life is what our thoughts make it."
—Marcus Aurelius, *Meditations*

SECRETS
of a
CHARMED LIFE

Part One

One

KENDRA

THE English cottage, bramble hedged and golden stoned, looks as timeless as a fairy tale except for the bobbing Mylar balloons tied to the front gate. Ivy scampers child-like across the house's walls—all the way to the gabled windows on the second story—and then is tamed to civil edges around the paned windows. Easter-hued holly-hocks stand in stately rows beneath the sills. As I pull up onto the driveway, the crunching of tires on gravel sounds like applause, which is fitting since the woman I am to interview is celebrating her ninety-third birthday. I set the brake on the borrowed car and reach for my messen-ger bag on the seat next to me. I step out of the vehicle and into the postcard charm of April in the Cotswolds. I'm not expecting to be invited to stay for the day's fes-tivities but I hope I will be just the same. I've come to adore the way the British celebrate a happy occasion in the afternoon.

Isabel MacFarland is a stranger to me, though I've been told that I've surely walked past her watercolors for sale in Oxford gift shops. I've yet to even hear her voice. She agreed by way of one of my professors to let me interview her about her experience as a survivor of the London Blitz, and only because the first person I had arranged to speak with had died in her sleep at an assisted-living facility in Banbury. Today happened to be the time that worked best for both of us while still allowing me to meet my deadline, take my finals, grudgingly say good-bye to Oxford and my studies abroad, and return to California.

I get out of the car and silently congratulate myself for arriving safely in the village of Stow-on-the-Wold and without having ruined anyone else's day in the process. In the four months I've been a visiting student at Oxford's Keble College, I've borrowed this car three times before today: once to see whether I should dare try it a second time, then again to prepare myself for the third time, and the most recent to drive my parents and sister out to Warwick Castle and Stratford-upon-Avon when they came to visit me at midterm. Statistically, I'm not owed any kudos for having gotten here in one piece. Apparently a Yank's first few experiences driving on the wrong side of the road are actually her safest. It's after a dozen trips behind the wheel that she becomes dangerous. Lets down her guard. Forgets where she is. That's when she'll make a fatal turn into oncoming traffic; when her senses have been dulled by familiarity.

Today's outing, the fourth time I've driven a car in England, is well below the multiple experience mark, and I will likely not drive again before the term ends. I wouldn't necessarily have needed to drive today, as there's a train station in nearby Moreton-in-Marsh, but there's also a five-mile walk on narrow country roads between the two villages, with an occasional bus making the rounds. Penelope, my dorm mate and a British national from Manchester, who has had the guts to repeatedly loan me her car, insisted I take it.

I stop for a moment outside the car and breathe the scents of grass and sky and dew—refreshing after weeks of city exhaust. All around me are velvety fields quilted by clumps of trees and scattered dwellings oozing storybook quaintness. Some of the nearby roofs are thatched, some not, but all bear exterior walls of golden-hued stone that look as though they would taste like butterscotch if you licked them. A figure appears at an arched front door that is festooned with climbing roses. The woman is wiping her hands on a towel and smiling at me. Her graying hair is stylishly cut with one side longer than the other. I am guessing she is Isabel MacFarland's live-in caretaker and housekeeper, Beryl Avery, and the woman who gave me directions.

"You found us!" she calls out to me.

I shut the door on Penelope's aging Austin-Morris. "Your directions were perfect. Okay if I park here?"

"Yes, that's fine. Come on in."

The balloons are pogo-sticking this way and that as I open the gate. One of the balloons attempts to attach itself to the strap of my bag as I pass. I gently nudge it away.

Mrs. Avery holds the front door open for me—it is painted an enameled cherry red. "I'm so glad you made it. Beryl Avery. Please call me Beryl." She thrusts her free hand toward me as I step inside.

"Kendra Van Zant. Thanks so much for letting me

come, especially when you have so much going on later today. I can't tell you how grateful I am."

Beryl shuts the door behind us. I am guessing she is in her late sixties. She smells like cake and cream and other sweet things. A smudge of flour dusts one side of her jawbone.

"It's no trouble," she says brightly. "I'm happy you're here. Auntie doesn't talk much about her experience during the war and we all wish she would, you know. When anyone else asks about it, she shoos the question away as if no one could possibly be interested in anything that happened so long ago. But of course we are interested. Terribly so, considering what happened to her. It's such a nice surprise she said yes to you."

I don't know what to say to this because it's a surprise to me, too, that the old woman said yes. Professor Briswell told me Mrs. MacFarland, a noted local artist and friend of his late mother, is known to have been bombed out of her home during the Blitz, but also that she never speaks about it.

"I would ask her why she said yes if I weren't afraid I'd jinx it for you and she'd change her mind," Beryl continues.

I'm about to ask why Mrs. MacFarland has been so reluctant to talk about the war so that I will know which questions to avoid, but Beryl fills the tiny space of silence before I can.

"I must tell you, though, that she seems a little lost in thought today. You might need to give her some extra time to answer your questions. It's probably all the hullabaloo with the party and all."

"Is she still okay that I am coming today?"

Beryl cocks her head. "I think so. Hard to say if

'okay' is the right word. Auntie isn't one to be overly demonstrative. I'd say she's content regarding your being here. I think she's more worried about the party this afternoon. She didn't want a fuss and I'm afraid that's exactly what she's getting. No one wanted to listen to me when I said she didn't want a big to-do."

We move out of the narrow entryway into a sitting room that looks as cozy and inviting as one of Tolkien's hobbit holes. A fat, fern-green couch and its matching love seat are situated in the middle of the room, while glass-topped tables laden with books and jonquils in vases separate them. Persian rugs cover the wood floor. A tea cart sits in one corner, a curio cabinet in another, and an L-shaped bookshelf in a third. Enchanting watercolors of young girls holding polka-dot umbrellas line the walls.

"Are the paintings Mrs. MacFarland's?" I ask.

"They are," Beryl replies. "They're all over the house. She's quite an accomplished artist, but you probably already know that. The Umbrella Girls are her trademark. Her arthritis is too bad now for painting. She had to stop a while back." Beryl sighs. "*That* was a hard day. She's had too many hard days, if you ask me. Far too many." The woman shakes her head slightly as if to dislodge the weight of the anguish she has observed. "Why don't you have a seat here on the sofa and I'll go fetch her?"

Beryl leaves the room and I settle onto the love seat, moving a few of the tightly stuffed throw pillows from behind my back. I can hear voices from other areas of the house now, and laughter in the back garden. A child squeals. Another one yells that it's his turn to have a go. A more calming adult voice, grandmotherly in tone, instructs someone named Timmy to share the glider with another someone named Garth or he'll be sent inside.

I pull my voice recorder from my bag and set it on the table in front of me, hoping Isabel won't mind if I record our conversation. I look over the questions on my notepad and decide I will let her answers guide me. I don't want to sabotage the interview by asking too much too soon. As I pull out a mechanical pencil, I hear the sound of shuffling feet.

"I'm fine, Beryl," a voice says, low toned and honeyed with age. "The tea is ready?"

"Oh yes. The tray's all set," Beryl says from the hallway, but out of my view.

"Lovely. You can bring it straight in."

"And your medicine?"

"Just the tea, thank you."

"But you didn't take it yesterday, either."

"Now, don't fuss, Beryl."

Isabel MacFarland steps into the room. She is a wisp of tissue-thin skin, weightless white hair, and fragile-looking bones. She is impeccably dressed, however, in a lavender skirt that reaches to her knees and a creamy white blouse with satin-covered buttons. Black ballet flats embrace her slender feet. A gold necklace rings her neck. Her nails are polished a shimmery pale pink and her cottony hair is swept up in the back with a comb of mother-of-pearl. She carries a fabric-wrapped rectangle, book shaped and tied with a ribbon.

I rise from my seat to see if I might need to assist her.

"Miss Van Zant. How very nice to meet you." Her English accent is not like Beryl's. There is something about it that seems stretched.

"Can I help you?" I take a few steps forward.

"No. Thank you, though. Please sit."

I return to the love seat and she lowers herself slowly

to the sofa across from me. "Thank you so much for agreeing to see me," I say. "And on your birthday, too."

She waves away my gratitude. "It's just another day."

Beryl appears at the doorway with a tea tray. "Ninety-three is not just another day, Auntie."

Isabel MacFarland smiles as if she has just thought of something funny. Beryl sets the tray down and hands Mrs. MacFarland her cup, already creamed and sugared. Then she hands a cup to me and I add a teaspoon of sugar to it. The stirring of a silver spoon in an English china teacup is one of the sounds I will miss most when I head back to the United States.

"Thank you, Beryl," Mrs. MacFarland says. "You can just leave the tray. And can you be a dear and close the door so that we aren't in anyone's way?"

Beryl glances from me to Mrs. MacFarland with an unmistakably disappointed expression on her face. "Of course," she says with feigned brightness. She heads for the door and looks back at us with a polite smile that surely takes effort. She shuts the door softly behind her.

"I think she was hoping she could stay," I venture.

"Beryl is a sweet companion and I could not live here on my own without her, but I'd rather have the freedom to say whatever I want, if that's all right with you."

I am not prepared for such candor. "Um. Of course."

"When you get to be my age, your physical frailties cause people to think other things about you are frail as well, including your ability to make your own decisions. It's my decision to meet with you today. And my decision to say what I will about what happened during the war. I don't need or want dear Beryl patting my hand or telling me I'm not properly addressing your questions. May I call you Kendra?"

"Yes. Yes, of course."

Mrs. MacFarland sips from her cup and then sits back against the couch. "And you will call me Isabel. So how are you enjoying your studies at Oxford, Kendra?"

Her interest in my life has an amazingly calming effect. "I will leave here kicking and screaming at the end of next month. I've loved every minute of it. There's so much history compacted into one place. It's intoxicating." I suppose I have spoken like a true history major.

"And is there no history where you are from?"

"There is. It's just different, I guess. Not quite so ancient. Where I'm from, the oldest building isn't even two hundred years old. It's just an ordinary house."

She smiles at me. "I've come to appreciate ordinary houses."

I redden just a bit. "That's not to say your house isn't charming, Mrs. MacFarland. Your home is beautiful. Has it been in your family a long time?"

"Just Isabel, please. And yes, you could say that it's been in my family for a very long time. You are a history major, then?"

I nod my head as I sip from my cup.

"And what is it about history that interests you?"

I've never understood why I am routinely asked why history interests me, as though the subject has no appeal to people who didn't major in it. All during my last year of high school when well-meaning adults and even other students asked what I would be majoring in and I answered them, the next question was invariably a request to explain the reason why. I still get asked three years later.

"How can a person not be interested in history?" I crack a smile so she won't take offense. But really, how can someone who survived the London Blitz not see the significance of an appreciation of history? The writer

Michael Crichton said, "If you don't know history, then you don't know anything. You are a leaf that doesn't know it is part of a tree."

Isabel finds my question back to her amusing. "Ah, but what is history? Is it a record of what happened or rather our interpretation of what happened?"

"I think it's both," I answer. "It has to be both. What good is remembering an event if you don't remember how it made you feel. How it impacted others. How it made them feel. You would learn nothing and neither would anyone else."

Isabel's mouth straightens into a thin, hard line and I am wondering whether I offended her and just ruined my last chance at an interview.

But then Isabel inhales deeply and I see that she is not angry with me. "You are absolutely right, my dear. Absolutely right." She takes another sip of tea and her mouth lingers on the rim of her cup. For a moment she seems to be very far away, lost in a memory—an old and aching place of remembrance. Then she returns the cup to its saucer and it makes a gentle scraping sound. "So, what will you do when you return to the States, Kendra?"

"Well, I've another year at USC and then I'm hoping to head straight to grad school," I answer quickly, eager to be done with pleasantries and get to the reason I am here. "I plan to get my doctorate in history and teach at the college level."

"A young woman with plans. And how old are you, dear?"

I can't help but bristle. The only time a person asks how old I am is when they think the answer is somehow relevant to him or her. It usually never is.

"You don't have to tell me, of course. I was just wondering," she adds.

"I'm twenty-one."

"It bothers you that I asked."

"Not really. It just surprises me when people ask. I don't know why it should matter."

"But that is precisely why it does bother you. I felt the same way once. People treat you differently when they think you are too young to know what you want."

The bristling gives way to a slow sense of kinship. "Yes, they do."

"I understand completely. You are the oldest in your family?"

"I have a sister who's four years younger."

"A sister. Just the one?"

I nod.

She seems to need a moment to process this. "I'd surmised you might be the oldest. We firstborns are driven, aren't we? We have to be. There's no one leaving bread crumbs for us on the trail ahead. We blaze our own trail. And the younger ones, they look to us. They watch us— they take their cues from us, even if we don't want them to." She drains her cup and sets it carefully on the tray.

I'm not sure what she is getting at. "I guess. Maybe. I'm not sure my sister would agree. She's got pretty strong opinions of her own. I think she'd say she's leaving her own bread crumbs."

Isabel laughs and it is light and airy. It's the kind of laugh that spills out when a memory is triggered; the kind of memory that perhaps was not funny in the slightest when it was being made.

"What is your sister's name?" she says as her laughter eases away.

"Chloe."

She closes her eyes as if tasting the word. "What a lovely name." Her eyes open. "Have you a photo?"

I pull my cell phone from my messenger bag and find a photo of Chloe and me taken in front of Christ Church on the last day she and my parents were here. My sister is a brunette like me, wears her hair shoulder length like I do, and has the same gray-blue eyes. But she puts ketchup on everything, plays lacrosse and the violin, and wants to be a civil engineer. We are close, Chloe and I, but none of those things interest me. Not even the ketchup.

I extend the phone and she studies Chloe's and my smiling faces.

"She favors you," Isabel says.

"We look like my dad, actually." I take the phone back and find a picture of my parents from the same day. My mom's red curls are dancing a ballet in the breeze and she is smiling so wide, her eyes have narrowed to slits. Dad, blue eyed and brown haired with a brushstroke of gray at the temples, has his arm around her. Their heads are nearly touching.

Isabel studies this picture as well, memorizing it. Then she hands the phone back. "You have a lovely family, Kendra. I hope you know how lucky you are."

I've never known quite what to say when someone says I have a lovely family. It's nothing I can take credit for, so saying thank you seems silly. But that's what I say as I smile and slip the phone back inside my bag.

"Now, then," Isabel says, and I sense she is at last shifting the focus from me. "Charles tells me this interview is more than just for an essay for a class."

It takes me a second to make the connection that Charles is Professor Briswell. "Yes. The seventieth anniversary of VE Day is next month. The professor for one of my other classes has made an arrangement with a London newspaper. The five best term papers will be published in the paper the week of May eighth."

I watch her face carefully to see whether this additional information is going to spell trouble for me.

"So what you write will be read widely?'

"Only if mine is one of those chosen. And I don't know that it will be. Is that okay with you if it is?"

"You will write to win one of those spots, yes? You'll be happy if yours is chosen."

"Well, yes."

"This other professor, he is friends with Charles? Can you count on him to judge your essay on the strength of your writing alone? Be a shame if he discounted yours because a fellow professor assisted in helping you secure an interview."

I am still not sure whether it is helping me or hindering me that this paper I am to write might be published in a London paper. "I don't know that they are friends. I suppose they are since they teach at the same college. I happened to mention to Professor Briswell that I was in a bind for another class. He was nice enough to want to help me."

Isabel leans back and I can see she is satisfied with my answer. "What did Charles tell you about me?" she says.

I'd done all the research on the effect of the Blitz on London's female population and had needed only the interview to write the paper and be done with it. When the woman I was to interview died, it was too late to change the subject matter without setting myself so far back that I would never finish the paper on time. I had mentioned as much to Professor Briswell, just in passing, and he had told me that an elderly friend in his family might be convinced to help me out. This person was one to decline interviews, though, even regarding her watercolors for which she was known throughout the southwest of England. He'd ask her anyway and tell her I was in a tight spot. But he said I should expect her to say no.

"He told me that you typically decline interviews," I say.

She smiles. "That's all?"

"He said you are known for your watercolors. I love your work, by the way."

"Ah, yes. My Umbrella Girls."

I turn my head in the direction of one of the more prominent paintings in the room: A young girl in a pink dress is walking through a field of glistening-wet daisies and holding the trademark red-and-white polka-dot umbrella. A brave sun is peeking through clouds that are plump with purpose. "Have you always painted girls with umbrellas?"

"No. Not always." Her answer is swift and without hesitation. But the way she elongates the last word tells me there is more behind the answer. She doesn't offer more even though I wait for it.

"Tell me, Kendra," Isabel says after a pause. "What is it about the Blitz that you would like to know? I should think there are dozens of books out there. What information do you lack that you cannot read in a book?"

I fumble for an answer. "Well, uh, aside from that I'm required to interview someone, I think . . . I think information is only half of any story about people. Personal experience is the other part. I can't ask a book what it was like to survive the bombs."

Isabel cocks her head to one side. "Is that what you want to ask me? What it was like to have my home bombed?"

It occurs to me that I posed a rather elementary

question with surely an equally elementary answer. I am suddenly superbly underconfident about all my questions. I glance at the notepad in my lap and every bulleted sentence looks superficial to me.

What was it like in the shelter night after night?
Were you afraid?
Did you lose someone you loved or cared about?
Did you wonder if it would ever end?

"Are you going to turn that thing on?"

I snap my head up. Isabel is pointing to my little voice recorder on the coffee table. "Do you mind?"

"You may as well, seeing as you brought it."

As I lean toward the table to press the RECORD button, the notepad falls off my lap and onto the thick Persian carpet at my feet.

As my fingers close around the tablet, I realize that there is really only one question to ask this woman who for seventy years has refused all interviews, and who told me not ten minutes ago when she told Beryl to shut the door that she would say only what she wanted to.

I place the pad on the seat cushion next to me. "What would you like to tell me about the war, Isabel?"

She smiles at me, pleased and perhaps impressed that I figured out so quickly that this is the one question she will answer.

She pauses for another moment and then says, "Well, first off, I'm not ninety-three. And my name's not Isabel."

$\mathscr{T}wo$

❧

EMMY

London, England
1940

THE wedding dress in the display window frothed like uncorked champagne, bubbling toward Emmy Downtree as she stood on the other side of the broken glass. Glittering shards lay sprinkled about the gown's ample skirt, sparkling as if they belonged there. Yellow ribbons streamed from behind the pouty-lipped mannequin, simulating a golden, unaware sun. At Emmy's feet, jagged splinters were strewn on the sidewalk at menacing angles. A hand-lettered Help Wanted sign, still partially taped to a fractured edge, pitched forward onto the frame, and fifteen-year-old Emmy knelt to pull it gingerly from the glassy ruin. She could hear the owner inside Primrose Bridal talking on the telephone to the police, demanding attention be paid her. Someone had crashed into her storefront during the night.

Julia, Emmy's seven-year-old sister, looked up at her. "Why don't the Germans like wedding dresses?"

Emmy didn't laugh at her sister's assumption that the Luftwaffe had blown the window to bits. For the past year they had lived with wailing air raid alarms, drills at school, and mandatory blackout curtains. Several uncomfortable nights had been spent with Mum huddled in the shelter nearest their flat with a dozen of their neighbors when a raid had seemed imminent. Both girls had carried a gas mask to school the past term. It was not so far off the mark that Julia saw the destroyed window and concluded that what they'd been told for a year could happen at any moment had at last happened.

Emmy rose to her feet with the little sign in her hands. "The Germans didn't do this, Jewels. None of the other windows on the street are broken. See? A car probably hopped the sidewalk. Hit the gas instead of the brake. Something like that."

Julia's gaze hung on the wreck of the window. "You sure?"

"Positive. We would have heard the sirens, right? It was quiet last night."

In fact, the sirens had not whined for more than a week, and the buzzing hum of the Luftwaffe over their heads hadn't been heard in twice that long. It was as quiet as it had been almost a year ago when the war was new and undefined.

"No one will want that dress now," Julia said, apparently satisfied that the Nazis didn't hate wedding dresses after all. "It's got glass in it."

"It can be shaken out. I bet the bride who buys it will never even know." Emmy flicked away a sliver of window glass from the Help Wanted sign and read the smaller words beneath it. *Hand-sewing and alterations.*

Eight to ten hours a week. Inquire within. She hadn't seen the placard before and wondered how long it had been taped to the window. Surely it had only been within the last few days. Emmy was familiar enough with the window at Primrose to know the sign was new.

"I wouldn't wear that dress. I like your brides better anyway. Yours are prettier."

Emmy laughed easily. "Think so?" She looked past the ruined display to the woman inside who was becoming more adamant that a policeman come that very moment.

"No, I haven't been burglarized." The woman's voice easily reached the two girls on the sidewalk. "That's not the point! Someone has run into my window and smashed it."

"This one's too poufy," Julia continued. "Yours are much nicer."

"Mine are just drawings, Jewels. Hard to know what they'd look like if they were real." Emmy looked to the chemist's across the narrow street and saw Mum through the window at the register. She'd be coming out soon. Emmy replaced the placard, but lowered it to the display window's floor facedown. She would come back later—when the owner wasn't so distracted—and with her best bridal gown sketches in hand, just in case she needed extra proof that she was worth considering.

"Yours are still prettier," Julia said.

Their mother stepped out onto the sidewalk across from them. Annie Downtree walked between slow-moving cars toward her daughters. A man in a shiny blue Citroën tipped his hat as he stopped for her. Emmy watched as the driver's eyes traveled past Mum's honey brown curls, her slim waist, to her long legs and slender ankles. With only sixteen years separating her mother and Emmy, they had lately been taken for sisters. Emmy had been annoyed at first, but realized quickly that such a mistake meant she came across as the adult she was so ready to be. The sooner she was independent of Mum, the sooner Emmy could chase her own dreams. Mum behaved as a sister toward Emmy most of the time anyway, confiding secrets one moment and withholding them the next, reading magazines and smoking cigarettes while Emmy made dinner, coming home late at night when the mood struck her, asking Emmy for advice when it came to dealing with Neville, Annie's on-and-off-again lover and Julia's father. Mum's intermittent displays of maternal competence were largely spent on Julia, who had never been mistaken for Mum's sister.

"Let's go, then," Mum said when she reached them. She slipped a little white parcel that she had picked up for her employer into her handbag.

"Look what happened to the bridal shop, Mum," Julia said urgently.

Their mother cast a disinterested gaze toward the ruined window. "Well, that's too bad. But no one's getting married these days, anyway. Come on. I still need to go to the butcher before work. Mrs. Billingsley demands a ham."

"That's not true," Emmy said.

Mum, already several steps ahead, turned halfway around. "Yes, it is true. I told you yesterday that I had to work today."

"I mean it's not true that no one's getting married. If that were true, this shop wouldn't still be open." And the owner wouldn't be hiring.

"For the love of God, Em. There's a bloody war on, in case you've forgotten." She swung back around to resume her hurried pace.

"But the Germans didn't break this window!" Julia chirped.

Mum turned in midstride, her frown deepening. "What are you filling her head with, Emmy?"

"I'm not filling her head with anything. She asked if the Germans bombed this place and I told her they hadn't."

Mum sighed but kept walking.

"We like looking at the wedding dresses," Julia said. "We don't want to go to the butcher."

"Yes, well, I like looking at the crown jewels," Mum called out over her shoulder.

Emmy pulled her gaze away from the remains of the window, the yards of organza, and the placard lying on its face.

Julia slipped her hand into Emmy's as they stepped away from the shop, their shoes crunching on silvery slivers. "I don't like the butcher. His store smells like dead things. I don't like it."

"We can wait outside."

The girls had taken only a dozen steps when Emmy heard the swish of a broom and the tinkling of glass against the edge of a dustpan. And then a voice cried out, followed by a murmured curse. Emmy turned to see a broom hit the pavement. The owner of the shop held one hand in the other and her face was wrenched more in annoyance than in pain. The broom and dustpan lay at her feet.

"Catch up with Mum." Emmy turned from Julia and retraced the few steps to where the owner stood. A crimson line crisscrossed her palm where a piece of glass had cut her.

"Are you all right, ma'am?" Emmy asked.

"Yes, yes," the owner mumbled as she yanked a handkerchief from a dress pocket and shook out the folds. She pressed the cloth to the wound. Emmy bent to retrieve the broom and dustpan.

"Careful there! No sense in both of us slicing our hands to ribbons," the woman said.

"Would you like some help with this? I can sweep this up while you take care of your hand."

The woman peered at Emmy, as if unprepared for such spontaneous kindness from a stranger. Then her eyes widened in recognition.

"I know you. I've seen you looking in my window, haven't I? Many times."

Heat rose to Emmy's cheeks. "Yes, ma'am. I like . . . I like your gowns. I hope to have a bridal shop of my own someday."

The woman smiled as she wound the handkerchief around the cut and a scarlet thread of blood began to seep through. "Well, I surely hope for your sake happier times are in your future." She nodded toward the broken display window. "As you can see, it isn't always a charmed life, running a business on your own. Especially with a war going on. If you'll excuse me, I need to find some gauze. I'll get to that mess later. But thanks." She started to head back into her shop.

"I see that you're looking to hire someone," Emmy blurted.

The woman turned, her head cocked in negligible interest. "I am."

Emmy swallowed back her nervousness. "May I come back later today and speak with you about the position?"

The woman hesitated. "How old are you?"

"Nearly sixteen." The little lie flew out of Emmy's mouth before she could stop it. Her birthday was nearly a year away. But a fifteen-year-old was still a child. A fifteen-year-old could still be evacuated.

"Have you any experience?"

Another swallow. "I've some."

Pressing the handkerchief tighter to her hand, the shop owner nodded once. "Come back at closing time and we'll talk. Six. I'll need references."

"Oh. Um, okay. Six, then. Right," Emmy stammered, her mind already reeling with the prospect of convincing this woman that her sketches of wedding gowns would have to serve as references.

"My name's Mrs. Crofton and I don't like it when people are late. Just leave the broom and dustpan there."

"I'm Em-Emmeline Downtree. I will be here at six. Thank you, Mrs. Crofton."

The owner stepped into the shop with a wordless tip of her head. Emmy set the broom and dustpan against the glassless window frame and walked away, amazed at the turn of luck that had come her way. For the better part of a year she'd been peering into Primrose Bridal's windows on market day, captivated by the gowns that hung fairylike from mannequins and padded hangers. This newfound affinity had eclipsed her fondness for doodling dress designs during math class and making countless paper dolls for Julia. Mum was one to walk right past Primrose Bridal; not so much in a hurry as in indifference. Mum had never married, and if perhaps someday she would marry, Emmy doubted she would wear white. For a half second Emmy wanted to thank the scoundrel who had run into Mrs. Crofton's window and set in motion the events that had resulted in her being granted an interview.

She rounded the street corner and nearly ran into Julia.

"Why aren't you with Mum?" Emmy gasped.

Julia frowned at her. "I don't like the butcher's. I don't like the way his store smells."

Emmy grabbed her sister's hand and pulled her down the sidewalk. "You should have done what I said."

"Why were you talking to that lady?"

"Never mind that now."

"But I saw you talking to her."

"I was just offering to help her sweep up the glass."

"She cut her hand."

"Yes."

Emmy quickened their pace. Mum would surely give them grief about taking so long. But she likely wouldn't ask why.

Mum wasn't interested in why Emmy liked gazing into bridal shop windows.

Three

⸙

EMMY stood before the mirror in the upstairs bedroom she shared with Julia, analyzing the dress she'd plucked from Mum's wardrobe. She had pressed away the wrinkles, but there had been no way to iron away the trailing scent of Mum's perfume—a flowery, musty vapor that smelled like an invitation to other things. The midnight blue frock with its ivory collar and sleeve cuffs wasn't Emmy's favorite dress of her mother's, but it was more fashionable than anything hanging among her own clothes, and she was unashamedly hoping there was luck still lingering in its threads. Mum had worn the dress two years ago when she interviewed to be a kitchen maid for the millionaire widow Mrs. Billingsley and had come home with the job. Emmy might not have remembered that detail about the dress except that Nana was still alive then and had been visiting.

It had been a roasting-hot day in July, and the war then was nothing more than a nasty disagreement between a couple of countries on the Continent. Mum's mother, visiting from Devonshire, was teaching Emmy to embroider. The girls saw their grandmother only when she made the trip to visit, which wasn't often. Emmy liked it when Nana came, even though Nana and Mum fought about nearly everything. She was always sad when Nana left except for the fact that the arguing stopped. On that particular afternoon, Mum had emerged from her bedroom wearing the midnight blue dress, and she posed like a model in front of the girls and her mother. Julia laughed and Mum laughed with her. Nana shook her head and told Mum it wasn't wise to get her hopes too high. Mum had worked in a hotel laundry room up to that point. To Emmy's knowledge, she had never been a kitchen maid before. And she had certainly never worked for someone with money.

"And why shouldn't I?" Mum opened a compact mirror and ran a tube of lipstick across her lips. She sounded as confident as Emmy could ever remember.

"An upstanding heiress is a different employer than a busy hotel."

Mum snapped the mirror shut. "And what is that supposed to mean?"

"You're an unmarried mother," Nana murmured, as though the walls of the kitchen might hear the scandalous truth and broadcast the news to the whole of London. "It matters. If this Mrs. Billingsley checks your references, she is sure to find out your daughters were fathered by two different men, neither of whom you were married to."

Mum had narrowed her eyes and grinned at Emmy

conspiratorially—the way an older sister might. She thanked Nana for such loving and motherly advice, and slammed the door as she left.

Nana had asked Emmy where her mother had gotten the dress.

Emmy hadn't known. Sometimes new clothes just appeared in Mum's wardrobe.

"Don't you wonder where she gets them?" Nana asked.

"She says the people she works with give them to her when they tire of them," Emmy answered.

"Sure they do," Nana muttered, and then she proceeded to show Emmy how to sew a perfect satin stitch.

An hour later, while Emmy worked on a dresser scarf and Nana showed Julia her wooden box full of colorful skeins of embroidery floss, Mum returned exuberant, and with a fancy black uniform over her arm.

Nana went pale. "They hired you?"

Emmy was astonished at the fear in her grandmother's voice.

"Don't act so surprised," Mum said. "I bloody well know how to boil water."

"I'm sure there are a lot of things you know how to do," Nana said, softly. It was almost a whisper, but not quite.

Mum turned from laying the uniform over the back of a kitchen chair. "What did you say?"

"Nothing."

Mum calmly walked to the front door and opened it wide. "I want you out."

Emmy had looked from one woman to the other; surely she had missed something.

Nana's lips flattened to a thin line. She slapped the wooden box of floss shut and slid it toward Emmy. "You work on those stitches, Emmeline," she had said. "It will give you something constructive to do while your mother is out earning her keep."

Nana kissed Julia good-bye and left. It was the last time Emmy saw her. Four months later she died of a massive heart attack. A telegram came to the flat from Mum's uncle Stuart, Nana's older brother and a man Emmy had never met, bearing the news of her passing. Mum read the telegram, lowered the piece of paper to the kitchen table, and then went into her room. Emmy didn't see her for hours. When she emerged, Emmy was full of questions. Julia, at five, had only one. Where was Nana now? But Mum didn't answer any of Emmy's questions. And to Julia, she said Nana was in heaven where everything was perfect, so she ought to feel right at home. Emmy didn't understand what her grand-mother and Mum had fought about that last day. As far as she could tell, Mum had been hired to be a kitchen maid, and that was exactly what she became. Nana made it seem as though Mum was doing something bad in exchange for her new job but Mrs. Billingsley wasn't running a brothel; she was a respected widow. And there were no men in Annie Downtree's life; not since Julia's father had walked out on her a year before.

Not long after Nana died, Emmy was at the kitchen table embroidering asters onto a pillowcase. Mum, on her way out the door to go to work, had stopped to stare at the colorful collection of flosses in the box and then whacked the lid shut. Emmy kept the box in her and Ju-lia's room after that.

Julia now appeared in the doorway as Emmy studied her reflection in the mirror. "I want to come to the bridal shop with you."

Emmy reached for her hairbrush on the dresser. "I need you to stay here."

"I don't want to."

"I'll be back soon, Jewels. I promise," Emmy said, running the brush through her hair with quick strokes.

"Take me with you."

Emmy replaced the brush, and then knelt by her sister and took her hands. "I'll only be gone for a little bit. I'll be back before you know it."

"But it will be dark soon."

"And I will be back before dark."

Julia's fear-filled eyes glistened with stubborn tears. Nights were the hardest. The sirens, when they whined, nearly only whined at night. They sounded like the agonized wail of the desolate.

"Be a love and get Nana's box of embroidery floss," Emmy said.

"Why?"

"I'll show you."

Julia walked to Emmy's bed, dropped to her knees, and thrust her hand under the bed skirt. She withdrew the wooden box and brought it back.

"Can you take all the threads out for me? Just dump them on my bed."

While Julia obeyed, Emmy reached for the satchel that she used for school, and then walked over to the bed and sat down next to her sister. In between them lay the pile of skeins, a tumble of color. From the satchel Emmy withdrew a folder marked *Geometry*, opened it, and pulled out a sheaf of sketches.

"What are you doing with your brides?" Julia asked.

"I might need to show them to the lady at the bridal shop."

"Why?"

"When I tell this lady that I've never worked in a dress shop, she might not want to hire me, but if I show her the brides, maybe she will."

Emmy reached for the empty box in Julia's lap. Its hinges and clasp, at one time golden-hued, had aged to a mossy brown. Etchings of flowering vines scrolled the front and sides, as did scuffs and scratches from its earlier uses. Emmy thumbed through the sketches, pulled out her earliest attempts, and then tossed these on the bed. She opened the lid and placed the best ones—a dozen of them—inside the box.

"There. That's better than a geometry folder."

"What if she says no?"

"Then I will be no worse off than if I hadn't shown them to her, right?"

"What if she takes the brides from you?"

"She won't."

"But how do you know?"

"I don't think she's that kind of person. Besides, I won't let her. I won't let anyone take my drawings from me, okay?"

Julia nodded but a trace of doubt lingered on her face. It was as if she already knew good things had a way of being taken from someone—especially in a time of war.

"What about those?" Julia pointed to the rejects on the bed.

"How about while I am gone, you give those brides some bouquets to carry? You can use my colored pencils and put flowers in their hair and bouquets in their hands. Yes?"

Julia seemed pleased with this assignment. "What if

I want to give them something else to carry? Does it have to be flowers?"

Emmy kissed the top of her sister's fair head. "It can be whatever you want. Give them kangaroos to hold if that suits you."

Julia laughed and Emmy pushed herself off the bed. "Do I look all right?"

"You look like Mum."

Emmy nodded. Good enough. "I'll be right back. Keep the door locked. Don't answer the bell. Just work on those brides."

She tucked the box under her arm and headed for the front door, her feet lifting slightly out of Mum's too-big shoes with every step.

Four

⚮

THE broken glass had been swept away and several long sections of wood had been nailed to the window frame at Primrose Bridal. Emmy stepped inside the shop and the tinkling of two silver bells attached to the handle announced her arrival. Mrs. Crofton looked up from a white French provincial writing desk situated along the left wall. Two Queen Anne chairs upholstered in cobalt blue velvet sat opposite her. Emmy imagined one was for the bride, and the other for the bride's mother or sister or maid of honor. Mrs. Crofton had probably consulted with a thousand brides from behind the desk.

"Flip the Closed sign, will you?" she said. "And set the latch."

Emmy turned back to the door and did what Mrs. Crofton asked, using the few seconds to still the niggling nervousness that had suddenly bloomed inside her chest.

"Please have a seat, Miss—I'm sorry I've forgotten your name," Mrs. Crofton said as Emmy completed the task. "Too maddening of a day."

"Emmeline. Emmeline Downtree." Emmy closed the distance between them and sat down on one of the chairs.

Mrs. Crofton finished making notations in a leather-covered ledger and closed it gently with a bandaged hand. "Eloise Crofton. If it's not a drunkard crashing his car into my window, it's daft suppliers who think just because there is a war, women aren't getting married."

Emmy had said as much to Mum earlier that day and nodded.

Mrs. Crofton set her pen down. "War makes brides as easily as it makes widows, Miss Downtree. And do you know why?"

"Because people still fall in love?" Emmy said hopefully.

"Because people need to believe love is stronger than war. A soldier marries before he marches off so that the ring on his finger will remind him who he is when he's crouched in a trench with his weapon raised to kill. You don't want to forget who you are then." She opened a drawer and slipped the ledger inside it. "Now, then. Tell me how long you've been admiring my shop?"

"I guess as long as we've lived in Whitechapel. We moved here two summers ago when my mother got a new job."

The woman waited for more and Emmy knew in an instant she'd probably already said too much. To mention a mother's new job and say nothing of the father meant there was something amiss.

"Oh. I see. How very nice." Mrs. Crofton tipped her head and Emmy saw the unspoken question in her eyes.

"Yes, I've walked past your shop every Saturday morning since then. I love your gowns. They're just so beautiful. And . . . so full of promise."

Mrs. Crofton regarded the dresses hanging all around them on hangers and dress forms and lithe mannequins. "Yes. They are very pretty. The prettiest dress a girl will ever wear on a day like no other." She turned her focus back to Emmy. "And what is your experience?"

Emmy cleared her throat of the knob of anxiety bobbing there. "Well, my grandmother taught me all the stitches for hand-sewing. I know the satin, cross, whip, running, chain, blanket stitch—all of them, really."

Mrs. Crofton leaned forward and steepled one hand under her chin. "What I meant was, what kind of retail experience have you had?"

The nervous knob bubbled its way back and Emmy tamped it back down. "None. But I'd be happy to show you my stitches. Your advertisement says you need someone to do hand-sewing and alterations, not someone with retail experience."

Mrs. Crofton smiled. "Fair enough. Come with me."

The woman rose from her chair and Emmy followed her into a back room. A long table was set up in the middle and a gown was lying across it. A black and gold Singer sat in one corner. Bolts of tulle and lace crowded into one another. Baskets of white thread, cards of silvery hooks and eyes, and little glass bowls of pearl buttons and rhinestones sat on the top of a cabinet in the farthest corner.

"I'll give you twenty minutes to finish the blind hem on that wedding dress. If I like what you do, I'll hire you on a trial basis. If I don't, you have to take out all the stitches before you leave so that I can do it later. Deal?"

It took supreme effort not to hug Mrs. Crofton when Emmy told her yes.

"I'll come back in twenty minutes, then," Mrs. Crofton said.

Emmy sat down in front of the dress, a feather-soft chiffon, and placed her box of brides at her feet, a bit disappointed that she hadn't needed to show them to Mrs. Crofton. The hem was a quarter of the way completed, the tiny pricks of the needle nearly invisible. Emmy lifted the gown to her lap, prayed to God Almighty for divine favor, and took up where the stitching had stopped. She made her stitches as even as the ones before hers, and as weightless. She was finished in seventeen minutes.

Emmy found a hanger and was just placing the dress on a hook on the wall when Mrs. Crofton came back into the room with a blue-and-white teacup in her hand. The air immediately became fragrant with the aroma of Earl Grey.

"My, my. Done already?" She set the teacup down, lifted the skirt, and studied the hem. "You've a nice touch with a needle, Emmeline."

"Thank you."

"Did your grandmother happen to also teach you how to use a sewing machine?"

Emmy gazed at the Singer in the corner. "I didn't get to see her very often. She died a couple years ago."

"Ah." Mrs. Crofton released the skirt and studied the way it fell from the hanger. "Very nice. Quite nice, actually. Perhaps you might work out after all."

Emmy looked at Mrs. Crofton's face to make sure there was no joking sentiment behind the words. "Are you hiring me?"

"Let's say Tuesdays and Thursdays, two to six. A

Saturday or two a month, depending. Twenty shillings a week. At the end of the month, we'll see where we're at. It's an uncertain world right now."

"Thank you, Mrs. Crofton. You won't be sorry." Again Emmy's eyes were drawn to the Singer in the corner. "Might I be able . . . That is, perhaps you wouldn't mind if . . ." But she couldn't finish. Surely it was too soon to beg for favors.

Mrs. Crofton followed Emmy's gaze. "You want to learn how to use my machine?"

"If it's not too much to ask."

"I can teach you a few things if you like. I'm thinking you'd pick it up fast enough. It would actually be better for me if you knew how to use it."

The opportunity to learn to sew on a machine was more than Emmy had hoped for. She felt her mouth drop open in grateful wonder.

And then out of Emmy's mouth burst words she hadn't needed to say. They seemed to gush from the spring of elation that was bubbling inside her and there was no stopping them. "Mrs. Crofton, may I show you something?"

"Yes? What is it?"

Emmy reached for the box at her feet, undid the clasp, and handed the woman the sketches.

After paging through a couple of the drawings, Mrs. Crofton cocked her head, intrigue etched in her expression. "Where did these come from?"

"They—they came from me." Emmy was unsure whether Mrs. Crofton's wide-eyed gaze was one of delight or dismay.

"Are you telling me you drew these? You didn't copy them from a magazine?"

Emmy nodded.

Mrs. Crofton leafed through the sketches a second time. She stopped at the one Emmy liked best, a form-fitted gown that fell from a ruched bodice with a dropped waistline into a petaled skirt. "This one reminds me of a dress I had in the window this past spring."

"The one you had had a scooped neck and high waist. It was pretty but no one with long legs would have looked good in it." Emmy's heart skipped a beat. She had said too much.

Mrs. Crofton raised an eyebrow, but her eyes were smiling. "Is that so? And how did you come to that conclusion?"

"Because I look at how women wear dresses. I always have. Even when I was drawing paper dolls for my sister. All dresses start out the same. A bodice, sleeves, skirt, and waistline. But not everyone can wear the same dress. A wedding dress is still a dress."

Emmy felt she was rambling but Mrs. Crofton seemed to be fascinated.

"And you've never touched a sewing machine?"

"I can learn. I want to learn."

Mrs. Crofton looked down at the drawings in her hand. "It's no small feat to sew a gown that you have to make the pattern for. You'll have your work cut out for you, that's for sure, if you want to sew one of these. Is that what you're thinking?"

"I am. That is, if you think they're good enough?"

"I like this one. And this one." Mrs. Crofton held up two sketches, one of a billowy tea-length gown with an Empire waist and bell-shaped push-up sleeves; the other of a full-length draped confection with an open back and sleeves of illusion. "Where did you learn to sketch, if I may ask? Do you have an art teacher at school? Or maybe one of your parents taught you?"

A laugh crawled up Emmy's throat and she squashed it. "No. No art teacher."

"And your parents?"

She cleared her throat so the laugh wouldn't escape. "My mother doesn't . . . She doesn't draw."

"And your father? Does he?"

"I wouldn't know."

An awkward silence followed. It was a wordless tension Emmy was familiar with when someone asked her a question about her father and she had no answer. Since she had already fibbed about her age easily enough, what was another fabrication of the truth? And she wanted Mrs. Crofton to have no reason to regret hiring her. "He's dead."

"Oh. I'm so sorry to hear that."

"I don't even remember him. It happened a long time ago. I taught myself to sketch, Mrs. Crofton. I checked books out of the library and I practiced on any blank piece of paper I could find. And then we moved here and I saw the dresses in your shop and I knew I wanted to design my own wedding gowns. This is what I want to do with my life."

Mrs. Crofton paused for a moment before continuing. "I'm afraid I can't help you make any of the patterns you'll need. That's a different skill. You're going to need a dressmaker to help you with that."

Emmy didn't know any dressmakers and told the woman so.

"I know one. My cousin Graham. He might be persuaded to take you under his wing. He does that with young designers if he thinks they have potential. I can ask him, if you're interested."

It had been so long since someone other than Julia had taken an interest in anything important to Emmy that tears sprang to her eyes, stinging and sweet. Words failed her.

Mrs. Crofton smiled as if she knew Emmy was not used to favors. "Look. I know what it's like to have other people stand around staring at you when they could just as easily help you, Emmeline. Who knows how long any of us will be around to think about bigger endeavors than just our own insignificant lives? Don't thank me yet. I can teach you to use my sewing machine. And I will contact my cousin to see if he is interested in taking you on as an apprentice. But in the end, only time will tell if a future in bridal gowns awaits you."

"I don't know how to thank you."

"You can help someone else down the road, when the time comes."

Emmy fingered away wetness at her eyes. She knew she would remember that moment for the rest of her life, that moment when someone who barely knew her fulfilled every childhood wish she'd ever had to feel she mattered.

"I'm so sorry about your window." Emmy's voice sounded young in her ears.

The swift change in the focus of the conversation seemed to surprise Mrs. Crofton. "Oh! Well, glass can be replaced. Will be replaced. It could have been worse. It can always be worse."

Emmy thanked her again and Mrs. Crofton walked her to the door to let her out. The sky had turned purple and ash, and Emmy would be rushing to get back to the flat before the sun set completely. Mrs. Crofton's many kindnesses to her in the span it took for twilight to fall suddenly weighed on her like bricks.

"I'm not nearly sixteen, Mrs. Crofton," Emmy blurted

as Mrs. Crofton lifted the latch. "I just turned fifteen in April. I've eleven months until my next birthday. And I don't know who my father is. I don't even know if he's dead or alive."

The woman said nothing. For a second Emmy was sure her late honesty had done her no favors. Then Mrs. Crofton swung the door open. "Good thing I'm not hiring him, then. I'll see you on Tuesday, Emmeline."

Emmy returned home floating on air, barely aware that the inky shroud of London at night was enveloping her. She ran the last block in darkness.

When she opened the door to the flat, Emmy saw that Julia had fallen asleep at the kitchen table. Colored pencils lay strewn about. She peered over her little sister to see how Julia had occupied the hour Emmy had been gone.

Instead of bouquets, the brides Emmy had left in Julia's care now held enormous red polka-dot umbrellas.

Five

❦

AFTER securing the blackout curtains and then gently shaking Julia awake, Emmy made toast for them and shared her news. Julia seemed happy, but was clearly unsure what Emmy's new job meant for her: Emmy saw the uncertainty in her eyes. Emmy had always known that the age spread between them meant that she would be out on her own long before Julia would. It likely hadn't occurred to Julia until she was sitting there licking marmalade off her fingers that Emmy had plans for the sketches that had very little to do with her. But Julia could see it now. She and Emmy were to be parted and it was the brides that would take Emmy from her. Emmy didn't treasure for a moment the thought of leaving Julia when the time came. The sisters washed and dried the dishes in silence.

After Julia got ready for bed, Emmy read to her from

a volume of fairy tales that was Julia's favorite, and the girls waited for Mum to come home from work.

With no sign of their mother by ten o'clock, Emmy tucked Julia into bed. She held the drawings Emmy had given her like a storybook.

"Do you like their umbrellas?" Julia fanned the brides out on her blanketed lap.

"I like them very much."

"Polka-dot umbrellas are my favorite. I want a red polka-dot umbrella. With a curly black handle that looks like licorice."

"That sounds splendid."

Julia pointed to one of the brides. She had drawn cartoonlike features onto the blank face, including a toothy smile and curling eyelashes that extended past the bride's hairline. That particular drawing was Emmy's second attempt at anything bridal. The skirt resembled a lacy lampshade that someone had stepped on. Julia's embellishments made it look even more amateurish.

"If it rains on her wedding day, she's going to need an umbrella," Julia said.

"You're smart to think ahead like that."

"So where will I go when you are working at the bridal shop?"

This was a detail Emmy had not wanted to ponder, though it had crossed her mind several times since she'd returned to the flat. She reminded herself that Julia was her sister, not her daughter. This was Mum's complication to work out, not hers. Emmy had a pretty good idea it would not take much persuading for Thea from the flat next door to look after Julia for the few hours Mum and she would be gone every week. Thea, a quiet, unmarried recluse who spent her days taking care of her senile mother, doting on her cat, and reading books about the sea, adored Julia. Emmy would suggest it if Mum hadn't a better idea.

"Mum will make sure you are looked after, Jewels. That's what mums are for."

Julia looked at Emmy, an unspoken question in her eyes. Emmy didn't want to know what that question was, so she did not ask.

"Why aren't you coming to bed?" Julia asked a moment later.

"I want to wait up for Mum and tell her about my new job."

"But why do you need a job, Emmy? You're not a mum. Only mums need jobs."

Emmy took the drawings Julia held in her hands and set them on the little table in between the beds. "Mrs. Crofton is going to teach me how to sew, Jewels. And she knows somebody who might be able to help me take my drawings and make real dresses out of them. Real dresses. That's why. Say your prayers now." Emmy rose from the bed and turned out the light. Darkness swallowed the room.

"Don't close the door all the way," she said.

"I won't. Sweet dreams."

Emmy settled onto the sofa with a magazine and waited for Mum but she fell asleep. Hours later in the gray light of dawn, the lock turned and she startled awake. Emmy sat up quickly and Mum, equally startled, half fell against the door frame.

"Good Lord, Emmy," Mum said as she caught herself. "You scared me. What are you doing there on the sofa like that?"

Emmy smelled pipe tobacco on her, even from ten feet away.

"Where have you been?" Emmy said, knowing how ridiculous it sounded that she was asking that question instead of the other way around, as she had heard other mothers do.

Mum pushed the door shut and smoothed a curl that had worked free of her white maid's cap. "It got late last night and it was too dark to walk home. It wouldn't have been safe."

Mum strode into the room and then into the kitchen, clicking on the light above the table. She set her handbag down and pulled the hairpins from her cap. Emmy joined her. In addition to the stale aroma of tobacco, she now smelled men's cologne.

Not Neville's. Wherever she'd spent the night, it wasn't with Julia's father, whom they hadn't seen in months. Emmy was both relieved and disgusted. She didn't like Neville but at least she knew who he was.

"So you had to spend the night at Mrs. Billingsley's?" Emmy said, only minimally masking her sarcasm.

Her mother tossed her cap onto the table. "I told you. It was too dark to walk home." Mum turned to the sink, grabbed the teakettle, and began to fill it with water. That was her standard practice when she didn't want to be bothered by anyone or anything. She would turn her back on whatever the nuisance was and make tea.

Emmy crossed her arms in front of her chest. "So Mrs. Billingsley's taken up smoking, then? And wearing men's cologne? Must drive you all batty."

Mum switched off the tap and just stood with her back to her daughter, holding the kettle by its handle. A few seconds later she plunked the kettle down on top of the stove. She switched on the burner and then turned to Emmy. "Let's get one thing straight. I don't report to you. You're not in charge here. I am."

"So you don't deny it? You weren't at Mrs. Billings-ley's last night?" The volume of Emmy's voice doubled but she didn't care if she woke Julia.

"I don't have to explain anything to you." Mum swung around to the cupboard to gather the tin of tea and a cup. Emmy saw her slender build under her maid's uniform, the fullness of her bosom, the shapeliness of her legs and thighs, and the graceful curve of her neck. Emmy saw how pretty Mum was, but how broken. She was only thirty-one, with not a wrinkle or blemish or so much as a strand of gray hair. Emmy didn't know what her mum had wanted to be at this stage of her life, but it came to her with crashing clarity that surely she hadn't dreamed of becoming a rich woman's kitchen maid. Emmy was never more aware of how much her very existence had marooned Mum to this scrabbling life than at that moment, though it wasn't the first time she had contemplated how her birth changed the trajectory of Mum's life. On truly terrible days, like when Neville left for good, or when her mother ran into someone she knew who lived a carefree life of normalcy, Mum would stare at Emmy and she would feel the weight of those lost years. Nana had told Emmy when she was ten that it was not her fault she had been born. It was Mum who, at sixteen, let herself get carried away by smooth talk. That was as much as Emmy knew about the man who had fathered her. He was a smooth talker. Nana had known more than that, Emmy believed, although she had acted as if she didn't. Emmy's birth certificate read that her father was unknown.

"How can you not know who my father is?" Emmy had asked Mum once, when she was old enough to know how babies were made but too naïve to figure out "unknown" could also mean "unnamed."

Mum had said Emmy was to think of herself as someone who had only one parent. Just a mum. There was no one else. In more recent years, Mum had explained that there had been a party and she'd had too much to drink. A man she barely knew told her she was pretty on a night when she felt ugly. It was as simple as that. Emmy wasn't to give that man another thought.

But how could Emmy not think about the man who was her father? He had made Mum what she was—an unmarried mother and a kitchen maid who, as near as Emmy could tell, would struggle the rest of her life to make ends meet.

"Don't you ever take on blame for something you had no control over," Nana had said, and Emmy had sensed in her tone that she'd given herself the same counsel often enough. That advice came back to Emmy now as she stood there, watching Mum make tea; then the years blended in Emmy's mind and the last words Nana said to her filled her head.

You work on those stitches, Emmeline. It will give you something constructive to do while your mother is out earning her keep.

Those words had embarrassed Emmy when Nana said them. At thirteen, Emmy knew what Nana was implying. But Mum had been so angry, and the charge so appalling, Emmy had kicked the notion away. Nana and Mum had often said terrible things to each other. Things that weren't true.

But now it was as if a bright light had been switched on and the blackout curtains had fallen from their rods.

Mum had thrown Nana out of the house because her mother had accused her of sleeping her way to a job in a rich woman's house.

Emmy now watched as Mum poured water into a chipped Royal Doulton teacup, a castoff from Mrs. Billingsley. She stirred in the sugar with a spoon that had also been a Billingsley hand-me-down. Emmy took in the small kitchen, with its pretty tile floors, reliable plumbing, and cabinets of hardwood. Their dining table was nothing special but it was not a rickety tumble of sticks, either. The sofa, just a few feet away from Emmy, was not moth-eaten and the rugs were not threadbare. She and Julia had warm blankets in the winter and comfortable beds to sleep in. Mum had her own bedroom. They always had food in the cupboards and shoes on their feet and clothes on their backs. Their existence was not extravagant, but they never lacked for the basics—and all this on the paycheck of an unmarried kitchen maid.

A kitchen maid who'd landed the job with no experience.

How could she have not seen it before? How could she have been so stupid to think a kitchen maid with no husband and two children could manage to afford this flat and its modest but adequate furnishings?

Someone had arranged for Mum to get the job at Mrs. Billingsley's house when Neville left. That was why Mum had been so confident the day of her interview. What kind of person would do that for a woman like her mother? Emmy suddenly understood why Nana had been so fearful when Mum came home with the uniform over her arm. Surely Mum was being compensated for something else besides boiling water for tea and shopping for hams.

"How could you do that?" Emmy whispered to Mum's back.

Mum turned around, the teacup poised for a sip and her gaze on Emmy defiant. "How could I do what?"

"How could you do *that*?"

Her mother lowered the cup. "You don't know anything about anything, Em," Mum said calmly, "so shut your mouth."

It was almost as if she were admitting to Emmy outright that someone was paying her for sex. Emmy looked at her with revulsion. "Is it Mrs. Billingsley's butler? Her chauffeur?"

Mum laughed but without mirth. "Really, Em. Is that what you think?"

"Tell me I'm wrong!"

She lifted her cup to Emmy in a salute. "You're wrong." Mum walked past her daughter and Emmy followed her into the living room. Mum parted the blackout curtains covering the window by the front door and a sallow sun seeped into the room. She took a long drink of her tea.

"Then explain all this!" Emmy yelled. "Explain how you can afford this flat and the clothes in your wardrobe! Explain how you got a job as a kitchen maid when you hadn't ever been one before! Explain where you were last night!"

Mum whipped around and hot tea sloshed out of the cup and onto her hand. She didn't even flinch.

"How dare you talk to me that way after all I have done for you?" Her voice was even and controlled, but her eyes glistened with anger. "After all I have *sacrificed* for you!"

"I never asked you to degrade yourself for any of this!" Emmy swept her arm in front of her to include the room's furnishings.

"*You* have no business scolding me for what I do for you."

"And *you* can't keep blaming me for your mistakes!"

Emmy and her mother stood there glaring at each other for several seconds. Then Mum brushed past Emmy and walked back into the kitchen. Emmy followed her. Mum poured more tea into her cup, but a second later she hurled it into the sink. The teacup shattered and bits of porcelain flew up like ocean spray.

"You can't keep blaming me for your mistakes," Emmy said again. It was all she could say.

Mum placed her hands on the countertop and lowered her head. Her chest was heaving but she made no sound other than the inhalation and exhalation of air in her lungs.

"I have paid for everything I have ever given you, Emmy," Mum said calmly. "I have paid and paid and paid."

The accusation slid into Emmy's core like a steel blade. "It's not my fault you got pregnant." Tears spilled down her cheeks.

"Just because it's not your fault doesn't mean you're not a part of this. Leave me alone, Em."

Emmy started to walk away but then abruptly turned back. Mum was not going to ruin anything for her ever again. She was through. She would get out of the flat and out of her way as soon as she could. Emmy would prove herself worthy to Mrs. Crofton and the woman's cousin. She would move heaven and earth to make something of herself. As soon as she had her feet under her and her own place to live, she would come for Julia. Mum would be free to live whatever kind of life she wanted or had been denied. They would both have what they wanted most.

"I got a job working for the lady at the bridal shop," Emmy said.

Mum faced her. "What?"

"I said I got a job. At the bridal shop. Two after-noons a week and some Saturdays."

"The bridal shop."

"Yes, the bridal shop. The owner is going to teach me to sew. She also looked at my sketches today and she said I have talent."

"You and your brides," Mum said derisively, under her breath but loud enough for Emmy to hear.

"She said I have talent! She likes my wedding gowns!"

"Pieces of paper, Emmy! They're just pieces of paper. Just wait until you grow up and you see what real life is like. You can draw all the dresses you want and imagine your life an endless parade of perfect tomor-rows. But wishing it won't make it happen and neither will all the white bridal lace in the world. You're chasing after moonbeams, Em. Someday you're going to remem-ber I told you this. You'll thank me then. Just you wait."

"I *am* grown-up. And I'm not like you." The words felt like poison off Emmy's lips, distasteful even to her. This time, Mum flinched but she held Emmy's gaze.

"Everybody's like me," she said.

Emmy turned from her.

"I didn't say you could take on a job!" she called after Emmy, almost like an afterthought.

"I'm not asking for your permission."

"What am I supposed to do with Julia while you're working?" she yelled as Emmy and her mother reas-sumed their roles.

"I'm not her mother. You are," Emmy shouted back.

Emmy headed for the stairs that led to the bedrooms to get dressed for the day. She met Julia halfway.

"Why are you and Mum yelling?" Julia's eyes were half-closed with the remnants of sleep. She hadn't heard much.

"Mum broke a teacup. She's just sad about it. Let's leave her alone for a little bit."

Emmy led her sister back up the stairs to their room and shut the door.

Six

THE first month at Primrose Bridal was magical despite the air raid sirens going off nearly every night and the friction between Emmy and her mother.

Emmy had relented and suggested Mum talk to Thea about caring for Julia when Emmy had to work, an arrangement to which their childless next-door neighbor was clearly happy to agree. Julia didn't seem to mind much, although Thea's aging mother thought Julia was a classmate from the Welsh village where she grew up, a state of affairs Julia didn't quite know what to make of.

Still, the situation couldn't have been more ideal. Thea was dependable, as she hardly ever left her flat, she doted on Julia, and she refused to be paid any money. The easy fix tamed Mum's annoyance over Emmy's taking a job without having consulted her. Her attitude toward Emmy's good fortune quickly dissolved into the ambivalence Emmy was used to.

After their fight that early Sunday morning, Emmy thought she began to understand why indifference suited Mum when it came to her older daughter. Surely it was because Emmy reminded Mum of herself. Emmy was nearly the age Mum had been when she became pregnant; Emmy's unfolding life mirrored hers before she had found herself a mother at sixteen. Emmy wanted to think that her mother involved herself so little in Emmy's life so that her bad luck wouldn't rub off on her, but it was perplexing to think Mum was doing something as noble as that on Emmy's behalf. Mum's way of showing love, if that was what it was, was mystifying.

When Emmy entered the bridal shop, she could forget about what was going on at home. Mrs. Crofton was easy to work for, provided Emmy arrived on time and stayed on task. As Emmy sewed in the back room, she could hear her waiting on anxious brides-to-be, helping them choose a dress off the rack—no one wanted to wait to have a dress made—and assuring them that war or no war, they could have a beautiful wedding even with just a gown and a groom.

Mrs. Crofton was also a patient instructor on the Singer, an impressive machine that seemed to have a mind of its own. The needle moved so fast and was so precise. On Emmy's first Saturday afternoon, when the morning crowd died away and the afternoon shoppers had yet to appear, Emmy threaded and rethreaded the needle fifty times so that she could do it confidently with her eyes closed. And then she sewed ten straight lines and ten figure eights, half on easy muslin and half on unforgiving crepe. When she was finished, Mrs. Crofton said Emmy had performed better than she had when she first learned and that, with practice, Emmy would be able to master crepe, satin, chiffon, taffeta, and all the other fabrics that floated like air or swam like water when a seamstress tried to guide them past a slender needle the width of a cat's whisker.

On the first Saturday in June, after showing Emmy how to alter a bodice to fit a woman with far less cleavage than the dress provided for, Mrs. Crofton told Emmy she had heard back from her cousin Graham Dabney.

"His father-in-law is very ill and he's up in Edinburgh with his wife taking care of him. I don't know when he'll be back in London. Soon, he thinks. But he said if your sketches are as good as I told him they were, he'd like to meet and discuss perhaps mentoring you."

Emmy wasn't sure what that meant. It sounded wonderful but also beyond what she could afford. "Does that mean . . . Would I need to pay him?" she asked.

"Graham said if you've the raw talent, he will teach you how to make your patterns in exchange for working in his studio here in London. He designs for several theaters on the West End and he always needs extra hands who understand formal wear. He's done this before with young designers who lack instruction and experience. Does that sound agreeable?"

It sounded amazingly perfect.

"A thousand times yes," Emmy said.

"I didn't tell him you were not yet sixteen. You might want to keep that to yourself for right now. And if school starts up again, you will have to work out a schedule with him that he will be happy with if you choose to continue with your schooling. He can be a little demanding when there's a show in production. And of course I will still expect you for the ten or so hours that you work for me. Will your mother have a problem with your being gone so much?"

"I make my own decisions about my time," Emmy said, and then quickly added, "My mum treats me like an adult."

"You're fortunate she does, Emmeline. I doubt this would work if she didn't."

Perhaps Emmy was fortunate. Up to that point, she hadn't seen the benefit of Mum's casual parenting.

"One more thing," Mrs. Crofton said. "Graham has asked to see a couple of your sketches. I'd like to send him by post the two that I liked the best."

As much as Emmy wanted to have all that Mrs. Crofton had just promised, the thought of handing over two of her best designs to a man she had never met made her instantly anxious. Her eyes must have betrayed her panic.

"You don't have to worry about sending them to him, Emmeline," Mrs. Crofton said. "He's a designer, too. He knows how to safeguard the work of a colleague. If I were you, I might be a little afraid, too, but I wouldn't let that stop me from sending them. This is a tremendous opportunity. He wouldn't ask to see them if he wasn't intrigued by what I told him about you."

For a breath of a second Emmy considered telling Mrs. Crofton she wasn't interested in having Mr. Dabney's offer if it meant sending him two of the designs before she'd even met him. But Emmy had no sooner imagined herself saying these words than she realized she had been brought to a life-changing fork in the road. If she chose to keep all the brides in the box and never trust them with anyone, it was likely they would never leave it. Mum had said wishing something didn't make it happen. Emmy had to do more than wish.

"All right," Emmy said. "I'll bring them on Tuesday."

It was going on early evening when Emmy got back

to the flat. The air inside was stuffy and hot even though a metal fan swung its neck from side to side from the windowsill by the front door. Other than the hum of the fan, the flat was eerily quiet for a Saturday at near twilight. Emmy stepped into the kitchen and found Mum still in her uniform at the kitchen table with a juice glass in her hand. In the middle of the table, a bottle of whiskey, a crumpled handkerchief, and the day's mail all touched one another in a triangle of unspoken woe. She looked up at Emmy and her eyes, red rimmed from earlier tears, glimmered from the numbing effect of alcohol. Pins had come loose in her hair and one long lock curled over her shoulder in a graceful way. The light above the table tossed a mellow and compassionate light onto Mum, the bottle, the handkerchief, and the two opened envelopes.

"Expected you home earlier," Mum murmured with no trace of anger in her voice. It was almost as if she were jealous Emmy had the lucky fortune of having been somewhere other than the flat.

"I was learning how to use the sewing machine. What's wrong? Where's Julia?" A band of sweat broke out on Emmy's forehead. The kitchen was sweltering. She walked over to the window above the sink and opened it to let in a breeze, but only hot stale air met her. She turned back to face Mum. "Why are you drinking? What happened?"

Mum downed the last bit of amber liquid in the glass and set it down gently. She fingered the corner of her mouth. "Neville was in a car accident. He's dead."

Emmy's gaze darted to the two opened letters on the table. "How do you know? Who told you? Where's Julia?"

Mum looked up. "His *mother* wrote to me. That's right, his mother. She's not dead after all. Neither is his father. You were right about him, weren't you, oh wise Emmeline? You tried to tell me he was a lying cheat. But I wouldn't listen." She picked up the glass, stared at its emptiness, and set it back on the table. "His last name isn't even what he told me it was. Black was his stage name."

Emmy closed the distance between them. "Mum, where is Julia?"

Mum waved Emmy's concern away with one hand and picked up the handkerchief with the other. "Next door at Thea's. The cat had her kittens. She doesn't know." Mum reached for the bottle and sloshed another mouthful into the glass. "She's not going to know."

"What do you mean?"

"I mean exactly that. She's not going to know." Mum downed the whiskey and grimaced. She wiped her mouth with the handkerchief. "You're not to tell her, Em. I'm not going to do to her what I did to you."

"Mum—"

"I mean it, Emmy. Don't you tell her! Let her think what she wants about him. She has every right to think what she wants." Mum reached for the bottle. Emmy leaned over her and moved it away from her outstretched hand.

"Stop it," Emmy said.

"Julia has every right to think whatever she wants!" Fresh tears rimmed Mum's glassy eyes. "Don't you tell her! I mean it, Emmy!"

Emmy placed the bottle atop the fridge and used the moments when her back was turned to assess her own reaction to the news of Neville's death. She felt nothing. Neville, most of the time an unemployed actor, had lived on and off with them for four years, starting when Julia was two. Emmy didn't like the way he treated Mum and she didn't like the way he looked at her when she started to develop a woman's body. But Julia loved that Neville could sound like an old man or a French painter or an American cowboy. She loved his outlandish stories and crazy songs. He was the kind of father every kid thought she wanted. He never raised his voice to Julia, never corrected her, never made her mind. After he'd disappear for months on end, he'd come back with a fanciful tale of the adventure he had been on, bearing trinkets for Julia and excuses for Mum. He could see that Emmy saw straight through the lies and pretense, so he brought her nothing. He was handsome and talented. He was also an opportunist and a playboy. Emmy celebrated the day he said he was moving out for good, even though Julia and Mum both cried.

They hadn't heard so much as a word from him in nearly a year. Julia believed he was somewhere in India on a movie set.

His death meant nothing to Emmy.

"Did you hear what I said?" Mom railed. "Don't you tell her, Emmy."

Emmy turned from the fridge. "Someday Julia won't be satisfied with vague answers about where he is."

"Today's not that day." Mum held out the juice glass.

Emmy took the glass and placed it in the sink where the breakfast dishes were still soaking. "I never said Neville was a lying cheat."

"You knew I shouldn't have trusted him. You were just a kid and somehow you knew. God, isn't that ironic."

Emmy opened a cupboard and pulled out a tin of corned beef, a loaf of pumpernickel, and a jar of peaches, as Mum apparently had no plans for their supper. "What's done is done, Mum."

"Why did he tell me his parents were dead? What

was the purpose of me thinking that?" Mum crumpled the handkerchief and tossed it onto the table next to the mail. "Why would he do that?"

"Does it really matter now?" Emmy withdrew six slices of bread, picked off a few flakes of mold, and set them on a plate.

"It matters to me! Why would he tell me his parents were dead?"

Emmy could think of a number of reasons why Neville had lied to Mum about his parents, not the least of which was that when he wanted to move in with them; it was a lot easier for Mum to welcome him when she thought he had nowhere else to go. "Because he wanted you to feel sorry for him. Or because he liked lying to see if he could get away with it. He was an actor, Mum. He made his living pretending to be something he wasn't." Emmy opened the fridge and pulled out a jar of mustard.

"Aren't you Miss Know-It-All," Mum murmured.

"You asked me. I'm just answering your question. He lied to you because it suited his ends."

"He told me he didn't have the money to marry me. Did I ever tell you that? What a fool I was. His father is a professor! He probably has all kinds of money. What a daft fool I was. You'd think I'd know better. . . ." Her voice trailed off.

Emmy opened the tin and the greasy-sweet odor of canned meat permeated the air in the little kitchen. "If you don't want me to tell Julia right now, I won't. But if she asks me why he's taking so long to come back from India, or wherever else she thinks he is, I'm not going to lie to her."

Mum inhaled deeply. "You won't have to. I'll tell her my own way, on my own day. If she asks you where he is, you tell her you don't know. Because you don't."

Her mother was staring at the letters on the table. It occurred to Emmy that if Neville's mother knew about Mum, she might also know Neville had a daughter.

"How did his mother find you?" Emmy asked. "Does she know about Julia?"

"She knows," Mum said slowly, her tone calculating. "He told his parents as he lay dying in a hospital in Dublin that he had a daughter in London. That's where he was. Dublin. Living with a woman half his age, no doubt."

"And?"

Mum swung her head around. "And, what?"

Emmy set the tin down. "Do they want to see her?"

Mum picked up the top letter and pocketed it. "Doesn't matter if they do."

"What's that supposed to mean?"

"Just that. It doesn't matter if they do. They're not going to. I want them to want to for a good long time. I want them to *want* to see Julia and not be able to. I want them to want it so much, it drives them near crazy."

Emmy forked out a watery slice of meat and slapped it on top of one of the slices of bread. Juice spattered on the counter. "Brilliant idea, Mum. So very fair to Julia."

Mum rose on unsteady feet and yanked on Emmy's arm, forcing her to look at her. More meat juices erupted from the tin in Emmy's hand and speckled the floor.

"That's right. It *is* a brilliant idea. It's my brilliant idea. Julia deserves to have what is rightfully hers. Just like we all do. Just like you do, Emmeline." Mum let go of her arm. "And I intend to see she gets it."

Emmy watched as her mother kneeled down and used the handkerchief wet from tears and whiskey to mop the meat juice off the floor.

"They obviously know where you live, Mum. Do you

really think you will be able to keep these people from seeing Julia until you have what you want from them?"

Mum rose to her feet in one swift movement. "Is that what you think? That this is about what I want? When has anything ever been about what *I* want?"

Emmy turned back to the sandwiches. "That's all it ever is," she muttered.

Mum pulled at Emmy's arm again, more gently this time. Her calm touch surprised Emmy.

"You're wrong, Em." Mum reached up to touch her daughter's face and Emmy involuntarily flinched. Mum tenderly tucked a curling wisp of hair behind Emmy's ear. "Someday I am going to prove it to you."

For a moment, there was no age difference between the two of them, no crossed purposes, no opposing forces. They were just two women trying to chisel a happy life out of a giant hulk of rough-edged circumstances.

Then the moment passed. Mum pulled the letter from her pocket, held it over the rubbish bin, and saw that Emmy was watching her. She shoved it back inside the pocket and sat down again.

"There's a designer who wants to teach me how to make patterns for my wedding dresses," Emmy said a moment later. "He's Mrs. Crofton's cousin. He wants to see a couple of my sketches. He might mentor me in exchange for some hours working in his studio. He designs costumes for the West End, Mum."

Mum furrowed her brow in consternation. Emmy could see that her mother was forming a response that Emmy would not want to hear.

"I'm nearly sixteen. Practically an adult," Emmy said, already in defense mode.

"Nearly isn't is, Em. You're not an adult yet. Not in the eyes of the law."

"But I know I can handle the extra work. Even when school starts in September. I can handle it. I've only a year left, anyway." Emmy's voice was rising in pitch and volume, and she tempered it to prove she was the rational adult she was claiming to be. "It's not going to be a problem, Mum."

"School isn't starting in September."

"What do you mean? Of course it is," Emmy said.

Mum picked up the other envelope that had come in the day's post and held it out.

Emmy wiped her hands on a dish towel and then took it.

The stationery was crisp and smelled of ink and importance. The return address was the school's. Emmy sensed as soon as her fingers touched the paper that the letter would change everything that had happened that day. Her eyes caught the words "invasion" and "safety."

"You and Julia are being evacuated to the countryside, Emmy," Mum said. "They're serious about it this time. You're leaving London next week. All the children are."

Seven

THE first time London's children had been evacuated, nearly a year earlier, Mum had flat-out refused to send Emmy and Julia away. Her attitude then had been that there wasn't a war, not on English soil, anyway, and she was not going to put her daughters on a train to God-knows-where. Emmy remembered her saying as much to their teachers at school, Thea next door, and anyone else who asked why Julia and Emmy were still in London. Emmy also remembered seeing something else in Mum's eyes besides the defiance. Mum had felt it wasn't in her best interest to send them off into the countryside, but for reasons Emmy was unsure of. There seemed to be more to Mum's refusal than just outward unwillingness to be parted from her daughters.

There was no precedent for London being emptied of her children; no previous war had demanded it. The last time there had been an exodus for safer homes was during the plagues, and then it was only the rich who fled the cities. The adversary this go-around was not a disease but legions of army planes carrying bombs. It was an astounding concept that Germany could strike England by air and subdue her without even setting foot on her soil. But Mum had scoffed at the idea that the only way to ensure Emmy's and Julia's safety was to entrust them to strangers.

"You and Julia aren't going anywhere," she had said when the letter had arrived in August 1939, advising her to prepare her daughters for evacuation. When the other children in the neighborhood trudged to school carrying suitcases and gas masks, their weeping mothers trailing after them, Emmy and Julia had stayed home and played checkers. Some mothers, who had looked down their noses at Mum the day before, apparently hopped over the police cordon at the train station and snatched their children back before they boarded. Those who bravely waved good-bye got postcards from billeting officials a week later advising them of where and with whom their children were living. Emmy found out after many of her classmates started coming back to the city that foster parents arrived at designated churches and community centers in rural villages to look over the trainloads of London children and then they chose the ones they wanted like buyers at an auction. One of Julia's six-year-old friends had been parted from her older brother because, so the story went, he could work a field and she could not. That little girl still had nightmares six months later. In the end, it had all been for nothing. The doomsayers who foretold that the Luftwaffe would flatten London had been wrong.

Emmy and Julia weren't the only children whose parents could not or would not bow to the notion that evacuation was the only course of action that made any sense. There was a set of parents just down the street from the Downtrees who kept their children back, and on the next block over, a couple more. The sisters and these other children had gathered at the home of one of the houses for impromptu lessons since the schools closed after the children left the city. But within a month, the schools had all opened again because most of the children had been brought back home. At the time, everyone had concluded that Britain would win the war on the fields of France and in the air over the English Channel.

But when Dunkirk fell some months later, the air raid sirens began to wail a little more often and the doomsayers began to raise the specter of a second evacuation of London's children. Emmy gave it little thought. Mum had kept them back during the first one; she'd do the same if there was another.

Emmy had been happy to stay behind during the first evacuation.

And now she was insistent that she stay behind for the second.

But this time, Mum would not hear of it.

For half an hour Emmy argued with her.

Emmy was too old to be evacuated.

There was no real danger.

How did Mum know they would be safe just because they weren't in London?

And the real reason, of course. Emmy had a job. And a dress designer interested in seeing her sketches.

Emmy was not going.

Mum had an answer for every excuse Emmy gave her. The letter in her hand said every child fifteen and younger was to be evacuated. The danger was genuine. The only safe place was in the country.

As for Emmy's little job, as Mum called it, did Emmy really think there would be fittings for wedding dresses with the war looming for real now, overhead?

Besides, Julia could not go alone. Not after what they had seen happen to classmates the last time.

"You have to go with her," Mum said. "We're done talking about it. You're going."

"Please don't make me, Mum."

"It's not up to me!"

"Yes, it is. You can do what you did last time. Just refuse to comply."

Mum's eyes had glossed shiny with emotion. "This time it's different. You really must go, Emmy. It is for the best."

Emmy wanted to grab her mother by the shoulders and shake her. Shake her until she told Emmy everything.

"The best for you, you mean," Emmy said instead. "Now you can spend the night with whomever you wish, whenever you wish, and as often as you wish."

Emmy waited for the slap across her face. She wanted it. She wanted to feel the sting of Mum's reproach. She wanted the welt to rise on her skin and blossom crimson in front of Mum.

Mum raised her hand slightly and Emmy braced herself for the impact.

But the slap didn't come. Mum lowered her arm and a second later it hung loose at her side.

"You and Julia are leaving on Wednesday," she said.

"Don't tell her about Neville. She doesn't need to know right now and this is going to be hard enough. You have to go with her, Em. Hate me if you want, but you know I can't send her away alone. You know I can't."

Mum turned and walked out of the kitchen.

Emmy felt as if she had been slapped anyway.

EMMY dreaded telling Mrs. Crofton that she was being forced to leave London. For the next two days after Mum got the notice, she imagined herself arriving for work on Tuesday and telling Mrs. Crofton she was being evacuated. She pictured Mrs. Crofton replying that she would not be able to keep the job open until Emmy could return. Emmy rehearsed hearing Mrs. Crofton say that there was no way now to hide Emmy's age from her cousin, and that Emmy would have to hope she could win him over when she was older, assuming he still had any interest. Emmy pictured Mrs. Crofton muttering she should never have hired Emmy in the first place. She didn't want to keep hearing those words in her head, but they played and replayed over and over until it seemed like she had already told Mrs. Crofton and the dream was already dead. Everything about the situation seemed so ridiculously unfair. Emmy couldn't completely blame Mum for the turn of events, but she needed to blame someone for the war and Emmy was angry at her mother for insisting she evacuate for Julia's sake, as though Emmy's own safety were not a consideration.

Mum came home Monday evening from a meeting at the school with a list of things the girls were to bring and not bring. Julia, excited to be going on a train to the country like some privileged heiress, was full of questions. She was enthralled at the idea of spending the autumn at a country home and riding a horse—as if all country homes had one—and growing her own pumpkins and skipping stones over a pond and counting stars. Emmy had only one question. How long would the evacuation last? The year before, the children began returning within a month. She could only hope it would be the same this time around. She had to get back to London. This opportunity for her and her designs would not wait for her.

Wishes didn't come true by wishing.

On Tuesday afternoon before work, Emmy took Julia next door to Thea's as usual. Their neighbor was in the middle of getting together a box of supplies for her Anderson shelter, a hut of corrugated steel covered in earth and half-buried in the ground in her back garden.

The Downtrees' flat was connected to Thea's and six others so that their brick, two-story homes looked like one long house with the same front door repeated seven times over. Each of the narrow flats had a splash of lawn in the front and a tiny garden in the back. Brick partitions separated the gardens. The neighbors had little flower beds and tomato vines and pots of pansies in their tiny gardens. The Downtrees had a stone slab, overgrown hedges, and dirt. Thea had erected an Anderson shelter in her minuscule garden when she was told her cat would not be welcome in the public shelter the neighbors all shared in the cellar of the shoe repair shop at the end of the street. Her private shelter nearly filled the space from garden wall to garden wall. The Andy looked like a dog kennel made by someone who had no idea how to construct one and so the builder decided to bury the evidence of ever having tried. Mum thought it was hideous; Julia was plain terrified of it.

"Oh my goodness, do you still need me to take Julia today?" Thea's eyes were shining with agitation. The news of the second evacuation had everyone on the street preparing for the worst, whatever that was.

"I still have to go to work today. It's my last day—at least for a while," Emmy said. "I'm hoping we'll be back soon."

Thea stared at Emmy as though she had spoken in a foreign language, one Thea didn't understand.

"Soon?" she asked.

"Yes. I'm hoping this evacuation will be like the last one."

Thea was holding a wicker basket filled with biscuits, tins of sardines, and bottles of soda water, but she set this down and told Julia, who was standing next to her, that the mother cat had moved the kittens into a bureau drawer and she should go see how cute they were. As soon as Julia had dashed upstairs, Thea turned to Emmy.

"Has your mother not told you how things are, Emmeline?"

Her tone made Emmy feel instantly young and uninformed, just like the child that everyone kept insisting she was. "What do you mean?"

"France is occupied and—"

"I know that," Emmy interjected. It wasn't as if she never read the papers or didn't listen to the radio.

"Yes, but that means now the Germans can reach *us*. They can fly their planes right across the Channel from France. It's not like last time. They're saying the Germans plan to bomb London."

"They said that a year ago."

"Yes, but a year ago, the Germans didn't have France."

Now it was Emmy's turn to stare at her as if she didn't understand the language Thea was speaking.

"We're on an island," Emmy said. "The Nazis can't roll in here with their tanks like they have everywhere else."

"But that's why no one can say how long this will last. I would hate for you to leave here thinking you'll be back in a month. The papers say—"

Emmy didn't want to hear any more. She was tired of everyone and everything deciding what was to become of everything that mattered to her. She cut Thea off in midsentence. "I have to go, Thea, or I'll be late. Sorry. I'll be back for Julia before six thirty."

Emmy knew she had been abysmally rude, but she simply had to get away from Thea and her box of supplies for her bomb shelter, and from the fear in her eyes. She went back to the flat for the two sketches she had promised Mrs. Crofton and held them to her chest for a moment. These would keep her place, if not in Mrs. Crofton's shop, then in Mr. Dabney's future plans. They had to.

She headed for the bridal shop, passing sandbag walls on street corners that she and everyone else had been walking past for a year and hardly noticed anymore. Everyone on the sidewalk seemed distracted by unspoken ponderings as they dashed about without a word to one another, not even a tip of the head or a weak smile. It was as though the imminent departure of a quarter million children meant London was poised to lose her innocence and no one quite knew what to do on the eve of that loss.

Emmy arrived at Primrose Bridal and opened the door. The store was empty except for one young woman buying a veil.

And only a veil.

Emmy surmised from the conversation the woman

and Mrs. Crofton were engaged in that she was to marry on Friday morning at Saint Martin–in–the-Fields wearing the veil and a dress of white dotted Swiss that she had worn to a piano recital in April. Her husband-to-be was shipping out with his platoon on Saturday afternoon.

While Mrs. Crofton finished the transaction, Emmy went into the back room to see what hand-sewing was lined up for that afternoon, but the long table was empty. A few moments later, Mrs. Crofton joined her. She looked haggard, as if she hadn't slept well or perhaps had eaten something for lunch that now roiled inside her.

"Are you all right, Mrs. Crofton?" Emmy asked.

She produced a wan smile. "Ask me that question when the war is over, Emmeline, and I might have an answer for you." Mrs. Crofton looked down at Emmy's hands. "You brought them."

"Of course." Emmy held the sketches out to her.

She hesitated for a moment before taking them. "Do you have something to tell me?"

The words startled Emmy, but a second later she was glad Mrs. Crofton had suspected she was to be sent away.

"My mother is making me leave. I'm so sorry, Mrs. Crofton. I had no idea this would happen when I took this job."

The woman nodded once and cast her gaze to the sketches in Emmy's hand. "I really thought I could pretend there was nothing to worry about as long as I just went about my business and sold wedding dresses to happy young women."

Emmy hadn't rehearsed a response from Mrs. Crofton that had nothing to do with her, so she had no words at the ready.

"Do you still want me to send these to my cousin?" Mrs. Crofton's voice was void of emotion and strength, as though it really didn't matter anymore that she had met Emmy and liked her sketches and wanted to help Emmy embark on a future as a wedding dress designer.

"I most certainly do. The evacuation doesn't change anything."

Mrs. Crofton looked up at Emmy. "Except that you won't be in London."

"But I am going to return as soon as I can. I very much want you to send the sketches to Mr. Dabney and I want to know when he will be returning to the city."

The woman laughed, a short little chortle shrouded in lassitude. "Oh, the confidence of the young! You would have us all drinking victory champagne by Christmas. My neighbor's son is in the British navy and she told me he has no idea how long this will last. I'm not getting any more dresses from my suppliers in Paris. It will be hard to sell wedding gowns when I haven't any to sell. And if all the London designers head to the hills, where will that leave me?"

"You could sell mine."

Her laugh this time was full and loud. "Made from what, hospital sheets? And who's going to spend money on a wedding dress if food gets really scarce like they're saying it will? Or if bombs are dropping every night? Don't they teach you current events in school?"

"School's not in session. And war makes brides as easily as it makes widows. You told me that yourself."

"But not as plentifully. I've had no customers yesterday or today, except for the young woman who bought that veil."

"Give your cousin the sketches, Mrs. Crofton. Please? I promise I will come back as soon as I can. War or no war."

She exhaled heavily. "All right."

"And you'll let me know when he returns to London."

Mrs. Crofton nodded. "Send me your address when you're situated."

They stood there for a moment looking at each other.

"I don't have any work for you today, Emmeline," Mrs. Crofton finally said.

"You can teach me how to line a bodice."

She lifted up the corners of her mouth in a half smile. "I almost envy you. Getting out of here like you are. Away from all this. You don't know how good you have it."

"I'll trade places with you."

Mrs. Crofton laughed gently. "If you were my daughter, Emmeline, I would do the same as your mum. I'd send you away to safety, too. I had a daughter once, you know."

Emmy didn't.

Mrs. Crofton stared at the wall behind her as if it were a window to the past. "She died of a fever when she was six."

"I'm so sorry, Mrs. Crofton."

Her employer hovered there, on the edge between the present and past, and then she turned toward the wall and plugged in the electric teakettle that sat on a little table by the door to the loo.

Emmy waited to hear more about the daughter who had died, but Mrs. Crofton only said she was terribly sorry that she'd run out of sugar and there wasn't any more at the grocery.

Eight

THE day Emmy and Julia left London, the June sun spilled cheerfully out of the sky, dousing everyone with extravagant and unnecessary warmth. A somber fog would have suited Emmy better, or a pelting downpour. She didn't want the heavens affirming this plan as she and her sister trudged to Julia's school, suitcases in hand, nor as they waited in a sunny sea of emotional mothers, wide-eyed tots, and uniformed officials pretending that what they were doing was perfectly normal. From the school, the sisters would continue by bus, then by train, and lastly by motor car or delivery truck or gypsy cart—who really knew?—to wherever it was they were to call home.

Emmy's solitary consolation as she packed her satchel was that she had discovered the key to Primrose's back door, which she had forgotten to return to Mrs. Crofton when they said their good-byes. It was like an omen that she would have to come back to London to return it to Mrs. Crofton. She slipped the key into her skirt pocket, letting her fingers linger over its shape before she withdrew her hand.

They arrived at the school fifteen minutes after the time Mum was told to have them there but their tardiness didn't seem to matter. The queues of parents waiting to register their children were long and curlicued, and the general feeling, despite the happy sun, was one of quiet desperation. The animated chatter of nervous adolescents was only slightly louder than the agitated voices of parents who wanted more information than anyone in charge was prepared to give them. The billeting officials to whom they appealed sat behind long tables and scarcely looked up from their piles of paper, so intent were they on making sure they didn't lose someone's child into the abyss of this second evacuation scheme. The youngest children clung to their mothers' hands. Some of them knew from the first evacuation what trauma was about to befall them, and they buried their heads in their mothers' skirts. The oldest evacuees—teenagers like Emmy—gazed about in disbelief, looking for all the world like they wanted to disappear into a separate dimension while the adults played war with one another. Emmy didn't see anyone she knew, probably because they were meeting at Julia's school, not hers.

Mum returned from waiting in one of those snaking queues with stringed, cardboard tags for Emmy and Julia, and luggage labels that bore their names, ages, Mum's name, and their London address. Julia's tag went promptly around her neck.

"I'm not wearing this," Emmy said, handing the name tag back to Mum.

"You have to," Mum said, ignoring her daughter's outstretched hand. She bent down to attach the luggage labels to the suitcases at their feet.

Emmy looped the name tag around the handle of the gas mask box that all the children were made to carry. Mum stood up, saw that Emmy didn't have the string around her neck, and huffed.

"Emmy, please. Just do it."

"I'm not five, Mum."

"Then don't act like you are."

Mum yanked the tag off the handle of Emmy's gas mask box and slipped it over her head.

"What does this say?" Julia peered at the small type-written words below her name and Mum's on the tag.

"Moreton-in-Marsh," Mum said, straightening Julia's barrette. "That's where your train is headed."

"What's a marsh again?" Julia furrowed her brow.

"It's an oozing swamp," Emmy said under her breath.

"Moreton-in-Marsh is a nice town in Gloucester-shire," Mum said to Julia, after a quick frown Emmy's way. "It's a sweet little place, the registrar told me. In the Cotswolds. There are others from your school going to the same place, Julia, so you'll already know people."

"And my school? Are there others from my school?" Emmy asked, her voice terse with cynicism.

Mum faced her. "There are plenty of people your age being evacuated, Emmy. Plenty. Look around. Stop making this so difficult."

Emmy wasn't making anything difficult. Everyone else was making things difficult. This was not her war. Nothing about what was happening was her doing or had anything to do with her.

A uniformed official speaking through a public address system called for those headed west to Gloucestershire and

Oxfordshire. It was time to board the bus that would take them to the train station.

Emmy lifted her suitcase and Mum laid hold of her arm. "Don't let them separate you," she said, softly but urgently. "If anyone tries, you give them hell. Promise?"

Emmy's suitcase, the gas mask, and the brides box in her arms suddenly seemed weightless compared to the burden of being forced to release all the good fortune that so recently had come her way. It was as if her dreams were spiraling out of reach, past the barrage balloons that hovered in the sky like enormous dead and bloated fish. Emmy was letting go of so much and yet her heart felt so heavy.

Mum squeezed Emmy's arm when she did not answer. "Promise me, Emmy."

"She's *your* daughter," Emmy whispered, and tears sprang to her eyes. She loved Julia, but she would not have agreed to leave London if she did not have to consider Julia. Mum should be evacuating with Julia, not her.

"And you're her sister."

The man called again for their bus.

The little tag around Emmy's neck fluttered in between her and Mum, lifting off her chest for a second as a breeze ruffled it.

Emmy looked into Mum's tawny brown eyes. "You ruin everything." The words fell off her tongue as easy as a song, but the minute she said them, she wanted to pull the words back and shove them to the dark place where they'd been hiding since Mum got the evacuation notice.

Mum arched one eyebrow, just the one, and only slightly so. "I didn't ask for any of this." She let go of Emmy's arm. "None of it. Be careful what you hate, Em."

Mum now bent forward toward Julia, whose face was awash in uncertainty. "You stay with Emmy, now, and don't give her trouble, pet. All right?" Mum drew Julia into her arms. When she let go of her younger daughter and stood, Mum's eyes were glistening. "Mind the people who will be looking after you. I'll come and visit you as soon as I can. I'll write you. And you can write me."

Julia nodded, pleased, it seemed, to think of writing Mum a letter—something she had never done—and getting letters from someone in the post, also a new and exciting concept. But then in an instant her eyes widened in alarm. "Wait. What about Neville? What if he comes back? He won't know where I am!"

"Yes, Mum. What about Neville?" Emmy echoed, with none of Julia's distress but plenty of cheek. Just how long was she supposed to pretend Julia's father wasn't dead?

Mum ignored Emmy. "I'll take care of that, pet."

"So you'll tell him?" Julia asked, less alarmed but still worried, and perhaps a little upset with herself for not having thought of this before.

"Yes, I'll take care of everything."

Mum answered Julia's question without answering it at all and then turned to Emmy. She did not hold out her arms to embrace her. Instead, she cupped one hand under Emmy's chin. "Don't forget what I said, Emmy."

Emmy didn't have to be told to watch out for her little sister. She was more of a mother to Julia than their mum was. She always had been, even those rare times when she resented the responsibility. "Do you really think I would let anything happen to her?" Emmy said, pulling her chin out of her mother's slight grasp.

Mum let her arm drop. "I'm talking about what I said about what you choose to hate. You don't know everything. I know you think you do, but you don't."

"And you think *you* know everything. You don't know what Mrs. Crofton said about my drawings because you don't want to know. You haven't even asked.

They mean nothing to you. Well, they're everything to me, Mum. Just so you know."

Mum shook her head. "For the love of God, Emmeline. You're so young—"

"Just because I'm young doesn't mean I can't make my own decisions about my future. You of all people should know that."

An official walking by saw Emmy's and Julia's name tags and where they were bound. "Come along, then, lasses. Right here, now. You'll see your mum soon enough. Off you go, then."

With the official's hand gently on her back, Emmy reached for the book of fairy tales that Julia had in one hand, and then looped the handle of her gas mask box over her wrist. Emmy added the book to what she already carried in the crook of her arm.

"Carry your suitcase in one hand and grab hold of my skirt with the other. Don't let go," Emmy told her. They walked away from Mum, carrying luggage that had appeared in the flat the previous day—out of nowhere—and which smelled slightly of men's aftershave. In her other arm Emmy carried Julia's book, the brides box, and a sack lunch that Mum said Mrs. Billingsley had bought for her and Julia from her favorite sandwich shop.

Julia turned back to wave to Mum as she stepped up to board the bus, a red double-decker that had been pulled from its usual task of ferrying tourists around London. Emmy turned as well. Mum stood unmoving, her arms folded across her chest as people scurried about, her expression unreadable. She unhooked one arm to return Julia's wave and to blow her a kiss. When her eyes met Emmy's, she lifted her chin slightly as if to communicate she was pleased that Emmy had realized they weren't so very different from each other after all.

Nine

EMMY had traveled on a train outside the heart of London only once before. During one of Neville's stretches of living with Mum, he took them all to Brighton Beach for a weekend at the sea. He wanted to take only Mum; Emmy remembered that had been obvious. But they hadn't lived in Whitechapel then, so they hadn't had Thea for a neighbor. There was no one who could take the sisters for the weekend. Mum didn't like any of their neighbors at the time and they didn't like her, according to Mum. Emmy believed what they didn't like was Neville floating in and out of the flat, sometimes with an actor friend or two, and that they often loudly rehearsed lines at three o'clock in the morning from the bawdy shows they were in. The only other friends Mum had were fellow laundry maids at the hotel where she was working, but none of them had wanted to babysit a three- and an eleven-year-old for an entire weekend.

Emmy had liked the train ride.

She'd loved the sea.

The rest of the weekend was forgettable.

As she and Julia now sat side by side on the train, she wanted to stay angry at Mum, at the Germans, at the British War Office, at God Almighty himself for whisking her out of London when she was on the very edge of having everything.

But as the city sights fell away, and the landscape relaxed to rolling hills and fields of yellow, she found herself unable to stay angry. The rumbling of the train, the scenery outside her window, and even the lunch Julia and she shared—the nicest they had ever had—calmed Emmy to a state of ordinary melancholy. When they changed trains in Oxford for the last leg of the trip by rail, Emmy's anger had mellowed to something more like grief.

There were seventy evacuees on the train to Moreton-in-Marsh, accompanied not by one of the schoolteachers, as the larger groups had been, but by a uniformed matron who reminded Emmy somewhat of Nana. Her build was the same, as was her silver-brown hair. She allowed Emmy, the oldest in their group, to call her Alice instead of Mrs. Braughton. As they were about to pull into the station at Moreton-in-Marsh, Alice asked if Emmy would keep an eye on the trio of young boys—all classmates of Julia's—who were seated behind the girls and who had spent the forty-minute journey from Oxford laughing, poking one another, and kicking the back of the girls' seats.

"Just see that they don't get separated from the group," Alice said as the whistle blew and the train began to approach the station. "We're being met at the station and from there we'll walk to the town hall. Just a short stroll. I'll bring up the rear. If you wouldn't mind staying in the middle, that would be grand."

Emmy nodded in soundless compliance.

"There's a brave girl," Alice said, mistaking Emmy's quietness for timidity. She squeezed Emmy's shoulder before making her way back to the front of the train car.

Once they were off the train, it took some doing to corral the boys and convince them to stay where Emmy could see them. Then the lot of children formed a queue and a billeting official counted heads, comparing names with a list she had in her hand. Their suitcases had been loaded onto a truck so that they would not need to carry them the three blocks to the hall where they were to be sorted out. And then the young Londoners were off, like soldiers marching to the battlefield, or prisoners to their cells, Emmy thought.

"I have to go to the loo," Julia murmured, her hand tight in Emmy's.

"You just went at Oxford."

"That was a long time ago."

"Think about something else. As soon as we get to the next place, I'll find one for you."

"I can't think of something else!"

"Yes, you can."

The three boys ahead of them stopped to look at a dead bird on the sidewalk. "Come on, boys," Emmy said.

"I dare you to touch it, Julia," one of the boys said.

"I dare you to eat it!" Julia challenged, her hand tighter now in her sister's.

Emmy kicked the tiny carcass with her shoe. It landed in the gutter. "You can compose dares later. Off you go."

They continued on their way, past shops and cafés and businesses. The town was like Brighton in some ways. The buildings were close to one another, and there were few taxis and no red double-decker buses. But there was no fragrance of the sea, no one selling pasties or ice-cream cones on the sidewalk. And in Brighton, no one seemed to even notice when they had arrived or cared when they left. Here, everyone stopped whatever they were doing to look at the line of children, from the barber sweeping his front step, to the grocer standing by wooden crates full of turnips, to women in unremarkable dresses going about their afternoon errands.

Two young mothers pushing prams on the sidewalk moved aside so that the group could stay together. Emmy heard one whisper to the other, "Oh! These are the London children. The poor dears!"

And the other one replied, "Can you imagine sending your child away like that?"

"Or taking one in? Good heavens, you wouldn't know anything about them."

"Nor do we know anything about you," Emmy whispered as she and Julia walked by them.

She heard nothing else from the two pram pushers and did not look back at them.

After another block they were at the town hall on High Street. The curbs were crowded with parked cars on either side. A few adults, mostly women, were standing outside on the steps, watching as the children made their way past them.

"Welcome to Moreton-in-Marsh," one of them said, but her tone suggested she was nervous about the children being there. The young evacuees were the evidence that everything was different now. The war was no longer phony, as some had called it. It was real. And here were London's children to prove it.

They were ushered into a large reception room filled with tables, folding chairs, and people talking in small groups. The luggage had arrived, and two men were now unloading it from a cart and lining the suitcases like dominoes against the back wall. At one table officials sat with their papers and clipboards. At another were cups of water, tea biscuits, and meringues. The boys in Emmy's care rushed to the food table and she let them go. She had done what had been asked of her—she got them there without losing them.

Emmy looked around for a sign indicating a privy, found one, and started to head in that direction, Julia's hand in hers.

"You need to stay with your group," a woman wearing an armband said to her.

"My sister needs to use the loo," Emmy said, and kept walking.

"What are those people doing back there?" Julia asked as Emmy led her down a narrow hall to one of two doors marked WC.

"They're here for all of us." Emmy opened the door for her.

"But why are they looking at us like that?"

"They've never seen children from London before, so you and I are like two princesses to them. That's why."

This satisfied her. She let go of Emmy's hand.

When they returned to the big room, Julia said she was hungry. They made their way to the refreshments, and Emmy could not help but notice how the people in the room watched as she and Julia approached the table, studying how the girls respected their hospitality. For one crazed second Emmy wanted to lean over and lick all the meringues.

"Just take one," she murmured to Julia. "Until you know everyone's had something."

"I know how to share, Emmy," Julia murmured back, her brow crinkled in annoyance.

A woman stepped up to a microphone and tapped it. A loud clunking and a short squawk followed. "All right, then," she said. "If all the children could stand behind me here, we can get started. If you are here to collect an evacuee or two, if you could please make your way to my left so that we can keep everything in order. Splendid."

Everyone did as they were told.

As the crowd of adults moved to stand where they could face the children, Emmy noted that the expressions on the faces were no different from those she had seen hours ago in the school yard. These country people wore the same look of apprehension mixed with hope. They wanted to believe, just as the parents in the school yard did, that this was without a doubt the course of action to take; the evacuation was how their nation would do battle and yet protect the blameless. Some would have to release a child into the care of a stranger, and some would have to take in the beloved child of someone they had never met. The war demanded that strangers could no longer exist in England.

It wasn't until the villagers began to pick whom they would take home that Emmy saw how the two groups were different. The parents in the school yard had not been able to choose anything; not which bus their child would board, not which town they would go to, not which family would take them in. These people, on the other hand, looked the evacuees over as though they were shopping for their Christmas goose.

The foster parents, as the woman at the microphone called them, were invited to come speak with the children so that they could "all get to know one another."

As the people began to move toward them, Julia grabbed Emmy's hand. Her little sister's fingers were sticky from the meringue.

A couple approached the girls. They were older than Mum, younger than Nana would have been. The woman smelled like furniture polish and the man had a giant mole on his cheek that looked like it was made of roast beef.

They told the girls their names, Mr. and Mrs. Trimble, and said how nice it was to meet them. Then they asked the sisters for their names.

"I'm Emmeline Downtree and this is my sister, Julia," Emmy said. Julia, wide-eyed, said nothing.

The woman bent down and touched Julia's corn silk hair. "My, aren't you a pretty little cherub."

Julia looked up at Emmy. She could see her question in the little girl's eyes. *What's a cherub?*

"Say thank you," Emmy whispered.

Julia obeyed.

The woman peered at Julia's tag and then crinkled her brow in pity. "Oh. So, you've only a mum, then? What happened to your dad, little one?"

"He's in India," Julia said. "He's making a movie about the treasure of the seven lost princes."

"What's that?" said the man.

Julia proudly repeated the answer to the question.

Mr. and Mrs. Trimble swiveled their surprised faces to look at Emmy.

"What is it exactly that your father is doing in India?" the woman said to her.

After a morning of not knowing what anything was about, to be asked something about which she had ample knowledge loosened Julia's tongue. "Neville's not her dad," Julia said without a hint of embarrassment. "He's only mine. But I just call him Neville. We don't know where Emmy's father is."

The couple stared at Emmy, thoroughly scandalized. Emmy didn't care. Maybe if no one wanted her, she and Julia would be put back on a train to London. Several long seconds passed before Mr. and Mrs. Trimble recovered.

"Aren't you a little old to be sent off to the countryside?" Mr. Trimble finally said to Emmy.

Emmy laughed; she couldn't help it. For the last five days she had tried to convince everyone of this exact thing and no one would listen to her. Now here she was in a strange little village, standing in front of a couple obviously appalled by the details of her existence, and the man had pronounced—with no urging from Emmy—what she had so desperately wanted everyone else to say.

"Oh my!" the woman murmured. Emmy's ill-timed chuckle only added to Mrs. Trimble's growing impression of Emmy as an undesirable foster child.

"I couldn't agree with you more," Emmy said, reining in her amusement. "Believe me, I'd much rather be home than standing here talking to you."

Seconds of silence.

"Well, we'll just take little Julia here, then. Can't we, Howard?"

"No," Emmy said before Mr. Trimble could respond.

"I beg your pardon?" the woman said.

"I said no."

Alice, hovering nearby, sidled up to the girls, her expression anxious. "We try to keep siblings together if we can," she said, looking from Emmy to the couple.

"We can only take the little one," the man said.

"Then you'll need to keep shopping," Emmy said. "Julia stays with me."

Alice admonished Emmy with her eyes. She could read what the woman was communicating to her. It was something along the lines of *Can you please try to be nice?*

"Come along, Margaret." The man put his hand on his wife's back to guide her away from the sisters.

"But, Howard, I want the little one," the woman protested.

Howard Trimble ignored his wife but turned his gaze on Emmy. "A word of advice," he said with feigned courtesy. "You'll get nowhere with that attitude. You should be thinking about your little sister."

"That's exactly what I am doing," Emmy replied, matching his tone. "She stays with me."

Their conversation had attracted some attention. As Howard and Margaret Trimble moved away, Emmy noticed other conversations had stilled. People were staring at her.

Alice leaned in close. "I can see that you're not happy about being here, Emmeline, but please try to be polite or I'm afraid no one will want to take you."

"I don't care if no one wants to take me. And who are these people to look down on all of us and decide which of us they want. We should be choosing them."

Alice shushed her. "Keep your voice down."

All eyes were on Emmy now. She and Julia would be back on the train in no time; she was sure of it. "I will *not* keep my voice down. I will not allow my sister and me to be trafficked like slaves. This is debasing."

"Now, now. I'm sure these are good people."

"And all of us forced out of our homes, are we not good people? Do we really deserve to be picked over and poked like melons on market day?"

There wasn't a sound now in the room except Emmy's voice.

Howard Trimble, a few feet away, was shaking his head. It was no surprise to him that Emmy was mouthing off like she was. What could one expect from someone like her—an illegitimate urchin of a girl.

For a long moment there were only silence and wide-eyed stares.

Then Emmy saw movement out of the corner of her eye. And then there was a voice.

"You are absolutely right, my dear."

Emmy turned. The woman who had spoken was older than either of the Trimbles. Her silver hair, flecked with hints of a former coffee brown, was bound in a braid that lay across her shoulder and then trailed down past her left breast. She was tall and slender, and her skin was wrinkled but in a nice way, as if she had one day started smiling and then had never stopped. She was wearing a cornflower blue blouse and twill skirt with a smudge on the hem that suggested she had been gardening that day. The spectacles on her face were slightly skewed; perhaps she had recently sat on them and had to bend them back into shape.

"Please forgive our thoughtlessness?" the woman said.

Emmy didn't detect a hint of sarcasm or a patronizing tone, but she said nothing.

"Please?" she continued. "My name is Charlotte Havelock. It would be my great honor to welcome you and your sister, Julia, at Thistle House during this distressing time of war. I have a nice bedroom for you to sleep in, and a garden to play and read in, and I promise to treat you with all the respect that you are due. That is, if you will have me."

Again silence reigned in the room. Emmy felt Julia tugging on her shirt. She looked down at her little sister.

"I like her," she whispered.

The woman smiled.

The room was library-quiet and Emmy still had everyone's attention. Alice nodded to Emmy, a wordless gesture of desperation. She wanted Emmy to be wanted by someone; it made her job easier. There was no going back to London; Emmy could see that in her eyes, too. She would have to find a place for the girls, if not here in Moreton-in-Marsh, then in some other little town. Emmy could not return to London by refusing Charlotte Havelock's invitation.

But she *would* return to London.

One way or another she would return. It was just a matter of time.

"All right," Emmy said.

Charlotte Havelock extended her hand and Emmy, after a second's hesitation, took it. Charlotte's grip was warm and firm.

"Shall we take care of the paperwork, then?" She released Emmy's hand, and an openmouthed Alice led them all to the billeting table to complete the process. Several seconds passed before the hum of conversation resumed.

Charlotte filled out her contact information so that Mum could be notified where Emmy and Julia would be staying. Emmy looked over her shoulder as Charlotte wrote. Her home, Thistle House, was located in Stow-on-the-Wold, a village Emmy had never heard of.

Charlotte set the pen down and turned to the sisters. "Let's go home."

Ten

*

THE road between Moreton-in-Marsh and Stow-on-the-Wold was narrow but straight, taking them past rock walls, grazing sheep, fields of hay, and cottages of fawn-colored stone. London and all that Emmy had left behind seemed remarkably distant. It was as if they were traveling back in time or maybe to an entirely different world. There were no sandbags here, no air raid shelter signs, no barrage balloons in this endless sky. Emmy wondered how anyone out in this vast countryside knew they were even at war.

She and Julia sat up front with Charlotte in a dusty blue jalopy that sputtered like a steam engine as she drove. It was a four-and-a-half-mile jaunt between the two towns, Charlotte said, but since she lived on the edge of Stow, it would seem more like five.

The woman filled the silence inside the car by telling

the girls about herself, which allowed Emmy to sit back and memorize the route they were taking so that one day soon, if she had to, she could make her way back to London on her own.

Charlotte was sixty-six, a retired schoolteacher, and a widow of five years. She and her husband, Oliver, hadn't been blessed with any children, but she had a younger sister, Rose, whose disabilities made her childlike in many ways, so Charlotte felt as though she'd been gifted the chance to mother someone.

Oliver, bless his soul, had owned a hardware store in Stow-on-the-Wold, as had his father before him, and his father before him. He had been quite handy and liked to build things. She had an indoor loo before anyone else she knew did, thanks to Oliver. The century-old house had been in Oliver's family all that time, and had a lovely name, Thistle House. Many houses in the Cotswolds had names.

"What is a cot's wold?" Julia asked.

Charlotte Havelock smiled. "The Cotswolds is everything you can see out the window. For lots of miles. A hundred of them. Think of England as a very large book. The Cotswolds would be an unfussy chapter in the middle somewhere where there is lots of limestone and even more sheep."

"But what is a cot's wold? I want to see one."

"Oh, I know exactly what you mean. I'd like to see one, too. Here's the thing. Everyone agrees 'wold' means 'hills' but not everyone agrees what the 'cots' are."

"That's easy," Julia said. "Cots are little beds."

"Indeed." Charlotte's smile was broad. "Right you are, Julia."

Charlotte then told the girls that she had been born

in Cornwall, near the coast, and that she met Oliver at his brother's wedding in Bristol in 1893. They fell in love, and married a year later, and she moved to Thistle House. It had been her home ever since. She and her husband took in Rose eighteen years ago when Charlotte and Rose's mother died.

"I know I wasn't born here in the Cotswolds, but I feel like I was. This place has a way of welcoming you in, even if you are a stranger."

Her words were meant to convey welcome, but Emmy didn't want to imagine she could belong there, even for a little while. Still, she sensed the subtle embrace of Charlotte's seemingly warless world where everything appeared to be bathed in butter.

"I've never seen so many houses and buildings all made of the same yellow stone," Emmy said.

"That's Cotswold stone. We are sitting on a vast blanket of limestone here. Loads of it. They've been building with it for centuries. When it's been out in the weather decade upon decade, it turns a lovely honey color, which is rather nice. Can you imagine if it turned pink with age?"

"I like pink," Julia chimed.

"A lovely color for flowers, but not so much for houses," Charlotte said.

"It's—it's pretty here," Emmy said, unable to stay disconnected from her new surroundings.

The woman nodded. "I think so, too, Emmeline. I know it's not your home. And I wish there weren't a war. But I do want you to feel it *is* your home for as long as it must be such for you."

Her words were heavy with the weight of what could happen. No one knew how long the war would last or how long England could defend herself. But Emmy refused to give in to such negative thinking on the first day of the evacuation.

"I'm sure it won't be for very long," she said.

"I hope you're right. I really do."

The three of them were silent for a few seconds.

When Charlotte spoke again, her voice was bright. "Now, then, would you girls like to call me Mrs. Havelock or Aunt Charlotte?"

"I like Aunt Charlotte," Julia answered.

This woman, kind though she was, was not Emmy's aunt. "I prefer Mrs. Havelock," she said.

Charlotte regarded Emmy for a moment, taking her eyes off the road ahead for a second or two. "You know, Emmeline, you're very nearly an adult. How about you call me Charlotte?"

"Fine with me."

"Right, then. That's settled. So here's Stow."

They entered a village that was what Moreton might have been like fifty years before. Stores and offices made of Cotswold stone lined both sides of the street that led into the center of town, some with thatched roofs, some with shingles. They passed a town hall, a pub, a grocer, a bank, a butcher, a dentist. There seemed to be one of everything needed for a town to survive on its own without any interaction from the outside, ever.

"There's the hardware store," Charlotte said, pointing to a toast brown building with a shiny red sign with black lettering in front. "It's called Browne and Sons Hardware now. Used to be Havelock Hardware. We sold it the year Ollie retired. I used to have tea with him Saturday afternoons before Rose came. I'd bring it down in the basket of my bike. Down that way is our train station, so if your mum wants to come see you, she can come straight here. Oh, and there's my church." Charlotte nodded toward a castlelike structure with a bright blue door and a steeple arrowing past the treetops. "And down that way is the primary school. The secondary school is back behind us a bit. I'll show them to you sometime if you want."

"That's all right," Emmy said as politely as she could. She didn't see much purpose to that. It was June. The school term was three months away.

Then they were back in the countryside, on a narrow, treelined lane.

"This is the Maugersbury Road," Charlotte said. "The village officials had to take all the road signs down because of the war, but everyone here knows this road leads to little Maugersbury. Rose and I live on the edge of both towns. Maugersbury is small, just a few houses, some farms, and the manor, really. Now, tell me about you. What do you girls like to do when you're not in school?"

Emmy nodded to Julia so that she could answer first. "Well, I like going to the park and playing with my paper dolls and I like Thea's cat and kittens and I like going to my friend Sybil's house because she has lots of toys. And her own tea set."

"Well, how lovely." Charlotte beamed. "My back garden is sort of like a park. I've lots of fruit trees and a little pond and a vegetable garden and chickens. And I have the tea set that was mine when I was a little girl. I'll have to get it out for you."

"Do you have a pony?" Julia said, as animated as Emmy had seen her since Thea's kittens were born.

"I don't have a pony. But my neighbor has two goats. Edgar and Clementine. And my other neighbor has a miniature horse named Jingles."

Julia whipped her head around to face Emmy, her eyes bright with anticipation and an "I told you so" gleam.

"How about you, Emmeline? What do you like to do?"

"Emmy draws brides," Julia said before Emmy could answer, her attention fully back on Charlotte.

"She draws brides?"

"Their dresses. She has drawn a whole bunch. She gave me some. I have them inside my book. You want to see?"

"Well, perhaps when I am not driving." Charlotte glanced at Emmy, hoping for a fuller explanation.

"I like to sketch bridal designs," Emmy said. "I am hoping, I mean, I am planning to become a designer. I had a job at a bridal shop. Until today."

"Oh. I see. I'm so sorry you had to leave it, Emmeline."

Her empathy was genuine and full, almost too much for Emmy to handle.

"Her dresses are really pretty," Julia continued, and Emmy was happy for the interruption. "She has them in the brides box. I like to look at them and Emmy lets me whenever I want as long as she is there with me. I'm not supposed to get them out when she's not home."

"I would love to see them sometime," Charlotte said. "If you don't mind showing them to me, that is."

"Um. Sure," Emmy said. Charlotte's interest, almost maternal in nature, was strangely welcome.

"If you like, I can show you my wedding dress sometime," Charlotte said, her smile broad. "Oh my goodness, Emmeline. Just wait until you see what was in style back when I got married. Would you like to?"

Emmy nodded, and a smile tugged at the corners of her mouth. She found she could not speak.

Charlotte seemed to pick up on this. It was as if she

knew Emmy needed the topic of discussion to shift to something not so desperately personal.

"So, we are almost to Thistle House," Charlotte said. "I need to tell you girls that my sister, Rose, is a dear soul, but she's a bit forgetful and simpleminded. She's only a year younger than I am, but you would do me a great favor by thinking of her—if you don't mind—as if she were five."

"Why does she think she's five?" Julia asked, genuinely concerned.

"She doesn't think she's five. She just has a difficult time thinking like an adult would think. Rose was in an accident a long time ago. It was very bad and we thought she might die. She finally came back to us, but she came back different. When she woke up from her injuries, it was as if she were a little girl again and she just stayed that way."

"How old was she when that happened?" Emmy's sympathies had been aroused as only a fellow sister's would.

"She was thirteen. A very long time ago."

"I'm sorry." Emmy didn't know what else to say.

"It's all right. My parents and I just learned to love the new Rose. It actually wasn't that hard to do." Charlotte laughed nervously, as though the accident was still fresh in her mind. "Once we let go of the old Rose. Here we are."

They turned down a narrow gravel path wide enough for only one car, which, after a slight curve, led to a house constructed of Cotswold stone, with wood trim painted forest green. Climbing roses rioted across the front gate and ivy crawled up the sidewalls. Gabled windows on the second story boasted window boxes of white and pink geraniums. A brass oval nailed to the stone framing the doorway read THISTLE HOUSE. It was such a charming, storybook place that Emmy instinctively reached into her skirt pocket to touch the ticket stub from Paddington station and the key to Primrose nestled behind it. She needed to remind herself that she really had awakened that morning in London. Julia was similarly awestruck. There was no house like this in their little corner of the world, and that corner was all her sister knew. Julia held her fairy tale book close to her chest, her eyes wide with wonder and doubt.

They got out of the car.

Charlotte, carrying Julia's suitcase, walked up the stone pathway to the front door and opened it wide. "Welcome to Thistle House, Emmeline and Julia. My home is yours."

The short, narrow entryway led to a sitting room and a staircase straight ahead, a kitchen and pantry and the privy on the left, and a dining room and living area on the right. In Charlotte's absence, Rose had been looked after by a neighbor who lived nearby. Mrs. Tinley bid them all welcome and then left by the garden door to return to her home.

Rose looked a lot like Charlotte; she had the same nose and chin, the same eyes, even the same long silvery braid. Their voices had the same tone and timbre. Their sameness seemed to accentuate Julia's and Emmy's differences. Julia's fair skin, green eyes, and blond hair were all Neville. Emmy's brown hair was darker than Mum's, and so were her eyes.

Charlotte led the girls to the table where Rose sat surrounded by a pile of magazines. "Rose, these are the children from London I was telling you about. This is Emmeline and this is Julia."

Rose languidly blinked at the girls. "Are they staying in my room?" she finally said, frowning.

"No, they're in the guest room. Remember?"

Rose studied the sisters for another long moment. "The green towels are mine. But I'll share them." Then she bent over her magazine.

"How about I show you to your room and then we'll have a nice tea out in the garden?"

They made their way back to the main entry and to the staircase that led to the three bedrooms upstairs. The guest room was decorated in shades of yellow with dormer windows graced with eyelet valances and the familiar blackout curtains. So they did know about the war here, Emmy thought. Two four-poster beds were side-by-side, both covered with daisy-patterned quilts and ruffled bed skirts. Each one was paired with a bedside table. Directly across from the beds and on the other side of the door was a tall wardrobe, painted white and decorated with sunflowers. A tall bureau painted white with yellow glass knobs filled one slanted wall, and a desk with a little gooseneck table lamp sat along another. A waist-high, lace-covered table stood next to the desk. It was the prettiest bedroom Emmy had ever seen.

"I've emptied all but the bottom bureau drawer for you," Charlotte said. "And more than half the wardrobe. And I've put some writing paper in the desk for you so you can write home to your mum or your friends as often as you wish. I wrote down my address on a little card there so that you can let people know where you are."

"Thank you," Emmy murmured, the most she could say at that moment.

A long pause followed as Emmy and Julia stared at the room that was to be theirs.

"Would you like to settle in and unpack first? Or would you like to do that later and come outside to the garden for a little tea?" Charlotte said.

Julia finally found her voice. "May we see the chickens?"

Charlotte laughed. "Of course! Right this way."

She turned to leave and Julia was right on her heels, grabbing Charlotte's hand as she stepped out of the room.

Watching Julia so easily reach for Charlotte's hand took Emmy aback for only a moment.

Half a moment, really.

That was how long it took her to realize this situation was perfect—for Julia.

She would write a letter that very night and give Mrs. Crofton her new address. When the day came that Mrs. Crofton informed Emmy that Mr. Dabney had returned to London, she could sneak away, and leave Julia here with no reservations whatsoever. Julia would be happy here. And Emmy would be happy to be returning to London and getting on with her life. Everyone would be happy.

Emmy followed her sister.

Eleven

⁂

WITH teacups in hand, Charlotte and Emmy settled onto padded metal chairs in the shade of a towering poplar tree while Julia scampered about the garden. Rose trailed after Julia with casual but undeniable interest. Paved in Cotswold stone, the little terrace where they sat sipping tea was surrounded on three sides by more trees, flower beds, a sizable vegetable garden, orchard trees, a chicken coop, and, beyond the perimeter of Charlotte's property, a murky pond that ended in reeds and a horizon of pearl-blue sky.

"I don't need to worry about Julia getting too close to the pond, do I?" Emmy said as Julia skipped after a pair of wood ducks waddling toward the water.

"It's quite shallow at the edge. Unless you think she will run headlong into it," Charlotte replied. "I'm sure she will be fine. And Rose will get after her if she goes too close."

"She will?"

"Well, not necessarily because she senses danger. She just knows how I feel about muddy shoes in the house."

Emmy took a sip of her tea and sat back in her chair.

"You've felt responsible for your sister for a long time, haven't you?" Charlotte said, but her gaze was on Julia a hundred yards away.

For a second Emmy wasn't sure how to respond. She sensed admiration in Charlotte's tone, or maybe solidarity as she had obviously taken on responsibility for her own sister, Rose, albeit to a much greater extent. "I suppose I have. It's not like I had a choice. Our mum's not . . . She's not like most mothers. She's . . ." Emmy's voice fell away. She didn't know what word she was looking for.

"She's ill?"

Emmy shook her head and a tiny laugh escaped her. "No. She's not ill. She's . . . She was only sixteen when she had me. She's never been married and Julia and I don't even have the same father. Her mother—my nana—was hard on her. They didn't get on very well. I think maybe Mum's getting pregnant—both times—was something my nana never forgave her for."

"And yet it takes two people to create a baby," Charlotte said gently, pouring more tea into her cup from the teapot sitting on a little table between them. She offered the pot to Emmy, who silently extended her cup.

Charlotte's soft but candid tone surprised Emmy. Mum had spoken to her from time to time about men, mostly how Emmy should not trust the ones who liked to say nice things about how she looked. Mum never talked about sex with Emmy. Everything Emmy knew about how babies were made she had learned from classmates at school in hushed conversations peppered with twittering laughter.

"Did neither father provide for your mother?" Charlotte continued when Emmy said nothing.

"Uh, well. Neville—that's Julia's father—he liked being a father when it was convenient for him and when it didn't get in the way of things he liked better. And he didn't know how to handle money, if that's what you mean. Whenever he had any, he spent it as soon as he got it. He was an actor. And was unemployed a lot of the time."

"Was?"

Emmy looked to Julia running up and down the bank of the pond. "He died in a car accident in Dublin not too long ago."

"Oh. I'm very sorry."

Emmy brought her attention back to Charlotte. "Julia doesn't know he's dead. She thinks he's still in India. Mum has always made up stories about where Neville was when he would disappear, so that's where she thinks he is. It's been a year since she's seen him."

Charlotte nodded thoughtfully. "I see. And Julia doesn't ask about him?"

"Sometimes. She can go for weeks without mentioning him, and then she will see something that reminds her of him and she'll ask when he's coming back."

"Strange that she calls him by his first name, isn't it?"

Emmy shrugged. "It suited him. And Julia didn't care. She liked him because he'd bring her trinkets and toys now and then, and he never did any of the things that little children wish their parents wouldn't do, like make them mind or insist they eat their vegetables or demand they clean their room."

"So you don't think she should be told he has died?"

"It's Mum who thinks she shouldn't be told. She found out he was dead the same day the evacuation notice came. Mum said it was too much for Julia to handle all at once. She made me promise I wouldn't say anything. So I haven't."

Off in the distance, Rose knelt down and Julia followed suit. Rose was showing Julia something in the water.

"One of the turtles, probably," Charlotte said, as if reading Emmy's mind. "We've several that prefer our edge of the pond."

Emmy watched as Julia put her hand in the water, squealed with delight, and drew it back out.

"And what about your father, then, if I may ask?" Charlotte said.

Emmy hesitated a moment before answering. "You can ask, but I haven't much to say about him. I don't know who he is. Mum said he was not someone I ever needed to think about."

Charlotte furrowed her brow. "So she was not in love with him?"

Again, Emmy shrugged. "I guess not. I don't know. She met him at a party, apparently. And she had been drinking."

"At such a young age?"

"It happens."

"And no one held the young man responsible?"

Emmy had always pictured Mum having met someone a bit older than she was at the party who had changed the course of her life, not another teenager like herself. It wasn't until Emmy was sitting there with Charlotte, discussing the very thing Mum and Nana never talked about, that she suddenly realized that if her father was a few years older than Mum, then he'd taken advantage of an underage girl, and that was against the law. He would have been arrested if Mum had named him. That Emmy had never given this any thought irritated her.

She looked up at Charlotte, and her face must have revealed that she had realized something she hadn't considered.

"What is it, dear?" Charlotte said.

"Nothing." Emmy drained her cup.

It all made sense. No one had held her father responsible because Mum hadn't identified him. That was why there was such animosity between Mum and Nana. Any parent whose barely sixteen-year-old daughter ended up pregnant would want to know who the father was. If Mum had refused to say, which surely was the case, it could only have been for one of three reasons that Emmy could think of: She had been protecting the man, she was embarrassed to admit she didn't know his name, or she had struck a deal with him.

Emmy set her cup down on the little table, angry that she had let herself be satisfied for fifteen years with such vague answers about who her father was.

"Emmeline?"

"Can we talk about something else?"

A slight pause. "Of course."

At that moment Julia called for Emmy to come look at the baby turtles. She and Charlotte rose from their chairs, and Emmy was thankful that the conversation she had wanted to end fell away, but only partially so. She knew she would revisit it in her strange bed that night.

A few seconds later they were all at the water's edge, and Julia was pointing to several young turtles swimming in the shallows, their little armored backs glistening. A few feet away, the wood ducks that Julia had followed paddled toward the pond's center. A pair of dragonflies darted past them and skimmed across the water's surface.

Surrounded by such pastoral splendor, Emmy found it hard to believe there was a war going on.

Her presence there at a pond in the middle of nowhere was the only proof that there was.

WHEN they came back inside the cottage, Emmy and Julia went upstairs to unpack and put their clothes away. Charlotte told them that for this first night they could relax in their room while she prepared supper downstairs, and that tomorrow the three of them would sit down and decide who would do what chores.

As Emmy hung up one of Julia's dresses, her sister asked what Charlotte had meant by that.

"I imagine she expects we will do our fair share here. Setting the table, clearing it, taking out the rubbish. That sort of thing."

"Do you think she will let me feed the chickens?"

Emmy slid the hanger onto the rung inside the wardrobe. "I am sure she will. Hand me your jumper."

Julia handed the sweater to her and snapped her suitcase closed. "It's not as bad here as I thought it would be. Aunt Charlotte's nice. And her house smells pretty."

"Pretty isn't a smell, Jewels. Slide your suitcase under your bed like I did with mine so you won't trip over it."

"Why don't you want to call her Aunt Charlotte?" Julia asked as she pushed the suitcase past the bed skirt.

"I'm too old to call someone 'aunt' who is not my aunt. But you're young. It's fine for you."

Julia rose from her knees and sat heavily on her bed. "What are we supposed to do now?"

Emmy closed the wardrobe door. "What would you like to do?"

"Can I look at the brides?"

"Not now."

"Why?"

Emmy didn't have a good reason other than she was tired and it was near the end of a very trying day. "Maybe later. Why don't you write a letter to Mum instead. You can tell her all about the ducks and turtles."

"All right, but I'll need help with the big words."

Emmy told Julia she would help her with any word she didn't know how to spell. She opened the desk drawer. Inside, Emmy found three different shades of writing paper, several sharpened pencils, and a fountain pen. It was exciting to think that she now had plenty of paper to continue sketching dresses. Emmy had planned to buy some drawing paper with her first month's pay, but specialty paper was also being rationed and thus becoming harder to find. She decided she would make it a goal, starting the next day, to sketch a new gown every week so that she would have something to look forward to. For the moment, though, Emmy withdrew two pieces of paper—one for each of them—a pencil for Julia, and the fountain pen for herself, to write letters.

Emmy let Julia have the desk while she sat on her bed with Julia's fairy tale book on her lap for a writing surface. While Julia wrote about the train ride, the dead bird in the street, the yellow bedroom, Charlotte's and Rose's long braids, and their lovely garden, Emmy penned a letter, too.

Dear Mrs. Crofton:

My sister and I are staying with an older woman named Charlotte Havelock in a tiny place not far from Stow-in-the-Wold in Gloucestershire. I would be very much in your debt if you could let me know when your cousin returns to London so that I might meet with him as we planned. I will continue to work on new sketches and I will ask Mrs. Havelock if she has a sewing machine that I can practice on while I am here. I hope to see you again very soon and I trust you will be safe.

Yours truly,
Emmeline Downtree

Thistle House
3 Maugersbury Road
Stow-on-the-Wold,
Gloucestershire

P.S. I still have the back door key you gave me.

They were called to supper just as Emmy was finishing addressing their letters. She brought the envelopes downstairs to be posted in the morning. Charlotte had set the table in the dining room for their first meal to mark the occasion. When Emmy asked about how to post the letters, Charlotte seemed pleased that the girls had been upstairs writing home.

"Your mum will be glad to hear from you girls," she said as she placed a dish of parsleyed potatoes on the table and motioned for them to choose chairs. Rose, already seated, was unfolding and refolding her napkin.

"Emmy didn't write Mum. Only me," Julia announced as she plopped onto a chair.

Charlotte raised her head slightly to look at the two

envelopes in Emmy's hand, surely wondering to whom Emmy had written. "We can post your letters tomorrow. Perhaps we can walk to town and do that. It's only half a mile. Be good to stretch your legs."

"I need new wellies," Rose announced, not looking up from her folding.

"Your wellies are in fine shape, Rose. But we'd love for you to come with us. Emmeline, dear, please do have a seat."

Emmy took the chair next to Julia while Charlotte brought in a plate of sliced ham, something the sisters hadn't seen since Christmas.

When Charlotte was seated as well, she held her hands out to her sister, and to Emmy on her other side.

"Shall we thank God for your safe arrival?"

It had been a long time since Emmy and Julia had been in the same room with someone who spoke to God out of reverence. She took her sister's other hand and bowed her head, peering at Julia to see whether she was doing the same.

Charlotte's prayer was brief and to the point. She thanked God for the girls, asked that they and everyone they loved would be kept safe during this uncertain time, and that they all would be always thankful for God's gracious provision. While they ate, Julia chattered about what their flat was like in London, the long-ago trip to Brighton Beach, and how much she hated the air raid sirens. Emmy let her carry the conversation, which Charlotte and Rose seemed to enjoy very much, leading her to believe the two elderly sisters had little exposure to the animated prattle of a child.

After the girls helped with the dishes, the four of them settled in the parlor to look at Charlotte's family photographs. Night fell. Charlotte switched on several lamps and pulled the blackout curtains down, shutting out a sky full of stars.

Twelve

DESPITE the lovely room, Emmy had trouble getting to sleep that first night at Thistle House. She had gone to bed when Julia did, though she could have stayed up later with Charlotte and Rose if she had wanted. Julia had grown pensive as they looked at Charlotte's and Rose's family pictures. For the first time since they had been notified of the evacuation, it seemed as if Julia understood more fully that she and Emmy had been sent away because London was not safe. That meant Mum was not safe. She did not want to go to bed alone in a strange house with such heavy thoughts.

Emmy pulled the curtains open when she turned out the light so that the bright moon, which had become London's enemy in recent months, could bathe the room in lustrous half-light and keep away the deepest dark.

She had sat on the edge of Julia's bed and stroked her

back to lull her to sleep, but it was a long time before her sister stopped asking questions such as "Why didn't Mum come with us on the train? Why isn't she here with us? What if the Germans come to London?" and closed her eyes.

When Julia was at last asleep and Emmy was finally in bed, she had her own troubles to keep sleep elusive, primarily the loss of her job, the meeting with Mr. Dabney that she did not want to miss, and the notion that Mum had willingly chosen to bear all the responsibility of raising her.

The more Emmy thought about it, the more she understood what she had simply failed to notice before.

What kind of man would sixteen-year-old Mum have agreed to leave unnamed on a birth certificate? A man who didn't want to be charged with statutory rape, that was who. And how else could this man have secured Mum's silence unless money had been involved? Surely that was how she had financed those first few years of her life as a single mother. There had been a payoff. That was how she was able to stay in London with a new baby instead of moving with her mother to Devonshire. How long had the money lasted? Emmy wondered. Because at some point Mum had met Neville and she had let herself get pregnant again. But this time she was twenty-four. Since she would not be paid off, perhaps she was hoping she could at last be married off. The trouble was, Neville hadn't had a keen sense of responsibility. A pregnant girlfriend wasn't exactly a problem, and it certainly wasn't *his* problem. Mum had been wrong about herself, too, because she fell in love with the man who fathered her second child but didn't want to marry her. And when that happened, it didn't matter that Neville had lots of money one day and nothing the next, or that he had no scruples. She was in love with him until the day he left her for good. Love had not worked out like Mum had hoped.

Love had failed her. But money had not.

Was that what she had returned to, then? Was that why they had moved to a nicer flat than a kitchen maid could afford after Neville left? Was that why they had warm beds, hot water, enough food to eat, and suitcases to pack their clothes in for the evacuation?

Because someone was giving her money on the side? And what else could it be *for* but for sex? Mum didn't have anything else to offer but her lovely body.

Emmy sat up in bed, both repulsed and heartbroken by what her mother had become. For several long minutes she sat there, drawing breaths in and letting them out, as she sought to calm her thundering heart. She swung her legs over the side of the bed and reached underneath it for her brides box. Emmy opened the latch and withdrew the sketches, laying them across her rumpled blanket now awash in moonlight.

A translucent glow draped the gowns with the sweet white radiance due them, such that each one seemed touched by magic for just that moment.

It did not matter that there were no faces on the penciled-in heads: The gowns themselves exuded elation and perfection, exactly what you would expect a bride to radiate on the day of her dreams, on the day everything was right in her world.

No wonder Emmy loved these dresses so. Each one was an emblem of all that she wanted for her miserable life.

Emmy didn't hear Julia rise from her bed, nor did she feel the tears on her own cheeks. Her sister was just suddenly at her side, crawling up next to her and laying her head on Emmy's shoulder.

Julia's small arm curled around her sister's back and Emmy lowered her head to Julia's.

"I miss Mum, too," Julia whispered.

THE next day over breakfast Charlotte made a list of the girls' chores so that they would feel Thistle House was their home. Guests didn't do chores, Charlotte said. And she didn't want the girls to feel like guests; nor did she want them to get bored. School would not be in session until September, which meant they had nearly three months to occupy themselves. Emmy couldn't quite grasp the idea that she would still be with Charlotte come September, but she said nothing.

Julia got her wish to be able to feed the chickens, and to water them, change their straw, and gather eggs. Emmy would take care of their laundry, bedding, and towels, and she would do the sweeping and run the Hoover. Rose, sitting at the table while the chores were divvied up and wanting to be a part of the conversation, was placed in charge of using the feather duster, although Emmy did not think she would actually remember that she had asked for a chore to do. The sisters would take turns setting and clearing the table and drying the dishes.

The vegetable garden and fruit trees were best kept by all four of them, Charlotte said, since both required constant vigilance against weeds and pests and inclement weather, and because the gardens and fruit trees might be what kept them all fed if rationing continued to become more strict. Butter, bacon, and sugar had been rationed since the beginning of the year, and meat, cheese, and fruit had followed not long after, when fewer and fewer supply ships could get past the German U-boats patrolling the English Channel. No one in London had a garden the size of Charlotte's. It was amazing to think that here in the country, a ration book didn't determine what you ate or didn't eat, but rather the state of your vegetable garden and henhouse.

Charlotte also decreed that Julia and Emmy should read a book every week to keep their minds fresh, and that they should write Mum twice a month, or as long as the stationery held out. Paper had also recently been rationed, Charlotte said, and Emmy could not help but frown at this. She could afford no reject gowns if the writing paper was to last. And while Charlotte had ample books in her sitting room, Emmy doubted she'd let her tear out the blank pages in back to sketch bridal gowns.

The four of them walked into town after lunch to post the letters, stop at the library so that the girls could check out books for the first week, and to buy meat, dried beans, and other staples Charlotte could not grow in her garden. The townspeople on the streets and in the stores regarded Emmy and her sister with friendly but wary smiles. It was obvious no one knew what to expect next. If the evacuation was complete and all the children were safely out of London, then what could possibly follow but the brutal attack everyone feared? Two of the women Charlotte introduced them to told the girls that their sons were far away fighting hard so that they could be reunited with their mum and dad. It was as if they needed the girls to know that although they couldn't see the war there in the Cotswolds, they could still feel it.

There were other London evacuees in the village; not just from their train, but from others as well. Just as she was about to enter the library, Emmy saw two evacuees she recognized, a sister and brother from their train car. Their eyes met from across the street and an unspoken communication passed between them. Somehow in that wordless exchange they were able to ascertain that neither of them had been taken in by a lunatic or a tyrant. The woman they were with was younger than Charlotte and held the hand of a little boy who was clearly hers. Emmy was glad in that moment that she and Julia didn't have to compete for attention from a foster mother's own child.

At the post office, Charlotte introduced them to the postmistress, easily the tallest woman Emmy had ever met. She handed her the letters and the postmistress accepted them with a confident nod, saying it took only two days for mail to reach London. As the letter to Mrs. Crofton passed from Emmy's hand, she unashamedly prayed for God's favor. She knew how selfish it was to ask for something so self-serving as an appointment with a dressmaker in light of the war, but she also knew the war could not last forever. One day it would be over. And they would all be able to go back to doing what they had been doing before—dreaming what they had been dreaming, and planning what they had been planning.

Emmy was already plotting how she would be able to sneak away unnoticed back to London. That daunting process had to begin with receiving Mrs. Crofton's letter of response and without Charlotte's asking about it. And she could not begin the journey there in Stow where someone would recognize her. She would need to get herself to Moreton where she would attract far less attention.

After leaving the post office, Charlotte stopped for a copy of the *Daily Mail*, which she said she liked to pick up every other day or so. Emmy quickly offered to add to her list of duties walking to town to get it for her. A trip to town away from watchful eyes would allow Emmy to post as many letters to Mrs. Crofton as she needed to without drawing attention to it. Charlotte seemed to think that the London newspaper might seem like a small tether to Emmy's real home. She also had no reason to mistrust Emmy's motives.

"Of course," she said.

The last stop before returning home was the variety store. While they waited outside with Rose and their armload of library books, Charlotte went inside for Epsom salts and a bottle of aspirin. She emerged a few minutes later with those items, plus several strange-looking pencils and ten sheets of card stock.

"So that you can keep drawing your bridal dresses." Charlotte handed the paper and the pencils to Emmy. "The pencils are special for sketching. They're what artists use and they're supposed to be just what you need."

It took Emmy a second to find her voice. "Thank you," she muttered, surprise making her gratitude sound halfhearted.

Julia stared at the pencils and the tissue-wrapped paper and then turned to Charlotte with an unmistakable "what about me" look.

Charlotte tousled her hair. "I have something for you back at the house, Julia."

"Really? What is it?"

"Let's go home and I'll show you."

Julia brightened and happily took Charlotte's hand. As the two of them walked ahead, Rose fell in step with Emmy.

They hadn't taken more than a few steps when Emmy felt Rose's hand in hers.

Back at the house, Julia could scarcely wait until what they had brought home with them was put away.

"Just let me get Rose settled with her tea and then I'll show you," Charlotte said as she put the kettle on. Emmy took the drawing paper and pencils to her room and laid them on top of the brides box on the bedside table. Back downstairs, she got out the cream and sugar while Charlotte poured Rose's tea and placed the hot kettle in the tea cozy. She handed Emmy two digestive biscuits.

"Give those to Rose, will you, dear?" she said to Emmy, then turned to Julia. "All right. Let me get a torch." Charlotte grabbed a flashlight from the shelf near the back door and then headed out of the kitchen. "Come along, Miss Julia."

Julia skipped after her.

Emmy brought the biscuits to Rose, and the two of them watched as Charlotte and Julia left the room.

"Where are they going?" Rose said, her brow furrowed.

"I don't know."

"I don't want them going in my room. They shouldn't be going into my room. It's my room."

Emmy could hear Charlotte and Julia on the stairs. So could Rose.

"It's my room. My things." Rose didn't sound agitated and she made no move to rise from her chair. Hers was the weirdest opposition Emmy had ever seen. Resistance without effort.

Emmy's own interest in what Charlotte was planning to give Julia was also piqued, and not just because of Rose. She turned to the older woman.

"Want me to go see what they're doing?" Emmy asked.

Rose picked up her cup daintily. "For heaven's sake, yes. It's my room. And my things."

Happy to oblige, Emmy made for the stairs.

But Charlotte and Julia were headed into the yellow room, not Rose's. Charlotte turned to Emmy when she appeared behind them, happy, it seemed, that Emmy had followed them.

"Rose wanted me to make sure you weren't traipsing about in her room," Emmy volunteered.

Charlotte just smiled. She turned back to face the far wall and the desk. She lifted the lace tablecloth off the waist-high table next to it, revealing a crawl space door between the wooden legs.

Charlotte sank to her knees and clicked on the flashlight. "Been a while since I've had any need to root about in here. Want to make sure no spiders or such have taken up residence." The door protested as she opened it, the hinges squeaking at the disturbance.

She bent forward and poked her head in the space, shining the flashlight about. "Hmm," she said. "Fancy that. Just a few cobwebs." She pulled her head back out. "Julia, you're young and small. Could you crawl inside and hand me the box with the pictures of canning jars on the sides? And then the bigger one underneath? I promise neither one is very heavy."

Julia didn't need to be asked twice. Charlotte moved out of the way and Julia dropped to her knees. Charlotte handed her the flashlight, and then Julia scooted inside the crawl space and disappeared inside it. Emmy heard scraping on wood and then the first box appeared, and then the second one.

"There's a box of books in here," Julia called out.

"They're just old schoolbooks. They can stay," Charlotte said, brushing her hand across the dusty surface of the first box. Motes took to the beams of afternoon sunlight slanting in the room.

Julia reappeared, her long blond hair mussed about her face.

"Well done, Julia," Charlotte said as Julia crawled completely out and Charlotte swung the door closed. She took the flashlight from Julia and switched it off.

"What's in them?" Julia asked, fully intrigued.

Charlotte smiled and opened the first box. Inside were little lumps of thin muslin. Charlotte withdrew one of the lumps. Inside the fabric was a child-size china teacup patterned in autumn leaves.

"Oh!" Julia exclaimed.

"It's my tea set from when I was a little girl. I want you to think of it as yours for as long as you're here, all right?"

Julia was speechless with wonder as Charlotte continued to unwrap the pieces. There were four cups with their saucers, four plates, a creamer and sugar bowl, and a squat little teapot with a swanlike spout.

Then Charlotte opened the next box, which held two dolls, one golden-haired and one brunette, and a smaller box of tissue-wrapped doll clothes.

She placed the dolls in Julia's arms.

"This one with the brown hair I called Guinevere and the other one Henrietta, but you can call them whatever you want. They are also yours to play with while you're here. But I want you to take good care of them. No leaving them outside or tearing the clothes or bringing them to the table. Can you do that?"

Julia nodded solemnly, astonishment in her eyes. "I promise," she whispered. She pulled the dolls close to her chest and kissed each head. "I love their names, Aunt Charlotte."

Charlotte got to her feet and picked up the smaller box with the unwrapped tea service resting at odd angles inside it. "I'll just wash the tea set and then it will be ready for you to use. That sound all right?"

Julia nodded, enraptured beyond words. It was the happiest Emmy had ever seen her.

She sought Charlotte's gaze. "Thank you for doing that," Emmy said softly.

"I've something to show you, too."

Emmy followed Charlotte to her room across the hall. The woman set the box with the tea set on her bed and walked to a wardrobe. After opening the door, she reached for a long, deep box on a shelf above the rod of hanging dresses and blouses.

This box Charlotte also set on her bed. She lifted its lid, pushed away the tissue paper, and pulled out an ivory gown, its skirt glistening with tiny seed pearls that had aged to twilight gray. Lacy sleeves that buttoned tight to the elbow ballooned to the shoulder in Victorian elegance. A close-fitting bodice completed the top half, and the crushed full skirt hinted at the gown's former glory.

"My wedding dress," Charlotte murmured, gazing at the gown, not at Emmy.

"It's beautiful."

She turned to Emmy. "I thought it might inspire you. Sometimes an old design will spark a new idea. You— you can take it apart if you want. If it helps you."

Emmy touched the fabric, a low-luster satin that nearly murmured hello back to her. "I couldn't do such a thing," she whispered.

"It is of no use to anyone sitting in a box," Charlotte continued. "It's no longer in style and I have no daughter to give it to. Wouldn't it make more sense for you to take it apart and study the construction? You could use the parts to reinvent it, or come up with your own design. Not just a drawing but an actual dress."

"You would let me do that?" Emmy was incredulous.

"It would make me very happy if you did. Now, I don't have a sewing machine. But I've sharp scissors, several spools of white thread, and lots of sewing needles. You'll have to do it all by hand, but I'm thinking you're probably going to have the time during these long summer months."

Emmy, like Julia, found she could not express the right words of gratitude. To say a simple thank-you to such generosity seemed too shallow.

So she thought of something else to say.

"Would you like to see my sketches?"

For the next few minutes, while Julia played with Guinevere and Henrietta in the other room, Charlotte and Emmy sat on the bed and looked at the sketches in the brides box.

Charlotte said they were the loveliest dresses she had ever seen.

A day that could not have been more surprisingly pleasant for Emmy and Julia became even more so. Late in the afternoon when it was time to take care of the chickens, a gentle rain started to fall. Charlotte let Julia use her umbrella: a red polka-dot umbrella with a curly black handle that looked like licorice.

Thirteen

❧

THE days at Thistle House fell into a routine as days always do. After the beds were made and breakfast things put away, mornings were spent tending the vegetable garden, weeding the berry patch, pinching off the heads of spent blooms, and watering the flower beds and the apple, plum, and pear trees, of which there were several each. Even though being outside made the girls hot and sweaty, it was Julia's favorite part of the day and the work made the morning fly by. After lunch on Mondays and Fridays, Emmy would walk to town to buy Charlotte a newspaper. The afternoons were spent inside reading, working on puzzles, or writing to Mum. Late-afternoon tea was often enjoyed at one of the neighbors' homes. All of the neighbors seemed to be Charlotte's age or older. Julia and Emmy were the only children among Charlotte's friends, and that they were London evacuees made them especially interesting. In the evenings, after listening to the BBC for a bit, Charlotte and Rose would knit, Julia would play with the dolls or the tea set or both, and Emmy would work on dissecting Charlotte's wedding dress—her favorite part of the day.

Some days Charlotte loaded everyone into her blue jalopy and they headed to Moreton or Cheltenham, to see Rose's doctor or to shop in stores that had more in the way of staples to offer, though the queues were longer. On Sundays they attended services at the church with the blue door that Charlotte had pointed out the day they arrived. Emmy liked the vicar well enough, and she enjoyed the way their voices echoed when they sang hymns or recited the creed and prayers. The stone floors and walls made the sound bigger than it really was. And more eloquent. Church was also one of the few places where they saw the other London children all at the same time. They, like the girls, seemed to have settled in to their new surroundings. Emmy felt no need to converse with these other children, but she was a bit surprised that they didn't, either, even though most were younger. It was as if they had all struck a careful balance between where they lived now and where their true homes were. To speak to one another was to trifle with that balance.

Emmy had summoned the courage and snipped away every seam of Charlotte's wedding dress, a process that took her nearly a week. She then laid out the pieces so that she could study their structure and also compare them with the brides box sketches. Some nights Charlotte would sit with her while she worked, and sometimes Rose would, which was always a bit unnerving as Rose was convinced the dress in pieces was for her wedding and she worried Emmy wouldn't get it sewn in time.

Mum's first letter came at the end of June, nearly two weeks after they had arrived at Stow. She wrote that she missed her daughters, that the entire city seemed out of sorts without its children, and that there had been annoying air raid warnings nearly every night since the girls had left. Emmy didn't think this was quite true. She read the newspaper that Charlotte had her buy. The rest of June had been relatively quiet in London. Julia and Emmy had left one week after Mr. Churchill announced on the radio that Britain would fight the Germans on every beach, street, hill, and field, and never, ever surrender to them. That had been as near an invitation to Hitler to come see if Britain would do just that as anyone could have given. And yet the attack on London did not come. The few bombs that had fallen in the open country, like those at Addington and Colney, had been so insignificant and so far from the city center, some wondered if London wasn't the safest place after all. There were no landing fields to strafe, no troops to engage, no planes to shoot down. London was a city of civilians—shopkeepers, firemen, watchers, and mothers without their children. But the girls wrote Mum back and told her they missed her, too, to keep the blackout curtains pulled tight, and to mind the sirens.

Only one letter came from Mrs. Crofton, in late June, which Emmy read as she walked to town and then hid inside her pocket. Mrs. Crofton had heard again from her cousin. He was much intrigued by the two sketches she had sent him, and he had an idea he wanted to run past Mrs. Crofton when he returned to London, which probably wouldn't be until sometime in August. She didn't know what the idea was or even if it had to do with Emmy, but she thought it might. She also wrote that she missed having Emmy at the shop and that business was dreadfully slow. Emmy wrote her straightaway, posting the letter at the post office before she walked back to Thistle House. She wrote that she missed her job at Primrose Bridal and that she was keeping up with her sewing skills by hand.

In mid-July, Charlotte planted a winter squash garden, something she had wanted to do for several years but hadn't because she hadn't known what she would do with so great a harvest. Now there would be plenty of people in the cities to whom she could give the squash if they had more than they would need. They also moved tomato plants that Charlotte had started in May into the main vegetable patch and harvested the early potatoes, beets, and carrots.

One day in late July, Charlotte brought home from the fabric store in Moreton a bolt of checked muslin that had been stained and that the owner of the store could not sell. It wasn't the entire bolt; the flaw hadn't shown up until the owner had already sold half of the yardage. But it was more than enough for Emmy to try her hand at making her own pattern pieces. It didn't matter if she made a mistake and cut pieces she could not use. Charlotte had acquired it for next to nothing because the owner was a close friend.

It was slow going, sewing everything by hand, but Emmy found she made fewer mistakes than when she was using Mrs. Crofton's impressive Singer. And she sketched two new dresses in July, one based on the basic design of Charlotte's dress and another on one of the dolls' ball gowns.

As the days leaned into August, Emmy found herself feeling sad that she would have to sneak away from

Thistle House to meet with Mrs. Crofton's cousin and that perhaps she would not be returning. If Mr. Dabney planned to offer her an apprenticeship, Emmy was prepared to accept and to ask him if she might be able to sleep on the floor of his studio at night. She would not be going back to Mum's flat. Emmy didn't even want Mum to know where she was if it came to that. Emmy was not bothered that Mum would likely be furious or even that Julia would miss her, because Julia would be safe and cared for at Thistle House for as long as the war lasted.

But Emmy was bothered that she would be disappointing Charlotte. She didn't think Charlotte would be angry like Mum would be, nor even sad like Julia. Emmy was afraid Charlotte would be hurt. Emmy didn't want Charlotte to think that, after all her kindnesses, Emmy wasn't grateful. At night in her bed, Emmy would imagine what she would write in the notes that she would leave behind for both Julia and Charlotte. She would have to be vague as to where she was going so that neither one would alert Mum to the location. And she had to communicate that it was simply wise and practical to think ahead to the life that she would live when the war was over. The time for Emmy to prepare for that life was now. The opportunity was now. There was no way for her to know whether a chance like this would come again.

If it came.

Mr. Dabney might not have any interest in mentoring Emmy at all. Perhaps his idea was to buy her designs. She would not sell them.

What would happen then? Would that be the end of it?

Emmy refused to consider that that was all he wanted.

A few more letters came from Mum. She hadn't

much to tell them, and she didn't speculate on when she might come to visit, even though the Moreton billeting official, a Mrs. Howell, had told them she was free to do so as often as she wished. Emmy wanted to believe it was because seeing them in the environment Julia had described in detail—with a lot of help with spelling—would be hard for Mum. Charlotte had provided for their every need, given them chores to do, a schedule to keep, goals to meet, and encouraged their budding talents. And she hadn't had to resort to anything disreputable to do it.

The more time chipped away at August, the more restless Emmy was to hear from Mrs. Crofton.

Two things happened at the end of that month. On the night of August 24, a Saturday, the Luftwaffe dropped a collection of bombs on London, destroying several homes and killing a number of civilians. Until that Saturday night, Londoners had heard distant gunfire, and seen the far-off vapor trails of dogfights in the sky over the English Channel. They had heard about the ongoing war in newspapers and on the radio. But this was the first time that London was bombed at night. Bombs fell at Aldgate, Bloomsbury, Bethnal Green, Finsbury, Hackney, Stepney, Shoreditch, and West Ham. Emmy heard on the radio the next day that fires had broken out all over London's East End, with blazes belching out of factory windows and walls crashing down as if they were made of paper. Ramsgate was also hit. Thirty-one people were killed in the seaside city and more than one thousand houses were destroyed and damaged. Emmy assured Julia, who managed to hear people discussing these terrible details despite her and Charlotte's attempts to shield her from them, that the bombs had fallen nowhere near Whitechapel and that Mum was quite safe.

For a few tense days after that, everyone waited to see what would happen next. The BBC announced that the RAF retaliated with attacks on Berlin. And then London was quiet again.

Which was exactly what Emmy wanted to hear, because on September 2, a Monday, she received her second letter from Mrs. Crofton.

Dear Emmeline:

My cousin, Graham Dabney, has at last returned to London. His father-in-law, God rest his soul, passed away two weeks ago. His wife is settling the last details and then taking over ownership of the house he left behind. I have some exciting news for you. At least I hope you will find it exciting. You wrote in your last letter that it would be no trouble for you to return to London to meet with my cousin about an apprenticeship. If possible, I would like you to meet me at his flat in Knightsbridge at four o'clock on Saturday, September 7, so that we might discuss our idea. Bring all your sketches, dear. And do bring your mother along, too, as she will need to give her permission for what we would like to do.

Running out of room on this notepaper. Will explain all when you get here. For now, just know that my cousin and his wife and I wish to do our part in the war effort and the protection of its youngest citizens. If you are to be evacuated somewhere, why not be with someone who can mentor you for the duration of your time away from home? Graham's address for now is 14 Cadogen Square.

Safe journey,
Eloise Crofton

Emmy read the letter three times, needing to convince herself every few seconds that she was not dreaming and that at last her patience had been rewarded. Mr. Dabney not only wanted to mentor her; he and his wife wanted to be her foster family. They wanted to be her Charlotte. Mr. Dabney wanted Emmy to bring her sketches to a meeting in London.

But they also wanted her to bring Mum, the very thought of which set Emmy's heart to skipping beats. She could not think of that now.

She would not think of that now.

Her only focus was getting herself to London on Saturday without anyone noticing.

Fourteen

❦

THE plan began to form in Emmy's head as she lay in bed that night.

She had to be at the Knightsbridge station by four o'clock in the afternoon. From their travels to get to Stow, she knew that meant she had to be on a train out of Moreton no later than noon. It was an hour to Oxford, where she would have to change trains, and then an hour and a half to Paddington station in London, and then another twenty minutes from Paddington to Knightsbridge, plus the transfer times in between. If she left any later than twelve o'clock, she would be at risk of missing the appointment.

Emmy was sure there was at least one train bound for Oxford that left Moreton before noon. That detail didn't cause her concern. Getting to Moreton on Saturday morning without being seen was going to be the most difficult leg of the journey.

There was only way to accomplish it that she could see—she would have to sneak away in the middle of the night and walk the five miles to Moreton in the dark. If she left at three in the morning, she wouldn't be seen by anyone; not even the milkman was out and about that early. She would take only what could fit inside her satchel. Emmy estimated she would need no less than two hours to walk in the dark to Moreton, which would put her at the train station a bit before sunrise. She would have to lie low for an hour or two and then when the station opened, buy a ticket to London on the first train out. If everything went as planned, she would be at Knightsbridge before one o'clock, a good three hours before she was to meet with Mrs. Crofton and her cousin.

All she had to do between now and then was write the two letters—one to Charlotte, and one to Julia—and think of a way to convince Mr. Dabney that he didn't need to involve Mum, and manage to pretend for the next three days that nothing out of the ordinary was happening.

Writing the letters was more difficult than Emmy initially thought it would be. With so little privacy at Thistle House, she'd have to write the letters by candlelight in her room or find a quiet spot during her Friday visit to town. Since she didn't know where Charlotte kept her candles and couldn't think of an excuse for why she wanted one, she opted to write the letters in the little triangle-shaped bit of parkland in Stow, just across the street from Charlotte's church. Friday afternoon she left for the village right after lunch, barely saying a word to anyone lest Julia or Rose ask to come with her. After stopping for Charlotte's newspaper, Emmy settled herself on the lone bench in the little park. She was still in view of anyone walking past, but surely she appeared as only a young woman writing an ordinary letter to a relative or friend. Once she was settled with pen and stationery in hand, the difficulty became not finding the privacy to write the letters but the words to put inside them. Julia's had to be worded simply and so that she would not panic, and that proved to be the stiffest challenge.

My dear Julia,

I have been called away because someone very kind wants to help me make my brides box dresses real. Just think! They won't be just drawings anymore but real dresses! I wish I could take you with me; truly I do. But Mum would worry about you too much and she would be very cross with me. I want you to stay here with Aunt Charlotte while I am gone. She will take good care of you. Before you know it, all the children will be going back home to London and I will come see you at the flat and show you the dresses. Won't that be lovely?

Be a good girl and mind Aunt Charlotte. The time will pass quickly, I promise.

Love,
Emmy

As Emmy read the letter back to herself, an ache swelled in her chest at the thought of leaving Julia, perhaps for the duration of the war. Would it be months before Emmy saw her again? Years? Would Julia forgive her for leaving her in the middle of the night? As she folded the letter and put it inside the envelope she had brought, she prayed that Julia would one day understand why it had to be this way. She printed Julia's name on the front of the envelope and then blew the letters dry. Emmy touched the

J to make sure it would not smear in her pocket, and her index finger lingered on the swirl of the letter's tail. It looked very much like the handle of an umbrella. The ache in her chest threatened to morph into something more like dread at the thought of leaving Julia behind. Emmy quickly slipped the letter into the pocket of her skirt so that she would not have to look at it anymore. Then she took the second piece of stationery and began to write.

Dear Charlotte:

I am so very sorry that I must return to London in a way that I am sure will disappoint you. You have been nothing but kind and generous to my sister and me, and I will always be in your debt. I have been given an opportunity to work alongside someone who can help me turn my bridal sketches into real gowns. It is an opportunity I cannot pass up. I mean no disrespect to you, and I ask that whatever feelings you have toward me for what I have done, please spare them from my sister. Please hold nothing against her because of my actions; just watch over her and keep her safe.

Thank you for everything you have done for me and will continue to do for Julia.

I hope you can forgive me.

You can rest assured that I am in safe company.

Yours,
Emmeline Downtree

Emmy read the letter over a few times to make sure there was nothing else she could add that would lessen Charlotte's distress. She could already feel the weight of Charlotte's displeasure as she folded the letter, placed it in its envelope, and wrote Charlotte's name across the front. When the ink was dry, Emmy placed the second letter in her skirt pocket along with the first.

When she got back to Thistle House, a surprising sense of melancholy swept over her as she realized that in less than twenty-four hours she would be gone, perhaps never to return. Ever. The war would end eventually, Julia would be sent home, and Emmy would have no need—and perhaps no invitation—to return to Thistle House. She took the stairs slowly as she went to her room to hide the letters in the brides box for the time being.

The rest of the day passed too slowly. Emmy found herself unable to concentrate on simple tasks or finish anything she started. Though she tried to project an unburdened state of mind, Charlotte asked her late in the afternoon if she was feeling all right. Flustered, Emmy answered that it was just her time of the month, and Charlotte promptly made a tea of soothing herbs that she said she used to brew for herself "back in the day."

Emmy thanked her and took the tea to her room to further the ruse that she wasn't feeling well. When she opened the door, Julia was sitting on Emmy's bed with the brides box in her lap. The letter addressed to Charlotte lay open and tented near her knee, likely unread because of the cursive handwriting. The letter addressed to her, however, she held in her hand. Though Julia startled when Emmy walked into the room, guilt at being caught with the brides box without permission evaporated quickly into accusatory shock. Emmy could tell by her expression that Julia had read the letter. Emmy had printed the words carefully so that she would be able to do just that.

"What are you doing?" Emmy exclaimed, though it

was plain as day what Julia had been doing. And what her little sister now knew.

Emmy strode toward the bed, spilling hot tea over her wrist and onto the floor. She put the sloshing cup on the bedside table and grabbed the letter out of Julia's hand.

"What have I told you about getting out the brides box when I'm not around?" Emmy scolded, reaching now for Charlotte's letter and the two envelopes, and scooping up the brides box in her other hand. "You're not supposed to get it out unless you ask me first!"

Emmy's heart was pounding and her hands shook though she desperately willed them to stop. She stuffed the letters inside the box and snapped it shut.

"Where are you going?" Julia's voice was whisper thin.

"You're supposed to ask me first," Emmy said again, ignoring Julia's question.

"Where are you going? What's that letter for? What are you doing?"

With each question, Julia's voice got louder.

"Keep your voice down! There is nothing you need to know right now."

"Are you running away? Is that what you're doing?"

"Julia—"

"You were going to take the brides box and leave me here, weren't you? That's what you were going to do!"

"Julia, please!" Emmy begged, all anger gone. Fear filled the empty space it left behind. She sat down on the bed next to her sister, the brides box clasped close to her chest. "Please keep your voice down. Please?"

"You can't just leave me here! How could you leave me here?"

Emmy laid the box down between them and gently took hold of one of Julia's hands. "Julia, listen to me.

You have to trust me. Sometimes grown-ups have to do things that don't seem to make sense and—"

"You're not a grown-up!" Julia snatched her hand away.

"Yes, I am. I'll be sixteen on my next birthday. I'm not a little child anymore. I have to think of my future and what I am supposed to do with my life."

"You're supposed to be with me." Julia turned from Emmy, frowning.

"Julia, look at me." Emmy waited until Julia had turned her head back to face her. "You know how much I love my brides dresses. You of all people know how important they are to me. I have a chance for them to become real. Some chances in life you only get once. Just the one time. I have to go."

Julia stared at the brides box that lay between her and Emmy. Her expression was part loathing and part desire. At that moment Emmy could see that Julia hated the brides inside that box as much as she loved them.

"Take me with you," Julia said.

"I can't."

"Yes, you can!"

"Julia, think for a moment. You are happy here. You have a lovely room. And Aunt Charlotte and Aunt Rose. You have the tea set to play with and Guinevere and Henrietta and all their beautiful clothes. Next week school starts, and you'll get to play with all the little girls you have seen at church and in the village. You have the chickens to take care of. And the pond and the turtles. You love it here. I know you do."

A tear had formed in the corner of each of Julia's eyes. "Don't you love it here, too?"

Emmy moved closer and put an arm around her.

"This is a lovely place. And Charlotte and Rose are wonderful people. I am not leaving because I don't like it here. That's not it at all. If I didn't have this chance to make my dresses real, I would stay. But I have to go. Someday when you're my age, you will understand why."

"I want you here with me."

"And I would stay if I could. But I can't. And you will be fine here without me." Emmy tightened her arm around her sister.

For a moment Emmy thought she had Julia convinced, but then she felt her stiffen in her half embrace.

"No."

"Julia."

"Take me with you or I'm telling Aunt Charlotte."

Emmy's breath caught in her throat. She put both hands on Julia's shoulders to turn her sister toward her. "Julia, I can't take you."

Julia wriggled out of Emmy's grasp, climbed off the bed, and stood in front of her. "Take me with you or I'm telling Aunt Charlotte right now." Julia's gaze on Emmy was like steel.

"Don't do this, Julia. Please?"

"Don't go, then. Stay here."

"I have to go!"

"Then take me with you. Or I'm telling Aunt Charlotte."

Emmy wanted to scream at her. Throw something. Pound the wall. She could do none of those things.

She could only agree to take Julia and then hope that when she got ready to leave in the middle of the night, Julia would not hear her and she could steal away unnoticed.

"All right," Emmy said. "I'll take you."

Julia stared at her for a moment, wondering, it seemed, whether she had heard Emmy right. She had expected Emmy to tell her she would stay; that was clear.

"When?" Julia asked.

"Very early tomorrow morning, before the milkman comes. But you can't pack anything, Julia. You can't bring your suitcase or your fairy tale book. They're too heavy. Do you understand? You have to leave those things here and you might not see them again. I'm leaving all my things here. I'm only taking the brides box. Do you understand what I'm saying?"

Julia nodded, a pensive look on her face.

"And you can't be looking at me strangely tonight at supper or asking me questions or anything. You have to act like everything is normal. All right?"

Julia seemed deep in thought. She didn't answer.

"All right?" Emmy said again.

"I know how to be normal," Julia said, crinkling an eyebrow.

From downstairs the girls heard Charlotte calling Julia's name. It was her turn to set the table.

Julia stepped to the door and opened it. "I'm coming!" she yelled.

"Not a word, Julia," Emmy murmured.

"I know how to be normal," Julia said again, and was gone.

For the rest of the afternoon and evening Julia kept her word. She gave no indication at all that she expected to run away with Emmy that night, not even the slightest of nervous behaviors. They listened to the BBC for a little while after dinner. But there was nothing except news of air battles raging over the English Channel. Charlotte switched it off and the four of them worked on a puzzle. Finally, a little after nine, Julia was sent up to bed and Emmy joined her. Thinking Emmy was still having menstrual cramps, Charlotte thought nothing of it. She sent her to bed with another cup of herbal tea.

Up in their bedroom Emmy laid out on her bed what she could fit in the satchel. The coin purse that held the only money she had—all of her paycheck from her two months' work at Primrose and the little bit Mum had sent with them—a package of biscuits she had taken from the pantry, changes of underwear, toothbrush and paste, and the brides box, which she wrapped in a shawl so that the corners wouldn't bite into her side as she walked the five miles to Moreton with the satchel over her shoulder.

The envelope inscribed with Charlotte's name she had already removed from the brides box and it now lay on the bed.

"What did you write in Aunt Charlotte's letter?" Julia asked.

"The same thing I wrote in yours." Emmy picked up the letter and set it on the nightstand so that Charlotte would see it in the morning.

"But you have to tell her I went with you. She won't know I went with you unless you tell her."

Emmy had hoped Julia would not think of this. But as she stood there staring at Emmy, she knew she would have to do exactly what her sister said. Julia and she had been together every minute since she'd opened the brides box and found the envelopes. She knew Emmy hadn't written anything additional in the note to Charlotte. Emmy decided it didn't matter. In the morning when Julia awoke, Emmy would be long gone. Charlotte would put two and two together. She would understand why in the first part of the letter Emmy asked her to watch over Julia and in the postscript she told her Julia was coming along, especially since Julia would be there to fill in all the blanks.

"Get me the pen off the desk."

Julia did as she was told. Emmy retrieved the letter, lifted the single sheet of paper out, and smoothed it onto the nightstand.

Underneath where Emmy had signed her name she added:

P.S. *Julia has asked to come with me.*

She put the note back inside its envelope and repositioned it on the nightstand. Then she told Julia to put on her pajamas.

"Why aren't we sleeping in our clothes?" Julia said, frowning.

"Because they will wrinkle. We don't want to draw attention to ourselves, do we?"

Julia shook her head gravely. Then she changed out of her clothes, draped them on the bedpost, and hopped under the covers.

Emmy had gotten into her own pajamas and was about to crawl into bed also when Julia sat up. "I need a drink, Emmy. I'm too excited. I'm thirsty."

"You'll have to use the loo if you drink too much."

"Just a tiny sip, please? I won't be able to sleep if I don't have one. I'm too excited."

Sighing, Emmy got up out of bed, opened the door, and headed downstairs. Rose had already gone to bed and Charlotte was locking the back door and turning out the lights.

A wave of guilt rushed over Emmy as Charlotte smiled at her and asked if there was anything she needed.

"Just a sip of water for Julia," Emmy said.

Charlotte laughed lightly, grabbed a juice glass from the cabinet, and filled it half-full from the tap. "That enough?"

"Perfect," Emmy said, taking it from her.

"Good night, Emmeline."

"Yes. Good night. And thank you."

Emmy could feel Charlotte's gaze on her as she left the kitchen. Emmy wanted badly to run from those compassionate eyes. But she walked calmly with Julia's water in her hand, took the stairs slowly, and opened the bedroom door.

Julia was sitting up in bed, eager for her drink. She gulped it down in one swallow.

"Won't Mum be surprised to see us?" Julia said as Emmy took the glass from her.

Emmy stroked her sister's head. It was difficult to stay angry with her. "Yes," Emmy said, unable to say anything to the contrary.

She tucked Julia in.

"Wake me up when it's time to go," Julia said, yawning.

"Sweet dreams," was Emmy's answer.

She turned out the light and got into bed, turning her back to Julia so that her sister would not see that Emmy kept her eyes open.

When Julia's breathing was slow and even, Emmy turned over, parted the blackout curtains, and watched her sister sleep in a spill of moonlight. She gazed up at the sky outside the window, thankful for the cloudless blanket of stars and generous moon.

She did not mean to doze at all, but the next thing Emmy knew, the clock downstairs was chiming two.

She sat up in bed, grateful it was only two and not

later. Emmy could not risk falling asleep again. She got out of bed quietly and listened for any sounds in the house that would indicate that Rose or Charlotte was awake. Hearing nothing, Emmy slipped off her nightgown and stuffed it into the satchel. She dressed in the same clothes she had worn the day before, grabbed her jacket from the back of the desk chair, and bent to retrieve the satchel. When her knees straightened, an owl hooted outside their window and Julia's eyes snapped open.

"Is it time to go?" she whispered.

Emmy's mind raced for a way out of this predicament. She had time. She could wait a little longer.

"Not yet. Go back to sleep."

Julia sat up. She saw Emmy's made bed, and that her big sister was in her street clothes. "Why aren't you still sleeping?"

"I—I just can't sleep anymore."

Julia tossed her legs over the side of her bed. "Me, neither."

"Jewels, it's not time to go yet."

"But I'm not sleepy anymore."

As Emmy pondered her response, the voice of reason seemed to murmur just at the edge of sound that this was a moment that demanded she weigh the consequences, consider the possible outcomes. She stood at a crossroads, half-aware that her choice would send her down a path from which there could be no turning back.

But instead of two choices, she saw only one—because it was all she really wanted to see.

Emmy mentally shooed the whispering voice away.

She would look back on that moonlit night and wonder and wonder and wonder what she would have done had she considered that the owl that awakened Julia was divinely sent so that she wouldn't leave Thistle House that night. Had it been summoned to the tree outside the window and called her little sister out of sleep so that Emmy might stop and consider that there is always, always the other road to choose, even if it seems to be nothing more than an unpaved path in the middle of nowhere?

On that night, the night Julia could not fall back asleep, Emmy saw only what she wanted to.

"All right," Emmy said, sighing as loud as she dared. "Let's go, then. Don't make a sound, Julia. Not a peep."

As Julia dressed by moonlight and Emmy made her bed, Emmy decided she would take Julia straight to the flat. If Thea wasn't home, she'd tell her sister to wait for Mum to get home from work. Emmy would still have plenty of time to make it to Knightsbridge by four. She would deal with Mum's anger later, if she had to. And as for Julia . . . Well, Mum could easily get her sister back to Thistle House on Sunday. Easily.

Mum had the address.

She had the day off.

She owed Charlotte a visit anyway.

There was nothing to worry about.

Emmy grabbed her satchel, and together she and Julia tiptoed soundlessly down the stairs, out the front door, and into the sparkling night.

Fifteen

KENDRA

A rap at the door startles me, but Isabel merely turns her head toward the sound.

The door opens slightly and Beryl pokes her head inside the parlor. "Can I freshen the pot for you ladies?" Her words are polite, but the tone and her facial expression are fraught with worry. I can see that she's concerned the interview is taking too long, that I am exhausting Isabel and potentially sabotaging the party.

"I am quite happy with the two cups I've had," Isabel replies without a moment's hesitation or a hint of fatigue. She turns to me. "Kendra? Would you care for more tea?"

"No, I'm good. But thank you very much."

Isabel directs her attention back to Beryl. "You can take the tea tray, dear."

Beryl enters the room, her anxiety only slightly lessened

as she hoists the tray. "Is there anything else I can get for you? Are you needing to rest, Auntie? Do you want your medicine now?"

"No, but thank you. We're fine."

Beryl turns toward us before she leaves the room. "If I can bring you anything else—"

"We'll be sure to let you know. Don't worry about us. You attend to the party details, Beryl."

"Right, then," Beryl says, obviously unconvinced as she closes the door behind her.

I turn my attention back to Isabel. She doesn't exhibit signs of fatigue and yet surely she must be tired after having talked without stopping for the last hour or so. I am thankful for the full charge on my recorder's battery. I have written nothing on my notepad, so spellbound have I been. From behind where Isabel sits, I see one of her Umbrella Girl paintings and I know now where the polka-dot umbrellas came from, though I don't know how. I only know that Isabel is somehow connected to the story she is telling me about the two sisters, one named Emmeline and the other, Julia.

Furthermore, we are sitting in Thistle House. Part of the story she is telling me happened right here in this room.

Isabel inhales deeply, as if needing a fresh charge of oxygen to continue. I am about to ask her if she would like to take a break after all, when she speaks.

"You, being a history major, probably know what these two sisters were headed into, don't you, it being the seventh of September."

I nod. "The Blitz began that day."

Isabel takes a handkerchief out of her skirt pocket and blots her nose, gently and with practiced gentility. "Indeed it did."

"But Emmy couldn't have known that."

"No. No, she could not." She folds the handkerchief and places it on the table next to her.

Then she laughs gently. "It is strangely amusing how proud Emmy was for getting herself and her little sister to Moreton, in the dark, after carrying Julia when her feet and legs got tired. And then they had to hide in the ladies' room like mice until the ticket office opened. Emmy had thought of a good excuse for needing train tickets to London while they walked, not that it should have been anyone's business. But she knew the station master would be curious. Children didn't travel to London those days; they left it, by the thousands. So she told the ticket man their mother was deathly ill and that their aunt had called them back to the city to say a quick good-bye before she passed from this life to the next. Oh, Kendra. Such looks of sympathy they got then. The porter—whom they didn't need because of course they had no luggage—and the conductor, and everyone went out of their way to be kind to the poor girls whose mother lay dying. So convincing was Emmy that she had to whisper several times to Julia while the train rumbled down its tracks that she'd made it all up. Julia was nearly convinced Mum was on her deathbed, too.

"And when they stepped out of the Tube at the station near their flat, you'd have thought Emmy had pulled off the greatest feat in modern history. That's how proud of herself she was." Isabel laughs with more energy. "And all the while the greatest feat was actually happening already as hundreds of Luftwaffe pilots climbed into their cockpits."

Her smile dies away slowly. Then she turns to me.

"Did you know, Kendra, that the RAF pilots who

saw the German bombers headed for the coast of England had never seen so many aircraft in the air all at the same time? Never had they seen the likes of it. Their coming was like a sheet of black across the sky."

"I—I can't even imagine." I am at a complete loss for words and already anxious about what she is preparing to tell me. It can't be anything good.

"No. Of course you can't. The radar station at Foreness was the first to pick them up, even as Emmy was making her way to Knightsbridge. Isn't that astonishing? Those planes were already in the air, already streaming toward London, as Emmy walked to her appointment, and no one had any idea."

Isabel seems to withdraw into a protected place where the details of that seventh day of September are kept. She learned of these details after the fact, perhaps months later, maybe years later, and it appears that she filed them away, to bring them out now, with me.

"There was all of London, going about its Saturday afternoon business. A WAAF corporal at the radar station was confused by the size of the formation on the radar screen and she called for one of her superior officers. She couldn't believe what she was seeing. 'What is that?' she probably said, pointing to the monstrous cloud on the screen. Can't you just see her, Kendra?"

I nodded. I could see her.

"Then the Dover radar picked up the giant shadow, and then Rye," Isabel continues. "And oh, the chatter as they took to their radios to warn their brothers at arms that an armada from hell was streaking across the Channel toward them."

She pauses for a moment. I can almost hear the throaty hum of all those engines.

Isabel turns to the window as a breeze catches the lace and lifts it in our direction, almost in greeting. The laughter of a child outside wafts into the room.

"It started on the south side of the Thames at about half past four." Her voice seems almost detached from her body. "Emmy was already finished with her meeting with Mr. Dabney when the sirens began to scream. And then everyone was running for shelter, and they heard the planes, and they felt the impact of what was happening at the docks. It was . . ." She stops and shakes her head as she struggles to find the right words. "It was as if the end of the world had begun. The end of everything."

Then Isabel slowly raises her head to look at me. "For a long time, Emmy wished it had been the end of the world. A very long time."

Part Two

Sixteen

❧

EMMY

WHEN Emmy and Julia arrived at the flat, it was as if they had never left it. The two and a half months they had been at Thistle House had seemed much longer until they stepped over the threshold, and then the days with Charlotte immediately took on the form of a prolonged dream. Everything seemed to whisper to Emmy that they had been gone only a day; everything except the evidence of Mum's lonely nights without them. The sitting room sofa was a tumble of pillows, unfolded laundry, and scattered magazines. Teacups and biscuit wrappers lay about, as well as plates and bowls with food remains clinging to them. A collection of nearly empty nail polish bottles was pushed together on the coffee table, looking like a tiny mob of dissidents.

"Mum is messy," Julia said as the girls made their way from the sitting area to the kitchen, which was just as unkempt as the front room.

"She misses us," Emmy said. "There's no one to clean the flat for without us here. That's all."

"I'm hungry." Julia frowned at the bits of dried egg and toast on a plate on the kitchen table.

Emmy checked her watch. It was just one o'clock—plenty of time before she needed to be back on a train toward Knightsbridge. "Run some soapy water in the sink and put Mum's breakfast dishes in it to soak," she said. "I'll see what there is to eat."

Mum had little by way of food in the cupboards, but Emmy did see that there was half a loaf of bread and a can of beans so that she could make Julia beans on toast. While the beans heated on the stove, the girls went about the flat, picking up the dishes Mum had strewn about and bringing them to the kitchen to soak. They also tidied up the sofa, put the laundry away, and straightened the magazines and newspapers. The truly empty nail polish bottles Emmy tossed into the bin. The couple with still a bit of polish inside them she set on Mum's bureau, which she found to be also littered with papers, hosiery, hair combs, and handkerchiefs.

Emmy sat Julia down with her lunch and then went next door to see whether Thea was home. There was no answer at their neighbor's door.

Back inside the flat, Emmy sat down next to Julia, who was halfway through her meal.

"Jewels, Thea isn't home right now, so I need you to be a brave girl and wait here for Mum to get home from work. It won't be long. If you take a little nap, it will seem like no time at all. Then you can surprise her when she comes inside and sees you."

Julia licked bean juice off her fork. "Where are you going?"

"I have to be somewhere else this afternoon."

Julia looked down at her plate and poked a piece of toast with the tines of her fork. "Is this about the brides?"

"Yes."

"Mum doesn't know where you're going, does she?"

Emmy paused only a second. "No. Not yet. This is our secret. Yours and mine. I want to surprise her."

"Surprise her with what?" Julia sounded skeptical.

Emmy leaned forward in her chair, wanting Julia to catch her excitement. "When my bride dresses are real, when people can buy them in stores, and women can wear them on their wedding day, she will be proud of me."

Julia swirled a cube of toast in the beans and then skewered it. "What time are you coming home?"

The less Emmy said about that the better. "I'm not sure."

Julia was thoughtful as she chewed, almost as if fitting something together in her head. "Mum's going to be cross with you."

Emmy rose from the chair and reached for the electric bill that was among the other pieces of opened mail on the kitchen counter. She pulled the bill out and brought the empty envelope and a pen back to the table.

"At first, yes, she will probably be cross with me," Emmy said as she sat back down. "I'm going to write her a note. When she gets home, you can make sure she sees it. All right?"

Julia nodded but the doubt in her eyes was alarming. Emmy had always been able to sway Julia her way, on just about everything. But at that moment Julia looked thoroughly unconvinced that Emmy was on the doorstep of her dreams.

"You'll make sure Mum sees it, right?" Emmy said, this time with more force.

Julia nodded slowly, a hundred little thoughts behind

her unreadable expression. The nod wasn't good enough for Emmy.

"Promise me you'll give it to her," Emmy pressed.

"I promise," Julia replied, without so much as a second's hesitation.

Emmy could not spend the time to figure out what Julia was thinking. Her sister looked tired. Perhaps that was all her strange behavior was, the result of too little sleep the night before.

"I'll write the note real quick and then I'll get you tucked onto the sofa to wait for Mum, okay?"

"Okay."

Emmy uncapped the pen and turned the envelope over to its back side.

Mum—

I had to come back to London to take care of something that matters a great deal to me. Julia insisted on coming with me. I had no plans to bring her and I am sorry if it makes you angry that I did. She misses you. Have no fear about taking her back to Thistle House if you want to. Mrs. Havelock is a very kind woman and Julia likes it there.

I don't know exactly when I will see you again. Please know that I am doing exactly what you said I should do. You said wishing something doesn't make it come true. Doing it does.

Someday I hope you will be proud of me.

Emmy

She set the envelope against a teacup on the counter. Then she reached for Julia's plate and set it to soak with the other dirty dishes. When Emmy turned back to her sister, she offered Julia her hand and she took it.

They walked into the sitting room. Emmy arranged the pillows. Julia crawled up onto the cushions and lay down at once. The missed hours of sleep and the long morning of travel had caught up with her.

Emmy smoothed Julia's hair away from her face, suddenly grieved that she wasn't sure when she would see her sister again. After the war, certainly, but how long would that be? If Mr. Dabney and his wife planned to evacuate her to the countryside, perhaps she could convince them to take Julia as well. But . . . Thistle House was such a lovely place and Julia had been so happy there. She didn't know the Dabneys at all. Emmy had no idea what to expect from them as foster parents. Indeed, she didn't care. She would suffer through any kind of parenting to be able to learn what Mr. Dabney could teach her.

No, the best place for Julia for as long as the war lasted was with Charlotte.

Emmy bent to kiss her forehead. Julia was already on the edge of sleep.

"Mum will be home in no time."

"Okay," Julia whispered.

"Don't open the door to anyone unless you hear Thea come home, okay? Stay right here on the sofa."

"Mmm."

Emmy stood and her sister did not move. "I love you, Jewels."

But Julia was asleep.

Now that Emmy could concentrate solely on herself, she realized how disheveled she probably looked. She went into Mum's room to borrow a dress that she hoped her mother wouldn't miss. She found one near the back, a red jersey knit patterned in tiny geometric designs and three-quarter sleeves. Mum had not worn it in a long while. As Emmy slipped out of her wrinkled dress to put on the fresh one, she figured out why. It was a bit snug, even on her. But it was ten times better than what she had been wearing, and definitely a woman's dress. She smoothed her hair in her mother's mirror, using one of Mum's hair combs to tame her curls. Then she took her wrinkled dress, folded it, and went into Julia's and her room and laid it on her bed. Back in the front room, Emmy gave her sleeping sister one last peck on her forehead. Then she retrieved her satchel from where she had stowed it by the front door and left the flat, putting the key back under the mat where she had found it.

Knightsbridge was two miles away: a walkable distance if Emmy had not already covered five miles that day and had more time.

She made for the Tube station, drawing no more stares from passersby. Having Julia in tow had made them noticeable. Now that she was traveling alone, she knew she didn't look like a child. And she didn't feel like a child. She wasn't about a child's business.

Twenty minutes later Emmy was at Knightsbridge station, with plenty of time to find Cadogen Square. She consulted the wall map posted underground and saw that the street she was looking for was only a half mile away. Emmy emerged from the station on Brompton Road and walked to Pavilion, passing walls of sandbags and signs for shelters. Above her the barrage balloons, hovering soundless, threw weird shadows onto the sidewalk.

Knightsbridge was a well-to-do area very much like Mayfair, where Mum went to work every day. Emmy didn't know how well-off Mrs. Crofton was: She had never mentioned to Emmy where she lived, but Mrs. Crofton's cousin apparently had money—or had married into wealth. As Emmy approached Cadogen, the residences became more and more elegant and stately. She found Mr. Dabney's home, a Georgian town house flanked on either side by half a dozen matching, three-story, wedding white homes. Each was flawlessly kept with window boxes of flowers and ferns, and ocean blue front doors that glistened in the late-afternoon sun.

She had five minutes to spare, but she didn't have the patience to stand outside and wait. Surely the Dabneys and Mrs. Crofton would find her punctuality an asset. Emmy could not stop her hand from shaking as she pressed the bell.

The door was opened by a uniformed maid not much older than Emmy.

"I've an appointment with Mr. Dabney. My name's Emmeline Downtree." Emmy's voice squeaked as she spoke her name.

The maid swung the door wide. "Please. Won't you come in?"

Emmy followed her into a tiled entry. A golden chandelier hung from a tall ceiling. Potted ferns flanked a tall wardrobe, one of only two pieces of furniture in the foyer. A round, marble-topped table in the center of the room was the other. A vase of silver-pink roses adorned it.

"May I take your . . . jacket?" The maid cocked her head and held out her hand. It was a nice day outside. No one was wearing or carrying a jacket.

Emmy handed it to her as her cheeks warmed.

"And your bag?"

Emmy's hand instinctively felt for the padded corners of the brides box inside her satchel. "I'll keep this with me, thank you."

She nodded. "Right this way, miss."

Emmy was shown to a sitting room that wasn't a

great deal bigger than Mum's, but the furnishings could not have been more different. Chintz-covered sofas were arranged in the center of the room on top of a thick rug in shades of mauve and russet. A marble fireplace graced one wall, a tea cart another, and an escritoire the last. Paintings of parks, woods, and rose gardens decorated the walls. French fashion magazines from before Paris fell were fanned out on the coffee table. Emmy had never been in such a pretty room before, except on school field trips to royal residences and museums.

"If you'd like to have a seat?" The maid motioned to the tableau of sofas and Emmy sat down, grateful to be off her trembling legs.

The maid left the room and Emmy took several long breaths to quiet her nerves, reminding herself that she had been asked to come to this elegant room. She was *invited* here.

Emmy reached into her satchel to remove the brides box from the shawl she had wrapped it in so that she would be ready to show Mr. Dabney the sketches. She pulled the bundle onto her lap and unfolded the layers of cloth.

The careful work she had done to calm her anxious heart disintegrated in a blinding instant.

Inside the shawl was Julia's book of fairy tales.

Seventeen

FOR several seconds Emmy could do nothing but stare at the book. Then she closed her eyes, willing the brides box to be on her lap when she opened them, because surely, surely, what was inside the shawl was not Julia's book.

It couldn't be.

Couldn't be!

Emmy opened her eyes slowly and the book's honey-gold cover met her gaze.

Julia.

Julia!

How could she have done such a thing? She knew there hadn't been room for her book in the satchel. She knew how important this day was to Emmy. She knew Emmy was meeting with someone who wanted to see the brides box. She knew—

And then clarity slammed into Emmy. Of course

Julia knew. That was why her behavior was so odd while she ate her lunch. She knew Emmy wouldn't be showing anyone her brides today. Emmy had said the day before that she had only this one chance with the brides. Julia had deduced that if this chance was eliminated, she would never have to worry about the brides box parting them. Ever. She knew Emmy would arrive at this meeting, thinking she had her brides, and would discover that she didn't. Emmy would have to leave the meeting. No brides, no meeting.

No meeting, no parting.

Emmy would have to come back to the flat. To her. Yes, Emmy would be livid, but she would have to come back to her. Julia knew where the brides box was, and Emmy didn't.

Julia hadn't been thirsty the night before at Thistle House when she sent Emmy downstairs for a drink of water. She had needed a few minutes to remove the brides box, wrap her fairy tale book in the shawl, and stuff it into the satchel. The brides box had no doubt been shoved under her bed as Emmy climbed the stairs with her cup.

It all made perfect sense. Julia never wanted to leave Thistle House, and she hadn't wanted Emmy to, either. Emmy would now have to take her back to Charlotte's if she wanted her brides returned to her. Upon their return, Charlotte would surely be vigilant so as not to let the girls out of her sight again.

Emmy wouldn't be allowed any more solo trips to town. She wouldn't be allowed solo trips anywhere.

Julia had concocted a brilliant plan. Emmy wondered if she even knew how brilliant it was.

She heard voices from outside the room; one was Mrs. Crofton's. Emmy had no sketches to show Mr.

Dabney, and no way of getting them back without returning to Thistle House. The room suddenly felt very
warm. A ribbon of sweat dampened her forehead as
Emmy hammered her brain to think of an excuse for
coming to the meeting without the designs.

Emmy could think of nothing. The sketches were the
reason she was there. It would be ridiculous to say she
had forgotten them and unthinkable to say she had purposely left them behind.

The door opened and Emmy rose to her feet.

Mrs. Crofton came into the room, followed by a man
and woman who looked to be in their late fifties. The
man had a groomed goatee and wire-rim spectacles, and
he wore a gray-striped suit. The woman wore a pale yellow chiffon dress with a dropped waist and lace sleeves.
Her hair was as black as night; his, pearl gray and brown.

"Emmeline, how good to see you again." Mrs. Crofton crossed the room and clasped Emmy's hands with
hers. "I am so glad you could come. May I introduce my
cousin and his wife, Graham and Madeleine Dabney."

The couple came forward to shake Emmy's hand.
Mr. Dabney's grip was firm and warm; Mrs. Dabney's
soft and cool. Both smiled politely and said how pleased
they were to meet her.

"I'm so very happy to meet you both as well." Emmy's voice sounded strange in her ears.

"Please, have a seat." Mr. Dabney motioned to the
sofa as he and his wife sat down opposite her. Mrs.
Crofton sat on a third sofa, the smallest of the three.

The young woman who had answered the bell came
into the room with a tea tray as they took their seats.
She set it down on the table in the middle and poured tea
into four bone china cups.

"So, Miss Downtree," Mr. Dabney began, stirring sugar into his teacup, "I hear you hope to have your own line of wedding dresses someday. Perhaps one day your own boutique."

"Oh. Yes, sir. Yes, I do." Emmy's cup trembled on its saucer. She took a sip to stop it even though the liquid burned her mouth.

"Tell me how you came to have such a vision for your future."

Emmy set the cup back on its saucer and placed it on the table to free herself of having to hold it steady. "I have always been drawn to women's fashions. Dresses, especially. The more elegant the dress the better. I don't know of a more beautiful and elegant concept of a gown than a wedding dress. They are so . . . flawless."

"I quite agree with you there, Emmeline," Mrs. Crofton said as she looked at her wristwatch. "So do you know how much longer it will be before your mother arrives?"

The pleasantries regarding why Emmy loved drawing wedding gowns had been to fill the time while they waited for Mum to join them. Emmy swallowed back a bolt of panic. "Um. Well, she is working today, actually. But I, uh, thought I'd see what kind of situation you are proposing and then I can present it to her, uh, when she gets off work."

"Oh." Mrs. Crofton looked to her cousin.

Mr. Dabney's mouth became a thin line. "I had rather we took care of this in one meeting, Miss Downtree," he said politely but with authority. "We are leaving London on Tuesday. What my wife and I are proposing will require your mother's approval."

"Well, my mother, um, looks upon me as an adult, you see. So I am able to make my own decisions regarding my future as a . . . as a designer."

Mr. Dabney smiled. It was a grin that made Emmy uneasy. He had found what she had just said amusing, not enlightening. "To be sure, but still. You are just fifteen, Miss Downtree?"

Emmy nodded.

"Then you can see that Mrs. Dabney and I must have your mother's permission to take you under our wing, so to speak. Did my cousin tell you what I am proposing?"

"I only hinted at it, Graham," Mrs. Crofton interjected. "I wrote the letter in a hurry and told her we'd explain it all when she got here."

"Ah." Mr. Dabney leaned forward and sandwiched his hands together, the pose of a man about to broker a deal. "Eloise sent me your two sketches and she told me that you've had no formal training either in designing or sewing. That is what most interested me. The sketches I saw were surprisingly good, considering. That you created them with no training is most remarkable. I am eager to see the rest of your designs. If I'm not mistaken, it would appear that you have an innate gift, Miss Downtree."

Emmy's heart took a stutter step and she forced herself to say calmly, "Thank you, Mr. Dabney."

"Now, it's been my practice to employ an apprentice or two in my studio throughout the year. I design costumes for theatrical productions here on the West End and elsewhere in Britain and North America. I like to do my part in encouraging the up-and-coming young designers, and I teach them while they help me construct my costumes. I believe Eloise has told you this?"

"Yes."

"When my cousin saw your sketches, she, too, was impressed with your untrained eye for design, which is why she sent me those two sketches. She thought I might wish to consider offering you an apprenticeship."

"Yes, I told her that," Mrs. Crofton said, offering Emmy a reassuring smile that wordlessly said all was going well and that Emmy didn't need to be so nervous.

"Now, Mrs. Dabney and I wish to do our part in the war effort, you see. Eloise tells me you have been evacuated to Gloucestershire and have spent the last few months there?"

"Yes, that's correct." Emmy could scarcely breathe. What was she going to tell him about not having the sketches?

Graham Dabney nodded to his wife, who smiled at him. "Mrs. Dabney and I have discussed taking in a London evacuee. It occurred to me that, depending on the strength of the rest of your designs, we might offer to take you with us on Tuesday to my wife's estate outside Edinburgh. That way I could teach you about dress construction, pattern making, all that. And while you learn, you can assist me in the creation of a series of costumes for a production of *La Bohème* in Boston. I think you would find the work as entertaining as it would be educational. The gowns for *La Bohème* are quite impressive."

Emmy swallowed hard. "The strength of the rest of my designs?"

Mr. Dabney sat back, distancing himself a little from her. "Yes, of course. It would be unkind of me to bring you on as an apprentice if you've not the natural talent that I am hoping you have. I already know you do not have the sewing experience. You would have to have one of the two." He laughed lightly, expecting Emmy would also.

Mrs. Crofton offered a half chuckle, surely meant to keep the conversation light. "I think you'll be quite satisfied with the rest of her work, Graham. Perhaps now would be a good time to show us the rest of your sketches, Emmeline?"

Emmy looked from Mrs. Crofton to Mr. Graham and to his lovely but obviously shy wife. Which of them could she appeal to?

"Emmeline?" Mrs. Crofton said.

Emmy closed her eyes as the truth, the only thing she could think to say, bubbled out of her. "I don't have them with me today."

"Did you not tell her to bring them?" Emmy could hear the disapproval in Graham Dabney's voice as he addressed his cousin.

"Of course I did," was Mrs. Crofton's quick reply. "Emmeline?"

Emmy opened her eyes to look at her.

"Why didn't you bring them?"

Please God, let the truth be enough, she prayed to the Almighty.

"I had them in this satchel, inside the box I carry them in. My sister—she's only seven—was worried that she might not see me again if I went to this meeting, and then became your apprentice. She substituted her fairy tale book for the box." She lifted the book out of the bag and placed it on her lap. "I just now discovered this, as I heard your voices outside the door. I am so very sorry. She— she's only a child. I promise I can get the sketches back. If you would allow me a couple days to retrieve them."

"A couple days?" Mrs. Crofton echoed. The other two adults stared at Emmy, apparently still trying to absorb what she had said.

"My sister made the switch when we were still in Gloucestershire. I need to travel back to the house where we've been living and get them."

Mr. Dabney still seemed to be processing Emmy's excuse. "But we are closing up this house and leaving on Tuesday."

"Please," Emmy pleaded. "Just give me tomorrow to return to Gloucestershire and get them. I can be here on Monday to show them to you."

"With your mother?" Mr. Dabney replied. "There is no point in returning on Monday without your mother. I do not wish to be arrested for kidnapping."

"Graham, dear." Mrs. Dabney touched her husband's arm, but her eyes were on Emmy. The woman could obviously see the turmoil that was raging inside her.

"Madeleine, we cannot take a fifteen-year-old girl to Scotland without her mother's permission."

"Of course we can't." Mrs. Dabney offered Emmy as compassionate a look as someone could. "Do go retrieve your sketches, Miss Downtree. And come back Monday at this same hour with your mum." She turned to her husband. "That will work, won't it, Graham?"

"We've a lot of arrangements to make, but I suppose it can, yes. But you must remember, Miss Downtree, I cannot take you with us unless I see the rest of your sketches. The work will be too daunting for you if you've no natural flair for it. I must be convinced you have it. It would not be good for either one of us if you don't."

"Yes. Yes, thank you," Emmy said, not much louder than a whisper. She felt on the edge of bursting into tears and she did not want even one tiny drop to find its way out of either eye. Emmy stood so that she could take her leave. She had an enormous task ahead of her.

The others stood, too. Emmy shoved the fairy tale book inside the satchel. "I'm so sorry to have wasted your time today, Mr. Dabney."

Mrs. Crofton reached out a hand to touch Emmy's arm. "It's not entirely your fault, Emmeline. You didn't know your sister switched out the box with her book at the last minute."

Emmy was certain Mrs. Crofton said this for her cousin's sake. It was becoming clear to Emmy that Graham Dabney was not one to overlook shortcomings. He demanded excellence, which was exactly what Emmy needed and wanted in a mentor. She could not risk disappointing him again.

"I wouldn't say it was a complete waste of time, Miss Downtree, but we leave on Tuesday. It's already been arranged."

"I will be here, with my mother, on Monday at four o'clock. I promise."

Emmy had not wanted to involve Mum at all but now everything had changed. She desperately needed her.

Not only did she need Mum to come with her to the next meeting with the Dabneys; Emmy needed Mum to accompany her to Thistle House on Sunday so that they could take Julia back and retrieve the brides box. And it was imperative that she return with Mum so that she could keep her word and be at Cadogen Square at four o'clock on Monday. Only Mum could make that happen.

Surely Emmy could convince Mum—a woman whose own dreams had been cruelly warped by circumstances she hadn't orchestrated—to let her go with the Dabneys to Scotland.

Surely Mum would be able to see Emmy had the opportunity to become more than the illegitimate child who had stolen Mum's life away from her. Emmy could become a creator of beautiful things. She could be someone Mum was proud of, instead of what Emmy currently was: a constant reminder that whatever plans she'd had for her life had ended when Emmy was born.

Emmy really did want Mum to be proud of her.

She had to find a way to persuade Mum to help her.

"I'll show you to the door, Emmeline," Mrs. Crofton said.

After retrieving her jacket, they walked to the front door without saying a word. When Mrs. Crofton opened it, she reached for Emmy's arm. "Make sure you have your sketches when you return, Emmeline," she said softly. "I can't stress it enough. Graham is very good at what he does, but he is also very demanding. And your mother must give her permission. Whatever differences you and your mother have, you must lay them aside. She has to come with you."

"I understand," Emmy whispered back. "Thank you. Thank you for making this happen."

Mrs. Crofton squeezed Emmy's arm. "I don't have any other family besides Graham. I want you to go as far as you can, Emmeline. I really do. You will always have a place at Primrose."

Emmy hugged her, grateful beyond words.

When she pulled away, Mrs. Crofton's eyes were shimmering. "See you Monday."

The door closed behind her and Emmy took off down the street.

Eighteen

EMMY rushed as quickly as her legs could take her back to Knightsbridge station and then sailed down the stairs to the train tracks. It was just a few minutes before four thirty. If a train came quickly, she could be at Oxford Circus station within ten minutes. She would have to run to Mrs. Billingsley's home a few blocks away to catch Mum before she left at five o'clock. But she had to try.

Emmy knew if she caught Mum as she was getting off work, she could prepare her for coming home to Julia on her sofa. She could also use the time they would be together in public transit to appeal to her. Mum's main reason for Emmy's accompanying Julia to Gloucestershire in the evacuation was to make sure Julia didn't end up in a terrible placement with ogres for caregivers. Mum had nothing to worry about now. Charlotte was every inch the ideal foster mother.

There was no reason for Mum to decline the Dabneys'

kind offer except for spite. Mum had her flaws, but malice was not one of them.

If Emmy could get her to agree, then perhaps a few years down the road, when the war was long over, Emmy's gowns would be hanging in a lovely boutique. She would have the money to get Mum out of whatever degrading situation she was trapped in. Emmy could get them all a nice flat on a quiet street and Mum wouldn't have to be a kitchen maid anymore. She could work in the boutique with Emmy. Julia could, too. The three of them would be surrounded by lace and loveliness and happy young women shopping for the day when they would look like and feel like princesses.

These thoughts propelled Emmy as she switched trains for the Oxford Circus station and then sprinted for Mrs. Billingsley's home off Regent Street. She had been to the home only once before. The previous Christmas, Mrs. Billingsley had invited her staff for a tea party on Boxing Day. Instead of serving, Mum got to sit in the parlor while hired hands poured tea and passed around platters of sweets and sandwiches. Emmy wasn't entirely sure she could find the house again, but she would ring the bell on every doorstep on the block before she'd give up.

When she turned the corner onto Regent Street, Emmy scanned the homes, at once certain that the glistening gray mansion with ironwork on every window halfway down the block was Mrs. Billingsley's. Relief flooded her; it was twenty minutes to five. Plenty of time.

Emmy rang the bell and waited, using the seconds to catch her breath. The door was opened by a woman Emmy had met on Boxing Day nearly nine months before. She remembered the woman's name was Gladys. She seemed quite surprised to see Emmy.

"Hello. I'm Emmeline Downtree," Emmy said. "I

am wondering if I might wait for my mother, Annie Downtree, to get off work?"

"Oh, my gracious. Is everything all right? I thought you and your little sister had been sent to the countryside."

Emmy's breath still came in ragged swells. "No. Yes. I mean, yes, everything is all right. We just . . . We just had to make a trip into London today to take care of a few errands. May I wait for her, please?"

"I'm afraid she went home early today. Are you sure you're all right?"

"She's left already?" Emmy's rapidly beating heart did a somersault. Of all the days Mum had to leave early, it had to be today?

"Yes. I'm afraid so. She left at four. Maybe even before. I think she—"

But Gladys didn't finish her sentence. Sirens suddenly pierced the air. The sirens never sounded during the day and so the two stood there dumbfounded for a moment, as if they had no idea what the strange keening meant. The Luftwaffe didn't fly during the day when antiaircraft guns could pick the planes off. The Luftwaffe flew at night, using darkness as a cover. Yet the sirens wailed.

"What the devil—" But Gladys's words were cut short by a series of loud booms that punched the air somewhere in the distance. Both women turned toward the sound. And then there were more thundering wallops. Smoke began to rise from the direction of the Thames, south and east of where they stood.

Several seconds passed before Emmy realized the sounds she was hearing were bombs. Dropped in daylight.

As she processed this knowledge, more bombs fell. Gladys reached for her. "Come inside, dear! We've a cellar!"

Emmy instinctively stepped back from her grasp. "I

have to get home." Emmy turned from her even as Gladys yelled for her to come back.

"You can't leave now!" the woman shouted.

But Emmy was already off the doorstep, out the gate, and then running back the way she had come. And all the while the sirens kept wailing, the horizon ahead kept filling with smoke, and a cacophony of explosions kept rocking the air in the distance.

She could no longer hear Gladys bellowing for her to return. She was only barely aware of the other people on the sidewalk who, like her, were rushing to be somewhere. Emmy's sole focus was getting on a train headed southeast toward home.

Emmy rounded a corner and nearly ran into a man coming from the opposite direction. They skipped the courtesies due each other and kept charging ahead. Emmy could see the steps to the Underground.

As she closed the distance, she heard herself saying aloud, "Thank God, thank God, thank God."

Thank God Mum had left early. A few moments earlier, Emmy had been perturbed that Mum wasn't at Mrs. Billingsley's, and now she was nearly crying with relief that she had gone home at four.

That meant Julia wasn't alone.

Thank God Julia wasn't alone.

People were cramming themselves onto the steps of the station to get belowground. Emmy pushed her way forward down the stairs to get on a train. Surely one or two were still running. The sirens had been wailing for only ten minutes. She pressed her way to the tracks, surrounded on all sides by women with shopping bags, men with briefcases, grocers and bus drivers, wardens and waitresses, bankers and beggars.

She could feel the incoming rush of air as a train

approached and the people moved forward as one, crushing her to the wall so that she could not take a step toward it. As soon as the train slowed to a stop, the people inside the station were at its doors. When they slid open, a few of the people on the train attempted to disembark.

"What's happened?" one of them yelled.

"There's an air raid!" someone in the crowd shouted back. "The Luftwaffe is attacking the East End. The whole bloody sky is filling with smoke!"

Some got off the train; some stayed on; others boarded until there was no more room. Emmy could not make her way forward to be among those who got on. It didn't matter, though, because the train didn't move after that.

She turned around and pressed through the crowd to get back to the stairs, but there was no way to ease or push her way through. The station was full of people, elbow to elbow, and outside she could still hear the wail of the sirens, the thunder of explosives, the crackling of antiaircraft guns, and even the buzzing hum of planes.

"What's your name?" a woman said. She was clutching a little dog to her chest. Her hair had worked itself free of its pins and spilled about her shoulders in a wacky, unkempt tumble.

"Emmeline."

"I'm Mrs. Grote. Do you live around here?"

"Whitechapel."

A muted boom punctured the sheltered air inside and Mrs. Grote jumped, knocking herself into Emmy. "So sorry," she said as she righted herself. "I am not good with loud noises. Percy doesn't like them, either. Do you, Percy? Oh, I'm so glad I was walking my dog when the sirens started," she said, now sniffling into the scruff of the dog's neck. "I'm so glad. He'd be home alone if I had gone to the market instead. Can you imagine?"

Emmy wanted to get away from Mrs. Grote and her dog and her chatty demeanor, but there was nowhere to go.

There was nowhere for any of them to go. The people in the station could only lean against one another and wait for the thrashing outside to stop and the sirens to fall silent.

For more than an hour Emmy hunkered in the station, listening to the muffled sounds of a battle raging above. Finally, a few minutes after six, the world outside grew quiet compared to what it had been before. The crowd of people waited expectantly for the all-clear signal but did not hear it. After several minutes, a few people began to venture out anyway, despite a warning by a civil defense official who had dashed inside with them that no one should leave until the all-clear signal. Following those who pushed past, Emmy emerged back onto the street. The sky to the east was a bright blaze of gold and gray. The barrage balloons that hovered in the distance looked pink in the strange light of smoke and fire.

Emmy didn't want anyone asking her any more questions about who she was or where she lived. She didn't care if the all-clear hadn't sounded and the Germans were merely circling to come back and have at them again. All she knew was the flat was in the direction of the fires and smoke. She had to get home to Mum and Julia.

She took off on foot as at last the all-clear sounded. She wasn't sure where she was until she saw a landmark sign for Saint Paul's two miles away. If she could find Saint Paul's, she could find her way home.

Others who had been sheltered and wished to be home or at least somewhere else were also on the streets. Emmy could hear snippets of their conversations. Someone had been listening to a radio. Fires at the docks were raging. Warehouses were engulfed in flames. Stores, houses, churches, and schools all across the East End were demolished, damaged, or burning.

Emmy turned to a man who said it was most severe by Tower Bridge. "Which neighborhoods? Which streets?" she asked him.

He shook his head. "I don't know, love. All over. Look at the sky." He nodded toward the direction they were headed. The rosy orange hue seemed to suggest the earth had swung off its orbit and now the sun was preparing to set in the east.

The long walk to the Moreton train station that morning seemed like a lifetime ago as Emmy dodged her way closer and closer to home in the sickly hued twilight. She knew from Mum that it was three miles from the flat to Mrs. Billingsley's in Mayfair. She tried to hail a taxi but none of them stopped for her. Everyone and everything moved at a frenzied pace as emergency vehicles raced to the East End and survivors made their way west. When Emmy could see the dome of Saint Paul's, she knew she was two-thirds of the way home. Just a mile to go.

And then the sirens came again.

Louder this time.

Or maybe it was just that she so desperately did not want to hear them.

Antiaircraft guns began peppering the sky over the river. She felt the drone of the approaching planes in her chest.

The scattering of people searching for cover erupted all around her but she did not join them. Emmy doubled her pace for home, despite her weariness.

"Run, run!" someone shouted. Emmy heard a whistle, almost like a flute, and then the sound became an orchestra of angry flutes. Then there was a shattering *whack*. Her feet were off the ground and Emmy marveled for a split second at the weightless sensation of flying. And then her head slammed against bricks and the world went silent and dark.

Nineteen

✑

I'M so thirsty.

This was Emmy's first thought when the darkness lifted.

She heard a woman singing softly, a lullaby. Emmy was not alone.

A trio of booms echoed from somewhere far above her. She smelled ash and dirt and sulfur.

Something cool and wet touched her forehead and she opened her eyes.

"There, now," a woman said as she held the compress to Emmy's head. "You're all right. You're safe."

Emmy looked about her and saw nothing but shadows and the dim outlines of men and women crouched like stowaways in the hold of a ship. She was lying on a cot. Her head pounded and her ankle throbbed.

A whistling sound, faint but recognizable from the

last moment she remembered, split the quiet, and Emmy half rose with a start before the woman gently pressed her back down on the cot. "Not to worry. You're safe here."

"Where am I?" Emmy croaked. "What happened?"

"You're in a shelter, love. You're safe. You were knocked out cold but a fireman brought you here. You're safe now."

For several seconds Emmy could not make sense of this information. All she could remember was that she had been on the street. And then there were sirens. And the angry flutes.

"What—what day is it?"

"It's still Saturday, love. What's your name?"

"Emmeline. Where am I?"

"You're in the basement at Saint Paul's. What's your last name, Emmeline?"

Emmy ignored her question. She had to think for a moment. She had been on her way home. Home. She was walking home. She had the satchel in her hand. She was walking home. Home.

Julia. And Mum.

Emmy bolted upright and her head spun.

"Hold on there, Emmeline. You've a nasty bump on your head. Let's take it easy, now."

"I have to go." A wave of dizziness swept over Emmy and her upper body fell against the woman. She lowered Emmy back down.

"You can't go back out, Emmeline. It's dangerous. There are bombs falling everywhere."

As if to prove her point, several booms pounded outside and the room shook.

"They're going to kill us all!" a man shouted.

"Hush, now!" the woman yelled back to him.

"But my mother and sister—," Emmy pleaded.

The woman's eyes narrowed in concern. "Were they on the street with you?"

"No. They're at home. I was on my way to them."

She patted my arm. "They are surely in a shelter, too, Emmeline. Just like you. They'd want you to stay safe. You can't go out there now."

"It's bloody Armageddon," another man said, sounding terrified.

The woman who was singing softly nearby stopped for a second and told the man to shut up. A child whimpered and she started singing again.

The satchel.

Julia's book.

"Where is it? Where's my bag?"

The woman held up the satchel. "Right here. It's right here. See? You've nothing to worry about. You're safe here."

"Nobody's safe," a voice grunted.

The angry flutes whistled outside, followed by a thunderous roar, and again the room shook.

From somewhere behind Emmy an old man began to recite the twenty-third psalm. The woman who held the compress to her head joined him. A few others did, too.

"I'm thirsty," Emmy whispered.

The woman reached behind her for a glass jar and poured water into a tin cup, which she held to Emmy's lips. The water tasted like metal. Emmy lay back down.

The woman unwound the shawl she had over her shoulders and folded it into a tight rectangle. Then she placed it under Emmy's head.

"Rest now," she said.

Emmy slept.

When she awoke, the room was in semidarkness and cloaked in an odd silence after so much noise hours before. People were walking about slowly, gingerly. Those who hadn't had a cot on which to sleep moved stiffly after having spent the night on the hard floor.

Emmy rose to a sitting position, her head protesting. She reached up to touch her forehead and felt a band of gauze, sticky with dried blood. The woman who had ministered to her the night before was asleep on the floor.

"Is it over?" someone asked.

"Who knows?" someone answered. "Who knows anything?"

Emmy reached for her satchel at the woman's feet and got up carefully, holding her head as she stood. A wave of dizziness nearly sent her toppling back to the cot. A man walking past steadied her and Emmy whispered her gratitude.

She wanted to thank the woman who had cared for her, but she had to get home to Mum and Julia. Perhaps she would see the woman again someday.

Perhaps.

Emmy slid the strap of the satchel over her shoulder and tested her footing. Her left ankle ached ferociously. She tried out a few small steps as she followed those also wanting to exit the shelter. They went down a hallway, through a set of double doors, and to a stairway that led upward. Emmy took the steps one at a time with a hand firmly on the rail. With each step, the smell of ash and fire and dust became more pervasive. The light at the top of the stairs was a sickly yellow, not from the morning sun but from a thousand fires still burning.

Saint Paul's appeared undamaged, but as Emmy gingerly made her way east toward home, the destruction from the day before began to reveal itself: crushed buildings, broken windows, blackened brick, roofs missing or caved in. Fire and rescue crews were rushing about with a hundred tasks to attend to; they had no time to bother with a fifteen-year-old girl who hobbled resolutely down debris-choked streets. The closer Emmy got to the flat, the more her heart began to pound. She passed the intersection that would take her to Primrose. She didn't know whether Mrs. Crofton's shop still stood but she could not take the time now to see. Her only aim was to make sure Julia and Mum were all right.

Emmy passed a rescue crew digging in wreckage. A dead man lay at their feet, his eyes open and vacant, his nose and mouth covered with dried blood. Another man was being tended to. His shoes had been blown off and his shattered legs hung from his pant legs like laundry on the line. "Where's my Lucy?" he was saying.

Two more rescue workers were pushing away rubble to get to an outstretched hand. "Hold on. We're coming for you," one of the workers said. He reached for the hand to assure the trapped person that help was on the way. The hand and half of its severed arm tumbled toward him at his touch.

Emmy turned away to vomit into the gutter. The paltry contents of her stomach landed on a baby's crib toy.

She wheeled away from the scene, holding a hand over her mouth and willing herself to look at nothing but her feet. Finally, she turned down her street. The first few buildings were fine. But then she could see that the row of flats across the street from where she lived had been flattened, squashed as if they'd been made of cardboard. With relief she saw that the flats on her side of the street still stood. But the explosions from across the street had taken out every front window. Whole sections of roof were missing and Thea's front door hung by one hinge.

Emmy hobbled up to her front door and felt for the key under the mat. She wrenched open the door, calling Mum and Julia's names.

Glass and ash covered the sitting room floor. She limped into the kitchen. More broken glass. She turned to hobble up the stairs.

"Mum! Julia!"

Emmy threw open Mum's bedroom door. Debris littered her bed. The blackout curtains from her window overlooking the street hung in tattered threads.

She limped into Julia's room, where she met the same scene.

They weren't there.

Emmy's head throbbed. She made her way back downstairs and pulled out a kitchen chair. She sank into it to wait for them to return from the shelter. She had eaten nothing in nearly twenty-four hours and she marveled that her stomach could growl for food after what she had seen that morning. But she was too tired to see whether there was anything edible left. There was no electricity. Whatever was still in the fridge was probably spoiled. She leaned forward to rest her head on the table.

Emmy startled awake when she heard a voice outside on the front step.

"Bloody mess this is."

Mum.

Thank God.

Emmy shot up out of the chair and had to steady herself when her injuries protested.

"Mum!" she called out.

Emmy stumbled into the front room as Mum stepped inside the flat.

She staggered toward her mother and wrapped her arms around Mum's neck. Tears that she'd kept at bay since the sirens first sounded yesterday fell freely.

"Good Lord, Emmy!" Mum's hand stroked Emmy's hair. She couldn't remember the last time Mum had done that.

"Oh, Mum. I was so worried."

"What in the world? What happened to you? Why are you here?"

Mum did not sound angry. She sounded surprised. Completely surprised. Emmy pulled back from her to study her mother's face.

"Didn't—didn't you see my note? Didn't Julia tell you?"

"What note? Didn't Julia tell me what? What are you talking about? Why are you here?"

"Mum. Didn't you come home yesterday? You got off at four o'clock."

"How did you . . . Why aren't you in Gloucestershire? Why are you here?" Mum's voice rose in pitch as she slowly realized that something was terribly wrong.

"Tell me you came home when you got off work. Tell me you have Julia," Emmy murmured, new tears already falling.

Mum went white. "Julia is with you. In Gloucestershire."

Nausea rose up inside Emmy. "Where did you go?" she whispered.

"Em. Where is your sister?" Mum's voice trembled. "Where is she?"

"Why didn't you come home?" Emmy cried. "You were supposed to come home!"

Mum placed her hands on Emmy's shoulders. Her nails dug into Emmy's skin. "Where is your sister?"

Thea.

Emmy freed herself from Mum's grasp and limped past her. She staggered across the rubble in between the two flats and swung open Thea's damaged front door. The destruction to Thea's flat was worse than theirs. In addition to broken glass and missing roof sections, the far wall was cracked and bulging inward. But the most disturbing detail was that her furniture was covered in white sheeting; the look of a place that had been sealed up and emptied of its people.

"Julia!" Emmy called. "Julia!"

Mum was now standing at Thea's doorstep. "What is going on? What did you do?"

Emmy wheeled around to face her mother. "Where's Thea?"

"What did you do?" Mum yelled.

"You were supposed to come home!" Emmy yelled back.

"What have you done with my baby?" Mum screamed.

"Are you two all right?"

The two women turned to the voice. A man stood on the sidewalk. Emmy recognized him as the pensioner who lived three doors down. He was staring at them, wide-eyed.

Emmy shuffled over to him. "Did you see Julia? My sister. Did you see her here last night?"

The man stared at her. "I thought all the children on this street had been evacuated."

"Did you see her?" Emmy shouted.

"No. No, I didn't."

Mum was at Emmy's side. "Emmy. I need to know what happened!"

Emmy ignored her. "Did you see Thea? The lady who lives here? Did you see her?"

The man blinked. "She and her mum left for Wales. A few days ago, I think."

"Did you go to the shelter last night? Did you see a little girl? She's only seven." Sobs garbled Emmy's words.

The man shook his head. "There were no children in the shelter last night other than a new mother with an infant who came in off the street."

Emmy pushed past him, calling Julia's name.

"Should I get a policeman?" the man yelled.

But Emmy could not answer him. She could only shout one word.

"Julia!"

Mum trailed after her, repeating a four-word phrase; four words that fell at Emmy's back like a mallet.

What have you done?

Twenty

THERE had been a time, right up until the Blitz had begun, when a missing child would have sent policemen scurrying to help. Neighbors and strangers alike would've stopped whatever they were doing to assist in the search. The moment a frantic parent or sibling sounded the alarm, caring strangers dropped everything to search nearby alleys and behind hedges, and they'd ask passersby whether they'd seen the child. It mattered when a child went missing.

But on that Sunday morning, when fires still burned and the dead were still being carried out and the extent of the destruction still could not be fathomed, a missing seven-year-old was just another calamity in a collection of calamities the likes of which no one had seen before. The police station where Emmy and her mother began their agonized search for Julia was filled with people who wanted information on the whereabouts of loved ones whose houses had been destroyed. An hour passed before a policeman took down their information. Emmy was asked twice why she had left Julia alone. "I had an appointment," she said. "And I thought my mother would come home after she got off work."

"And why didn't you come home, then?" the cop said to Mum.

"I had an appointment, too," Mum said, not taking her eyes off the policeman. "And I had already placed my children in the care of a foster mother who lives two hours away in Gloucestershire, so naturally there was no reason for me to think I was needed at home, now, was there?"

The cop shook his head, silently indicting them both for such a cavalier approach to responsibility. "All right, then," he said when he was finished. "We'll be on the lookout for her. Is your home still livable?"

"Barely," Mum said.

"You might want to stay close to it the next couple days in case she comes back on her own." The policeman removed the report from his clipboard, added it to the mountain of papers already on his desk, and then looked past to others waiting for help. "Next in line, please."

FROM the police station, Emmy and her mother went to the hospital, which was bursting with the injured. No one there had admitted a little girl named Julia. No one had seen a little girl who fit her description.

They appealed to their local warden, Mr. Findley, whom they found making the rounds with officials whose job it was to determine whether the houses in his sector that had been destroyed still had victims inside them. He wearily told them to try Julia's school, on the slim chance that someone had taken her there last night to be reevacuated out of London. But that suggestion also proved fruitless. The school was a burned-out shell.

Next they trudged to social services. They pounded on the door of the nearest children's home for orphans and crawled inside every shelter in a two-mile radius.

No one had seen the seven-year-old girl. And no one had time to stop what they were doing to help Emmy and her mother figure out where she was. No one could do more than ask the same questions everyone else was asking.

Did you check the hospital?

Did you contact the police?

Did you search the shelters?

Did you check all the wardrobes and cupboards at home? Under the stairs? In the attic?

The neighbors?

Everywhere they turned they were reminded that their little woe meant nothing compared to the compounded loss of London's East End.

Mum would not look at Emmy or speak to her after she had told her why she had come back to London and why she had brought Julia with her. In their search, Emmy and her mother went to each place together, but in silence. When they had exhausted all their options, they returned to the flat, hoping that Julia was waiting there for them, sitting on the stoop with her arms looped around knees folded to her chest. But the front step was empty.

Their neighbor to the left was covering her broken windows with pieces of plywood. When the woman, a quiet factory worker named Geraldine, saw Emmy and her mum, she paused with a hammer in hand.

"Did you find your little one?" she asked.

Mum shook her head. She went into the flat without a word.

"No one has seen her," Emmy replied.

"She has to turn up," the woman said, but her tone conveyed her doubt.

Inside, Mum was standing at the kitchen sink, looking out the broken window at the bit of dirt that was their back garden. Her hands were folded across her chest.

Emmy lowered herself into a kitchen chair, grateful to be off her injured leg, but not wanting to be in the same room with Mum and the crushing weight of her anguish.

She had already told Mum she was sorry, so very sorry, and there was nothing else she could say. She said it again anyway.

"I'm so sorry, Mum."

Her mother did not turn at the sound of Emmy's voice. She just stood there, looking at the dirt and the scattering of war debris that had landed in the garden.

"Mum?"

"I should have known something like this would happen," Mum murmured, more to the broken window than to Emmy.

"What?"

"I should have guessed that when you put you and me together, this is what comes of it."

Emmy didn't know what she meant. She didn't want to know.

"I sent you away with Julia when you didn't want to go and you came back with her when you should've left her where she was," she said, her voice strangely emotionless.

"I'm sorry, Mum," Emmy said for the hundredth time. "I didn't know this was going to happen. I thought she'd be safe. I thought you were . . ." Her voice trailed away.

"Yes, you thought I'd be coming home. To my empty house, like I do every night because that's the life I have."

Her detached manner scared Emmy. She said nothing.

Her mum turned to face her. "Don't you want to ask me where I was last night? Don't you want to know since it's my fault this happened?"

Emmy wanted the floor to open up beneath her and swallow her whole. She wanted to scream and scream until she had screamed all the oxygen out of the room and she could simply keel over dead in the chair.

"That's what you're thinking, isn't it? That it's my fault?"

"That's not what I'm thinking," Emmy whispered. "I didn't know this would happen. I just wanted to make something of myself. I just . . . I just wanted you to be proud of me."

Mum stared at Emmy for several long seconds, her arms crossed loosely over her chest. "Is that really what you wanted? Wasn't it instead to prove to yourself that you're better than I am? You've always been ashamed of what I am. No wonder you jumped at the first chance to get the hell out of life here with me."

"That's not true!" Emmy yelled.

"Of course it's true. And who can blame you. You were never meant for this. Not this."

She turned back to the window.

They were quiet for a few minutes, each lost in private regrets.

When she turned back around, Emmy could see that her mother had made a decision. She strode purposely past Emmy.

Emmy heard her on the stairs. She got up from the kitchen chair and limped up to the second floor. Mum was in her bedroom, looking through her wardrobe. Glass crunched beneath Emmy's feet as she walked in.

Mum pulled out a heather gray dress she'd come home with last spring. If she had noticed Emmy was wearing one of her dresses, Emmy couldn't tell. She said nothing.

"What are you doing?" Emmy asked.

Mum tossed the dress onto her bed, reached up to the buttons on her maid's uniform, and undid them. She stepped out of her work clothes and pulled on the dress. "I can't do this alone. I need help."

"But we've already been to the police and they—"

"I'm not talking about the police. They don't care about me or Julia. I'm no one to them. Just another pitiful soul they don't have the time or the means to pay attention to. I need someone who has connections."

She grabbed a hairbrush off her bureau, shook the dust from it, and ran it through her hair. Even after a night of hell and a day of torment, she still looked so beautiful.

"Where are you going?" Emmy asked softly.

Mum picked up a bottle of perfume and squeezed the ball. The room filled with a sweet scent. "Stay here," she said. "I don't want Julia coming home to an empty house."

She moved past Emmy, who turned to follow her.

"Where are you going, Mum?"

"If the sirens go off again, go to the shelter at the corner. When they stop, get back here as quick as you can."

"Mum!" Emmy rushed to keep up with her.

Her mother was down the stairs and reaching for her handbag where she had dropped it at the front door when Emmy reached for her.

"Mum, please! Wait."

Her mother turned to face Emmy.

"Please, Mum. Tell me where you're going."

Mum looked at her for a moment, studying her daughter's face as if seeing it for the first time in a long while. "I am going to get help."

It made Emmy sick to think she was going to whom-ever she was selling her body to; she was sure that was where her mum was headed. Emmy had brought her to this moment. It was because of her that Mum's options for finding Julia had been reduced to this.

"Mum, don't go," Emmy pleaded.

"I have to."

Then, from some crazed part of her, Emmy tossed out an offer that scared her breathless the second she uttered it, not only because it was so terrible, but because she was ready to make good on it. "Take me with you. I'll do . . . I'll do whatever it is you have to do. I'll do it. This is all my fault."

Mum's features softened into a look Emmy hadn't seen since Neville first came into her life to stay. Julia was a baby, and Mum was happy then. She reached out to touch Emmy's face, cupping her fingers gently under her daughter's chin. "No, it's not."

"Yes, it is! It is. Let me do what you have to do."

She smiled, dropped her hand, and looked away. A mirthless laugh escaped her. "Oh, Em. You're not like me. Deep down I've always known it. You're not like me. This is my doing. I will fix it."

When she turned back to look at Emmy, her eyes were glistening. "Find something to cover the windows."

"Mum—"

"Stay here. Watch for your sister. Don't go outside after dark. It's not safe."

Before Emmy could say another word, her mother stepped outside into the chaos of their broken street and she watched her walk away, a beautiful woman in a heather gray dress with whispers of floral scent trailing after her.

Twenty-one

AFTER Mum left, Emmy busied herself with looking for something to cover the windows in the front of the flat. Geraldine saw her poking about the ruins across the street for larger pieces of wood and brought over her last piece of plywood. She helped Emmy cover the front window downstairs, the biggest of the three that had shattered. And she let Emmy borrow her hammer and nails so that Emmy could cover the empty window frame in Mum's upstairs room, and the little one upstairs in the privy.

Emmy attempted to return the hammer but Geraldine asked her if she and Mum were staying that night at the flat. When Emmy nodded, she said, "You know there's no electricity, no gas, no running water?"

"Julia might come home."

"Does your mother keep a gun?"

Emmy shook her head, unable to reason why her neighbor was asking that.

"Hang on to the hammer, then."

She watched Geraldine trudge off with one suitcase to who knew where, the rest of her worldly belongings as secure as she could make them.

Back inside the flat, Emmy swept up the shards of glass, shook out all the sofa pillows, and waited for Mum.

At dusk she was still not back.

Emmy found half a package of biscuits and another of sardines and ate them.

Still Mum was not back.

She went upstairs to the room she shared with Julia, grabbed the coverlet and pillow from her bed, and took them downstairs. She arranged herself on the sofa so that she would hear if anyone came to the front door. The room quickly became inky black as the sun set and whatever residual light that crept in through the boards over the windows disappeared. She pulled the blanket up under her chin and clutched Geraldine's hammer. Minutes later, the air raid sirens began to wail, and the drone of planes overhead rumbled outside. Emmy grabbed the blanket and hammer, and headed for Thea's, pulling open the broken front door and running through the kitchen. When she flung open the back door, Emmy saw that Thea's cats lay dead on the back step, stretched out as if they had been arranged there by Death itself. Emmy grimaced as she stepped over the bodies and crawled inside the Anderson shelter. Emmy yanked the door closed and scooted as far back as she could in the pitch black of the damp shelter, knocking over a box of metal items that skittered across the dirt floor. The ground beneath her knees rocked as somewhere nearby a bomb connected with its target, and a spray of dirt fell on her.

"Stop! Stop it!" Emmy yelled, pressing her hand to her ears, while fear coursed through her veins.

She was now the girl home alone while bombs rained down all around.

Julia!

Emmy called for her sister. She called for Mum.

She could do nothing but cover herself with the blanket and clutch the hammer as the bombs fell. Emmy would learn that this second night was worse than the first. Four hundred people would be killed, and more than seven hundred injured.

Warehouses along the Thames were again easy targets, and buildings that had been afire on Saturday night were burning again. Hundreds of fires would join together to become one.

And all the while, Emmy huddled in Thea's bomb shelter, alone and afraid.

She didn't know when she fell asleep. She only knew that when she awoke, she heard the far-off sounds of emergency vehicles. She emerged from the shelter to a fog of smoke and ash and mist. Her row of flats was still standing but the unit on the end was now minus a roof and a second story. Emmy picked her way back to the flat, calling for Mum, calling for Julia. But the street, the flat, all that she knew, were empty of people and silent. Inside, she used the toilet, its water soured and stinking since it had been used but not flushed in two days. The food in the fridge, the little there was, stank as well. She found a swallow of brandy in the cupboard above the fridge, which she drank because there was nothing else. Then she opened a tin of beans and ate them cold with a spoon.

Sometime later Emmy saw through a slit in the plywood a man approaching the flat. The warden perhaps? Emmy could not let him see her. He would insist she leave and that was something Emmy could not do. She had not locked the front door. Before she could turn the latch, she heard him knock. Emmy sprang to the kitchen and let herself out the back door into the debris-littered garden where she concealed herself as best she could along the wall. She still held the hammer.

Emmy heard the man inside the house.

"Anyone here? Annie? Are you here?"

Emmy stood still against the wall. The voice didn't belong to Mr. Findley. She didn't recognize the voice at all. Still, he would only be able to see her if he came into the garden. And surely there was no reason for him to do that.

He called for Mum again. And again.

And then he left.

Emmy waited until she could see him over the garden wall, walking away. He wore a nice hat and a wool coat.

Should she have revealed herself? She wasn't sure. She didn't know him. What did he want with her mother?

Emmy watched the man until he was no longer in sight. Then she went back inside and waited.

Mum did not come back.

Emmy read Julia's book of fairy tales. She slept. She ate another can of cold beans. She watched the fires burning across town from the back garden.

When darkness began to fall, Emmy realized it was Monday. Mr. Dabney had expected her at his town house at four o'clock that afternoon with her mother and the brides box in tow.

He and his sweet wife were leaving for Edinburgh tomorrow. And she was to go with them, she and her brides box, because she was going to be Graham Dabney's apprentice.

It was now after seven.

And the sirens began to wail.

Once again, Emmy grabbed the hammer and her blanket and ran to Thea's Anderson shelter.

In that hellish cocoon Emmy did not know that fires were burning all around Saint Paul's and buildings were ablaze on both sides of Ludgate Hill. A women's hospital was hit as was a school being used to shelter homeless families. More than four hundred people were killed and more than a thousand injured on the second night that she huddled in Thea's shelter, the third night of the Blitz. There were a few tins of canned milk inside the shelter, which she drank, and a package of digestive biscuits, which she ate.

She fell asleep when exhaustion overcame her, to the rumblings of explosions that filled her dreams with terror.

In the morning, as the East End continued to burn, Emmy let herself back inside Thea's flat, hardly noticing the dead cats as she stepped over them.

She needed food and water.

Thea had emptied her kitchen of food in preparation for evacuating with her mother to Wales, but Emmy found a few jars of preserves, canned meat, and other items that would not spoil in their absence. She grabbed a market basket from Thea's kitchen and filled it with all the food she had left, even the cats' food.

She took the basket and her hammer back to the flat to wait for Mum.

But she did not come.

And Julia did not return home.

Rain began to fall in the late afternoon, a weeping, mournful downpour. Extending into the early-evening hours, it should have kept the Luftwaffe from continuing its assault. But no. The Luftwaffe made full use of the cloud cover. Bombers pounded the city once again and Emmy spent another night in Thea's shelter.

On Wednesday with no sign of Mum or Julia, Emmy

hid the basket of food in her wardrobe upstairs and ventured out to look for them.

She went back to the places Mum and she had been before. She also went to the shelters where the homeless were gathering. No one at the hospital had seen Julia and there was no record of either Julia or Mum having been admitted. Emmy returned to the police station, which was as chaotically busy as it had been three days before. A different policeman was on duty and she had to explain all over again how Julia came to be missing.

"And where is your mother right now?" this new policeman said, looking past Emmy. Emmy was a child and he didn't have time for children.

"She's out looking for my sister." It wasn't exactly a lie.

It was obvious he was perturbed that Emmy was at the station alone without Mum. "Look, I've heard nothing of a young girl turning up. Have your Mum check with all the neighbors, and the child's friends, and—"

Emmy cut him off. "We don't have any more neighbors! Our street has been bombed. Everyone has left. That is what I have been telling you. She went missing the first night of the bombing."

He frowned at the interruption. "You bring your mum here and I will make out an official report."

"We already did that!" Emmy yelled. "On Sunday. This is Wednesday. She's been missing for four days!"

The policeman wagged a finger at Emmy. "Do you think you're the only soul in London with a tale of woe today? Do you know how many people are dead or missing? You tell your mum to come next time. I'm done with you."

He turned from Emmy to help someone else.

She stood there stunned, unable to believe no one

could help her. An older woman sitting on a bench and looking as though she had been waiting a long time crooked a finger, beckoning Emmy to approach her.

"I heard what you told the policeman, and I'm very sorry your little sister is missing," she said. "I hate to be the one to tell you this, but you and your mum should check the casualty listings at one of the Incident Inquiry Points."

Emmy had no idea what she was talking about. "The what?"

She reached for Emmy's arm and squeezed it gently. "They have listings, my dear. The names of those who've been killed. They have a list."

Emmy felt the blood drain from her face. "I don't know what you're saying." But she did. She did know what she was saying.

The woman released her hold and patted Emmy's arm. "Tell your mum to check at the nearest Incident Inquiry Point, love. There's an IIP just around the corner from the police station here. Tell your mum to check with them."

The woman withdrew her hand and her attention. She turned from Emmy to stare at the queue of people waiting their turn for help, allowing Emmy a sliver of privacy to take in the idea that Julia's body might be lying in a morgue somewhere, waiting for a family member to claim her remains.

Emmy left the station, numb with fear and dread.

Somehow she put one foot in front of the other and walked to the IIP office, as the woman had called it. Emmy stepped inside and fell in with the crowds of people seeking information. Her mind seemed to drift into that state between sleep and wakefulness as she waited her turn. Others ahead of her also wanted to see the lists. New copies of the latest reports of the dead were laid out on the counter by a green-uniformed matron of the Women's Volunteer Service. Those on an errand like no other moved forward to peer at them. The man ahead of Emmy looked and turned away, relief evident in his face. Emmy bent over to look, her gaze traveling over the letters of the alphabet. Past the As, the Bs, the Cs and then the Ds.

And then she saw it.

Downtree.

Emmy's heart slammed against her chest.

Downtree.

And then she saw the name following it, separated from *Downtree* with a tiny, gentle comma.

Anne Louise.

It wasn't Julia's name listed on the roll call of the dead.

It was Mum's.

Twenty-two

EMMY had never been to a morgue before, makeshift or otherwise.

The sheet-covered bodies lay on the school cafeteria floor, where only six months earlier children had eaten sausages and peas at sturdy wooden tables. The fallen were arranged in even rows, each one with a cardboard label affixed to the chest, identifying them by name—if it was known—and where they had been killed. Several officials moved about the rows, escorting next of kin to the draped body of the family member they'd been looking for, lifting a corner of the covering, and revealing just half the face; all that a mother or brother or son or grandparent needed to see to identify and claim their beloved.

Emmy would not be able to recall every step to the school-turned-morgue or how she managed to remember the directions after she was told how far she needed to walk to claim her mother's body.

She did remember being asked how old she was when at last her voice returned and she whispered to the volunteer at the IIP that Mum's name was among those on the list of the dead.

The first lie came off her lips as easy as air out of a burst balloon.

To have said she was fifteen and orphaned was to have sentenced herself to a children's home or worse. A social services worker would have been summoned. Emmy would have been escorted away. She wouldn't have been able to return to the flat. She wouldn't have been able to keep looking for Julia, whose name was not on the list.

Not on the list!

Emmy was all Julia had. She had to stay on her own. She had to.

"Eighteen," Emmy had said.

And where was her father?

The second lie came just as effortlessly.

"Recovering in hospital. We got separated Sunday night."

Kind condolences were offered to Emmy but she did not want the woman's sympathy. She wanted nothing from her that would give weight and substance to yet another grief.

Emmy was tired of weight and substance. Tired of fear, of anguish, of hunger, of thirst, of despair.

She wanted to feel nothing.

It had taken supreme effort not to press her hand to the woman's mouth and tell her to shut up about the terrible loss of her mother.

"Where is she?" Emmy had said, and the woman told her how to find the temporary morgue that had been set up near Holborn station for unclaimed dead.

Every step had seemed like the ticking off of the days and weeks and months the war was taking from her. With one word, she allowed her sixteenth and seventeenth years to be swallowed whole by the enemy—taken as swiftly and surely as the war had stolen everything else that was hers. This was all she had been aware of as she strode forward.

She could be a child no longer. Emmy had to be done with immature worries and juvenile hopes.

Orphan was a word to describe a child without parents. Emmy was not a child.

She was Julia's only living hope, and as such, her little sister's guardian.

Julia was Emmy's sole concern.

She would tell whatever lies she must to find her sister. Mum would want only one thing from Emmy now. To find Julia.

When Emmy arrived at the temporary morgue, she was eighteen. She felt eighteen. There would be no looking back.

She approached a haggard-looking city official with a clipboard who seemed to be in charge of receiving callers to the morgue. He looked as though he hadn't slept in days.

"I've come about my mother," Emmy said, surprising herself with how grown-up she sounded. "Her name is Annie Downtree. Anne Louise Downtree. I was told I would find her body here."

The man looked at his clipboard. "Are you the next of kin?" His voice sounded as tired as his body looked.

"I'm her only kin."

He looked up to study Emmy's face, wondering perhaps how old she was. But Emmy knew she no longer looked like a child.

"My father passed away when I was young." Again, the lie flew off Emmy's tongue with hardly a moment's thought.

"I'm so sorry for ye, lass. Truly I am."

Emmy did not want his sympathy. "Where is she?"

Again he consulted his clipboard, and then he checked a ledger on a nearby desk. When he looked up, he shook his head. "We aren't able to keep the unclaimed bodies more than a few days. We always make what inquiries we can. I am so sorry."

An odd sensation rippled through Emmy. Fear? Emptiness? Dread? "What did you do with her?" she said, restrained emotion thickening her words.

He consulted his clipboard yet again. When he looked up, he rubbed his chin with his hand, the gesture of one about to say something he was afraid to say. "She was buried proper; I can tell you that. In Tower Hamlets. Just this morning."

Emmy needed a moment to understand what the man was telling her. Mum had been buried already. She was buried. Buried. "What is Tower Hamlets?"

"It's the public cemetery, miss. Not far from Charing Cross. They were all given proper burials."

She swallowed a lingering sensation of loss and fear. " 'They'?"

"There were others what no one came for and who had no kin near as we could tell. They were buried proper. A vicar and everything."

"A vicar," Emmy echoed.

"Yes."

Emmy started to teeter and she steadied herself against the wall.

"Miss?" he said.

"Where—where was she found?"

The man checked the ledger; a different page this time. "In the basement of the Sharington Crescent Hotel. The place took a direct hit, I'm afraid. The upper floors collapsed into the basement, I hear. No one sheltering in the basement survived. I'm sorry."

A hotel. She was at a hotel.

"Where is this place?" Emmy said evenly.

"I'm sure it was quick, miss. I'm sure she didn't suffer."

He could be sure of nothing and he and Emmy both knew it. "Where is it?"

"Near Covent Garden, I think."

"And there were others?"

"Others?" He blinked, wide-eyed.

"Others in the basement? Was she with someone?"

He blinked again. "Oh, aye, there were other victims, I hear. A dozen or so."

"And they all came here?"

The man was trying to piece together why Emmy was asking so many questions. He stared at her. "No. Not all."

"Just the ones no one came for," Emmy finished for him.

He half nodded, embarrassed for her, possibly.

"We have what she was found with," he said. "Her handbag and such. Those haven't been stored away yet. Hold on."

He disappeared into the kitchen and Emmy heard him speaking to a woman.

The man told her whose effects Emmy was after and the woman asked who wanted them.

"It's the deceased's daughter."

"Daughter?" The woman sounded surprised. Emmy's pulse quickened as the woman appeared in the doorway, her brow furrowed.

"Are you Anne Downtree's daughter?" the woman asked as she approached Emmy.

Emmy felt a pulsing instinct to run.

"I am." She swallowed the rising alarm.

"Your foster mother already got the telegram and brought you here?"

A second ripple of fear coursed through her. "Y-yes."

The woman looked past Emmy to the door she'd come through. "We weren't told you'd be coming today. I'm sorry to tell you that I could not have released your mother's body to your foster mother even if I had wanted to. Is that what she was thinking? Is she outside waiting for you?"

Emmy had to get away.

But she had to pretend as if she didn't.

"She is," Emmy said slowly.

The woman frowned as if she'd been insulted. "And she sent you in here alone? Of all the—" She slammed the ledger shut and began to stride toward the door.

Emmy moved toward the woman, blocking her path.

"Please. I—I asked to come in alone. I wanted to see her on my own. My foster mother wanted to come in with me but I begged her not to."

The woman's disdain melted into something more like compassion.

"She's waiting for me at the chemist," Emmy continued. "My little sister has . . . She has asthma. We needed medicine. I'll go get her."

Emmy turned before either one could offer to ac-company her. She strode toward the door as unhurriedly as she dared, without Mum's handbag or whatever else she had on her when her body was found.

As soon as she was outside and around the corner, Emmy ran as fast as her legs could carry her.

Tears crept to the corners of her eyes as she sprinted down the street but Emmy savagely rubbed them away. After several blocks, and when her lungs were burning, she slowed to a walk, looking behind to make sure no one was coming after her.

So Charlotte had been sent a telegram that Mum had died. Would they come looking for her? Emmy wasn't sure. Would the woman at the morgue assume that once Emmy told her foster mother that Mum had already been buried, they would opt for the first train out of hellish London? She would, wouldn't she?

Even so, Emmy could not continue to stay at the flat, not now that she had been seen. Besides, there was no running water, electricity, gas, or food. She had to make other arrangements, but what?

Emmy had passed homeless shelters on the way back to Whitechapel, but whenever she had neared one of them, she smelled the fetid odor of unwashed bodies and makeshift latrines. She had no desire to stay in one. She could not go back to Mrs. Billingsley's. The widow and her staff all knew how old Emmy was. They would con-tact social services.

Perhaps, though, Mrs. Billingsley could be persuaded to help her find Julia. If Emmy begged her? The woman had money. Apparently Mum had believed money was needed to do what the police could not or would not.

But would Mrs. Billingsley do that?

Emmy could not chance it.

She could go to no one that she knew; no classmate from school, or even a classmate's family. She had to be eighteen-year-old Emmeline: a woman who did not yet exist in the eyes of anyone who knew her.

But where else could she go?

And then Emmy thought of Mrs. Crofton. Could Emmy convince her to let her stay with her? Emmy had missed the opportunity to become Graham's apprentice but perhaps Mrs. Crofton would allow Emmy to stay with her while Emmy looked for Julia. Emmy would promise her that when she found her sister, she would return to Charlotte's and she and Julia would stay in Stow for the remainder of the war, as they were supposed to have done. Yes, Emmy would do that. She would again have her brides box. She would find some way to regain the opportunity she had lost. Emmy would bring Julia with her back to London when the war ended. Perhaps Mrs. Crofton would allow her and Julia to board with her. Mrs. Crofton had had a daughter once, and she was fond of Emmy because of that. Emmy could tell that she was. She could pay for their room and board by working at the shop. And at night she would work on her gowns. Perhaps after the war, Mr. Dabney would give Emmy another chance. Emmy could still find a way to make Mum proud of her. Surely God allowed a dead mother glances from heaven at the children she had been torn from. . . .

Yes.

But Emmy didn't know where Mrs. Crofton lived.

Hoping the shop had not been bombed, she decided to make her way to Primrose Bridal. She still had the back door key. She would wait for Mrs. Crofton there or poke about her desk, looking for the woman's home address. Surely Mrs. Crofton would understand the need to do such a bold thing.

Emmy quickened her steps, impatient to take what she needed out of the flat and get to the bridal shop.

She arrived back home as the sun dipped low in the sky. Emmy pulled a travel bag from Mum's wardrobe and added to it the contents of her mother's top bureau drawer, which included her stockings, a nightgown, a felt-lined jewelry box, and a few trinkets. She also stuffed inside three of her mother's dresses, a pair of her slacks, gloves, and a pair of heeled shoes. Next, Emmy went into her old bedroom and took the remaining undergarments she had left behind, a few of Julia's clothes so that when she found her sister, she'd have clean clothes to wear. Back downstairs, Emmy grabbed her satchel and tossed what was left of Thea's food stores inside—and the hammer—and ran out of the flat and down the deserted street.

The sun was nearly gone from the horizon.

Emmy doubled her speed, running haphazardly with her awkward load.

Let it be standing, Emmy whispered to the heavens. *Let Primrose still be there.*

She covered the four blocks to the shop in less than ten minutes, dodging debris and collecting stares all along the way. She reached the street and her heart plummeted to her knees. The building on the corner of the street was a smoking hulk.

But Primrose, four buildings down on the opposite side, still stood among the ruins.

Twenty-three

⁂

EMMY let herself into the bridal shop by its back door, certain that Mrs. Crofton wasn't there, and yet she called for her as she stepped into the shadows.

She locked the door behind her and crept from the back entrance to the alterations room where she had first sewn a hem for Mrs. Crofton. Here, Mrs. Crofton had installed a blackout curtain for nights when she stayed late after business hours. Emmy lowered her belongings to the floor and reached up to the little window that overlooked the alley. She pulled the curtain down, securing it to the hooks Mrs. Crofton had nailed into the plaster. Emmy switched on the small table lamp by the sewing machine, grateful that the electricity on this side of the street had not been affected. A halo of sallow light fell about the tiny room. It was just enough brightness to see her way around but not enough to be detected by patrolling wardens and fire-watchers outside.

Emmy plugged in Mrs. Crofton's hot plate, filled the teakettle, and for the first time since she had sat in Mr. Dabney's elegant sitting room—a lifetime ago—she drank hot tea from a dainty, beautiful cup. Along with the tea, Emmy ate two slices of stale bread that she had taken from Thea's kitchen, spread with marmalade.

In her rush to be away from the flat, she had not considered that she might need a blanket and a pillow this night. It was too dark now to rummage around Mrs. Crofton's desk for her home address. Emmy would have to sleep at Primrose.

She stripped down to her underwear and, with water from the sink in the loo, she used a scrap of fabric from the alterations dustbin to wash the grit, dirt, and ash from her body. Then she stuck her head under the tap and washed her hair, repulsed by the swirls of dirty suds that accumulated at the drain as she massaged her scalp.

Emmy used a hand towel to dry off and then slipped on a pair of Mum's slacks and a blouse to serve as pajamas. As she started to comb out the tangles with the brush she'd grabbed from Mum's bedroom, she noticed it still held strands of her mother's hair in the bristles.

She pulled the brush away from her head. As she gazed at the mingled strands, hers and Mum's, a wave of grief swept over her. For hours, Emmy had kept the loss of her mother at a distance, refusing to acknowledge that Mum was dead. In her drastic measures to be able to keep searching for Julia, Emmy had not allowed herself to shed a tear for Mum. Not one. But now as she stood in the back room of the bridal shop, wearing Mum's clothes and holding her mother's hairbrush, the full weight of her loss came crashing in. Emmy sank to her knees, clutching the brush to her chest. The bristles pricked her skin like nettles through the thin fabric of her mother's blouse.

The tears began to fall, rivers of them, as Emmy sat back on her bent knees.

"Mum," Emmy murmured, as she thought of her mother's hand on her cheek and the last words she had said to her—the last words she would ever hear her say—floated into Emmy's mind.

Stay here and watch for your sister.

Don't go outside after dark.

It's not safe.

With those parting words, Emmy had suddenly been flung into an unfamiliar world falling apart all around her. She was alone in the very place where, only a few months ago, hope had been breathed into her dreams. Those dreams seemed thin as vapor now, spun by a different girl, someone Emmy barely recognized.

"Mum, Mum . . ." Emmy's voice was hoarse as she pushed it past the anguish in her throat. She raised her hand to wipe away tears and caught the faintest whiff of Mum's perfume on the sleeve of the blouse. Emmy folded herself to the floor and laid her head on the travel bag, clutching the hairbrush to her body just as the night before she had clutched the hammer. As she lay on the tiles, she began to shiver, and she screwed her eyes shut to take herself back to Brighton Beach, to that long-ago sultry weekend when Neville was still in Mum's life. The sand had been warm between Emmy's toes and a brilliant sun had been shining down on the water, making the surface of the sea look wired with tiny little flames. The white surf hitting the shore bubbled like bridal lace and Mum had been standing by Emmy as she dug her toes into the sand. They had been watching Neville and Julia play in the waves and Mum had reached down and laid a hand on her shoulder. Emmy had been reminded then of how it had been before Julia was born. When it was just she and Mum. Emmy had been flooded with the memory of her and Mum splashing in a London fountain and Mum stroking Emmy's hair and telling her someday she'd have everything she ever wanted.

And then Julia had squealed for Emmy to help her as Neville grabbed her around the middle and the two fell splashing and laughing to the water. Mum had laughed, too.

I guess you'd better go rescue her, Mum had said, nodding toward the water. *It's you she wants.*

For a moment, a solitary pinch of time, she and Mum stood in the sand, looking out past the happy swimmers to the vast and endless Atlantic.

You'd better go rescue her.

"I will, Mum," Emmy whispered now as the sensation of the warm sand and hot sun began to fade away, replaced by the cold tiles.

Emmy had no sooner murmured this promise than the sirens began their dreadful wailing and she was forced to contemplate her options. If she ran outside to join those sprinting for the nearest public shelter, she would be noticed by the local ARP warden whose job it was to account for the civilians in his or her sector. She could run for the nearest Tube station, but those inside would wonder where she had come from that she could suddenly materialize out of nowhere and be in need of shelter in a space they'd been hunkering down in for weeks.

As the first whistling bombs began to fall, followed by the thundering claps of their detonations, Emmy instinctively crawled under the sewing machine. Then an explosion rocked the world outside and she knew she needed something to cushion her against shattering walls, if it came to that. And Emmy knew where she could find that protection. She came out from underneath the sewing machine and stumbled into the dark store, yanking ebullient wedding gowns off their hangers as outside the air rocked with violence. She ran back into the alterations room, her arms overflowing with yards and yards of downy fabric. She scooted under the sewing table, then shoved the gauzy, generous gowns all around her until she felt she might suffocate. For the next seven hours, until four o'clock in the morning, Emmy crouched under the Singer as the Luftwaffe pummeled London, every word off her lips a promise to her mother.

When at last an eerie quiet signaled that daylight was not far away, she nodded off, enveloped by bridal gowns.

Emmy awoke midmorning and emerged from her white cocoon. Her head ached from mourning the loss of Mum, and a heavy numbness clung to her, but she still sensed relief that the street and the shop had not taken a direct hit. The toilet still flushed. The hot plate still worked. She could make tea. She found a bottle of aspirin inside a cabinet in the privy and took two.

With her teacup in hand, Emmy ventured out into the main room to steal a glance outside. As she was about to walk past the dressing room and Mrs. Crofton's consultation desk, Emmy saw a suitcase, standing as if at attention along the wall. A pair of gloves rested neatly on top and a neck scarf was draped over one side. Mrs. Crofton was prepared to go away. Perhaps she would be coming by the shop today to get her suitcase and flee London. Perhaps Emmy could convince her to delay her departure for just a few days so that she could help Emmy find Julia.

Emmy saw a neat pile of documents at the edge of the desk closest to the suitcase, and the unmistakable shape and color of a British passport. The other documents were folded. She picked up the little pile of documents and unfolded the first two. Mrs. Crofton's marriage license and her late husband's death certificate. The other three pieces of paper were her business license and her late daughter Isabel's birth and death certificates. Emmy noticed that Isabel would have been eighteen on the coming Sunday had she lived. Such history bound up in such flimsy pieces of paper. Private pieces of paper.

Emmy put them back where she had found them as her burning cheeks reminded her they were not her documents. A stamped but unmailed envelope lay next to Mrs. Crofton's private papers, addressed to Mrs. Talmadge, the woman who cleaned the shop on Friday mornings. Emmy reasoned that she needed to read what was written inside because she had to know what Mrs. Crofton's plans were. She needed to ascertain whether Mrs. Crofton would be able to be of any help.

The letter had not been sealed. Emmy lifted the flap, drew out the single piece of stationery, and read what Mrs. Crofton had written: It was dated Sunday, September 8.

Dear Mrs. Talmadge:

I am closing the shop for a while, perhaps a long while, and leaving London to wait out the war with my cousin and his wife in Edinburgh.

We are leaving Tuesday morning, so I shall not need . . .

Emmy stopped reading.

Today was Thursday.

If Mrs. Crofton had left on Tuesday with Mr. Dabney, why had she not taken her suitcase? And her important documents?

Had Mr. Dabney not left yet?

In her heart Emmy rushed to believe this was the case, that Mr. Dabney had been detained because of complications from the bombings, and that if Emmy just waited there at the shop, Mrs. Crofton would be by shortly to fetch her suitcase and papers.

Emmy could tell her what had happened. She could offer to wash by hand the gowns she had used for protection the previous night. Perhaps Mr. Dabney would allow her and Julia both to join them all in Edinburgh, once Emmy found her.

Mr. Dabney could write to Charlotte and have her send the brides box to him in Edinburgh.

It could all still work out. Maybe it was possible that Mum would one day, indeed, look down on Emmy from heaven and see that she had rescued Julia and made something of herself. Perhaps in heaven, a mother was allowed to feel pride in a child's accomplishments after her death.

Perhaps in heaven, you could see that your existence on earth hadn't been wasted.

Emmy just needed to find Julia and to have Mr. Dabney say he'd be fine with Emmy's coming later and bringing her sister.

But even as she entertained these idyllic thoughts, doubt began to creep into her mind. Today was Thursday.

Mrs. Crofton had written the note Sunday.

She wasn't going to be returning to the shop for her suitcase.

She had either fled with her cousin to Edinburgh without it, or she'd gone back home Sunday to get some forgotten thing, and the Luftwaffe had found her.

Emmy sank into a chair and dropped her pounding head into her hands.

There was a way to find out whether Mrs. Crofton had made it safely out of London. All she had to do was step inside the nearest Incident Inquiry Point and peruse its appalling list.

But not today.

Emmy could not look at that list today.

She kneaded her forehead with her fingers, wondering how much more she could be expected to take. She had enough food for only a few more days, no ration book, no money, a place to call home for only as long as she could stay undetected.

She had to find a way to search for Julia. But how could she without money? Without Mum?

Mum . . .

Emmy dug her fingertips into her temples. She couldn't think anymore about having lost Mum. She couldn't start thinking about having lost Mrs. Crofton. Grief sapped her of mental clarity and made her feel weak. She could not be a companion to it now. All that mattered was finding Julia. Somehow she had to insert herself into the workings of the war effort so that she could be privy to what became of lost or abandoned children. She needed to volunteer somewhere so that she was in the know. With the Women's Volunteer Service, perhaps. The women of the WVS were everywhere with their official badges, helping to ease suffering, administrating the evacuation of children to safety, serving food to the firemen, assisting the homeless and hurting. But how in the world was she going to pass herself off as an adult who had every right to be on the streets of London on her own in wartime?

Then out of the corner of her eye, she saw the little stack of papers.

And Isabel Crofton's birth certificate.

Twenty-four

❧

EMMY'S new life as eighteen-year-old Isabel Crofton began with a set of new routines.

She sheltered during air raids under the sewing machine at the bridal shop, covered in a dozen wedding dresses. She found she much preferred taking her chances under a table with easy access to the street rather than huddled in a claustrophobic shelter belowground. A bona fide shelter was no guarantee one could survive a bomb. Mum hadn't.

Emmy dared not be noticed coming and going from Primrose Bridal. The ARP warden for these city blocks was under the impression that the owner, Mrs. Crofton, had left London. If it came to pass that Emmy was noticed and questioned, she would just give the man her new name. She didn't think the warden would know that the real Isabel died twelve years ago. Mum had never volunteered much personal information to their warden. Surely the loss of a daughter all those years ago was a sad detail Mrs. Crofton had shared with very few people.

Afternoons were spent volunteering with the WVS, specifically with finding relatives or foster families to take in the orphans of the city. Emmy projected a particularly impassioned heart for the fatherless and motherless, an ardor that all the other WVS ladies in the relocation and evacuation scheme seemed amazed by. Her tireless efforts to find and relocate the most innocent and youngest victims of the war to loving foster families often meant she stayed the night at the office, sleeping on a cot in case an ARP warden during the wee hours brought in a frightened child who hadn't been evacuated and now was suddenly bereft of his or her parents. She ate her one meal a day at the WVS canteen, sometimes hiding a roll or two in her pocket for later, as she hadn't summoned the courage to apply for a ration book under her stolen identity and she had exhausted what was left of Mrs. Crofton's ration book.

She visited the hospitals looking for orphans and scouted out parks and alleys and abandoned homes, looking for children who believed they were safer on their own.

Emmy befriended the journalists and the foreign press, many of whom she could find drinking at the bar at the Savoy in the late afternoons or eating breakfast in the hotel dining room in the mornings. She told them to let her know if in their coverage of the war on London they came across children who seemed to be in the care of no one.

After a few weeks of being Isabel, and spending every waking moment either crouched under the sewing table or looking for Julia, Emmy began to forget her old dreams, and, in the forgetting, she found a numbing emptiness that she welcomed. The wedding dresses that had at one time entranced her were now wrinkled, smudged, and smelled of smoke and ash. And yet they protected her, cushioned her, were nearly a wall against the forces of evil. In the mornings when she pushed the dresses aside, they still swished a greeting, but it no longer had anything to do with any dream of hers other than to find Julia.

Halfway through the month, there was a turning point in the battle for London. Despite its relentless nightly attacks, the Luftwaffe was unable to flatten the British defenses and take London as Paris had been taken. The air raids continued past the middle of September, but they weren't as harsh, or at least that was how it seemed to Emmy.

Near the end of September, she finally went to an IIP and looked at the casualty list. She found Eloise Crofton's name on an older listing. Her employer had died, as Emmy had already guessed, on the evening of Sunday, September 8, before the Dabneys were to leave for Edinburgh, the same day as Mum. Her flat in Islington had been crushed by a bomb and she with it. The Dabneys, Emmy noted, were absent from the lists of the dead.

Emmy wondered only for a second whether Mrs. Crofton had been buried in Towers Hamlet along with Mum. But no, probably not. She had next of kin. Mr. Dabney surely came for her the next day, and saw her to Edinburgh just as planned, only on a different kind of train car.

Emmy left the IIP heavyhearted and yet strangely grateful. In her death Mrs. Crofton had unknowingly given Emmy a way to stay in London and look for Julia, as well as a new name and a new home, such as it was. A new life. Emmy didn't know when someone would come by Primrose Bridal to empty it of its contents but it was hard to imagine that would happen while the war raged.

By October, the weather turned cold and damp. Emmy finally opened Mrs. Crofton's suitcase—until that point she had revered it as the last vestige of the woman's presence on earth—hoping there was a winter coat inside since Emmy had left her own flat without even thinking about autumn's being on its way. She found a blue wool coat, as well as woolen stockings, several knitted sweaters, and flannel pajamas. Everything was a little big on Emmy but she would not complain. She would be able to stay warm at night and outside.

Again, Mrs. Crofton had gifted Emmy with what she needed to survive.

Emmy started visiting the Savoy on Monday mornings to talk to members of the foreign press as they prepared for the week ahead, to remind them to be on the lookout for orphaned children, and to pump them for information about any street children they might have seen but neglected to ring her about. She was often greeted warmly with a polite nod but more often it was a cocky, "Here comes Isabel the Crusader." Emmy didn't care what the reporters thought of her. She didn't care if they found that her passion for war orphans bordered on fanaticism. All that mattered was that one of them might possibly come upon Julia.

On one of those mornings near the end of the month, she was going about her usual stroll through the lobby and dining room when an American seated at a table with other journalists asked if she'd like to have a cup of coffee while she tutored them all on how to recognize street children. Emmy had not noticed this man on any previous visit to the Savoy and she wasn't sure whether he was taking her seriously or mocking her.

"Are you new here?" she asked.

"Not exactly," he answered, smiling broadly. "The place where I have been staying the last few months doesn't exactly exist anymore. So the Savoy is home now."

"And you think the plight of orphaned children living on the streets is amusing?" Emmy replied, one eyebrow arched.

"Watch out, Mac," one of the other reporters said. "Miss Crofton will have you looking for lost little ones in your sleep."

The American, ginger haired and handsome, gazed at her, wide-eyed, and his smile was even wider. "I definitely don't think it's funny, Miss . . . uh, Crofton?"

"Then why are you smiling at me?"

The other men at the table laughed.

"I wasn't aware that I was smiling at you, Miss Crofton."

More laughter.

"Yanks got plenty to smile about," one of the other reporters said, a British man who was grinning broadly. "They think this isn't their war."

"Hey. I'm here, aren't I?" the American said.

"You and your little radio aren't going to help us win the war from underground, mate."

"That's where you're wrong, *mate*. Every time we broadcast from here, your American friends across the pond are listening with bated breath. My little radio is already helping you win the war. You just don't know it yet."

The British reporter laughed and stood, as did the others around the table.

"You may as well take him up on the offer, Miss Crofton," the British reporter said, offering Emmy his chair. "The Americans still have good coffee to put into their cups."

"Yes, please, join me," the ginger-haired man said, feigning a serious expression.

Emmy stared at him as the other men walked away, talking to one another. "You are making fun of me," she said when they were gone.

He shook his head as he motioned for a waiter to bring another cup. "Not at all. Want to have a seat?" Her face was expressionless.

"What I want is to be taken seriously."

A waiter brought a cup of coffee to the table, unsure whom to give it to.

"It's for Miss Crofton," the American said, nodding toward the empty chair where the British reporter had been sitting.

The waiter smiled and set the cup down.

"Please?" the American said, cracking a tiny grin.

Emmy sat down in the chair. The coffee smelled dark and rich, and a half-eaten apple tart in front of the American was practically calling her name. He pushed the plate toward her.

"Would you like the rest? Not as good as my mother's but passable," he said, his smile growing.

Emmy hesitated only a second before picking up the fork that was already on the plate and plunging it into the sweet confection. The first bite was nothing short of heaven. "I can't believe I'm doing this," she murmured as she chewed a second bite and then realized that any respectable adult probably wouldn't. She put down the fork.

"You may as well finish it, Miss Crofton. I've had all I can eat. Be a shame to waste it."

Emmy retrieved the fork after a moment's pause. "It would be criminal. I can't believe the cooks at this hotel can get their hands on sugar and cream when the rest of the country is trying to pretend that carrots are candy."

The American laughed, and the sound of it caused Emmy to raise her head and stare at him. It had been a long time, or at least it had seemed so, since she had heard laughter.

"Sorry," he said. "I like to smile and I like to laugh. I mean no disrespect. Honestly. I know the rationing hasn't been easy."

Emmy slid another bite into her mouth. "The rationing isn't the worst of it."

When she swallowed, he put his hand out toward her.

"Mac MacFarland. My real name's Jonah. But everyone calls me Mac."

Emmy slowly reached her right hand toward his and shook it.

"Aren't you going to tell me your first name?" he said, smiling broadly.

"Em . . . It's Isabel."

"Isabel. Nice to meet you. May I call you Isabel?"

She brought the coffee cup to her lips and shrugged as she sipped, feeling warmed to her core. "You can call me whatever you like if you promise to let me know if you see any homeless children when you're out and about gathering news."

Emmy set the cup down, pulled a WVS card out of her skirt pocket, and handed it to him.

"Women's Voluntary Service," Mac said as he read the card.

"Just ring me there if you see any when you're covering the news. Little girls especially."

Mac pocketed the card and took a swallow from his own coffee cup. "Well, I am happy to obey but I am not out on the street as much as the other reporters here at the Savoy. I am a sound engineer and I spend most of my time three flights down in a bunker."

"A what?"

Mac went on to explain that he worked at nearby Broadcasting House for CBS, Edward Murrow, and a clutch of other radio journalists tasked with keeping the people of the United States informed about a war that was now just one ocean away from them. He also told her he was twenty-six, hailed from Minneapolis, and that he had actively sought a London posting after Britain declared war on Germany. He told her being there helped him feel like he was a very small part of holding back the Nazis, since America had yet to join in the battle against Hitler. He had worked at a CBS radio station in Manhattan before requesting to be posted in London when he learned a reporter friend of his from college would soon be in London himself.

"I see," Emmy said, finding that she was sad Mac would likely be of little help to her. She hadn't had anyone to talk to about something other than the war in weeks. Something about him was calming and inviting.

"What about you?" Mac said.

"What?"

Mac smiled. "I said, what about you? What were you doing before the war?"

I didn't exist before the war, Emmy thought as she pondered a suitable answer.

"Unless you don't want to tell me," he continued.

But she found she did want to tell him. She wanted to exist in someone's eyes. She wanted to be more than just a spectral vapor who lacked an endlessly long string of yesterdays. Pretending to be Isabel Crofton meant she was entitled to a past. It was her right and privilege now to come up with one.

"My mother and I owned a shop, Primrose Bridal, near Saint Paul's. She was killed the weekend the Blitz began and our flat was destroyed. I am living at the shop for the time being."

"Oh! I'm so very sorry. And your father?"

Emmy set the fork down on the plate, the ruse now feeling all too real. "He died some years back."

"Isabel, I'm so very sorry for your loss. Truly. I can't imagine how hard this must be. And here you are caring for the needs of homeless children when your own sorrow must be so great."

Emmy smiled wanly. "I know what it's like to have your parents taken from you and your home destroyed. I know what it's like to feel lost and alone. It's terrible."

He asked her about her work with the WVS and what were her favorite things to do before the war; as they talked, Emmy sensed that Mac seemed interested in her, *attracted* to her—an unnerving and stimulating concept. Emmy had never had a boyfriend before, and had been kissed only once, the spring before at a school dance. It had been a sloppy affair that she hadn't looked forward to repeating anytime soon.

Emmy could tell Mac thought she was pretty, also a new and intriguing concept. With Mum's clothes on and her comb nestled in her hair, it occurred to Emmy that she might actually look like her mother. Mum had always drawn the stares of men, even in her maid's uniform. Emmy liked that Mac thought she was pretty. She considered for only a moment that he was actually eleven years older than she, not the eight that he believed she was when she told him her age. But why should that matter? She was Isabel. She was eighteen.

When she left the Savoy a few minutes later, she could feel Mac's gaze on her.

By the end of October, Mac was hanging about the Savoy dining room on Monday mornings, making sure he didn't miss Emmy's visit. He would save a Danish or sweet roll from his breakfast and would invariably ask her to sit and enjoy it.

Emmy in turn started looking forward to those borrowed moments of pleasure. That anticipation caught her by surprise, and she suspected it was dangerous to feel that way about their visits, which was something Mac picked up on from the get-go and apparently found alluring.

On the morning of October 28, Emmy arrived at the Savoy feeling particularly defeated. Julia had been missing for nearly two months and Emmy was no closer to finding her than she had been the day she disappeared. Mac poured her a cup of coffee and asked her to sit and tell him what was wrong.

His compassion was attractive. In fact, everything about him was striking that morning. The stubble on his chin, the timbre of his voice, the muscles in his arms as he handed Emmy a Danish. She didn't want to admit she was drawn to him. She wanted to believe that only Julia mattered. But that morning Emmy could sense how weak she was. Resolve, her constant companion for the last two months, had apparently been left behind with the wedding dresses she had slept on. She was alone with a handsome man who reached out and squeezed her hand.

"Is everything all right?" he said.

The pretense that she had been carefully constructing threatened to crumble. She felt her old self clawing its way to the surface. Emmy made her hand a fist under Mac's as if to smash back down the girl she had been before.

"Isabel?"

Emmy shook her head to keep the ghostly remains of her former life from settling back into the folds of her mind. "No!" she said. To herself. Not to Mac.

But he thought Emmy was answering his question.

"What has happened?" he said, stroking Emmy's balled fist, forcing her to relax her fingers.

No! She could not go back. There was no going back. There was only the task at hand. She was Isabel.

"I—I'm just missing my mum, I guess," Emmy whispered. It was as good an answer as any.

Mac lifted her palm off the table and enclosed it in his. "I'm so sorry about that."

Emmy was mesmerized by the warmth and strength in his tender grip. She hadn't been touched—by anyone—in weeks; not since Mum put her hand on her cheek on the night she died. Emmy wanted to be in Mac's arms. She wanted Mac to pull her to his chest and kiss her forehead and tell her everything was going to be all right. She wanted to be enfolded in his embrace. And to disappear in it. For good.

A tiny exhale escaped her as she vented the tremendous pull of that desire to be held and loved.

"What can I do for you?" Mac said as he squeezed her hand.

Emmy summoned Isabel from the foggy place to which she had wafted away. She shook her head. "Nothing."

"There must be something I can do."

As Emmy felt Mac's hand strong and protective over hers, and as she saw in his eyes a longing to be close that she didn't need to be eighteen to recognize, she decided to trust him. To let him in, only halfway, so that she could have what she wanted—his help—and he could have what he wanted—a closer relationship with her.

"Maybe there is something," Emmy said.

"Yes?"

Emmy leaned forward, imploring him. "I'm looking for a young girl. Her name is Julia Downtree and she's seven. She disappeared on the first night of the Blitz. She was left home alone by accident and her street was bombed. None of the neighbors have seen her. She's not on any of the casualty lists. The police have not seen her. She's not in any hospital. She's just . . . gone."

"Is she someone you know personally?" Mac said, obviously puzzled by Emmy's interest in one particular child.

Emmy had a split second to decide how she would answer. She knew he would double his efforts to help her if she told him the truth. Emmy didn't have to tell him everything. But she could tell him this.

"She's my half sister. And I'm the one who left her alone. I didn't think she'd be alone for very long. It just . . . It just happened that way. I was on my way to her when the first bombs fell."

With his other hand, Mac reached into his shirt pocket, withdrew a slim notepad, and placed it on the table.

"Julia, you said?" He pulled his other hand off hers

and withdrew a pencil from the same pocket. He began to write.

"Downtree," Emmy replied.

Mac glanced up at Emmy, wondering, she supposed, whether she was going to explain how she came to have a half sister.

"We've the same father and that's all I am going to say about that." The less Emmy entwined her two lives with explanations, the better. Besides, a gentleman didn't need to know any of the supposed sordid details.

She said nothing else and Mac quickly lowered his gaze back to his notepad.

"She's only seven," Emmy continued. "Blond hair. The flat where she lived with her mother was off Queen Victoria in Whitechapel."

"And where is her mother, if I may ask?"

"She unfortunately died on the second night of the bombings," Emmy said, her voice breaking a bit.

Mac again looked up at Emmy, surprised at her re-action to the death of her half sister's mother. Emmy was fine with Mac thinking whatever he wanted. She did not try to mask the emotions etched across her face.

"I'm so very sorry, Isabel. Damn this war. Damn the Nazis to hell." He shook his head like people did when they were disgusted, and he slipped the notebook and pencil back inside his pocket.

"I just want to find her, Mac. I'm all she has. I've checked with the police and the hospitals and the IIPs. They have no record of her being found. None of the remaining neighbors have seen her."

"And you've thoroughly checked the flat?"

"Yes. I've been back several times. There is no gas or water or electricity."

"No other relatives or friends of the family could have come for her?"

For the first time it occurred to Emmy that Charlotte might have come back for Julia. Maybe that was why every search she had made on her own came up empty. Maybe Julia had been discovered by an ARP warden who managed to get her back to the foster home where she should have been all along.

But she had scoured as many evacuation and billeting records as she could since the night she and Julia returned to London. There was no record of a Julia Downtree being reevacuated to her foster home in Gloucestershire.

What she hadn't checked was whether a certain Charlotte Havelock had reported her evacuees as having run away. Surely Charlotte had notified someone when she awoke the morning of September 7 and saw that Emmy and Julia were gone. There would be a paper trail for that. There—

"Isabel?"

Emmy snapped back to the present moment. "What?"

"No one else?"

"No . . ." But her mind was far away. She had to find out whether Julia was safe and sound with Charlotte. Surely that was where she was. That was why she couldn't find any trace of her in London! Why hadn't she thought of this before? Just because she had found no record of Julia being reunited with Charlotte at the beginning of her search didn't mean that record didn't exist now.

Emmy rose from her chair and nearly knocked it over. "I need to get back."

Mac's eyes widened in surprise. "Just like that? You—you haven't even eaten your Danish."

"I—I forgot to take care of something important. I—I need to go."

Mac rose, too, unconvinced. "Did you remember something about your sister?"

"Yes . . . I mean, no. I mean, I need to go."

Emmy made for the lobby doors and she could sense Mac was right behind her. He sprang ahead of her so that he could open the door before the bellman did.

"Can I see you later today? A drink after work perhaps?" he said.

"I—I don't know." Emmy couldn't think about anything but her new task at hand.

"You don't know?" Mac smiled and held the door open wide.

They emerged onto the street. A light drizzle was falling but the air still stank of fire, ash, and ruin. Emmy turned to Mac to say good-bye.

"Thank you," she blurted, and stepped away from him.

"For what?" Mac called after her.

"For . . . the Danish!" she said.

"You didn't even eat it!"

But Emmy just smiled stupidly and dashed away into the rain.

Twenty-five

AFTER so many weeks of frustration, the prospect of knowing that Julia had been rescued from the nightmare in which Emmy had left her was almost too much to take in. She nearly sprinted back to the local WVS office to revisit her inquiry into the evacuees who had been billeted with Charlotte Havelock.

Emmy did not have direct access to all the billeting records for the children of the East End but she knew where to go and whom to ask. Isabel Crofton's reputation for fervently making sure every orphan with whom she came into contact was properly cared for had been made obvious to all, so it surely came as no surprise when Emmy appeared, breathless and rain soaked, at the offices where the East End billeting records were kept and announced she had a lead on an orphaned evacuee who might have been reported missing by her foster mother.

The WVS volunteer who was assisting the billeting officials offered to help Emmy, and together they pored over a pile of ledgers and files to see whether a Charlotte Havelock had reported weeks ago on September 7 that the two evacuees in her care had run away. After half an hour of careful searching, Emmy finally found a notation that Charlotte had called Mrs. Howell, the billeting official in Moreton-in-Marsh, who had notified the billeting headquarters in London that Emmeline and Julia Downtree had run away, supposedly back to their mother's flat in London.

Emmy and her companion continued to peruse the paperwork from September 8 onward.

There was no new record of the Downtree evacuees having been returned to Mrs. Havelock.

"Are you sure that documentation wouldn't be someplace else?" Emmy asked, a knot of dread rising in her throat.

"I don't see why," the WVS volunteer replied.

"Maybe you should ring up Mrs. Howell in Moreton and make sure."

"Make sure of what?"

"Make sure the sisters didn't return on their own and that no one recorded it!" Emmy replied, a little too forcefully. "I mean, perhaps the children returned on their own. I would just like to know for sure. I've—I've a report that the younger Downtree sister has been seen on the streets in Whitechapel. I . . . just want to know if that is possible. She's quite young."

The woman shrugged. "I suppose." She picked up the telephone and asked for the Moreton exchange while Emmy waited, trying very hard not to pace.

"Yes, this is Vera Brindle at HQ," the woman said a

few moments later. "I'm just checking to see if the two Downtree sisters reported as runaways in September have turned up. They had been billeted at the home of a Charlotte Havelock in Stow-on-the-Wold."

There was an interminable moment of silence as the woman listened to an answer that Emmy couldn't hear. She wanted badly to yank the receiver from the woman's hand and shove it next to her own ear instead.

"Oh. I see. Yes. Quite right," the woman said.

Emmy closed her eyes for a second to keep from pouncing on the woman.

"Yes. No doubt."

For the love of God . . .

"All right, then. Thank you very much." The woman hung up and looked at Emmy. "No sign of them, I'm afraid."

Emmy couldn't breathe. "Truly?" she finally eked out.

The woman closed the ledger they'd been looking at, as if that little matter was done for the day. Maybe forever. "Mrs. Havelock has been instructed to inform Mrs. Howell if the girls turn up. But they haven't. And their mother was killed, you know, so it's a very sad business. No one knows what became of those girls."

Hope that had filled Emmy's heart only moments ago was suddenly sucked away. A cold and ironlike dread filled the emptiness.

The woman patted Emmy's hand. "You did all you could."

Emmy felt as though she might vomit, and she raised a hand to her mouth.

"Really, now. You shouldn't take it so to heart, Isabel. You'll go mad if you do."

"Yes," Emmy whispered. "I just . . . I haven't eaten

anything yet today and I . . ." But Emmy's voice faded. The effort of pretending her nausea was just the result of having missed breakfast was too much for her. "Thank you for your help," Emmy mumbled, and moved away.

"You should go to a canteen right now and have something to eat!" the woman called after her. "It's not smart to work so hard on an empty stomach."

Emmy nodded and continued out of the billeting office and back outside into the rain.

She tipped her face up to the sodden clouds and waited for the icy downpour to cleanse her of her mistakes. But as people walked past her and stared, she knew she was just a girl standing in the pouring rain.

EMMY did not return to her afternoon duties for the WVS. She made her way slowly back to Primrose, on foot, hardly caring if anyone saw her. She let herself in by the back door, and, soaked to the bone, curled up on top of the wedding dresses that lay like mattress stuffing on the floor.

Tears did not come; she was beyond the uselessness of tears. But sleep finally did.

Emmy awoke a few hours later, freezing, her skin chafed from her wet clothes. She changed into dry clothes, made a cup of tea, and hung the damp wedding dresses she'd been lying on back on their tossed hangers to dry.

Hours later, when the sirens began to scream, Emmy did not crawl under the sewing table. She sat in the middle of the floor, shivering from the cold, and implored the heavens to give her what she was due.

But as incendiaries and bombs fell all over London, Emmy's frozen corner of the war remained stalwart and upright.

When she fell asleep again, she did not awaken until she heard a tapping at the back door. Her first thought was that the bridal shop had been hit after all and was on fire. Everything was hot. Burning hot. Maybe she was in hell, and the tapping was the sound of the damned banging on the walls of their prison. She found she didn't care.

And then someone said, "Isabel!" and she wanted to say, *There is no Isabel,* but her throat was coated in broken glass and she could utter nothing. The flames were covering her head, bursting out of her chest.

There was a loud noise and then she felt snakes on her arms. They coiled themselves about her and lifted her off the floor.

"I have her," one of the snakes said.

A snake had appeared to Eve in the garden, hadn't it? The snake was the devil. And now he had her. She had gotten her wish after all.

Emmy had been given what she deserved.

She felt a blast of piercing needles against her skin and then all was dark.

EMMY didn't know when she realized she was not in hell after all. Her body still burned but she was lying on a bed, not a lake of fire.

A cool hand soothed her brow.

She tried to open her eyes but it was as if they had melted shut.

Not from the fires of hell, but from fever.

Emmy slept.

WHEN at last Emmy opened her eyes, a dark figure stood beside her. The figure moved closer and took her hand.

Was she lying on the wedding dresses? All seemed white around her. But no, she was on a bed. White sheets covered her. There were white sheets everywhere. She was in a room full of beds with other people lying on top of them. A nurse moved into her peripheral vision and bent over a man wrapped in white bandages.

"Welcome back," the dark figure said. "Guess I came for a visit at just the right time."

Mac.

Emmy lifted her gaze to look at him.

"Where am I?" she murmured.

"At Royal London Hospital, cozy and warm."

Emmy knew this place. She'd been inside its doors many times over the last two months, looking for Julia.

"I'm afraid I've blown your cover, Isabel," Mac said.

"What?" A ripple of fear wriggled up from within her. Her cover? Did he know who she really was? Is that what he was saying?

"I came to your bridal shop on Tuesday to convince you to come have dinner with me. The ARP on your street said no one was there and I assured him someone was."

"Dinner?" Emmy couldn't think properly. "What day is it?"

"It's Friday, actually."

Emmy couldn't remember what day she had last seen him. When had she run off into the rain? What had happened that day?

Monday.

Emmy had seen him on Monday.

And then she had run to the local billeting offices where she had learned Julia was not at Charlotte's. Julia was nowhere.

"Your nurses tell me you'll live. They also say I am your hero." He laughed and squeezed her hand. "So maybe you'll forgive me, then?"

"Forgive you?" Emmy's head was spinning.

"You can't go back to your mother's shop, I'm afraid."

"What?"

"Actually, even if I hadn't blown your cover for you, you still couldn't go back."

It was too much to take in. Her place with the wedding dresses was her sanctuary, her secret haven. What did he mean, she could not go back? Had someone figured out that that she was posing as Eloise Crofton's daughter? Would she be arrested?

Emmy started to rise from the bed, but fell back against the pillows.

Mac was hovering over her in an instant. "Isabel, you're still very sick. I'm sorry. I shouldn't have said anything yet. That was stupid of me."

Emmy felt instantly woozy from having tried to sit up. "Water?" she murmured.

Mac reached for a glass at her bedside table. He slid next to her and raised her head off the pillow so that she could drink.

He lowered Emmy gently to the pillow and then reset the glass down on the table.

"What happened?" Emmy whispered.

"You mean after the warden and I found you? There were bombs, Isabel. Just a few hours later. I'm afraid the bridal shop was hit. All the shops on that street were."

Julia's book of fairy tales, Isabel's birth certificate.

Her death certificate . . .

They were all inside Mum's travel bag.

"I have to go back . . . ," Emmy whispered.

"Hold on, Isabel. It was hit by incendiaries. There's nothing left."

Mac didn't need to say more. She knew what had become of Julia's book. Mum's travel bag, her clothes, her trinkets. And she knew that Isabel's death certificate had also been reduced to ashes. At least no one combing through the rubble would find it and realize she was an imposter.

"Your bag is here," he said. "Although I'm afraid that's all I was able to grab the day I found you."

"My bag? Here?"

He nodded toward a chair in the corner. Mum's travel bag sat there like an old, wise friend. It was still clasped shut.

"Bring it to me!"

Startled, Mac was slow to respond, but then he let go of her hand, walked over to the chair, and grasped Mum's bag by its worn handles. He brought it to Emmy and she clutched it to her chest, embracing it as a child would cuddle a beloved toy. Tears of relief spilled out of her.

Mac stared wide-eyed.

"It was my mum's," Emmy said, hoping that was explanation enough. "Thank you for thinking to take it."

He returned to the chair by the bed. "You're welcome."

For a few minutes there was silence between them as Emmy held on to the last thing on earth that she owned.

"Isabel, the hospital is a little short on beds as you can imagine. The nurses want to know who will be coming for you," he said gently. "Is there a friend or relative here in London who can take you in?"

Emmy shook her head, closing her eyes against the thought that she had nowhere to go.

"What about any relatives elsewhere in England? Is there anyone I can ring for you? Anyone I can take you to?"

Emmy started to shake her head again. And then an image of Thistle House with its climbing roses and clucking chickens, its shining pond and gabled windows, and Charlotte with her long silver braid, filled her head. Charlotte. Would she take Emmy back? Or would she despise Emmy for what she had done? Emmy realized with a sickening thud in her heart that she no longer felt the urgency to stay in London and look for Julia. Her sister was lost to her. Emmy didn't deserve to be rewarded with finding her and she knew now that she wouldn't be.

The brides box was at Thistle House, though.

And although Emmy felt no tingling sensation of hope or aspiration at the thought of being reunited with her sketches, at least she would have them again.

"There is someone," Emmy said. "She's . . . an aunt. She lives in Gloucestershire."

"I'd be happy to telephone her for you," Mac said, then added, "or take you to her."

He said this last bit as if he wanted to take Emmy to Charlotte's himself, but did not want to appear too forward. The last thing Emmy wanted was for Charlotte to learn over the phone what she had done and then have to come to London to pull her out of the pit she had dug for herself.

"Would you? Take me there?" Emmy asked.

Mac smiled. "I'd be happy to."

Emmy nodded. Tears formed at the corners of her eyes at the kindness of this man who thought he knew her.

Mac leaned in, thumbing away the tear that had escaped and was now sliding down her cheek. He kissed her forehead.

It was not the first kiss of lovers, yet it felt just like that to Emmy. A gnawing desire to be wanted—in every possible way—surged up within her. Despite all the mistakes she had made, she still wanted to be loved.

Emmy reached up with one hand to touch Mac's face and he leaned into her palm.

"If London weren't a battleground, I'd be attempting to convince you to stay here with me," he whispered, kissing Emmy's wrist where it met his jaw.

He rose from his chair. "I've got to get back. We've a broadcast in less than an hour. But I'll see you tomorrow, Isabel."

Mac smiled at Emmy from the door, then turned and left.

As she listened to his footfalls on the corridor outside her room, she reasoned that it was okay for Mac to be attracted to her and for her to be attracted to him.

Because she wasn't foolish, immature Emmy who had abandoned her sister.

She was Isabel.

And Isabel had done nothing wrong.

Twenty-six

❧

EMMY didn't know how many hoops Mac had to jump through to borrow someone's car and drive her to Gloucestershire when she was released from the hospital two days later. When Emmy asked him how he managed it—and the cost of the petrol—he waved away her questions and told him he had a friend who owed him a favor.

The handful of women with whom Emmy had served at the WVS and who came to visit her at the hospital seemed genuinely sad to hear that Emmy was leaving London; at least as sad as they could be to say good-bye to someone who had volunteered with them for only two months. The war made every relationship seem temporary. Someone else would surely show up to take her place.

Mac offered to drive Emmy past the burned ruin of Primrose on their way out but she declined. She wanted to remember it as it had been, when it was a lovely shop on a bustling street back when the war was just a rumor, and even after the first bombs fell, when it was a dark and shadowed haven for a young woman who had nowhere to go. For the last eight weeks, Emmy had fought to stay in London so that she could find Julia, but on the day she left, she could not get away soon enough. As they drove out of the tattered city, gray from November clouds and never-ending smoke and ash, Mac assured Emmy that he would stay on the lookout for her half sister. He would continue to ask about her among his colleagues covering the many sides of the war. He had the connections Emmy did not have and none of the transgressions that she did. He was the perfect person to look for Julia.

He also asked Emmy whether it would be all right if he stayed in contact with her after he returned to London. She could tell Mac was growing fond of her—fond of Isabel the Crusader. Emmy did not hope for a minute that his affections would amount to anything lasting; he was an American stationed abroad. But she liked how he made her feel. She was taken with the notion that Mac preferred her over other women he knew—older, more experienced women. Emmy would enjoy his attentions as long as she had them. She told him she would like that very much.

The hospital had deemed Emmy well enough to be discharged as they needed her bed for the wounded, but cautioned her that she still required bed rest for a week or two. She began to get sleepy as the car rumbled out of the city, and when she began to nod off around High Wycombe, Mac told her not to fight it. He had a map. He'd get her safely to Stow.

So she slept.

An hour or so later, Mac shook her gently awake. They had arrived at Stow and he needed to know how to get to Thistle House from the village. Emmy told him which direction to head for and soon they were traveling down Maugersbury Road, the same narrow lane on which she and Julia had started their escape in the dark two months before. It seemed like such a long time ago. And then in no time at all they were pulling up to Thistle House. Smoke swirled from the chimney in delicate tendrils and soft lights glimmered in the front room windows.

"You can just let me off," Emmy said to Mac, unable to take her eyes from the cozy beauty of the house, its timeless perfection and stoic presence.

"What was that?"

Emmy turned to him. "You can just let me off." She needed to speak to Charlotte alone.

Mac laughed lightly. "Not a chance." He put the car in park and set the brake.

"Please, Mac. We, I mean, my aunt and I didn't . . . We didn't part on the best of terms. And I didn't ring her up to tell her I was coming."

He turned the car off. "Well, then I am definitely not just leaving you off. What if she says no, you can't stay?"

Emmy looked back at the house. She saw a face at the window. Charlotte's. "She won't say no."

Mac reached for her hand and squeezed it. "Then you've got nothing to worry about."

"Give me a second with her, please? Just wait here a bit. Will you?"

He frowned. "Well, if you think that's necessary."

"I do," Emmy said hurriedly, withdrawing her hand from under his. "Just give me a moment so that I can tell her why I am here. And what—what has happened. She probably doesn't know."

The red door opened and Charlotte appeared, wiping her hands on a dish towel.

Emmy opened the car door and the biting chill of the outside air prickled her. "I'll be right back."

She stepped out of the car, purposely keeping her back to the house as she maneuvered out. She closed the door, kept her head down, and walked up the stone pathway to the front door. Emmy was wearing Mum's second-best dress, Eloise Crofton's blue wool coat, and a knitted hat Mac had bought for her to keep her head warm. From a distance and with her gaze fixed on her heeled shoes, Emmy knew she did not look like the fifteen-and-a-half-year-old who had run away from this house just weeks before.

When Emmy was only a few feet from the door, she raised her head to look at Charlotte and their eyes met.

"Emmeline!"

Emmy's name came out of Charlotte's mouth like a breath, like a prayer. She bolted forward and drew Emmy into her arms. Weak from illness and so ready to be held by someone who cared for her, Emmy nearly collapsed into her tight embrace.

"Are you all right?" Charlotte said, and Emmy smelled pie crust and cinnamon and nutmeg in the woman's gray braid.

Before Emmy could answer, she pulled away and looked past Emmy, to the waiting car. Emmy saw in Charlotte's shimmering irises what her eyes sought.

Julia.

A blade seemed to slice into Emmy's chest. "It's just me, Charlotte," she whispered.

With her arms still on Emmy's shoulders, Charlotte

looked hard into her eyes. "Is Julia . . . Has she . . . ?" But Charlotte could not finish her question.

Emmy shook her head. "I don't know. I don't know where she is." The familiar nausea at saying these words swept over Emmy and she faltered. Charlotte caught Emmy as spots began to dance in front of her.

"Emmeline, are you ill?"

She nodded.

Charlotte's firm arms were around her again in an instant. "Who is that in the car?"

"A friend, the only friend I have, actually. He brought me here. His name is Mac. He's an American." Emmy leaned into her.

"Let's get you inside." Charlotte turned toward the car and motioned for Mac to follow them.

Emmy heard the car door open.

She let her head fall on Charlotte's chest. "Charlotte?" she whispered.

"Yes?"

"He thinks my name is Isabel."

MAC stayed less than an hour; long enough to have tea, which Emmy knew Charlotte would offer him, and to make sure Emmy had a place to stay. She had only minutes to explain to Charlotte why he believed her name was Isabel Crofton. She was thankful that, upon her introducing Mac to Charlotte, he'd asked to use the privy—it had been a long drive—and Emmy used those precious few minutes to tell Charlotte why she had taken on the name of someone a few years older. So that she would be free to look for Julia. Julia was missing, and had been since the night before Mum died. Charlotte asked Emmy who Mac was and it seemed she feared he had taken advantage of Emmy, or worse, that Emmy had become what Mum was: a woman who traded favors to get what she needed. As they heard the toilet being flushed, Emmy assured her that Mac was a good man who had been nothing but kind to her. She hadn't slept with him and he hadn't asked her to.

For the next forty minutes Charlotte attempted to make polite conversation with this stranger who had driven Emmy the eighty-plus miles to Thistle House. Her impatience to ask Emmy questions that needed to wait until Mac was gone made for a stilted performance on her part, however. And Rose, who seemed annoyed that Emmy had returned, sat in a chair by the window and frowned at Emmy the entire time they drank their tea. The tension in the room was palpable, but since Emmy had told Mac that she and her aunt had parted on less than amicable terms, the woman's unease around the pale Isabel Crofton surely seemed perfectly apropos to Mac, as did Rose's icy silence.

While they sipped from their cups, Charlotte learned how Mac had found Emmy delirious with fever on the floor of the bridal shop just a few hours before the entire block was set ablaze by incendiaries. And Emmy could see that Charlotte was flummoxed when Mac said he had been impressed with Isabel's relentless volunteer efforts to find and care for the orphaned children of London, especially her missing half sister, Julia, whom he promised to keep an eye out for. The wordless question in Charlotte's eyes was obvious. *So Isabel is the one with a half sister named Julia?*

When their cups were empty, Charlotte did not offer to make a second pot. Mac took the cue and rose from his chair, saying he had best be on the road.

Emmy had started to get up from the sofa, too, but Mac insisted she stay put, which seemed to surprise and impress Charlotte. When she went to get his hat and coat from the hall tree, Mac walked over to the sofa and leaned over Emmy.

"You sure you're going to be all right with these people?" he whispered as his lips brushed her forehead.

"I will. Charlotte and I just need to talk about . . . some things," Emmy whispered back.

He pressed a few pound notes into Emmy's hand. "Train fare if you need to hightail it out of here," he said.

Emmy started to laugh and the sound struck her as the most foreign thing in the world. She hadn't laughed in what seemed like forever. She stopped abruptly.

"It's okay to laugh again, Isabel," Mac said, touching her chin with his fingers as he stood.

At that moment Charlotte returned with his coat and a slightly alarmed expression on her face. "Thank you so much for bringing ah, Isabel, to me. May I pay you for your petrol?" she said, handing him his things.

"It was my pleasure, Mrs. Havelock," he said as he put on his coat. "You have a charming home here. And a lovely niece. I hope I may have the opportunity to visit again?"

"Oh. Um. Thank you. Thank you very much. Friends are always welcome at Thistle House," Charlotte said, struggling just a bit to sound completely convincing.

Mac put on his hat and tipped it to Emmy in farewell.

"Thank you, Mac. Safe journey. And do be careful back in London." It suddenly occurred to Emmy that Mac was returning to what was the closest thing to the front lines of battle that she had ever known. She instantly worried for him and for his safety.

Charlotte had turned away to walk toward the

entry. Mac winked at Emmy. "I'll be seeing you," he murmured. And then he was gone.

AFTER Mac left, Emmy found she dreaded the thought of recounting every terrible thing she had done and every horror she had witnessed in the weeks she'd been away. As Charlotte made her way back to the sitting room after seeing Mac to the door, Emmy resolved to answer with as little detail as possible the questions that were sure to come.

"What happened to your sister, Emmeline?" Charlotte asked as she sat down next to Emmy. "The authorities told me Julia wasn't sheltering with your mother in the basement of that hotel."

Emmy shook her head. "She was alone in the flat where I left her. It was only supposed to be for a little while. I thought Mum would find her there. But Mum didn't come home from work that afternoon. And I tried to get back to the flat when the bombing started, Charlotte. I tried. God knows I tried! I couldn't! After Mum died, I looked for Julia everywhere I could. I walked past the bodies and the blood and the mess every day, looking for her."

The ache of loss that had dulled while Emmy lay in the hospital now regained its vigor, and she clutched her chest.

"Why did you leave here like you did? Why?" Charlotte's eyes were full of tears.

Emmy closed her eyes against the sting of her confession. "I had an appointment with a designer who wanted to see my bridal sketches. Julia was going to tell you that I was sneaking away if I didn't take her with me. I swear to you I never intended to bring her. If I could go back in time and do it all differently, I would do it, Charlotte! I never intended to bring her with me."

As fresh tears streaked down her face, Emmy waited expectantly for the chastisement that was due her. She wanted to be berated for having been so foolish, so selfish, so shortsighted. She wanted Charlotte to raise her hand and slap her senseless, even though Emmy knew Charlotte had probably never slapped anyone before. Emmy wanted her to at least walk away in utter disgust. But Charlotte did not do any of these things. Instead, she wrapped Emmy's still-feverish body in hers and held her while they both wept. Emmy thought she had been done with tears. In London, they were useless. Here at Thistle House, it was as if the walls themselves wanted to weep with her. Emmy felt ugly and small in Charlotte's arms, and cheated of the reprimand she was owed.

"Someone will find her, Emmeline. I am sure of it," Charlotte said, and while Emmy desperately wanted that to be true, she bristled at the use of the name she no longer used.

"Please. Please don't call me that," Emmy said, unable to say the name herself.

Charlotte pulled back and blinked, her eyelashes silvery with tears. "Pardon?"

"Don't call me that. Please? Can you please call me Isabel?"

Charlotte studied Emmy's face, looking for the girl she knew from before. "But that's not who you are."

"It's who I am now," Emmy said. "That other name means only misery to me."

"But . . . you can't just decide to become someone else, Emmeline. Inside, you are still you. I know you've been through hell, but you will—"

"I don't want to be called that anymore."

Again, Charlotte held Emmy's gaze, and Emmy could

see fear, like an old neighbor, in the woman's eyes. "What happened to Julia is not your fault."

"Of course it is," Emmy said. "I took her to London with me when I ran away and I left her alone in the flat."

"But you didn't know that—"

"I *took* her with me when I ran away. And I left her. *Alone*," Emmy said again, louder and with a prickly vehemence that made Charlotte wince. Emmy could feel her pulse pounding in her head. Her hands were starting to shake.

"All right," Charlotte said soothingly. "I will call you whatever you want. If you want to be called Isabel, I will call you Isabel."

"Isabel is eighteen," Emmy said in a challenging tone that a ten-year-old would employ. But she wanted Charlotte to know she was not like the other fifteen-year-olds in Stow. She would never be like them.

Charlotte rested her hand on top of Emmy's. She flinched at first. "You, as Isabel, are more than welcome in my home," Charlotte said gently. "Thistle House is for people who love and care for one another. We respect one another in this house, Emmeline. We carry one another's burdens. We weep for one another and we laugh with one another. We hold one another by the hand when the lights go out and when the way seems hopeless. We work together and we share the table together and we pray together. No matter how old we are or what we are called."

She waited for Emmy to respond that she not only understood but was also willing to abide by this contract. Emmy hesitated only because she had never known a house like that. It wasn't that Mum was a terrible parent. She just never said words like that to Emmy. She didn't think Mum believed she was capable of creating such a home.

"Emmeline?" Charlotte said, for what would be the last time.

"Yes." Tears formed at Emmy's eyes and she wiped them away. "I understand."

"Then Isabel you shall be. But there will be conditions. I will need to inform Mrs. Howell in Moreton that you, Emmy Downtree, have come back and that you wish to continue to live with me. They must likewise be informed that Julia is missing so that they will be looking for her and will return her to us when they find her. Plenty of children here in the village finish their schooling at fourteen, so it will not raise an eyebrow if you do not attend classes here. But I insist you finish your education at Thistle House with me. And you *will* finish it. I will not allow you to stop learning just because you wish to be treated like an adult. Lastly, I must insist that you never run out of this house again without talking to me first. And I shall make that same promise to you. I won't budge on any of these things. Are we agreed?"

Emmy nodded.

Charlotte reached for Emmy's hands and clasped them in her own. "And I will pray every day that Julia comes home to us. I promise I will."

Emmy's voice felt thick in her throat but she wanted to express her gratitude to Charlotte, if nothing else than for a warm place to sleep that night. Emmy had grown used to expecting only as much good fortune as one day could hold. "Thank you," she said, the two words coming out thin and splintered.

Charlotte patted Emmy's hand under hers as if she had uttered her thanks with the boldness of a field general. "You're welcome, Isabel."

Twenty-seven

IT was nearing the middle of November before Emmy felt well enough to rise from her sick bed on the parlor sofa and take her meals in the dining room with Charlotte and Rose. The attending physician at the hospital in London had said she was suffering from an advanced case of pneumonia, although Emmy knew it was more than that. She hadn't the energy to climb the stairs, nor the courage to spend much time in the bedroom that she had shared with Julia.

Charlotte had driven out to Moreton-in-Marsh to inform Mrs. Howell that Emmy had returned, and as Emmy was too weak to accompany Charlotte, she did not have to go. There had been no word on Julia. It was recommended to Charlotte that she apply to be appointed as Emmeline's legal guardian so that she could make decisions on her behalf until she came of age. She asked Emmy if she was in favor of this and Emmy found it did not matter to her what Charlotte did or didn't do for Emmeline Downtree. If she thought it made sense, she should do it.

Charlotte didn't want to rush Emmy back into studies, so she allowed her to read what she wanted as she convalesced, and said that they would pick up on the sciences and mathematics after the Christmas holidays. Charlotte brought home a basket of books to her every Monday, even after she was well enough to go to the library in Stow on her own. Emmy preferred to stay with Rose and leave it to Charlotte to provide her with books to read. She had no desire to be seen in the village. Those who knew Charlotte surely also knew Emmy was that rebellious runaway who had lost her sister in the bombings. Emmy didn't want anyone looking at her, staring at her, whispering about her. She was Isabel, not that other girl they thought she was. So she stayed at Thistle House unless it was absolutely necessary to go out. If Emmy had to go into town, Charlotte agreed to take her to Moreton, where hardly anybody knew who she was. Visits to the doctor, the dentist, the clothing store, the shoe store, all took place in Moreton where, except to Mrs. Howell, whom Emmy avoided as much as she could, Emmy was viewed as a London refugee named Isabel who was helping an older woman named Charlotte Havelock take care of her handicapped sister, Rose.

On the day that Emmy was to move back into the bedroom upstairs, Charlotte sat Emmy down after breakfast and asked her how she felt about taking in two evacuees, now that she was finally well again. The need for homes in the country was still great and there was room at Thistle House. Emmy was flattered that

Charlotte asked, because in truth, she didn't have to. Emmy's first reaction was to balk at any kind of intrusion into the carefully scripted world she was rebuilding for herself, but when Charlotte said there was plenty of room for a second bed in her bedroom and that Emmy could join her, which would make the yellow bedroom available, Emmy saw the beauty of Charlotte's plan. She was handing Emmy a way of staying at Thistle House without having to sleep in the spare bedroom that she had shared with Julia. They both knew her plan was as much to insulate Emmy from the damning weight of her regret as it was to provide a home for evacuees.

When Emmy agreed, Charlotte asked if Emmy wanted to move her things from one room to the other, or if she preferred Charlotte did it. The wardrobe, desk, and bedside tables were still full of Emmy's and Julia's things. And the brides box was surely hidden in the crawl space in the yellow room; Emmy was sure of that, though she hadn't been upstairs yet. Charlotte, who believed the sketches had been lost in the bombings, obviously hadn't found the box shoved under a bed or stuck in a wardrobe after the girls had left, which meant the crawl space was the only place the box could be. Julia had had no time to hide it anywhere else.

As Charlotte waited for an answer, Emmy realized she wished the box *had* been lost in the bombings. She wanted it to have been blown to tattered bits. It would've been a fitting end to them. Emmy didn't know whether she had the courage to do what the bombs should have done, for surely that was what she would have to do with those sketches when she had them in her hands again. She knew she couldn't bear the sight of them, but would she be able destroy them? The burn pile out in the garden would be a willing partner if she was able to just toss them in.

"I'll take care of it," Emmy said to Charlotte.

Charlotte nodded and rose to begin making her inquiries.

Emmy headed up the stairs.

The room was cold and cheerless from having no warm souls sleeping in its beds at night. Emmy changed the linens first, stopping a time or two to stare at the little table along the wall as she assessed her readiness to be reunited with that which had parted her from her sister. The box was there; she needed only to crawl inside the narrow space and retrieve it.

She'd save that chore for last.

Emmy took a wicker basket and loaded up Julia's few clothes, the dolls Charlotte had given her to play with, and the tea set. She put this basket on the floor of a smaller wardrobe in Charlotte's room that had been emptied for Emmy to use. Then she moved her own things. Her satchel was gone, but she had Mum's travel bag with the few things she had grabbed from the flat: Julia's book of fairy tales, the felt-lined box of trinkets, and Geraldine's hammer.

She hung up Mum's clothes, which were hers now, put her box of trinkets on the extra bureau Charlotte and she lugged in from Rose's room, and placed Julia's book on the bookcase by the window. The hammer she held in her hands for a long time before sliding it between the mattresses of her new bed. She could not see placing it among Charlotte's tools in the utility cupboard downstairs next to the loo. It wasn't just a hammer to her. It was something else entirely: a steeled and weighted reminder of what she had been parted from.

Emmy went back into the yellow room and swept and dusted.

The room was clean now, and ready for its new

occupants. There was only one thing left to do. She propped the broom up against the wall and then moved the little table away from the wall, revealing the crawl space door. Emmy knelt before it and saw that it was slightly ajar, further proof that Julia had shoved the box inside in a desperate hurry. Emmy pulled the door open and its hinges squeaked a faint protest. She leaned forward on her knees and stuck her head inside, expecting to see the box lying there at an angle after being hastily shoved in.

It wasn't there.

She dropped to her elbows and crawled halfway inside, letting her eyes adjust to the shadowed light as she felt around. She touched dust-covered piles of books, the frayed top of an embroidered step stool, a hobbyhorse, old shoes, and their button hook.

But no box.

No box.

Emmy withdrew from the darkness and sat back on her bent knees, unable to fathom where else Julia could have hidden it.

A queer ache pulsed inside her at the cruelty of not being able to find the box, but the ache was quickly and surprisingly replaced with relief. She would not have to be the one to destroy the sketches after all. They were gone and it did not matter how. Somehow, the brides had been taken as atonement for her offenses.

She only had to offer the rest of what Emmy had once been.

Emmy had been given what every penitent thief wants more than anything: a merciful way to compensate for what she stole.

She turned her hands over in her lap, empty.

And outside, a light snow began to fall.

Twenty-eight

HUGH and Philip Goodsell, brothers ages six and eight, arrived on December 6. Emmy had not asked Charlotte to bring home boys, but as soon as she came into the house with them, Emmy was overwhelmed with gratitude that Charlotte had not brought home two sisters.

They were shy at first, having suffered a distressing period of homelessness after their flat near Horse Guards was bombed. Their parents had managed to find a place to live near Edgeware with a distant relative, but there wasn't room for the boys, nor, after so close a call, was their father willing to give in any longer to their mother's pleas that they stay together.

The boys took to Emmy like glue once she told them she had also lost her home in the bombings. After they managed to extract from Emmy that she had lost her mother as well, they took it upon themselves to find ways to cheer her. They made pictures for her to hang on her wall, and fought over who got to play cards with her and who got to hang the washing with her. Charlotte told Emmy this was evidence of how much they missed their own mother.

The boys' devotion at first surprised Emmy, but it soon became a soothing balm. She felt scraped and raw after her cleansing experience in the yellow room, as though she were knit together solely of the pink, fragile skin that was revealed when a sunburn sloughed off. Hugh's and Philip's affections lessened the sting of that newness.

Rose was jealous of the boys' attentions toward Emmy; another reason for her to scowl incessantly at Emmy. Rose knew enough to understand that Emmy was somehow an extension of the girl who had been at Thistle House before, and occasionally she would ask Emmy, "Where's the other one?" meaning Julia.

On several occasions Rose flat-out said to Emmy, as if it had suddenly dawned on her, that Emmy's name wasn't Isabel.

Once when she did this—in front of the boys, no less—Emmy leaned in toward Rose and told her she had a secret. Emmy had discovered that Rose loved secrets. She loved the word "secrets." Emmy told her she wanted to be called Isabel because it was her favorite name. And that she would call Rose by her favorite name if she would tell Emmy what it was. Rose's eyes glittered with the heady notion of being called by a name she loved far more than her own.

She leaned toward Emmy in return. "Ophelia," she murmured.

Emmy told her that was a beautiful name and that she would call her that.

Rose's reticence toward Emmy began to wane after

that. This was a good thing because since Emmy never wanted to go to the village, Charlotte went—most often with the boys in tow—and that meant Emmy stayed at Thistle House with Rose. Rose slowly began to prefer Emmy's company to Charlotte's, an oddity that Charlotte seemed to wish to find endearing and not a bit hurtful. She had cared for Rose for two decades, yet here was Emmy stealing away Rose's affections after only a few weeks. When Emmy caught Charlotte looking injured at Rose's continued deference to Emmy, she apologized for it, and Charlotte just said, "Don't mind me."

Rose seemed to think she and Emmy had a treasure trove of secrets between them now, when in reality they had just the one. And even that wasn't a secret, since everyone heard Emmy call her Ophelia. But that one secret seemed like a thousand to Rose. And it made her happy.

Between caring for Rose when Charlotte was away from the house, minding the boys, and getting the house ready for the holidays, Emmy's life seemed full of purpose. They prepared for Christmas—the five of them—by agreeing that they would only give one another presents they had made themselves. Emmy had long since put away the pieces of Charlotte's wedding dress and had no desire to trifle with her bargain with God by sewing anything for anyone, so she used the money that Mac had given her and bought watercolor paints and canvases at an art store in Moreton. Emmy had never painted before, but she had found creative release and joy in sketching, so wouldn't it stand to reason that she could find the same in painting?

At night, after the boys were in bed, Emmy would set up a makeshift easel in the laundry room by the privy, the only place where she had any privacy, and experiment with brushes, shades, and strokes. She painted what she saw in the laundry room, which, that first night, was Charlotte's umbrella, the very same one Julia had dreamed of owning one day. Over the course of the next few nights, a second painting took shape: a flaxen-haired nymph of a girl holding a red-and-white polka-dot umbrella with a curly licorice black handle, and walking in the rain down a flower-flecked path. It would be the first of many Umbrella Girls, though Emmy did not paint another for six years. That first one Emmy gave to Charlotte for their Christmas together at Thistle House. For Rose, she painted a trellis of roses, and for the boys, a horse for Hugh, and a sailboat for Philip.

She also helped the boys make gifts for their parents, and for Charlotte and Rose. They made calendars constructed from old greeting cards that the woman across the lane—the only one of the neighbors who didn't crinkle an eyebrow when she called Emmy "Isabel"—was going to throw out and instead gave to Emmy for the boys.

During these weeks, Mac rang up from London several times, to say hello and give Emmy an update on his continued search for Julia. Emmy knew he would be spending Christmas in the hotel, so with Charlotte's permission, Emmy invited him for supper. He rode the train with Hugh and Philip's parents, who had also been invited.

As they all sat around the dining table Christmas Day with one of Charlotte's fatter and recently retired laying hens serving as their Christmas goose, Emmy was astonished at how normal and wonderful the scene was. Even Philip and Hugh bickering over a chicken leg seemed perfectly sublime.

After dinner and before their train ride back to London, Mac asked to take a walk with Emmy. They bundled up against the chill and headed outside.

Emmy knew how the war was progressing; she and Charlotte listened to the wireless most nights after the boys and Rose were in bed, and they had a two-day-old newspaper once or twice a week to keep them abreast of what was going on. Emmy knew that more than twenty thousand ordinary people like her mum and Eloise Crofton had been killed in the Blitz since September, and that hundreds of thousands had been made homeless. Coventry had been decimated not long after Emmy returned to Thistle House, and terrible raids had been inflicted on Manchester and Liverpool in the days leading up to Christmas. More than forty thousand British soldiers had been made prisoners of war on the Continent.

Emmy did not particularly want to talk about those things as she and Mac stepped outside, but how could they not? The war was what had brought Mac and her together and the war was the only reason he was in England instead of at home in the States.

Mac told Emmy he was afraid the year to come— 1941—was going to be a long one. Things would get worse before they got better.

But then he took her mittened hand in his as they walked up Maugersbury Road. "I'm glad you're here in Stow, even though I hardly ever see you. London's no place for a young woman like you."

Emmy didn't know what to say to this. Mac didn't know her at all.

"I wish I had news of your half sister," he continued when she said nothing. "I hate to tell you that I don't. And on Christmas, too. The one thing you can hold on to is that there's no record of her death."

"I almost wish there was, because then I'd know." Emmy exhaled heavily, her breath puffing away from her in vapor.

They walked in silence for several seconds.

"You must be very close to her," Mac finally said.

"I am," Emmy replied. "She was—is—very fond of me. She looked to me for protection. I was more like a mother to her than an older sister."

"Her mother wasn't around much?" he asked.

"She . . . was around. She just struggled to make ends meet. It was hard. I think she did her best."

"And the father you shared passed away a while ago, right?"

The mingling of her lives in conversation made Emmy feel a little dizzy, as though she were spinning in a circle and if she stopped, she would topple.

"Right," she said simply.

"What was he like, your father?"

They were just short of entering town, a good place to stop. Emmy needed to be careful of what she said. And remember every word. She stopped at a picket fence that bordered a cottage of Cotswold stone and stared at the gray skies beyond.

If Julia and she had shared the same father—which was what Mac believed—then Emmy would have memories of him; she was the older by eight years. Emmy reasoned that if she could blend Emmeline and Isabel into one, she could certainly combine her nameless father with Neville.

"My father wasn't a very responsible person. He had charm and liked to be happy, but he didn't know how to think beyond the moment." As Emmy said this, she wondered how much was true of her own father, whoever he was. He had certainly charmed Mum with no thought to tomorrow.

"I'm sorry to hear that." Mac stood close to her.

Emmy shrugged. "I've not spent any time mulling over it."

He seemed surprised. "Really?"

"What good would it do? It won't change anything. He was who he was. I'm not going to spend the rest of my life wondering why."

Mac smiled. "Good for you." He paused a moment. "So what *are* you going to spend the rest of your life doing? Assuming the Luftwaffe doesn't kill us all." He laughed lightly.

Emmy stared at the pointed slats of the fence. She didn't have a plan for the rest of her life. Not anymore. "I really don't know."

A couple seconds of silence passed between them before Emmy realized she should ask him what his plans were. "What about you?"

Mac looked past the cottage, just as she had, to the colorless sky. "Well, if the Nazis don't blow me to bits, I want to move back to Minneapolis or maybe Saint Paul, buy my own radio station, make a lot of money, marry, have a couple kids, retire at fifty."

"That's all?" Emmy said, and Mac laughed.

"I like knowing what I want out of life," he said.

"Knowing isn't having." Emmy did not mean for it to sound bitter, but she tasted resentment on her tongue.

"But if you don't know what you want, you can't reach for it."

She wanted to tell him that reaching hard for something you thought you must have, having it nearly in your grasp, and risking all to get it, could lead you straight to the heart of utter ruin.

But what would Isabel Crofton know of that?

"Want to meet in Oxford for the New Year?" he asked.

Emmy coughed to hide the breath he had stolen from her.

"I don't mean at a hotel, Isabel. I mean at a party. A friend of mine in London has family there. It would be fun."

Her eyes were watering at the curious exchange of air and breath and voice taking place in her throat.

"Maybe," was all she could say.

But Mac did not make it to the party in Oxford on New Year's. London was bombed two days before New Year's Eve with such intensity that a firestorm swept across the city and nearly swallowed the East End whole. Five days passed before Mac rang Emmy and told her he was all right.

And so began 1941, the second year of the war.

Twenty-nine

❧

THE occupants of Thistle House spent 1941 adjusting to the odd sense of subtraction that was the war. Every day it seemed there was the loss of some small thing, like no more lemon curd or brass cleaner or toilet paper. Heeding the national call to plant a victory garden, Charlotte and Emmy doubled the size of the vegetable patch that spring, and they cared for it and the orchard trees all summer. They harvested, canned, and distributed in the fall and winter, making many trips to Moreton in Charlotte's coughing blue car with crates of food to be sent to the cities where the need for food was greatest. Hugh and Philip were the caretakers of the chickens and roosters, and they walked to town every morning on their way to school with two dozen eggs that Charlotte gave away. The reports from London and beyond tutored everyone to keep a perpetual eye to the sky as it seemed the enemy would soon be screaming over Gloucestershire as it had elsewhere and rain down its wrath.

An RAF airbase had been constructed near Moreton and a fleet of Wellington bombers was now taking off and landing only a few miles away, a new development that the boys loved as much as Emmy hated. She had heard enough of planes.

Emmy kept to herself and the house. She ventured out now and then to meet Mac in Oxford, but only in the company of other people. As the second year of the war ended and 1942 began, Mac made it clear he was hoping for more than just friendship from Emmy. He wanted to date her, for lack of a better word. Did anyone still date? Did the war allow for that? Emmy didn't know. And she didn't want to know. She was afraid to give her heart over to Mac. He assured her more than once that he didn't just want to take her to his bed. He also wanted the deeper emotional intimacy that a loving, caring physical relationship would bring to what he hoped was a very serious friendship with potential for much more. As the buried Emmeline within her aged, Emmy became aware of a pounding ache to be desired in that way. But how could she give herself body and soul to a man who had no idea she was an imposter?

Emmy finally told Mac she was not the woman for him, not the one he wanted to be with in *that* way, but that she very much treasured his friendship. And she did. He was still the only friend she had or wanted as she had purposely kept her circle of loved ones small. Charlotte. Rose. Hugh. Philip. Mac. No one else.

An awkward few months followed after that conversation when Mac didn't ring her up. She started to think her circle was down to four. But in the end, Mac agreed to friendship only, if that was what she wanted. He told Emmy he understood the war kept her from risking her heart on love, but that maybe when it ended, she would feel differently.

Emmy let him think what he wanted as it kept him from abandoning her completely. Perhaps she *would* feel differently in the distant future. She wanted to believe that maybe she would.

Mac did not come for Christmas dinner in 1942. Everything had changed for Americans, even those stationed abroad. Pearl Harbor had been bombed by Japan, and the United States had entered a war that now stretched around the globe.

The next two years were spent in a mindless routine, of "mend and make do" and hoping against hope that the forces united against the Allies would break and the beast be rendered powerless. As 1944 came to a close, it began to seem possible that the dark hand of war might lift.

It was wonderful to imagine that the madness and violence would end, peace would be restored, and simple joys like sugar and ham and nuts would find their way back to the pantry at Thistle House. And yet Emmy didn't want her time there to end. There was nothing for her in London, and she had given up hope of finding out what had happened to Julia, though whenever she saw a blond little girl, she did a double take. Emmy did not know what Isabel Crofton could do with a life not dictated by war. She didn't know what she was capable of doing as Isabel other than surviving.

Mac was only so much help in this regard. He and Emmy had come to an understanding of sorts. She told him she couldn't see ever leaving the Cotswolds; it was as if she was tethered to the area now. And he could not wait for the war to end so that he could return to America. They still enjoyed each other's company, but he no longer made romantic overtures toward her. What was the purpose? Emmy could see there was no future for them as a couple.

Mac began to see other women: a nurse he met at a triage center, a secretary he encountered at a cocktail lounge, a ballet dancer with whom he huddled in a Tube station during an air raid. He didn't parade them in front of Emmy, but he wanted her to know about them so that she would not find out another way. He did come for Christmas that year, but their easy camaraderie had been dealt a blow when she rejected his deeper affections. Mac was still her friend, but it was different. It was hard to describe how other than there was no expectancy. Nothing to anticipate.

The war was waning. Emmy's relationship with Mac was waning. Her time at Thistle House was waning. If she just stood still, would the walls of her existence fade to gossamer and then to nothing? Would she disappear into whatever world Julia had been spirited away to when she vanished?

Emmy had called herself Isabel for four years. No one knew her as Emmy except for Mrs. Howell in Moreton, and she had long since stopped paying Emmy any mind since she had aged out of the evacuation scheme for children several years earlier. And while at the beginning the ladies in Stow who knew Charlotte best also knew that Isabel's real name was Emmy, they seemed to forget it as the years passed. Isabel had proved to be a helpful companion to the aging sisters and their evacuees. And Emmy surmised that even though she seemed standoffish whenever she had to be in town, these women chalked it up to what the war had taken from her—a sister and a mother. So what if the Londoner wanted to be called Isabel.

Which was why on February 11, 1945, a cold, windy day, Emmy was surprised to receive a thick envelope in the post from Mrs. Howell, addressed to Isabel Crofton née Emmeline Downtree.

Hugh, just turned twelve, had collected the post that morning from the box at the driveway. He'd dropped it into the empty fruit bowl on the kitchen table on his way outside to work on a sailboat of tree bark that he and Philip were making at the edge of the pond.

Emmy saw the thick envelope peeking out from behind the smaller bills and letters and pulled on it to see what it was.

That Mrs. Howell would use Emmy's former name so publicly annoyed her for only a second, for that was the time it took Emmy to realize that perhaps inside the envelope there was news of Julia. She brought the envelope into the privy before anyone saw her with it so that she could open it and deal with its contents in private.

Emmy's hands were shaking as she slit the letter open and withdrew a sheet of paper and another sealed envelope. The piece of paper—a note signed by Mrs. Howell—notified her that a certified letter that had been crisscrossing the south of England had finally found its way to Emmy. Mrs. Howell hoped that it was good news.

Emmy laid the letter down on the sink and turned the other envelope over. It was addressed to Emmeline Downtree, at the old address in Whitechapel. The return address was a law firm in Chelsea.

Emmy tore it open, willing the documents to reveal the whereabouts of Julia, lost for nearly four and half years.

But the cover letter said nothing at all about her.

January 7, 1945

Emmeline Downtree
24 Great Trinity Lane
Whitechapel
London

It has come to our attention that the bequest to you of £30,000, as stated in the last will and testament of your father, Henry Thorne, has not been received by you. If you wish to claim your inheritance, it is suggested you appear at the law offices of Grimm and Bowker at your earliest convenience. Please kindly inform us when you shall be coming so that we may prepare your cheque.

Yours truly . . .

Emmy did not read the remaining few words. The letter fell from her open hand and glided to the tiles at her feet.

Thirty

EMMY had not expected to see London again.

It was not the lure of the money that drew her back, though she supposed few would believe that to be true. She hadn't any idea what it would be like to have that much money. Indeed, she could not imagine it. Instead, it was the notion that Emmy had been *known* that pulled her. The shadow man who was her father had a name, Henry Thorne. And Henry Thorne knew her. In his death—and in his will—he had acknowledged her as his daughter. He had provided for her, the only way the dead can: through what they leave behind.

Emmy wanted to know who he was, how he knew Mum, how he knew where to find her, what he thought of her. She wanted to know if he wished he could have been a part of her life and why he chose not to be. Surely this lawyer, who must have known her father, would have the answers.

Charlotte offered to come with Emmy, nearly insisted that she come, but Emmy thanked her and told her she would go alone. Rose and the boys would not like it if they both left for an entire day, and truth be told, Emmy did not want Charlotte to be any part of this meeting, even as a witness. Emmy would have to crawl back into Emmeline Downtree's skin to find out the answers to her questions. She didn't want anyone to see her as her old self.

She did not need Charlotte's assistance legally, either. In Emmeline years, she was nineteen, though Emmy felt every bit as old as Isabel's twenty-two years.

Charlotte drove her to the train station in Moreton early in the morning on February 16. When she hugged Emmy good-bye, her eyes glistened with tears, as though she were bidding Emmy farewell for a journey of ten thousand days.

"I'll be back this evening," Emmy said.

Charlotte nodded, laughed away her tears, and told her to be careful.

Emmy chose a seat where she could see Charlotte on the platform. She wanted to wave to her from the window, to smile, and assure Charlotte that she would be all right. And Emmy wanted the last thing she saw as the train puffed out of the station to be Charlotte's face, her raised hand, and that long silver braid.

Emmy had spent her whole life minimizing any thoughts or feelings she had about her father. Mum had never wanted her to contemplate him, which had always made Emmy think that to her mother, he was just a chance encounter she wished to forget. But as the train rumbled across the landscape, all Emmy could do was contemplate him. His name was Henry Thorne. He had provided for her in his will. He was a man of means. He had to be. Thirty thousand pounds was an enormous amount of money.

Had he made himself rich at a young age?

Or was he the son of a rich man?

How did he die? Was he a soldier in the war?

Did his parents know about her?

By the time Emmy arrived at Chelsea station three trains later, her mind was awhirl with ponderings. As she walked the blocks to the law firm's offices, she was insulated from contending with the evidence of London's four-and-a-half-year-long nightmare. She was only vaguely aware that the city's streets did not look the same, nor did its weary people.

At the threshold of Grimm and Bowker, a brick and ivy-covered building on a street lined with leafless trees, Emmy stood still for a moment to calm her anxious heart. She did not want to inundate Mr. Bowker with endless questions, yet she hoped the man would have time to speak to her. There was so much Emmy wanted to know.

As she stepped inside, a silvery bell announced her arrival. A woman in a tweed suit sitting behind an ebony desk looked up and offered a knowing half smile.

"Emmeline Downtree," Emmy said anyway. "I've an appointment with Mr. Bowker."

The woman nodded toward three upholstered chairs lined up against a paneled wall.

"Won't you have a seat?" she said.

As Emmy turned to follow her instructions, a door behind the woman opened. Standing there was a silver-haired man wearing a charcoal gray suit, wire-rim spectacles, and a trimmed mustache and goatee. He was expecting Emmy, yet she was aware that her presence startled him. He stared at her, undone, or so it seemed, by her physical features.

"Miss Downtree, this won't take but a moment. If you will follow me," he said a few seconds later, with the same forced politeness as his secretary.

Emmy sensed she was to take her money and leave. Her many questions hovered in her head. Which ones would she have time to ask?

She followed the man into a narrow hallway, past two closed doors, to a third door, which was open. He stepped inside.

Mr. Bowker's office was nicely appointed. Polished wood gleamed everywhere. Red- and brown-spined books were shelved on bookcases that spanned three of the four walls. Two leather-upholstered chairs faced his desk.

Emmy started to sit in one of them but Mr. Bowker stopped her.

"Actually, I have your check right here, Miss Downtree," he said, emphasizing her last name in a way that befuddled her. He reached for an envelope lying near the edge of his desk.

"I have a few questions," Emmy said, hearing a tremor in her voice and wondering whether he heard it as well.

He arched his silver-gray eyebrows. "I beg your pardon?"

Emmy lowered herself into one of his chairs, feigning confidence, but actually needing to sit to keep the world from spinning.

"I—I have a few questions."

Mr. Bowker stared at her. "I have not been instructed to answer questions, Miss Downtree."

Instructed? Who was giving him instructions?

"I would like to know when my father died, please. I was not told," Emmy said, attempting to sound merely like a grieving daughter.

His raised eyebrows lowered to become part of a thinly veiled scowl. "I have not been instructed to answer questions. If you feel you are entitled to more than this check—"

"Entitled?" Emmy echoed, feeling a strange indignation rising up within her. "You—you wrote to me that my father had provided for me in his will, Mr. Bowker. *You* wrote to me."

He opened his mouth to say something but the secretary poked her head in the room.

"She's on the telephone. She wants to speak with you. Says it can't wait," the secretary said.

Mr. Bowker frowned. He handed the envelope to Emmy. "I believe we are finished here, Miss Downtree."

Emmy hesitated, unwilling to leave without so much as a crumb of information. He took a step toward her, the envelope now just inches from her.

Emmy took it. What else could she do? She rose slowly from the chair, holding the slimmest of evidence that she'd had a father who had known who she was.

As the secretary ushered her back down the corridor, she heard Mr. Bowker speak into the receiver of his phone.

"That's not what we agreed," he said. And then, "I really don't think that will be necessary." And finally, just as the inner door to the corridor closed behind Emmy, "But she's already left."

Whoever he was speaking to was talking about her. The person on the other end of that call was surely the one who had instructed Mr. Bowker that Emmy was to be given her check and shown the door.

At that moment Emmy had the first inkling as to why Henry Thorne had waited until he was dead to provide for her the way any decent father should.

Emmy was the result of an illicit relationship that ought not to have been. She had long known that. But now she was putting the rest of the puzzle together. Wealthy Henry Thorne had not taken responsibility for her existence while he lived, but did so in death—hence the will—lest he be damned twice over.

Emmy wanted out of that office. She quickened her steps to the front door and pulled it open.

"Wait!" said a voice behind her.

She turned and Mr. Bowker stood at the connecting door.

"You've been asked to please wait for a car to come for you. You're wanted at the house." He said it as if he'd been forced to speak with a gun pointed at his head.

"Who wants me? What house?" Emmy replied, hardly able to comprehend what he was saying.

Mr. Bowker sighed heavily. "Mrs. Thorne wants to have a word with you. She's sending a car."

"His . . . mother?" Emmy said. A nervous mother cleaning up her son's mistakes? Her grandmother?

He looked at Emmy as if she were daft. "His *wife*."

The way he said it made her feel ugly and valueless. A pariah.

Emmy's hand was still on the doorknob as she vacillated between leaving and staying.

"She wants a word," Mr. Bowker said again, and it was obvious he'd been told to see that Emmy stayed and waited for the car to come for her.

"I've done nothing wrong," she blurted.

The man's hard features softened the tiniest bit. He had not been paid to look out for Emmy's interests, clearly, but a sliver of compassion for her was now etched on his face.

"You said you had some questions," Mr. Bowker said. "If you really want the answers, stay for the car. If you don't, leave. I will tell her I couldn't make you stay."

Emmy wanted so much for someone to tell her what to do. She should have brought Charlotte with her. It was her damnable pride that made her tell Charlotte she didn't need her. But Charlotte wasn't there. There was only herself, the lawyer, and his tight-lipped secretary.

"Would you stay, if you were me?" Emmy finally asked, a challenge in her tone.

He shook his head, almost as if to shake away the entirety of all the messes people made when they let their desires run amok. "Honestly, I'd take the check and leave."

Mrs. Thorne was not happy about this situation. That was clear.

"I never knew his name until you sent me that letter," Emmy said, her throat thickening with childlike sadness.

"She never knew about you until she saw his will."

It hurt Emmy to hear him say it that way. She felt at fault for having survived childbirth and taken her first breath.

But she was sure Mr. Bowker didn't include himself among the unaware. He had known about her. He had drawn up the will.

"Why not?" Emmy asked.

"You seem a reasonably smart girl. I am sure you can guess."

Emmy didn't want to guess. She wanted the truth. She took her hand off the doorknob and let the door swish closed.

She took a seat in one of the chairs and smoothed her skirt.

"When did he die, Mr. Bowker?"

Emmy expected the man to say a year ago or six months ago or even on Remembrance Day, three months before.

She did not expect him to say that Henry Thorne had died on September 8, 1940, in the basement of the Sharington Crescent Hotel, his arms wrapped around her mother.

Thirty-one

AT first Emmy refused to believe that her mother and Henry Thorne had been together in that hotel. That was impossible. If that was true, then it was also true that on the night Emmy was conceived, he hadn't been some passing teenage acquaintance that Mum had slept with after having had too many drinks. He wasn't a person Mum had long put out of her mind as she had led Emmy to believe.

Mum had had a relationship with him. A continuous one. A secret one. Emmy now thought of Mum in those few minutes before she left Emmy at the flat, the last time Emmy saw her. She was going to Henry Thorne for help. She had said they needed someone with connections. Someone with money to help them find Julia. When Emmy had offered to do whatever Mum was willing to do to get what they needed, Mum had laughed in a sad, funny way because she was going to Henry Thorne for help.

Emmy's father.

And she didn't even tell her.

"How—how long did they . . . How long were they . . ." But Emmy couldn't find the words to phrase so delicate and private a question.

Mr. Bowker gave a mirthless chuckle. "You really don't know, do you?"

Emmy shook her head.

"On and off since the day you were born. Your mother was a sixteen-year-old maid in your father's house. He was twice her age and unhappily married. When she ended up pregnant, he put her up in a flat across the river. Paid for the doctor, the hospital. Paid for your nappies and your blankets and your sitters. Found her new jobs when she needed them and got her out of jams when she got herself in them."

The air in the room felt warm with his indignation.

Or maybe it was just hers.

"Because he had to hide what he'd done to stay out of jail and keep his fortune and reputation?" Emmy said, hotly.

"Because he thought he loved her."

Emmy was stunned into silence.

Before she could summon words to ask him what he meant by that, the door opened, and an older man in a black suit and cap stepped inside.

"I'm here for Miss Emmeline Downtree," he said.

Mr. Bowker nodded to the world that waited outside the open door. "Watch your step, Miss Downtree." And then he pivoted to return to his office.

Emmy walked numbly to the sleek black car waiting

curbside. The driver helped her inside, but Emmy would later not remember whether he said anything to her, nor which streets they drove down before he turned into the curved driveway of a stately home that was as large as the entire row of flats in Whitechapel. The gray-stoned mansion was four stories high, trimmed in white. Miniature topiaries lined the walkway to the massive front door.

The driver parked the car and then came around to Emmy's side to assist her out. He motioned toward the wide steps that led to the entrance. The front door swung open, and a maid in a navy blue dress and white lace apron appeared on the threshold.

"If you will follow me, please," she said. Emmy took the steps slowly and then entered a marble-tiled foyer. Gilded mirrors and picture frames hung on walls that seemed endless.

The maid showed her into a room that appeared to be a study or library. Books lined the walls. Leather sofas and chairs were set about in cozy groupings. A fire danced in the grate and wherever there weren't books or leather, there was gleaming mahogany.

Above the fireplace was a portrait of a man who seemed vaguely familiar to her, seated next to a slightly plump woman who stood next to him with her arm around his shoulder. On his other side was a boy, about twelve, with his forearm draped over the back of his father's chair. The man in the portrait looked like Emmy. Or rather, she looked like him.

Henry Thorne.

Her father.

For several long moments Emmy just stood there and stared at the man who had fathered her. She didn't hear footfalls from behind. There was just suddenly a voice.

"Miss Downtree."

Emmy startled, and turned to see the woman in the portrait, older now.

"Yes," she answered.

"Agnes Thorne. Won't you sit down?" The woman's tone was cool, as though her words had been carved of ice.

Emmy took the chair Agnes Thorne offered her, and the woman sat down opposite, smoothing her wool skirt. Her brown hair held tints of gray, but her complexion was flawless, her lips full and red, and the pearls at her neck and ears luminescent. She was not beautiful, but she had a commanding air, a gracefulness born of a lifetime of privilege. Emmy caught a whiff of the woman's perfume. It smelled like something from another world altogether.

The world of the wealthy.

A tea tray was set between them. Agnes lifted the pot. "Tea?"

"Yes, thank you."

The woman poured and then handed Emmy a cup without so much as a tremble in her fingers.

"I want it to be clear between us that the check you were given is the end of the road." She spooned sugar—something Emmy hadn't seen in months and months—into her cup and stirred. "There will be no more after this."

"Pardon?"

Agnes laid the spoon carefully on the saucer that held her cup. "Your connection to this family—however small it may be—is done after this. We will not hear from you again. Is that understood?"

Blood rushed to Emmy's cheeks as humiliation bloomed inside her. She fought to stay in control and not let this woman see her shame. Emmy needed answers. She deserved answers.

"No. It's not understood, actually. I have a few questions."

The woman looked up, surprised. And instantly furious. "You are not in a position to ask questions, Miss Downtree. You have my husband's money. I suggest you take it and leave."

"Why did it take four and a half years for me to learn that my father is dead?" Emmy asked.

Agnes sniffed, put her cup down, and stood. "I thought we could have a civilized conversation regarding this. But I see now that we cannot. You will not get another shilling from me. Not a one."

Emmy was not leaving. Not yet. She stayed seated. "I don't want anything of yours—you can be sure of that. I just want a few answers. Why did it take four and a half years for me to learn that my father is dead?"

The woman sat back down slowly. "It's wartime. Very hard to locate people. You are no longer living at your last-known address. We couldn't find you."

She was being untruthful; Emmy felt sure of it. "You didn't try to find me, did you?"

Agnes Thorne crossed one leg over the other. "Be careful whom you accuse of lying, Miss Downtree."

Emmy saw hurt in the woman's eyes when she said this. And it occurred to Emmy that this woman had been lied to for years. Henry Thorne had carried on his affair with Mum up until the day they both died. And this woman had never known. Emmy felt a strange and instant kinship with Agnes Thorne. Emmy had been lied to as well, about the very same thing.

"I didn't know who he was," Emmy said, her heart aching for the two of them in a way that astounded her. "Mum never said a word. I didn't even know she was still seeing him."

"Don't you dare say a word about it," Agnes said, enunciating the first three words as if they were arrows. "Not a word!"

"But I didn't! I knew nothing."

The woman's chest was heaving as she locked her gaze on Emmy, her eyes wild with anger. "How could you not know? Do you think I am silly enough to believe you didn't know where your clothes came from? And your food? And the rent for your flat? And every toy you got for Christmas! I've seen the hidden ledgers, Miss Downtree. I know exactly how much money he wasted on you and your whore of a mother all those years. He paid for it all. So don't you tell me you didn't know!"

Emmy's mouth was open but no sound came out. She had no words to sling back in retaliation. She felt as though she had been tarred and feathered, right there in that beautiful room with its expensive furnishings.

The whore's daughter.

Agnes Thorne could see that she had Emmy now, defenseless, in her grip. She leaned forward. "I don't know how you found out about the will, but I am telling you, I am finished with you. You go to the press with this and I will spend every penny I have making your life as miserable as you've made mine."

"I didn't . . . I never . . . I was sent a letter informing me that I had money coming to me," Emmy finally sputtered.

"Liar."

"I swear it's true!"

"You lie!"

"I didn't even know his name until I got this letter. I didn't know anything!"

Agnes Thorne was at the ready to denounce Emmy when a voice broke through the heated exchange.

"She's telling the truth, Mother."

Emmy turned toward the sound of the voice. A young man, perhaps a little younger than she was, stood in the doorway. He was the boy in the portrait, grown up.

"Colin!" Agnes sputtered. "What did you do?"

The man came into the room. Emmy could see that he favored his mother in looks. But his eyes were not full of hatred and disgust.

"I did what I told you I was going to do when I turned eighteen. I told Mr. Bowker to find her. That money is hers. Dad left it to her."

Agnes seemed to deflate before Emmy. Where a minute earlier there had been a fiery warrior, now there was a beggar woman. The change in her was that remarkable.

"Colin, how could you do such a thing?"

Emmy could feel the pain behind her words, the sense of betrayal.

"Because it was the right thing to do. You know it is."

The man turned to Emmy and put out his hand. She shook it slowly and with little enthusiasm, she was still so astonished. "I'm Colin Thorne. Your half brother."

Agnes winced and turned her face away, as though she could no longer bear the sight of Emmy in her house.

Emmy looked from one to the other, from the half brother she didn't know she had who'd risked his mother's wrath to see that she was paid in full, to the wronged woman who'd learned too late that her husband had been unfaithful to her. And then there was Emmy in the middle, the whore's daughter. The ignorant child who couldn't see where the good things her mother had had came from, or rather, who chose not to.

Emmeline.

The girl she used to be.

She reached into her handbag, and closed her fingers around the check that had been made out to Emmeline Downtree.

Emmy pulled it out, laid it on the table by her teacup, and stood.

She started to walk away from the man who wanted her compensated and the woman who wished she had never been born. It was several seconds before either one of them realized Emmy was leaving them and their money.

Colin came after her. "Wait, Miss Downtree! Wait."

But Emmy did not wait.

"Miss Downtree!"

Her hand was at the door when Colin reached her. He had the envelope in his hand.

"It's yours. He wanted you to have it."

Emmy looked at the envelope. Such a thin little thing to have caused such grief today.

"But that's not what *I* wanted," she said.

And she left him standing there with the envelope in his hand, his fingers covering the word *Emmeline* scrawled across the front in Mr. Bowker's practiced script.

Thirty-two

OUTSIDE the Thorne mansion, the driver stood next to the vehicle as if he'd been told Emmy would only be a short while.

He snapped to action when Emmy emerged from the house and opened the car door for her. Emmy would have walked away from that place on her own two legs, but she had no idea where she was. She got inside.

"Paddington, miss?" the driver said when he was also back inside the vehicle.

Emmy did not want to go back to Thistle House right then. Not as Emmeline, and that was who she firmly was as she stepped out of the Thorne home slathered in recriminations. She wanted more than anything to go to Primrose and fall asleep on the heap of bridal gowns, and never open her eyes again.

She wanted to wake up in the arms of the angels and

have them tell her she was worthy of love—to give it and to have it given to her.

But there was no place like that in London. Not for her. Except perhaps . . .

"The Savoy," she said.

Thirty minutes later, Emmy was inside the lobby of the hotel where she used to go every Monday on her campaign to find London's orphans. Mac wasn't there; it was only midafternoon. He was no doubt in the underground studio at Broadcasting House, working dials and switches as someone leaned over a microphone and described the advance of the Allies across Germany.

She settled into a chair to wait for him.

Emmy was not aware she had fallen asleep until Mac was bending over her, gently shaking her awake and murmuring her name.

When Emmy opened her eyes, she saw a woman standing behind Mac, her hand on his arm, and the utter despair of that singular moment was nearly the end of her. But then the woman walked away, clearly having spied the party she was looking for. Mac was now alone.

"Is it really you?" Emmy said.

He laughed. "I was about to ask you the same thing. What are you doing here?"

Emmy stood and threw her arms around his neck and held him tight. It took him a moment to respond in kind, but then his arms were around her as well. She did not want to start crying into his shirt collar but she did, and once the seal was broken, the tears would not stop coming.

Mac cupped the back of her head in his hand and drew her closer. "Isabel. Is it about Julia?"

She shook her head.

Emmy wanted to tell him why she was suddenly at the Savoy, in tears, and wrapped in his embrace. But to repeat every ugly thing Agnes Thorne had said to her and about her, and relive it, held no appeal. Besides, that was Emmeline's story, not Isabel's.

"I just had a really terrible day. Awful." Emmy pulled away and he immediately handed her a handkerchief. "I don't want to talk about it."

"You're in London," he said, and it was a question that wasn't a question.

"There was someone I needed to see. It couldn't be helped."

He studied her. "And it didn't go well?"

"No. It didn't."

"Sure you don't want to talk about it?" he asked.

"Quite sure."

"Can I take you to dinner, then?"

"Will your girlfriend mind?" Emmy said, handing him his handkerchief and making no attempt to hide her disdain.

He laughed. "She's just a friend who's a girl, Isabel."

"Will there be a stiff drink?" Emmy wanted to drown the word *whore*, *whore*, *whore*, which kept echoing like a clanging bell in her head. Drown it in drink.

"Uh. Sure." Mac gave her his arm and they started to walk toward the lobby doors.

"You look beautiful when you cry, by the way," he said.

Emmy leaned into him as they stepped into the early evening. Surely there would be no air raids tonight. Germany had nothing left to send up into the air.

"I don't like it when I cry," she said. "Makes me feel weak."

He slid his arm around her waist and kissed her temple. "Oh, but it's our tears that make us human, Isabel."

Being on Mac's arm as they walked, and in his arms as they danced after dinner, and then as they walked past the ruins along the river, Emmy felt something being returned to her after a long absence. The fires had stopped burning, the bombs had stopped falling, the debris was being cleared away, the slabs where buildings once stood were being scraped clean to begin their second life, a life after the war. It was not far off, this new life. A few months, maybe by the end of the year, but she could feel that the turning of the tide was just beyond the horizon. She was ready to feel again. To feel something good. Chocolate on her tongue. New shoes on her feet. Holidays at the seaside. Blank canvases on which to paint. Kisses on her neck and lips.

They went back to the Savoy to see whether Emmy could get a room as she had missed the last train to Oxford. But the hotel was full.

"Come up to my room, Isabel," Mac offered. "I can sleep on the floor. Scout's honor."

And that was the plan.

Mac would have honored it; Emmy was sure of that.

But sometime in the night she dreamed that she was the one trapped in the basement of the Sharington Crescent Hotel, buried in rubble, and no one would help her. She was suffocating and darkness was closing in on her. She would be buried alive.

Worse, Julia was in the rubble with her, and her eyes were open, glassy, and unblinking, like the dead man on the street during the Blitz whose nose and mouth were spattered with blood.

Her screams woke Mac, who was at her side in an

instant, shushing her, calming her. And then kissing her. Everywhere. When he realized what was happening, he pulled away, an apology on his lips.

But she drew him back to his bed.

Emmy wanted to be with him. She wanted to feel as if she mattered.

As Mac entwined his body with hers, as close as two people could possibly be, Emmy suddenly understood why Mum had kept going back to Henry Thorne, even though he was married to someone else. It wasn't just about the money he gave her to survive as a single mother. He made her feel wanted. Desired. Precious.

Mum had made an exchange, just like everyone does when quaking under a load that seems far too heavy. She exchanged a transparent life of abject poverty for one of secrets and illusion that kept her and her daughters fed and clothed. Julia had likewise exchanged the brides box for the fairy tale book when she didn't want Emmy to leave. Emmy had exchanged Julia for her own aspirations when she didn't want anyone else telling her what she could and couldn't do.

And that very day Emmy had exchanged the absolution her father had willed to her for her own dignity.

This was how people balanced the scales their world was tipping, Emmy reasoned. It was only after time had passed that a person was able to see whether she might have been able to bear the load she was sure had been too heavy.

But life is lived at the moment you are living it, she thought. *No one but God in heaven has the benefit of seeing beyond today.*

In the morning when she awoke, Mac smiled at her in sleepy wakefulness and fingered a lock of hair away from her eyes.

"Good morning," he said.

Emmy was afraid to rise from where she lay. Time seemed to have stilled and she didn't want it to go about its relentless forward march. She didn't know which girl she would be as she rose from the bed. She whispered her reluctance to leave.

"Stay, then."

"I can't. You know I can't."

"Then marry me."

He said it so swiftly. Emmy waited for him to laugh and assure her he was joking. Surely he was joking. But the seconds flitted by and he did not laugh.

"I'm crazy about you. Marry me, Isabel."

Emmy stared at him openmouthed, not daring to imagine herself the happy wife of a good man. She was no friend of happiness. Mac had no idea whom he was proposing to.

"I'm not who you think I am," Emmy whispered. Tears gathered at the corners of her eyes.

He kissed them away. "You're the woman I love."

"But you will leave when the war is over."

"Everyone has to leave sometime, Isabel. Life is about coming and going. Come to America with me. I promise I will live every day to see that you don't regret it."

She closed her eyes to stop picturing herself pushing away from England, the only home she had ever known.

Pushing away from Julia, finally and fully.

"Isabel?"

"I don't know what to do."

"Do you love me?"

The moment the question was posed, she knew that she did. She did love him. But just because she loved him did not mean she was entitled to happiness with him, nor did it mean she had the courage to leave England and walk out on a promise she'd made to Mum years before on a sunny beach.

"What does it matter if I do?" Emmy said, rising from the bed and reaching for her clothes. Loving Mac changed nothing about who she was and what she had done.

"Isabel."

She turned to him.

"Please don't let the unhappiness you knew in the past keep you from accepting happiness now," he said. "Please don't."

The pulling and twisting of her two identities— Emmeline's past, Isabel's future—was making her head spin. "I have to get back. Charlotte will be worried."

"Isabel?"

"I—I can't think about the future right now, Mac. Please don't ask me to."

He said no more about it. He said hardly anything as he walked her to the train station.

Emmy returned to Thistle House and made her apologies for having stayed overnight without letting Charlotte know. Then she told Charlotte what had happened at the lawyers' office, and at the Thorne mansion.

She didn't tell Charlotte she'd slept with Mac.

But Emmy thought Charlotte knew anyway.

Mac rang her twice in the weeks that followed, and Emmy kept the calls short, something she had not done before, not when it came to Mac. But his unanswered proposal hung between them like a gift she was too afraid to reach out and take. Her heart ached for Mac, but sleeping with him had been reckless and selfish.

And not without consequence. Seven weeks after

returning from London, it was clear to Emmy that she was pregnant.

As Emmy vomited again and again into the toilet, and as Charlotte placed a cool cloth across the back of her neck, a terrible longing filled the emptiness that gripped her stomach. She missed her mother.

"I want my mum," Emmy rasped to Charlotte, between heaves.

Charlotte leaned over her and kissed the back of Emmy's head. "I know you do."

Through all the years of the war, Emmy had awakened each day as Isabel Crofton. But she was still Annie Downtree's daughter. Mum had stood where she was now: alone, pregnant, and reeling from choices made in weakness. Mum alone knew where to find the strength to keep putting one foot in front of the other despite the stares, the empty days, and the lonely nights.

Mum knew how to survive in a world without dreams.

"I don't know how to do this," Emmy finally whispered.

Charlotte sought Emmy's gaze, maneuvering her face close to Emmy's. "Tell Mac. He loves you. I've known it all along. And I think you love him, too. This child is as much his as it is yours."

Emmy blinked back threatening tears. "But . . . Mac is American. When the war is over, he will go back to America."

Charlotte looked down and nodded. "I know."

"You . . . would want me to go? Leave here?" Emmy could hardly form the words. Thistle House had been her refuge, a sanctuary after the war had taken everything from her.

"We're not talking about what I want." Charlotte

reached for Emmy's hand. "This is about your life, not mine. You need to make your way back into the world, Isabel. You've a place in it. You need to find what it is. I know you've said you won't ever sketch another bridal gown, and maybe you won't, but you were meant to do something with your life. I can't believe it's to sit in Thistle House and watch time pass you by."

"But I feel . . . safe here," Emmy said, scarcely breathing.

"Safe is not the same thing as happy. Trust me on this, Isabel."

They were quiet for a moment.

"I won't know what to do with myself in America," Emmy finally said.

Charlotte smiled. "You will build a life with the man you love and the child you created. You'll figure out the rest. That's what we all have to do."

Another stretch of silence passed as Emmy contemplated a future with the only man she could ever see herself loving. It seemed too grand a thing to imagine; it had been too grand for Mum.

Mum.

If she did this, this was where Annie Downtree's daughter and Eloise Crofton's would part. For good.

This was where Emmeline Downtree would fade at last into nothing, just like Julia had. Like Mum had.

Charlotte got to her knees and told Emmy she was going to make some chamomile tea to settle Emmy's stomach.

"You might consider telling Mac who you really are. I don't think it will matter to him," Charlotte said as she stood at the doorway.

Emmy murmured that if it didn't matter to him, then

there was no reason to tell him. Because it mattered to her. Life was about coming and going.

For Emmy, it was time to go.

ISABEL Crofton married Jonah MacFarland in a London courthouse on May 8, the day the Allies declared victory in Europe.

The end of hostilities.

The newlyweds left for America with Isabel's brand-new passport on a foggy morning in July after a tearful, long weekend at Thistle House where she said her farewells. The morning of their departure, Isabel found herself as she had been the day she left London after Mac had saved her life, desperate to be far from it. She felt the stitching of any last ties to her old life break away as London fell behind her. In her suitcase in the belly of the ship, she carried a small stack of maternity clothes, her watercolor brushes, her birth certificate, a felt box of trinkets, a book of fairy tales.

And a hammer.

She would not see England again.

The hammer would remind her, lest she forget, that she had made a transaction when she became Isabel.

Leaving England forever meant she could leave Emmeline Downtree and her terrible sorrows there with it.

It seemed a reasonable exchange.

Thirty-three

KENDRA

I look at the woman across from me on the sofa, framed by her iconic Umbrella Girls paintings behind her. Her hands are crossed in her lap and she is staring at them.

She is Emmeline Downtree. She is Isabel Mac-Farland.

"But you *did* come back to England," I say. "This is Thistle House, isn't it?"

She nods once. "It is."

"What—what made you return?"

Isabel raises her head but turns to gaze out the window. "Oh, I suppose the mighty hand of God. That's what it usually takes to move someone who is holding on to what doesn't belong to her." She laughs lightly, as though the details of her return still surprise her.

"I—I'm not sure I follow you."

Isabel tips her head to glance at me, but only barely.

"You haven't made the mistakes I have nor have you been flung into a tempest that forces you to make choices you are not prepared to make—I know that. But I hope someday you will remember I told you that you do not own your sins."

I am still at a loss. "You're not saying people aren't responsible for the wrong they do," I say, though I can't believe this is what she means. Not after all that she has told me.

She sighs gently, wondering perhaps how to make it clear to me.

She is revealing something to me, I think. Her purpose for having allowed me to interview her perhaps?

"I am saying, when you make a choice, even if it's a bad one, you've played your hand. You cannot live your life as though you still held all your cards."

"Is that why you agreed to let me talk to you today? To tell me this?"

Isabel laughs. "Good Lord, no. My reason is far more selfish than that." She smiles at thoughts I am not able to guess at. She shakes her head. "Far more selfish."

I wait for her to continue.

She looks at me. "You might have guessed I have not been very adept at being transparent with people. I agreed to let you interview me because I plan to leave my history with you."

"Me?"

Isabel crooks an eyebrow. "Yes, of course you. Why not you? You are a history major. This is history. My history. And only a handful of people know it."

"You . . . never told anyone who you are?"

She lifts the corners of her mouth in a half grin. "I told a few. Gwen knows. And Beryl."

"Gwen?"

"My daughter. Mine and Mac's. We only had the one."

I hear children outside the door on the staircase. Isabel hears them, too, and turns to the sound of innocence.

"Did you ever tell your husband?" I ask.

She faces me again. "Eventually. Took me twenty years but I finally told him."

"When you came back to England?" I had done my research. I knew the artist Isabel MacFarland had returned to England for a visit in 1958 with her daughter and stayed. Her husband joined her several months later.

"Yes," she says, drawing out the word and giving it an emphasis I don't understand. "When I came back to England."

Isabel reaches for the cloth-bound bundle that she came into the room with a couple hours earlier.

"Mac and I started out very happy," she says as she unties the ribbon on the bundle. "At least as happy as two people who have survived the horrors of war can be. We bought a little house in Saint Paul, Minnesota, and lived near his parents for the first few years. They were very sweet to me and utterly devoted to Gwen. They were far better at being grandparents than I was at being a mother. I worried all the time about her safety. I was sure that I would lose her like I lost Julia.

"Mac wanted to make it in broadcasting but for whatever reason, he didn't. He started writing children's books instead. Mysteries with a teenaged, aspiring journalist and his artsy next-door neighbor as the hero and heroine. Joey and Izzy."

"You and Mac?" I say, proud of myself for figuring this out.

"Naturally." She unfolds the fabric. Inside the bundle

are a yellowed envelope and a leather-bound notebook, tawny with age. "The books did well enough for us to live off that income alone," she continues. "I had my little studio, and I started painting the Umbrella Girls. At first they were just for me. I found that remembering Julia in this secret way assuaged the guilt I still felt. I missed this house, and I missed Charlotte and Rose, but I could not bring myself to visit them, not even when Mac's books did well enough that I could have. And then, one day in April 1958, I got a letter."

Isabel hands me the envelope. There is no name on the outside. Opening it carefully, I withdraw three sheets of lavender-hued paper. I read it aloud:

October 12, 1957

My dear Emmy,

If you are reading this letter, then you will know that I have passed on from this life and that I've left you Thistle House in my will. I have always known I would leave it to you, from the moment you returned to me seventeen years ago, after having lost so much. I knew that very day that you and I were bound together as surely and as irrevocably as those who share the same name, the same blood. You are as much my daughter as any child that could have been born from my body.

It does not matter to me that after you left England to begin your new life you felt it necessary to keep me at a distance, not just physically but within our souls. I know how precarious it can be to live the reinvented life. Your birthday cards and Christmas gifts to me over the years, while they may have seemed small and insignificant to you, have meant the world to me, especially after the passing of Rose. I wrote to you only as often as you wrote to me because I wished nothing to upset the careful balance you had struck with what was, what is, and what might be.

It is my hope and prayer that you consider Thistle House as your rightful inheritance. I wish I were able to maintain it as beautifully as it was when you last knew it. Underneath the peeling paint and chipped plaster and wild vines, the cottage is still a grand old friend who longs to welcome you back.

I have left Thistle House to Isabel Crofton MacFarland because that is the name you go by and I wish to make it as seamless as possible for you to take possession of it. But should you encounter any difficulty, my attorney has a sealed letter from me verifying your true identity that need only be opened if anyone doubts your claim to my property.

Please come as soon as you can to claim Thistle House, Emmy. I do not know how many months or even years will have transpired between my writing this and your reading it. The doctor says my heart is giving out and I find that I agree. It is my earnest desire to give the heart of my home to you, dear Emmeline.

And there is another reason I am hoping you will come back to see Thistle House. I shall not trouble you with the details of this reason if your wish is to sell the cottage unseen and be divested of your last tie to the person you were when first I met you. If you come, as I truly hope you will, then you will be able to do what you wish with the letter that is waiting for you in the top drawer of my bedside table.

I have prayed every day since you left twelve years ago that you would find the courage to forgive yourself for what seem to you to be unforgivable actions. There was a time, decades ago, when I felt as you do, and was granted the same courage because my dear husband prayed the same for me.

Rose's accident was my fault, Emmy. At least that is how I saw it. I was angry with her the day she went swimming alone. She liked the same boy I liked, and she knew I liked him. Rose was pretty and graceful and could have had the affection of any boy in our neighborhood. She chose Martin because I liked him. It was petty sibling rivalry, nothing more, but I let it get the best of me, in every sense of the word.

She asked me to come swimming with her the day of her accident. Begged me to. It was a sweltering-hot day and there was a lake near this summer place that we went to for holiday every August. I said no, just because I was mad at her. I was fourteen; she, thirteen. Since I was the older, my parents had always looked to me to watch out for her, a charge I had begun to detest. Rose was clearly the more confident, the more engaging, the more capable. And we were not little children anymore.

Our parents, schoolteachers on term break, had gone to the city that afternoon to pick up the post, get some groceries, pay bills. They had left me in charge. Rose and I weren't supposed to swim at the lake alone; that had been the rule since we were young. But she went anyway and told me if she drowned, it would be all my fault.

She didn't drown when she hit her head diving into the lake, but to nearly drown can be just as life changing. And for her, of course, it was. If the two boys who had been fishing had not walked by at just that moment, she would have died. As it was, she lived, but her brain had been deprived of oxygen for too long. She was different when she finally came home to us. And so was I.

And while I knew she should not have gone swimming alone, and that what she did was not my fault, I had wanted something bad to happen to her, Emmy. It was this fleeting but ferocious desire for harm to come to her that haunted me for years afterward. She did not remember begging me to come with her. I could not forget that she did.

In my more desperate times I let myself believe God kept me from having children to punish me for what I did to Rose. But in the end I came to see that we all make choices, Emmy. I made mine; Rose made hers. Our parents decided to leave us alone that day. Those boys decided to go fishing. I am not such a significant creature in God's universe that it is my decisions alone that can change the destiny of another.

We make our choices—you and I—in a world that isn't perfect. And while I wish I had made different choices, as I know you do, which one of us can say that if we had, nothing bad would have ever happened to the people we loved?

You are not to blame for what happened to Julia, any more that I am to blame for what happened to Rose. I have wanted to tell you this for many years, but I did not want you to think that I see my loss as comparable to yours. I know yours is the greater.

It has been a joy to know you and to love you, Emmeline. I am thankful every day that God brought you and Julia into my life.

I leave to you the only treasure I have in hope that it will bring you peace.

Yours always,
Charlotte

I look up from the letter. Isabel is staring out the window again, her eyes shimmering with unshed tears.

When she speaks, her voice is hushed. "Mac was sitting next to me at the kitchen table as I was reading that letter because it had not occurred to me when I opened it that I would need to hide it from him. He kept saying, 'Isabel, what is it? What's wrong?' I knew I could no longer keep the truth from him. I told him everything. It was a very complicated day after that. He was not happy with me. I had not trusted him with the truth about who I was and that hurt him to his core. We barely spoke to each other for the next few days. Weeks, really. Gwen could see that we'd had an argument and asked me repeatedly what it was about. I finally told her that a distant aunt had left me a one-hundred-year-old cottage in England and that we were at odds about what to do with it."

She pauses for a moment and then continues.

"By May, things were no better between Mac and me. We both decided it might be best if I came to Thistle House for the summer, assessed the future of both it and our marriage. Mac had a manuscript due, so it made sense to our friends and family that I would take Gwen for a three-month stay in England to check out an inheritance and that Mac would stay and work on his book. So that was what we did. Gwen and I arrived in June of that year."

"But . . . you stayed," I say, when she pauses. "Your husband joined you, right?"

"Yes. We stayed."

"Did you stay because of that other letter that Charlotte mentioned? The one in her bedside table?"

Isabel tips her head. "Oh, I suppose that had something to do with it. But it's not the primary reason we decided to stay."

I wait.

"You recall that I told you that once you play your hand, you can't live as though you still hold all the cards?"

"Yes," I said.

And she hands me the leather-bound notebook in her lap.

Part Three

Thirty-four

JULIA

June 8, 1958

Dear Emmy,

It's been so long since I've imagined you being alive that I don't really know where to begin.

My therapist, Dr. Diamant, said that I should pretend that I am writing you a letter. Think of you as alive and just start writing. It doesn't matter how I start, she said; it only matters that I do. She feels that writing to you like this will allow me to move on with my life, put you to rest, so to speak, so that I will not be haunted by your memory anymore. Actually, Dr. Diamant says you do not haunt me, Emmy. I haunt myself with everything that is left undone between us. This journal will allow me to say what I need to, she says. It will allow me to move on.

I think that's a very strange way of putting it. To move on. As if I were frozen in one place and therefore I must do something drastic to start moving again. When are we ever able to stop moving? You and I know better than anyone that the earth continues to turn, no matter what happens to you, and it takes you with it whether you want to go or not. You keep breathing, your heart keeps beating, the sun keeps traveling the sky, and the world just keeps spinning. When one day ends, you crawl into bed, and when you wake up, another day is there waiting for you. You really have no choice. If I truly had the power to stop things from moving, I would have exercised it a long time ago.

Dr. Diamant is not my first doctor, but she is my favorite. Simon likes her, too, and that's good. I think you'd like Simon. He's smart and kind and reminds me of Neville, except that he's dependable and honest and alive. He has curly brown hair, eyes like chocolate, and he looks like he's in a perpetual state of surprise. I think that's the feature I like best about him. He seems always on the verge of discovering something amazing. He's the one who found Dr. Diamant, actually. There was a long stretch of time when I didn't have a therapist. I guess I thought I had outgrown the need for one. When I finally decided I was ready to move back to London a few years ago, I figured that was proof enough I was done with needing one. It had been eighteen years, after all. Good Lord, you'd think I would have a handle on it, wouldn't you? But then I met Simon and fell in love with him, and the very prospect of being deliriously happy for the first time in my life just about drove me crazy. I nearly quit my job and moved back home to Granny's. But Simon, God love him, convinced me to stay. He found Dr. Diamant for me. Simon knows everything that happened to me. Well, pretty much everything. I don't think anyone knows everything. But Simon loves me despite my being a wreck and he says he will wait for me to be able to say that I'll marry him. Quite the fellow, right?

That's pretty much why he wanted to find someone like Dr. Diamant. He has also had a couple of appointments with Dr. Diamant himself, just so he can know what to say to me—and I guess what not to.

Dr. Diamant is probably forty, maybe older, smokes these skinny brown cigarettes, and wears wild prints that make me think of Morocco or Zanzibar. She's not like any of the psychiatrists I had when I was little. The first one was a dreadful pug-faced troll named Dr. Nielsen. He was supposed to have been this brilliant doctor who knew exactly how to cure a child chained to fear and anxiety. There were times when I wanted to throw that man off a bridge, Emmy. All he ever wanted to do was talk about *that* day, the last day I saw you, over and over and over. That was the *last* thing I wanted to talk about with him. I didn't want to talk about it with anyone. That was why I stopped talking, for heaven's sake. You know, I look back on it now and I think, what in the world was he doing, wanting me to relive that day in his office every time I was dragged in to see him. How did he think I got to be the way I was? It was from having to live that day the first time.

Granny eventually decided Dr. Nielsen wasn't helping me. She said it was because he was American and what did we expect? She didn't say this to me. She said it to her fellow British expats when she assumed that because I wasn't talking, I wasn't listening.

The next doctor was just okay. The third one, Dr. Hunt, I liked very much, but he got married and moved away after only two years. I saw him from my tenth birthday to just before my twelfth. He had been able to get me to utter a few sentences the last few months we were together, and he told me before he left for Texas that I honestly didn't have to worry about talking or not talking. It wasn't a big deal. When I was ready to resume communicating verbally, I would know it. He had never met a person like me, who didn't start talking again when she was ready. There wasn't a magic formula for it. When I was ready, I would just start talking again.

I'll never forget how I felt when he said he had met others like me. I even managed to ask him about it.

Yes, he said. There are many, many people like me. In fact, everyone is like me. We're all susceptible to loss and the effects of trauma. There isn't a one of us who could experience what I did and not struggle to find some way of coping with it.

I was so glad to hear that. I hated feeling like I was different. Weird. That's what kids call you when you don't talk, Emmy. They didn't call me weird to my face. But I knew what they whispered about me.

That's the English girl who doesn't talk. Except when she counts things.

How come she doesn't talk?

The Nazis killed her family and she's not even Jewish.

How'd she get away?

No one knows. No one will ever know.

Why does she count things?

Because she's cuckoo.

There were a lot of times I wanted to tell stupid kids like that the Nazis did *not* kill my family, but if I had, they might have asked, *Well then, who did?* I didn't have an answer for that.

After Dr. Hunt, I didn't want to see another doctor and I wasn't made to right away. The war ended just a few months later anyway and Granny wanted to go back to England.

I didn't want to come back initially.

In fact, the first time I had yelled anything in five years was when I told Granny I didn't want to go back to England. She was happy to have me yelling, but after she got over her joy, we had our first argument.

But it's where your home is, Julia, she said.

I don't have a home, I yelled.

Your home is with me.

I don't have a home!

Your home, Julia, is with me. I'm your family. Me and Gramps.

In the end, we went back. Of course we went back. We're not Americans. Granny and Gramps have a nice house in Woodstock near Oxford where Gramps, whom I had seen only twice in five years, taught literature. He had missed us. He wanted us to come home.

As we packed our things to leave Connecticut, I flat-out refused to go anywhere near London.

Granny said there would be no reason to. It was a wreck, anyway.

Ever, I said.

And she said if I never wanted to see London again, I didn't have to.

We sailed on a ship as big as a city, or so it seemed to me. And when we docked in Southampton, Gramps was there to meet us with his car.

He asked me how the crossing was. I told him it was fine compared to our departure when U-boats were trying to bomb us. He started to tear up when I said this and I worried that Granny hadn't told him how scary our first crossing had been. That wasn't it. He knew how terrible it was. He just had never heard my voice before.

I actually didn't like the way my voice sounded when I started to talk again. I had been going to school with American kids and hearing them talk, and even though I hadn't been doing much talking myself, their funny way of speaking had slithered into my head and mixed itself in with the way I talked five years before. What came out of my mouth when I started communicating verbally again was a weird half-British, half-American mush that made me sound like a psycho.

It does not make you sound like a psycho, Granny had said. *Where did you hear that word?*

I sound strange.

You just sound like all the other British children who were evacuated to America, Julia. That's what happens when you're immersed in another culture.

You don't sound like them, I said.

That's because I am fifty years older than you. You are young. It will come back, Julia. The way you talked before will come back.

And I guess it did. Mostly.

Granny was so happy to be back in England in her pretty house and with Gramps and all the friends she left behind when she evacuated with me to Connecticut.

And I guess I liked the house, too. You would like it, Em. There's a big garden in the back and rows and rows of raspberry bushes. I had my own room, the one that had been my father's. Granny still had a few of his toys in there and loads of pictures of him from when he was a baby and a schoolboy and when he started to do plays.

It made Granny sad to talk about Neville but she did it anyway. I think she has always been afraid that I would forget him because I was so young when he left Mum. But there are things you don't forget even if you are young.

She doesn't know I only ever called him Neville. Even all these years later, she doesn't know. She thinks I called him Daddy.

Do you know why I called him Neville?

Because you did.

I was afraid if I started calling him Daddy, then you would call him Daddy. And I didn't want to share him with you, Emmy.

I would now, of course. I would share anything I have with you.

Julia

June 11, 1958

Dear Emmy,

Today Simon and I tried to find the street where you and I and Mum lived in Whitechapel. It all looks so different now. I couldn't find it. I can't remember what the actual street was named and nothing looks familiar. Nothing at all. I know we lived close to Saint Paul's and that we were also near a Tube station. But even though we walked down street after street, I couldn't find it.

Part of me was relieved because I'm not completely sure I'm ready to see our flat again. And part of me was annoyed because what if seeing it would've brought me one step closer to being at peace with everything? You know?

Simon had done some checking and he knew the area east of Saint Paul's had been heavily bombed, not just the day I last saw you, but many other times after that. He said it might be that I couldn't find our flat because it had been destroyed and something new had been built in its place. There are so many new buildings in the East End. It's as if everything that made it ours is gone, Emmy. Saint Paul's is there, of course, but nothing else that I can remember.

When that search proved useless, we went looking for Mum's grave. She was buried in a plot of earth with a hundred other paupers on September 12, 1940. They didn't know what date to put for her date of birth, Emmy. It just says her name and the date she died. The day after you and I came back to London.

Do you know she's dead, Emmy? If I were to see you again, this would be hard for me to say, to tell you she's dead. She was in the basement of a hotel on that night. A bomb obliterated the building and sent it in pieces hurtling onto the basement, crushing the twenty or so other people who were sheltered there when the air raids started. I don't know why she was there. The tiny headstone doesn't say that. Granny said maybe she had been outside on the sidewalk and ran into the shelter when the sirens began to wail.

Granny didn't tell me right away that Mum had been killed because she was afraid I would disappear into myself and never emerge again. Neither did she tell me that Neville had died before Mum did, even before you and I were evacuated. It's true.

He was gone before we left London for Aunt Charlotte's. Mum didn't tell me, though. And Mum didn't tell me I had grandparents, either, which I still don't understand. Granny had offered to take us, Emmy. Before we went to Charlotte's. She wrote to Mum after Neville died and told her she would take us away from the war. We could have come together to America, you and I. Well, she didn't exactly offer to take you in that letter she wrote because she didn't know about you. But a long time later, she told me if she had known I had an older sister, she would have offered to take us both to America.

But Mum didn't tell me Granny had written to her. I was at Aunt Charlotte's, thinking Neville was still in India when he was already dead. And we spent all those weeks away and I never knew I had grandparents who wanted to see me.

When I asked Granny why Mum did that, she said I shouldn't ponder things I could only guess about. She said maybe Mum needed time to get used to the idea that I even had grandparents and that Neville was dead, and that before she got used to either one, the Germans started bombing London.

Why didn't Neville tell me I had grandparents?

Granny said she had to do the same thing as me: not ponder too hard things she could only guess about. She told me my grandfather and Neville didn't see eye to eye on anything. Gramps wanted Neville to go to Oxford and get a proper education, settle down, and have a respectable career. Neville didn't want any of that. He wanted to be in theater. So maybe he didn't tell them he had a daughter because he knew he hadn't become a father in the proper way, and he figured that would matter to Gramps.

I think Neville might have also wanted to keep me from his parents because he was afraid if I was around them, I would grow to be *like* them—unimpressed with who he was. I didn't come to this conclusion until I was much older. Because even though Granny told me not to ponder it, I did.

I pondered a lot of things.

You're probably wondering how I came to be with Granny.

First, you need to know that Neville was in a horrific car accident in Dublin. That's where he was, Emmy. Not India. He was living with a woman who owned a little theater. He was starting to direct plays and skits, and he was out one night after a performance that he had starred in and directed. He'd had too much to drink and he crashed the car he was driving into another car. The crash didn't kill him, but he was so badly hurt and he barely had any money for the hospital. No surprise there, right? The woman he was living with was afraid he would die if he didn't get the medical care he needed, so she looked up his parents and rang them. Gramps and Granny came out to see if they could transfer him to a hospital in Oxford. But his injuries were too severe. Right before he died, Neville told his parents about me. Told them where I lived and what Mum's name was. Granny said it was as if he knew he was dying and he wanted to give them something precious and beautiful in place of all the heartache.

And that's just what he did, Granny said.

She told me all of this before I was talking again, probably sometime in the second year we were in Connecticut. I remember I had already had my eighth birthday. I still didn't know about Mum. And I didn't know where you were. I've never known where you were.

It hurt to hear Neville had died long before, and worse still to be told a few weeks later that Mum was also dead, and had been dead for months and months. Both times I felt myself folding in like I was spinning a cocoon.

Granny knew what happened to Mum because Gramps discovered it and told her. Granny never really had Mum's permission to take me to America, but it wasn't like she could wait around to get it with the Germans bombing London every five minutes and Mum nowhere in sight. But I guess Gramps had

316 | SUSAN MEISSNER

been insisting all along that they *had* to find out where Mum had disappeared to. Gramps didn't feel right about Granny whisking me off without Mum's permission, even though I was now far from the war. Granny finally gave in and told him to see what he could find, though I know now that she was terribly afraid Mum was in turn looking for me and would want me back. Gramps hired someone to look for Mum and that person found out Mum had died in the bombings. Her name was on a list.

When Granny finally told me Mum was in heaven, I said three words. The first in who knows how long.

What about Emmy?

And Granny said, *Who is Emmy?*

My sister, I said.

A sister? Was she Neville's daughter, too? Granny asked, and she looked like she was about to have a heart attack thinking Neville had two little girls in London and she had rescued only one of them.

I shook my head.

From another daddy? Granny asked.

And I nodded.

I don't know where she is, Granny said. *But I can try to find her. Would you like me to?*

I was done with words for another few years. I just nodded my head.

But Granny never did find you. Sometimes I wonder how hard she looked. And I know it wasn't easy during the war to find out where someone was.

And then sometimes I wonder if she did find out and she just couldn't tell me.

Even now, when I could ask her, should ask her, I can't.

I have done my own searching. I've looked in every telephone directory I can find for an Emmeline Downtree. In my braver moments I've checked cemeteries and fatality reports from the war. I've even checked every bridal magazine, every design house, every wedding dress shop in London, and it's because I can't find you in that little universe that I fear you must be dead.

If I could have one wish, it would be that I hadn't switched out the brides box with my fairy tale book that night we left Aunt Charlotte's.

I would, Emmy. Even if it meant it was the only wish I could have.

I've looked for your brides everywhere. Every time I see a woman in a wedding dress, I look to see if she is wearing one of your gowns.

But how could she?

You don't have any of your designs.

I took them from you.

I'm so desperately sorry, Emmy.

If I could remember Aunt Charlotte's last name or the house where she lived or the town where the house was, I would see if the brides box was still there and I would spend the rest of my life looking for you so that I could give it back to you. But I can't remember where that house was or Charlotte's last name. When I tried to find out, I learned that the building where the East End evacuations records were kept was destroyed by a V-I flying bomb in 1944.

I can't make it right.

I wish I could take back what I did. I wish it all the time.

This is not helping me.

This is not helping.

Julia

Thirty-five

June 12, 1958

Dear Emmy,

I told Dr. Diamant today that the journal idea is not working. She wanted to know why. I told her that I didn't feel better after writing to you. I actually felt worse. She said sometimes on the road to healing, you must reopen an old wound. It will hurt again, maybe as much as or more than it did when it was first inflicted, but as you reconnect with and embrace the healing process, it will begin to hurt less. Sometimes a broken bone does not heal properly and there is unrelenting pain because bones that aren't supposed to touch are rubbing up against each other. The only way to fix it is to break the bone again and reset it. That's the only way it can heal properly. You have to break the bone again.

That was her way of explaining that as I write to you, I might feel worse before I feel better.

I suppose that makes sense.

But I didn't know what else to say to you. Dr. Diamant asked if I would feel okay if she read what I had written so far. I let her read it.

Dr. Diamant said she was very proud of me for being so honest with you and that I should keep going. *Keep going how?* I said.

She suggested that I start at the beginning where you and I left off because if I were to see you again, that's what I would want to hear from you. I'd want to know what happened to you after we were parted.

I admit I'm afraid to go back to that day, Emmy. I've placed it so far in the back of my mind. I worry that by dragging it up from that dark place where it's been sleeping, I will relive it. And if I relive it, then I will again become that silent girl who can't sleep at night. Dr. Diamant told me that little girl has grown up. I can speak to that seven-year-old inside me and tell her she survived this. I don't need to be afraid of looking back to the place where she was because that place is just a memory, and memories have no power but what I allow them.

I will try very hard to keep that in mind as I write.

Simon is sitting here next to me. He doesn't know everything about what happened the day my life changed, but he knows how hard this is for me. I told him I would let him read this journal when I am done so that he will know what he's dealing with. That seems only fair. In the meantime, we are sitting side by side at my kitchen table with only a teapot between us. He is reading while I write these words to you. And every so often he gently rubs my back and refills my teacup.

So here we go. Back to the beginning.

I awoke to the sound of sirens.

At first I thought you had not left the flat because it seemed you had only just been at my side a second earlier, fluffing the sofa pillows and telling me to stay where I was and that Mum would be home soon.

I called for you as the sirens wailed but you did not answer. I heard popping sounds, the far-off echoes of the antiaircraft guns, and thundering booms that seemed to come from up underneath the earth. You did not tell me what to do if the sirens went off. So I stayed on the sofa and covered my ears with the throw pillows. I screamed for you—and for Mum—even though I knew I was alone.

Then I heard the whistles of the bombs, some far away and some near, and I began to hear the explosions as they landed, despite the pillows over my ears. I felt them in my chest, in the very depths of me. This wasn't a drill. This was real. The Germans were bombing London.

Instinctively I knew I should run for cover but you told me to stay in the flat. Mum was coming. I scrambled to the corner with the sofa pillows and crouched there. I remember crying and how my wails sounded like the sirens outside.

But then a bright flash and a thunderous whack shook the flat. The front window shattered. Confetti-like glass blew into the room and fell on my hair and in my lap. Everywhere.

I screamed for you.

I screamed for Mum.

I tossed the pillows and sprang for the front door. When I opened it, I could see that the row of flats across the street was wrapped in a fog of powdered debris. A gaping hole stretched across where front doors and upper floors had been. The air was thick with smoke and fire and the buzzing of giant insects, which were the planes that I could not see. It was as if I had been transported to hell.

All I could do was stand there and scream for you.

Then there were arms around me. I heard a voice say my name. At first I thought it was an angel, come to pluck me out of hell. And then I thought it was you, Emmy, waking me from a nightmare. I fell into those arms and I felt myself being lifted.

I opened my eyes to tell you I was afraid and I saw that I was not dreaming. You were not holding me there on the sofa while I pulled myself out of a tormented sleep. I was in Thea's arms.

Where's your mum? Where's Emmy? she shouted as she carried me toward her house.

I could not answer her.

A boom split the air as another bomb fell not far away. Thea stumbled and then caught her balance against the door frame. She dashed with me through her front room and I remember all of her furniture was covered in white sheets. Then we were on her back step and I saw what Thea had been up to when the sirens went off. Her two cats and the four kittens, much larger now than they had been when we left for the countryside, were laid out on her back steps. They were lying so strangely still in the midst of all that chaos. I knew they were dead. She had gassed them with ether, Emmy. So that they wouldn't starve on the streets as she and her mother evacuated to a relative's home in Wales. I didn't know that many London pet owners euthanized beloved pets that they couldn't take with them when they fled the city. Thea and her mother were leaving London the next day. Her mother was already at a hotel near Paddington station. Thea had come back to the flat to take care of the cats so that her mother wouldn't have to see. She had just finished her dreadful chore when the sirens began to scream and so did I.

I learned all of this from Granny much later. All I knew then as Thea ran with me to her Andy was that the kittens I had loved and played with and called special names were dead.

It was dark and clammy inside the shelter. Every time a bomb shook the earth, the Andy's walls rumbled. Thea held me in her arms on a cot on the floor, rocking me back and forth while she sang Christmas carols. I don't know why she did that. Granny said later it was because she didn't have to concentrate on the words; they were just right there. Or maybe it was because Christmas carols made us think of presents, Father Christmas, peppermint, and Baby Jesus. Things that make us feel safe and loved and happy.

I don't know how long the raid lasted. I just remember there being a moment when the bombs stopped and the booms outside were replaced with the wail of emergency-response vehicles. When we crawled out of the shelter, we saw that the world around us had become colorless except for the orange hue of hundreds of fires. Ash and dust swirled.

Thea steered me past the cats. Their lifeless bodies were peppered with bits of roofing tile.

She led me back to our flat, calling Mum's name: *Annie*.

Julia, did your mum bring you back here from Gloucestershire? she asked as we stood in the living room.

I shook my head no.

How did you get back, sweetie? Did Emmy come with you?

I had no voice to tell her.

What are your foster parents' names? Do you know where they live?

I thought of the idyllic world we had left just hours before, where everything was perfect except that Mum wasn't there. I wanted to go back. I wanted to go back in time to that happy place before you left me. Before the bombs came. Before the dead cats.

Charlotte, I said. It was the only word I said for a long time.

Charlotte? Thea said. *What's her last name?*

I couldn't remember.

Sweetheart, where does Charlotte live?

I couldn't remember where she lived, Emmy. I still can't.

Thea took me by the hand into the kitchen.

Did you and Emmy write to your mum? she asked.

I might have nodded as Thea looked through Mum's recent mail for a letter from us.

Does your mum keep important papers in a special place? Do you know where she'd put your billeting card?

I said nothing. A blanket of numbness was replacing the fear.

We went upstairs, crunching on glass that had been blown onto the steps. Thea went into Mum's bedroom and opened her top bureau drawer. She looked inside and pulled out an envelope. Granny told me much later that Thea had thought she'd found a letter from us because she didn't recognize the return address.

But it wasn't a letter from you and me.

It was the letter Granny had written to Mum after Neville died. Thea read it while I leaned against her leg.

That was how I came to be with Gramps and Granny, Emmy.

Thea couldn't find our billeting papers that had Charlotte's name and address.

She didn't know where Mum was. She didn't know where you were.

And she was leaving for Wales the next day.

Thea took the letter and we left our demolished neighborhood. We had to walk a little bit before she was able to hail a taxi that could take us to her hotel.

The air raid sirens started again as we were getting out of the taxi cab. I think we spent the night in the hotel basement. That part is a bit foggy.

In the morning, Thea called Gramps and Granny. They talked for a little while, Thea in hushed tones. Then she called the widow Mum worked for, and I heard her ask if she could please try to get word to Mum that I would be at my grandparents' house. The next thing I remember, I was on a train with

Thea and her mother. They took me to the Oxford railway station on their way to Wales, and Gramps and Granny met us there.

I recall Thea telling Granny that Mum worked for a widow named Mrs. Billingsley whom Thea had called that morning. The widow's butler would try to locate Mum and let her know where I was.

When Thea knelt to say good-bye, I flung my arms around her neck and held tight.

Your grandparents will take good care of you, she said. *They are your family, Julia. They will help you find your mum.*

I tightened my grip around Thea's neck.

She had to pry me loose.

I crumpled to the pavement as Thea, crying into her handkerchief, walked away. Gramps lifted me into his arms.

I really don't remember anything else of that day, just Thea—the last link I had to the life I knew—growing smaller and smaller in my field of vision until she was gone.

My hand hurts, Emmy.

Everything hurts.

I must stop for now.

Thirty-six

June 18, 1958

Dear Emmy,

I had to take a few days off from the journal. Spilling everything about the bombing like that sort of took the breath right out of my lungs. I've been in a bit of a mental wasteland for the last few days— trouble concentrating at work, not sleeping well, things like that. Dr. Diamant told me this might happen and not to worry. It's perfectly normal to need some time to sort out these memories that I'm dredging up. That hasn't stopped Simon from worrying, unfortunately. He called Dr. Diamant and said that maybe this wasn't such a good idea after all. I don't know what Dr. Diamant told him but Simon said all right. All right. All right. Three times. Somehow she convinced him this was still a good idea. And so I am back.

It's two a.m.

I can't sleep, so I may as well write to you.

It's hard to fully recall those first few days with Gramps and Granny. It's almost as if there are rooms in my mind where all these memories are kept and some of those rooms have no doors. I know the memories are there but I've no way of getting to them. When Granny called Mrs. Billingsley on Monday, two days after the bombing, she was told Mum hadn't shown up for work that day. Mrs. Billingsley had sent her butler to our flat to make sure Mum was all right, but he'd found our street bombed and our flat empty. All of the flats on our side were empty. He found no one to even ask if they'd seen her. The butler had taken it upon himself to check with the hospital, but there was no record of an Annie Downtree having been admitted.

Gramps and Granny were worried about me because I wouldn't speak; the only time they heard my voice was when I screamed in my sleep. Granny told Gramps she wanted to take me to America to get me away from the war. Other family members of Oxford instructors had been evacuated to Connecticut under a private scheme, to the homes of Yale professors and staff members. Granny begged Gramps to see if she and I could go, even though everyone else had already left many weeks before. Gramps didn't like the idea because of the U-boats patrolling the Atlantic. One ship full of evacuees, mostly children, had already been torpedoed.

But Granny insisted. She had to get me away from the war or she'd lose me like she lost Neville, just in a different way. I heard her say this.

We were at the docks at Liverpool just two days later, boarding a ship that would take me away from England for nearly five years. I don't think Granny had any idea that's how long we would be away. I don't think anyone knew the war would last that long. On the passenger manifest I was listed as Julia Waverly. Granny said my father would want me to have his last name since he had been taken from me so early in my life. I didn't want a new last name but I was unable to argue that point. By the time I was able to speak my mind, I had been a Waverly for almost as long as I had been a Downtree and it didn't seem to matter as much. Being a Downtree would not bring you back. I have been Julia Waverly ever since.

What I remember of the crossing is the swaying of the ship like a cradle being rocked, but I also remember there being alarms, and donning our life vests as U-boats were in the area and at any moment they might close in on us and blow our ship to bits. I remember Granny having to cram my arms through the vest as I fought and kicked. I also remember her pacing the floor by my cot in our stateroom. I can still see her shoes going back and forth; just her shoes, because I am under the cot. I remember dreaming that it's not dead cats I see on Thea's back steps; it is you and Mum and Neville.

The first few weeks after we arrived are a blur. Less than a blur. Those memories are in one of the rooms with no door. I think it's odd that I can remember the smell of acrid smoke, the feel of broken glass under my shoes, and the open-eyed stares of those cats, but I can't remember the first weeks of my life in tranquil America.

There was no war there, no sandbags or barrage balloons or running for cover. We lived on the third floor of a brick colonial situated on a peaceful tree-lined street with a Yale professor of history, Dr. Bower, and his wife, Florence. Their twin sons, Charlie and Randall, were in the United States Army Air Corps, training to be pilots. Granny had the bigger of the two rooms, furnished with a lovely canopied bed, but she often slept in the armchair in my room. At least for a while she did.

My room reminded me of the room you and I shared at Aunt Charlotte's. It was nestled in the corner with a slanted roof that I could touch where it met the wall. After I had settled in, I would lie in my bed, close my eyes, and imagine that I was back at Aunt Charlotte's and you were just a few feet away. This was how I fell asleep every night for many, many nights—imagining you were in a bed next to me and that we were safe at Charlotte's, the brides box on the nightstand between us along with my book of fairy tales.

While the rest of that September and then October and November are lost to me, I do remember my first Christmas in America. Snow covered the ground, lights shone in every window, and there were presents under a lovely tree. Florence made gingerbread men and decorated them with frosting faces and buttons. We drank hot chocolate while Professor Bower read from the Bible by a snapping, happy fire. The professor and his wife didn't listen to the radio, as least not when I was in the vicinity, so there were no reports of doom telling us how terrible it was in Europe. School had been let out—I don't recall much of my first months of school, I'm afraid—and Granny bought me a plaid wool coat and a matching tam with a pom-pom on top so that we could go for twilight walks under violet skies. I remember feeling a sense of tranquility for the first time in weeks and weeks. But when I heard carolers outside my window, I was back under my bed again while Granny paced the floor of that pretty little room, begging me to come out.

She didn't find out for a long while why I couldn't handle hearing Christmas carols. In some ways I still can't. When I hear them now at Christmastime, I want to think only happy thoughts. But a niggling tug won't let me forget Thea singing carols in her bomb shelter as she held me tight and hell fell down all around us.

There was a terrible night of bombing in London that same Christmas. Worse than the day you were taken from me, but I didn't hear about it until later. Newspapers never made it home to the Bower house. The professor read them at the college and left them there.

I think I started to see that first troll of a doctor right after Christmas. I had begun to say a few words here and there. Mostly "no" and "I don't want to." Florence had a cute little spaniel named Pixie that I liked to play with and I would talk to her. But never more than a few sentences, and I always stopped when the adults froze like statues to listen to me. I knew if I started talking in full sentences to them, they'd start asking me questions.

So to Dr. Nielsen I went. I suppose he tried all the tricks he knew with me. But I didn't trust him, Emmy. I didn't believe that by telling him anything he could reverse time, and you and I could go back to that day at Aunt Charlotte's when I found those notes you wrote. If I could have lived that moment over again, I would have told Charlotte what you were planning to do. I would have run down the stairs and shown her those notes. And yes, you would have been hopping mad at me. Maybe for quite a while. But then you would have softened as you always did. You would have forgiven me for tattling on you. And then you and I would have spent those five years of the war together at Aunt Charlotte's. You would have continued to draw your lovely dresses. We would have celebrated our birthdays and Christmases without me under the bed. Mum would have come to visit us now and then. And when the war was over, we would have gone back to London. We'd be together and I would not have needed to count things to keep from going mad. You would have gotten your job back at that bridal shop you loved. (I've looked for that shop, too, but have not been able to find it.) And you would have made your wedding gowns and they'd be in the window just like all those other dresses had been, except yours would be more beautiful and I would have said, *I told you so.*

Could Dr. Nielsen have made that happen?

No, he could not.

He wanted me to talk about the horrible things that had taken place and which he could not change. What was the point of that?

I suppose Granny kept dragging me to him because he kept saying it might take time. By the end of May, she figured out he wasn't going to be the one to help me. School was about to be dismissed and she wanted me to enjoy a happy summer, even if it meant a silent one.

I was actually sad to see the school term end. Even though my teacher could barely get a word out of me, I did well in school. Learning was my place of escape. Not school itself, but the activity of learning. It gave my brain something to do that was unrelated to the war and my losses. When Dr. Troll suggested perhaps Granny needed to consider institutionalizing me, she showed him my report card and said—so she told me—that what I needed was a break from doctors like him.

We spent the summer at a cabin the Bowers owned somewhere on a lake. I don't remember what the lake was called. It was very beautiful there, Emmy. There was a girl in the cabin next to ours named Frannie who was a year younger than I was, and in Granny's words, a relentless chatterbox. Frannie probably loved that I said practically nothing when we played together, because that allowed her to fill every silent moment with her ceaseless prattle. I felt very much at ease with Frannie. She did all the talking and never hungered for me to say anything in return. Some days I very nearly forgot why I was there.

Amazingly enough, whole days passed when I didn't think of you and ache for a time machine.

Every summer we'd go back to the cabin on the lake and every year Frannie would be waiting for me.

The last time we went was the summer of 1944. I was eleven. Frannie wasn't there when we arrived. She came a few weeks into July and she was different. Quieter. More like me. One morning just after she and her parents arrived, we went out on the lake in her little rowboat. She had never asked me much about my life to that point. I figured Granny and Frannie's mother had talked and Frannie had been apprised that I was a British girl who had fled the war in Europe. But that day she asked me if I knew what the war was like.

I nodded.

Is it terrible? she asked.

Again, I nodded.

Then she told me her parents had been sent a telegram. Her brother was missing in action, somewhere in France. His plane had been shot down.

Do you think he's afraid? Frannie asked.

I thought about it for a moment and slowly nodded my head. Just because you're an adult doesn't mean you're not afraid. I'd seen fear in Granny's eyes.

Do you think he's okay?

She wanted what I wanted. To know that her brother was alive somewhere and would come back to her.

I spoke to her. Just one word.

Maybe.

She was no doubt surprised to hear my voice, but that I had offered a ray of hope was the bigger surprise.

The girl who knew what war was like was telling her not to give up hope.

Sometimes I wonder if that's what the journal is supposed to show me, Emmy. Perhaps it is so I can know if it is possible to hold on to hope and still move on.

Is that possible?

I don't know.

I am tired now.

Good night, Emmy.

Julia

Thirty-seven

❦

June 22, 1958

Dear Emmy,

Simon and I are going to the ballet this afternoon. *Swan Lake*. He has a cousin who is dancing in it. After the performance there will be a party at his aunt and uncle's house in Chelsea. I have met only his mother and father. Tonight I will meet everyone else. His brother, Dennis, and his wife, Trudie. His grandparents, both sets. Four sets of aunts and uncles and a dozen or more cousins.

I am a little nervous about it.

I never know what to say when people ask about my family. Maybe they won't ask tonight. Maybe Simon has told them everything already and I can avoid having to explain it ten times over. Except that if they all know, then I will be subject to the pathetic stares. When you're known as the young woman orphaned by the war and tragically separated from your only sister, you can't help but be rewarded with pathetic stares. No one really knows what to say to you, but they think hard to come up with something, and as they are blistering their brains to find the right words, they stare. They don't mean to, but they do.

Simon will watch over me, thank goodness. I doubt he will leave my side for a second. He's afraid I will get scared off and he'll have to go back to the beginning and woo me all over again. Did I tell you what he does for a living? He's an accountant for the company I work for. Our company makes maps and globes and atlases. I love working there. I love the idea that it's important to know there are many places other than the one where you are. I am an assistant to the art director. It's not like I am good at art, not like you. But I am good at maintaining the research files, and working with the surveyors and artists. I keep everyone in line, my boss likes to say. He told me he's never met anyone who can keep track of all the details like I can.

I think it's because during the war when I was forced to reinvent myself as Julia Waverly, I was highly aware of the details of my new life. I knew how many steps it was to the third floor of the Bowers' house. I knew how many tiles there were on the bathroom floor. I knew how many knobs were on the kitchen cabinets. And how many books Professor Bower had in his study. I had counted all these things. Counting things was how I kept hold of my new life since it was all I had that I could control.

When I would think of you and Mum and the flat and the kittens and home, I would have to start counting something to keep myself from going crazy. Sometimes Granny would hear me whispering the numbers and she'd pretend that she hadn't. One of the doctors she took me to told her it was my way of coping with what had happened and not to pester me about it. I think it worried her, though. Counting the rosebuds on the rug in the living room or slats in the blinds surely seemed pointless to her.

I no longer count to keep myself calm, but when I do have to count something, like presentation folders at work, it reminds me of how scared I was to come back to London when the war was over. Granny and I returned to England in June 1945. I was twelve but it was another four years before I saw London again.

Just as in America, school here in England wasn't hard for me, but socially I was an outcast. Those of us evacuees who spent the war years in America were treated differently from those who had spent the war years in the English countryside, mostly because of our Yank accents, but also because it was believed we had not suffered like those who'd stayed had. My teen years weren't the greatest. I am ashamed to tell you there were times when I wondered how much rope I would need and if it would hurt very much. . . .

I didn't see a psychologist for the first couple of years we were back, but Granny sensed I was having a rough go of it. So she found one for me. Dr. Bristol was thirty-something and handsome. I remember looking forward to Tuesday afternoons when I would see him. He coaxed out of me a lot of what I have shared with you here. He's the one who said I needed to visit London again, even if just for a few hours, so that I wouldn't be afraid of it anymore. He even offered to come with Granny and me, which I was all for, but Granny said she could handle it.

Granny decided we'd go for tea at Harrods. Just for tea. Harrods wasn't near Whitechapel or Saint Paul's, so I wouldn't have to see anything I didn't want to see unless we started strolling east.

Did you know, Emmy, that fear can feel like heaviness? I am sure you probably do.

The whole time we were on the train, I seemed to be carrying the weight of those nine years I had been away from London. It was as if time itself were a tangible thing that one could put on a scale and then watch the needle swing right.

When we closed in on Paddington station, I looked for something in our car to count. I could find nothing, so I closed my eyes and counted seconds.

The train stopped and everyone stood up to be on their way. Granny waited until I stood before she rose as well. She silently took my hand and we got off. I counted hats on heads as we walked through the station and out to the queue of taxis waiting at the curb. Inside the cab, with Granny still holding my hand, I counted buses and bicycles and black cars as we made our way to Knightsbridge, a couple miles away.

By the time we stepped out of the cab a few minutes later, I had slowed to counting just my own breaths, slow and even. Fear is worse than pain, I think. Pain is centralized, identifiable, and wanes as you wait. Fear is a heaviness you can't wriggle out from under. You must simply find the will to stand with it and start walking. Fear does not start to fade until you take the step that you think you can't.

I got out of the cab onto the street and I stood there balancing the weight of nearly a decade of regret. Granny somehow knew just to stand still next to me after she'd paid the driver.

After a moment I knew I could walk and carry it because you would have wanted me to.

We had tea and Granny found things to talk about that had nothing to do with anything important. We were just like any other young woman and her grandmother out for an afternoon of shopping. I sat in my chair and drank from my cup as one in a near-dream state. Fear is not only a leaden foe, but a liar as well. It was not as bad as I thought it would be, sitting there in a London department store on an ordinary Saturday.

We walked to the underground to take a train back to Paddington. There was a terrible moment when we walked past a bridal shop and I was reminded of what I had stolen from you.

I'm sure you know I hid the brides box in the crawl space of our bedroom at Aunt Charlotte's. When you went to get me a drink of water, I stuck it on a ledge that is over the frame of the little door. You can only see it from the inside.

I am so sorry, Emmy.

I wish you could know how sorry I am.

Dr. Bristol was immensely proud of me when I saw him the following week and told him about the trip. He said I had crossed a bridge, a big one. And now that I had crossed it, I could take more trips to London, which Granny and I did over the next couple years. We even went to a church service at Saint Paul's so that I could stand just a stone's throw from where you and I lived and not be undone by it.

I stopped seeing Dr. Bristol just before I turned eighteen, at his advice, since he was a child psychologist and I was certainly no longer a child. I also came to realize he was married and a new father, so the attraction I'd had for him had started to diminish. He was very happy with my progress. I was talking, counting only when something truly needed to be counted, and I was able to stand on the streets of a London being rebuilt. Not only that; I would be starting college and handling my adult life just like those of my peers.

Everyone has good days and bad days, Dr. Bristol told me.

I came to learn, though, that there are days that are neither good nor bad. There is a kind of day that is something else entirely.

On those days, you are restless for something. And that fidgety feeling doesn't make your good days bad or your bad days good.

It just makes you hungry.

That was when I knew I had to move back to London to live, not just visit.

It's time to get ready for the ballet.

Love,
Julia

June 24, 1958

Dear Emmy,

The ballet was wonderful. Beautiful, actually. And I had a surprisingly nice time meeting Simon's family. No one asked me about my own family except to say things like *So Simon tells me your grandfather is a professor of literature at Oxford?* I cornered Simon and asked him what he had told everyone about me. He just said he told them I was lovely and smart and that I lost my family in the war. You can say that and it answers a thousand other questions. The war is still spoken of here as if it happened yesterday even though it's been thirteen years since VE Day.

So instead of answering awkward questions about where was home for me and did I have any brothers and sisters, I answered questions about what it's like to be the granddaughter of an Oxford don.

Granny and Gramps had wanted me to go to college just like they wanted Neville to. I did try, Emmy. I tried to be the person they wanted me to be. But I found myself hungering for London. It was as if London were calling me to come back and become reacquainted with it again. There was unfinished business between London and me, and I needed to attend to it.

My grandparents, especially Gramps, weren't happy about my wanting to leave college before I graduated but they handled my decision better than they had handled my father's. They didn't cut me off, financially or personally, which is what they did to Neville. Sometimes you get a second chance in life. The thing was, as soon as I decided I needed to come back, I felt ready to come back. It was the strangest thing. It was 1953 and I had just turned twenty, the same age you were when the war ended.

I think that's why I had to come back then.

I looked for you in the faces of the people I saw on the streets.

I steeled my resolve, made a list of all the bridal shops, and I went to each one, looking for your name on the dresses or your face behind the counter.

The first job I had was with the telephone company, which made it easy for me to look for your name in all the telephone exchanges in England, but I did not find you.

Gramps helped me get the job at Masters & Sons Cartographers. He went to school with Reginald Masters, the owner. I've been there for three years, and Simon for two. We became friends and then he asked me to dinner. He's never had a steady girlfriend before. He's the studious type. I have dated, but I can't say I've had a boyfriend. I've had boys date me and boys dance with me, but I've never had a boy care for me like Simon does.

As I got to know him better, I learned that he'd spent the war far from his parents, in a Suffolk farmhouse, cared for by foster parents who hadn't a tenth of the affection for him and his brother that they had for their own children. If that were not hard enough, he was teased by the local children for the way he spoke, his city ways, and his bookish looks and behavior. When he returned to London after five years as an evacuee, he felt as displaced as I did when I came back to England. He isn't afraid to show his sensitive side, because it's really the only side he has. It took him forever to work up the courage to kiss me.

I like that about him, Emmy. I like that the very thought of kissing me makes him tremble.

He would marry me tomorrow if I said yes.

He has told me a hundred times he loves me.

But I struggle to say this back to him, even though I think what I feel in my heart for him is love. And that's what scares me. I know what it is to have loved. To have a life that is uniquely yours and to have people in it who are your sun and moon and stars. I know that feeling.

And I dread how weak it makes us.

Simon says love doesn't weaken us; it opens us. To love is not to be fragile; it is to be unlocked and open. And when something is open, other things can come in.

And things can be taken out, I said to him. When you're standing there doing nothing remarkable, all you love can be yanked out of your open arms.

What can be given in one moment can be taken in the next.

Which is why I agreed to start seeing Dr. Diamant. After five years without professional counsel, this is why I must lay it all bare before another psychologist.

I don't feel entitled to happiness, Emmy. I robbed you of yours.

Dr. Diamant says the war is to blame for what came between you and me.

I look around London and I see all the new buildings. It's obvious that what the war did has been fixed.

What I did is what I must fix.

I want to fix what I broke.

Julia

Thirty-eight

❦

June 27, 1958

Dear Emmy,

I am sitting here with a glass of sherry watching the rain sputter against the living room window. It's late and I should be in bed, but I know that if I crawled under the covers, I would not be able to sleep. I have too much on my mind.

I told Dr. Diamant today that I had written everything I could think of to tell you and that I'm no closer to being able to say yes to a happy life than I was before I started.

She asked what I thought was holding me back. I told her I had not been able to fix anything. Writing to you hasn't mended anything. I wanted to repair what I broke.

If I could fix it, what I would I do? she asked.

You mean aside from going back in time?

Yes.

Well, if I knew where Aunt Charlotte's house was, maybe I would rap on the door and ask if could have a peek in the crawl space of the bedroom to the right of the stairs.

I said it kind of snippy. Like I wasn't serious.

And if you knew where Aunt Charlotte's house was, would you do that?

A prickling sensation traveled up my spine as the hazy image I have of Aunt Charlotte materialized in my mind. Her gray braid, her smile with the little gold tooth at the back, and her blue car. She had chickens. She let me play with her dolls. Two of them. And a tea set. Beyond those images was nothing but fog.

But I don't remember where that house is, I said. *Only that it's in Gloucestershire.*

Thea told Granny that Aunt Charlotte's house was in Gloucestershire, Emmy. Mum had told her that much.

But then the prickling intensified. I suddenly remembered something else, something that had been hidden in mist for nearly twenty years.

Charlotte had a sister named Rose, I said.

Dr. Diamant seemed cautiously surprised that I remembered this. She furrowed her brow. I could tell she was ruminating on something, wondering if what she was about to suggest was a good idea or not.

Have you ever considered looking for the house where you hid your sister's sketches? she asked.

I shook my head. I hadn't believed it was possible to find Aunt Charlotte's house.

Then Dr. Diamant said that maybe if I retrieved the brides box—if I unhid it—I would put to right a physical wrong. I could fix, to some extent, what I had broken. And if I could do that, then maybe I would find enough peace to believe that I do deserve to be happy.

She told me to go home and think about what it might mean to me to have the brides box again. Was the thought of finding it comforting to me? Or frightening? Was I okay with the notion that I could very well find the house but the box wouldn't be there? Could I handle earnestly looking for the house and not finding it?

She told me not to rush to a decision either way. There was no wrong answer, she said. Just an A choice and B choice. Like two doors painted the same color.

What do you think I should do? I asked her.

She thought for a moment. Then she said that I had written to you that more than anything I wanted to undo what I did with the brides box. Retrieving it wouldn't bring you back, but symbolically I will have righted a wrong.

A righted wrong only matters if you can unhurt the person you hurt, I told her.

Yes, but what about your hurt, Julia? she said. *This thing you did hurt you, too. You believe you are undeserving of happiness because you robbed Emmy of hers.*

What I am supposed to do if I find it? I asked. *I can't give the brides box back to Emmy.*

She answered with this: *What would you like to do with it?*

This is what is keeping me up tonight, Emmy.

What would I do with your sketches if I could have them again?

Simon told me at dinner tonight that he will help me if I decide to go looking for Aunt Charlotte's house. He has a car. We can use our Saturdays to drive out to Gloucestershire and poke about, which is surely the least effective way to look for it. But the evacuation records from my school were all lost to a demonic V-1. Simon said if I want to do this, we could get a map of Gloucestershire from work and circle all the smaller cities that have train stations. We could check with the local officials of those towns to see if anyone knows of two sisters named Charlotte and Rose who took in evacuees from London at the start of the war.

Simon asked me if I would know the house if I saw it.

I told him I wasn't sure.

Then he asked me if I truly wanted to try to find it. *Because you don't have to do this, you know,* he said.

I could not answer him.

And now as I sit here trying hard not to count raindrops on the window, I am not sure if I want to try.

I think I'm sure that I want to find the brides box.

I'm just not sure that I want to try.

It's the trying that scares me. I'm afraid this quest will be like the search to find the flat and the bridal shop.

And you.

I failed in all of those.

But this I do know, Emmy. If I could find the brides box, I would do for you what you wanted all along.

If I can find your sketches, I will make the dream you had come true.

Julia

July 2, 1958

Dear Emmy,

I have decided to look for Aunt Charlotte's house. The more I've thought about it, the more I've come to believe it might actually be possible to find, so I can't imagine not trying. I asked Dr. Diamant what was the worst thing that could happen to me if I try to find the house and can't.

She returned the question to me. What did I think the worst thing would be?

I guess I would be no better or worse than I am now.

She said if that was an accurate gauge of how I'd feel, she thought I should give it a go.

So Simon and I got a map of Gloucestershire and spread it out on the lunch table at work. I remember that when you and I got off the train the day we left London, we walked outside and I saw that we weren't in a major city. It was more like a country town. The streets were not full of taxis and buses or tall buildings. I remember there being mums on the sidewalks with prams and a dead bird that you poked with your toe so that we could walk past it. Simon crossed off the larger cities like Gloucester, Cirencester, Cheltenham, and Swindon. We drew circles around all the towns that would have had a train station in 1940. So many of the railway stations have closed since the war; dozens in Gloucestershire alone, Emmy. People drive their own cars now.

Anyway, as we were studying the map, I saw the word "Cotswolds" written in block letters, which is the name of one of Gloucestershire's districts, and I had another prickling feeling. I pulled the map closer to me and whispered that word out loud. The second I did, I saw us back in Aunt Charlotte's car when she told us the golden-colored stone we were seeing everywhere was Cotswold stone.

The Cotswolds, Emmy. I am right, aren't I?

I turned to Simon and told him you and I were somewhere in the Cotswolds.

Simon started naming towns. Adelstrop, Bourton-on-the-Water, Chipping Camden, Moreton-in-Marsh, Stow-on-the-Wold. Fairford. Blockley. Naunton. The Slaughters. Oddington. Tewkesbury.

But nothing sounded familiar to me. I must have started to look a little overwhelmed. Simon said to never mind, that I was brilliant because I had just narrowed the search considerably. He mapped out a day trip for us for this Saturday, using Fairford as our starting point since it's one of the first places we will pass coming up from London.

I know Fairford isn't right. Somehow I know it's not. But we have to begin somewhere. I am both eager and hesitant to look for the brides box, Emmy.

It seems like the honorable thing to do. I hope God in heaven will look down on me and favor me with success. It seems such a little thing to request of him.

Simon asked me if I am going to tell Granny what I am doing. I don't think I will. All of this happened between you and me before I knew her. She can't help. And if I told her and then failed, she would know I tried and I would see my failure in her eyes every time we visited and she asked me how I was.

This is between you and me.

Julia

೩

July 5, 1958

Dear Emmy,

Simon and I are back from our first trip out to look for Aunt Charlotte's house. He is heating up soup for us to eat as I write to you. We are cold and soaked to the skin. The day dawned with sprinkles and then switched to rain just as we arrived in Fairford and began our first inquiries.

It didn't occur to us until we were under way that we could expect no help from city officials in these towns because it was Saturday. No city offices would be open. But Simon said not to worry. City officials might have been hesitant anyway to speak to two strangers asking about sisters whose last name they didn't even know.

The Fairford train station didn't look anything like what I remembered. We didn't even get out of the car.

We drove on to Kempsford where we got thoroughly drenched finding out there was no railway station there. We tried Lechlade, and then Burford because it was nearby, even though it's in Oxfordshire, not Gloucestershire. And then back in the car to Bourton-on-the-Water, a beautiful little place. I was so taken with it that Simon suggested we should ask about the sisters in the druggist's and the beauty shop and at the park. I'd decided that when I asked about Charlotte, I would say only that I wished to find my foster mother and thank her for taking my sister and me in, all those many years ago. Don't you think other evacuees have done this, Emmy? Gone back to the homes and mothers and fathers and siblings who sheltered them during the war years? I think they do. And this seemed to me a very polite and respectable reason for snooping about and asking strangers to tell me whether a Charlotte and a Rose live—or lived—nearby.

So that is what I did. I asked people, mostly older folks, if they knew of two sisters named Charlotte and Rose, because I had spent nearly three months with them at the start of the war, before my mother died.

There are a great many souls in Bourton-on-the-Water and the surrounding little towns that took in evacuees, Emmy. But no one remembers a pair of gray-haired sisters named Charlotte and Rose. We also tried at Upper and Little Rissington—tiny little villages brimming with houses made of Cotswold stone—because they are within a manageable walking distance of Bourton.

I remember that you and I walked from Charlotte's house to a train station the morning we returned to London. It was a long walk and you carried me part of the way. It was dark. And I was tired. Simon thinks it can't have been more than six or so miles that we walked because I was too young to walk farther than that in the middle of the night. And I was too heavy for you to carry the entire way.

But we found no one in these towns who knew the sisters.

Still, we drove down some of the lanes, looking at the houses, mostly all made of the same stone, and reminding me very much of Charlotte's house.

We didn't find it.

But I am strangely encouraged.

The sense of the familiar was too strong, Emmy.

Julia

&

July 12, 1958

Dear Emmy,

We went out again today. This time we made our way to Chipping Camden, which didn't look familiar at all when we first drove into town, and I had to remind myself that nearly twenty years have passed since the day you and I arrived in Gloucestershire. But as we neared the city center, I began to think perhaps we were to be lucky today. The railway station and the lay of the streets and the city hall—it addled my brain how familiar and yet not familiar they were. Again we asked about in the shops and the library and the bank if anyone knew of the sisters. We received mostly kind and compassionate responses. A few people looked askance at us or simply shook their heads with a wordless no when we asked. We had tea at a lovely café to refresh us and Simon noted on the map how many villages were within walking distance. And we went to them all, Emmy. Aston Subedge, Broad Marston, several others.

Every place looked like it could have been where you and I were. And yet no one knew of the sisters. We even strolled the cemeteries, looking for their names.

On the way home I was feeling tremendously discouraged. I wondered aloud if perhaps Thea had been wrong about where Mum told her we were. Maybe she assumed it was Gloucestershire. Or maybe Thea said we had been in Oxfordshire and Granny heard Gloucestershire, because there are Cotswold villages in Oxfordshire as well.

Simon just said, rather confidently, *Well, then we'll look in every village in Oxfordshire, too.*

The way he said this gave me pause. I couldn't see his face clearly because night had fallen and the only light on his features was from the headlamps of a few passing cars. But in the shadows I saw a determined look that surprised me. It did not matter to him that the search may have now widened to include another county. It only mattered that we pressed on, like a wise accountant would do to find the error in the ledger and adjust it. It was as if he was determined to find the house to fix *me*, which is different than the reason I want to find it. He wanted to find the house so that I could at last climb out of my regrets and marry him. I am not interested in fixing me. I want to fix what I broke.

It's completely different.

When I said nothing, he took my silence for anxiety that now we have even more towns to search and that he might lose interest in me because of it. He said not to worry, because I was the only thing that mattered to him. He reached for my hand.

I love him, Emmy, I do. And I know he loves me. But sitting there in the dark with the shimmer of London way off in the distance, I knew that I must continue on alone. If I don't, I fear I am the one who may lose interest.

I don't want to feel as if I am the broken thing that needs to be repaired even if that's what I am. Your lover should see you as whole even if you are in pieces, because that's what love does, doesn't it? It sees past the flaws. It forgets there are flaws.

Simon said my name.

I traced his hand in mine, wondering how to tell him. *Simon,* I said, *would you mind very much if next Saturday I went alone?*

What was that? he said.

I proceeded to tell him that finding the brides box was something I needed to accomplish on my own. I figured the word "accomplish" would sound good to his ears. I didn't think he needed to know that I was feeling he was showing less love for me rather than more by his ardent enthusiasm for the quest. That would only wound him. And there are already enough wounds in the world. I told him I appreciated with all my heart the help and support he had given me, but that I wanted to continue on my own.

But are you sure that's a good idea? he asked. *Going alone?*

I think he was suggesting that in my fragile state, maybe I would collapse at the shock of finding the house and the box, or be devastated at not finding them.

But I have survived much, Emmy. Haven't I? Haven't I survived the war and the loss of my childhood, my parents, and my sister? Haven't I come back to London? Haven't I looked for you? Haven't I agreed to write this journal? Haven't I embarked on the mission to find your brides? And haven't I done all that alone?

I squeezed Simon's hand. *This is something only I can do for me, Simon,* I said. *I will be all right.*

He attempted a couple more counterarguments but, in the end, because he loves me, he agreed.

I asked him if I could use his car, which he has loaned to me other times, and he said of course.

He seemed a little hurt when we said good night, but I don't think he feels injured by me. It's more that he's disappointed he can't be the one to rescue me.

I think I know how that feels.

Julia

Thirty-nine

July 19, 1958

Dear Emmy,

Emmy, I think I found the town where we got off the train and Charlotte met us! When I drove into Moreton-in-Marsh today, I felt as though I were being tugged through a tunnel. I was shaking when I parked Simon's car and walked into the train station. The station itself didn't seem familiar to me, but walking out of it and back onto the street nearly took my breath away. The scene in front of me was like a long-lost photograph that flitted down off a shelf in my mind. It was the same, but different. As I walked up the sidewalk toward the town center, I could see you and me, holding our cardboard boxes with our gas masks inside. I could feel the weight of my fairy tale book tucked under my arm. I could feel my hand in yours. There was a dead bird in the street, and the boys ahead of us from my school wanted to stop and poke it. They were daring *me* to touch it. You kicked it with the tip of your shoe and it flopped over into the gutter.

Oh, Emmy, the pull of feeling you so near almost yanked me to the ground.

This was the place. I knew it.

The first few people I approached in the grocery store and the stationers seemed dubious when I told them whom I was looking for and why, and I realized I was talking too fast and too frantically. I must have seemed like a madwoman escaped from an institution, intent on hacking to death the two sisters I was searching for. I knew I needed to compose myself. And I needed to sit down with the map and see where you and I could have come from that long-ago morning when we walked to Moreton. Charlotte didn't live here. She lived somewhere else. But I was close.

I went to a café, ordered a pot of Darjeeling, and used the warmth and floral notes of the tea to calm myself as I studied the map. I made a list of towns that you and I could have walked from to reach Moreton. Batsford, Draycott, Bourton-on-the-Hill, Blockley, Chastleton, Broadwell, Longborough, Stow-on-the-Wold, Oddington.

I drank my tea, got back in Simon's car, and headed to the northwest corner of my search area to work my way down. So today, I only got to explore Batsford, Blockley, Bourton-on-the-Hill, and the smaller hamlets Paxton and Aston Magna.

I did not find the house.

And I did not see the sisters' names in the local cemeteries.

I started home for London when the sun was setting and drove to Simon's flat so that he could take me home and have his car. He seemed a little sad that I'd so quickly discovered Moreton on my own. Not sad for me, but for himself. It was obvious that he wished he had chosen Moreton the first day out.

Still want to go alone next Saturday? he asked. Maybe I should have invited him to come; I could tell he wanted to. But I kissed him and declined.

I like it that it's just me.

Next Saturday I will head for Chastleton, Broadwell, and Longborough.

❦

July 26, 1958

Dear Emmy,

I am sick with some kind of flu.

It's Saturday but instead of getting into Simon's car and continuing my search, I am spending the day in bed with a fever. Granny insisted on coming out on the train to take care of me when I came home ill from work on Thursday, even though I was far from needing that much attention.

I haven't been out to see Gramps and Granny much since I started dating Simon. I think she was looking for a reason to come see me and to see how Simon and I are getting on. I'm twenty-five and never really had a boyfriend before. She and Gramps have met Simon only once, when he and I drove out to have Sunday dinner with them a few months ago. That was before Simon proposed to me and tried to offer me a ring, and I told him I wasn't ready.

No one really knows he did that. Well, maybe his parents do. I don't have many close friends at work or here in my building. I haven't wanted to trust many people with my friendship. I guess because of how awful my teenage years were. So I don't have chummy girlfriends to confide in. Maybe if I had a best friend, I would have told her Simon had proposed. But I don't really have one of those. Simon is my best friend. You can see how terrible it will be for me if he loses interest in me.

He says he won't, but I wonder how he knows he can wait for me. He's never done this before.

Granny stayed for two days, made me loads of soup, did my laundry, and went to the pharmacy for cough syrup. She asked more than once what I've been up to in my free time. I think she is wondering why I've not been home on Saturdays when she has called.

I almost told her what I've been doing.

I'm not sure why I didn't other than she'd worry that I'll wish I hadn't looked for the brides box when it's all said and done, whether I find it or not.

She left this afternoon on the five o'clock train back to Oxford. Simon is coming over in a little while, to read to me and fuss over me, no doubt.

I just want to shake this bug and get back to what I was doing before I got sick.

I am close. I can feel it.

Julia

❧

August 2, 1958

My dear Emmy,

I am not sure how to put into words what I am feeling. I am still a bit dazed. Numb, really. I don't feel at all like I thought I would.

I found Aunt Charlotte's house today.

But not the brides box.

I was inside the bedroom you and I shared. I found the crawl space. I opened the door that had been painted shut.

It wasn't there.

I am back home now, sitting in my flat and watching the telly with Simon. He's afraid to leave, thinking it will dawn on me after he goes that the brides box is lost to me forever and the last little bit of you with it.

But I am strangely numb.

I found the village to which Charlotte first took us to get library books. It's Stow-on-the-Wold, and it's four miles from Moreton-in-Marsh. I didn't remember the name of this little town, but when I saw the church and the library and even the post office, I knew this was the village Charlotte had called her own, and you and I had been to it—many times.

I started out by going into the library, mainly because I remembered it. I asked the more mature of the two librarians if there was an older woman in the village named Charlotte. In her eighties perhaps?

You mean Charlotte Havelock? the librarian replied.

I felt silly not knowing her last name, so I just asked if this Charlotte Havelock had a sister named Rose.

The librarian said yes, she did.

Oh, Emmy, how my heart thumped in my chest as I asked where I could find them.

She said she was sorry to tell me they were both deceased. She had attended Charlotte's funeral just three months ago. Rose died several years before that.

Three months, Emmy. Charlotte was alive three months ago.

I had to sit down for a moment to let that sink in. I knew no good would come from pondering why I hadn't begun the search sooner. But how could I not lament having just missed her?

The librarian felt bad for me and wanted to know if she could get me anything.

I told her I just needed to know if Charlotte's house was still standing.

She answered with a nod and told me she'd heard an American woman and her daughter were living there—at least for the summer. The woman was distantly related to Charlotte. Or something like that.

She asked if I wanted directions to Thistle House.

Charlotte's house has a name, Thistle House. You probably remember that. You probably remember everything.

It didn't take long to drive the half mile to the house. The moment I was standing outside it, it was as if the years had rolled back like a curtain and you and I were arriving on that first day.

I knocked and the door was opened by a teenage girl. She asked if she could help me. Her American accent was strange to hear coming from that threshold.

I told her that I had lived in this house during the war when it belonged to Charlotte Havelock. And then I asked if her parents were home. She said her father was still in the States and her mother wasn't due back until evening. I was so deeply disappointed. To have come that far—to have actually found the house—only to have to leave and come back another time was crushing.

I pulled a grocery receipt out of my handbag and scribbled my name and phone number on it. I asked the girl if she wouldn't mind giving my name and number to her mother when she got home and asking her to give me a ring.

Does my mother know you? she asked.

I told her she didn't. And then who knows why I did what I did next. I just blurted it all out, Emmy. I told the girl about you and your bride sketches and what I had done with them on the night we ran away from Thistle House. I told her how you and I were separated on the first night of the Blitz and that I was whisked away to America by a grandmother I didn't even know I had and that I never saw or heard from you again.

The girl's eyes were rimmed with tears when I was done and I realized with a shock that so were mine.

I began to apologize profusely when she opened the door wide and told me to come and see if the brides box was still there.

I didn't think I should with her mum not at home. But the girl said I looked harmless enough.

I'm not sure I should, I said.

I am plenty old enough to take care of myself. Come in.

So I did.

She told me her name was Gwen.

Emmy, from what I can remember, the house looks the same. The same furniture. The same green sofa in the living room. The same oak kitchen table. The same red carpet on the stairs and the same creak as we ascended them.

So you're related to the Havelock sisters? I asked, babbling as we climbed to calm myself.

Gwen shrugged and said she wasn't really sure how they were related. She said her mother was born in England but she moved to America when she married her father. Gwen said she didn't know very much about her mother's side of the family because they were all deceased and her mother never wanted to talk about them.

We got to the top of the stairs and I saw bursts of yellow. The room we slept in is still lemon hued. The two twin beds are gone, and now there are a settee and two armchairs upholstered in checked canary yellow. My gaze was immediately drawn to the far wall where the lace-covered table had been. A bookcase is there now.

I told Gwen the crawl space was behind the bookcase and she didn't hesitate. She walked right over to it and started to pull books off the shelves so that we could shimmy it away from the wall.

As we worked, I asked her if this was her first time to England and she said yes. Thistle House had been left to her mother when

Charlotte Havelock died and they were just staying the summer. Home and her father were in Minnesota. I asked if she liked it here. She said if she were allowed to go anywhere or do anything, she might like it. She said her mother worries too much about her and it drives her crazy. I felt sorry for her. She reminded me a little of you, Emmy. I'm not sure why. Maybe because she seemed so eager to be grown-up and to make her own decisions. I asked her how old she was and she said nearly thirteen.

When we had removed enough of the books, we pushed the bookcase out of the way and there it was: the crawl space door, painted shut. Gwen ran downstairs and quickly came back with a screwdriver. Before I could ask if her mum would want her to, she started to pry the painted seam open. The seal broke with a cracking pop. Gwen pulled the door open and then sat back.

She told me to go ahead and see.

My pulse was drumming as I crawled halfway in and reached up above the door frame. I felt dust and cobwebs and droppings but no box.

No box.

Gwen ran downstairs again and returned with a torch. She asked if she could give it a try. I worked my way out and she crawled in, clicking on the light as she went. I could see the beam dancing on the confines of the little space.

I told her I had placed the box on the ledge on the inside of the door frame. She swung the light around to shine it on the back side of where the door and the wall met.

It wasn't there.

She crawled out again and we both sat there looking at the dark space we had unearthed.

Sorry, Gwen finally said.

I was sorry, too. The numbness was already settling on me, like a heavy coat against wintry gusts that would chill to the bone if they could get to you.

We closed the door, and returned the bookcase to its rightful place and the books to their shelves. Then we went back downstairs.

There didn't seem to be a reason to stay, so I thanked her again and asked her if she was going to get into trouble for having let me in.

She shrugged like she didn't care.

I told her I'd be happy to talk with her mother by phone and let her know how kind and helpful she had been, but she just smiled and said I didn't have to do that.

I told her to give her mother my name and number just the same.

When I left, she was standing at the door, watching me drive away.

She's not going to give her mum that piece of paper with my name and phone number on it.

That girl is just like you were, Emmy. Wanting to make her own way in life, and the world isn't willing to grant her that freedom.

I guess I am just like her, too.

When I got home and told Simon what had happened, he asked me what I was going to do now. I know what he meant. He wants to know what this means for us.

I can't answer him.

I feel as if I am underwater. Suspended. Hovering between where I was and where I want to be. I am in no place to decide.

I am sorry I lost your brides, Emmy. I am so very sorry.

Julia

Forty

August 5, 1958

Dear Emmy,

I am trying very hard to do what I said I would do—and that is live with the fact that the brides box is gone. I told Dr. Diamant before I started looking that I would be okay with not finding it. I told Simon the same thing.

Simon said this evening he wished he had talked me out of looking.

But then I would always wonder, I said.

And he said sometimes wondering is better than knowing.

Dr. Diamant told me truth is a strange companion. It devastates one moment and enthralls the next. But it never deceives. And because of that, in the end, it comforts.

Julia

August 7, 1958

Dear Emmy,

I think we might be done here.

Simon thinks it might be a good idea to lay you to rest. He wonders if maybe I could use this journal to memorialize you. I could burn it, and its ashes could be your remains. He read in an article that people who grieve the loss of a loved one where there is no body often need something to burn or bury to find ultimate release. That's how we say good-bye to people. We clasp them to our chest, weep over their lifeless form, and then send them back to the earth.

I could do that with this journal.

I need to ask Dr. Diamant what she thinks.

Julia

August 11, 1958

Dear Emmy,

Dr. Diamant says the journal is mine to do with as I want. The journal has always been more about me than you. Isn't that funny? Here I am writing all these words to you, words you will never read. And it's not a problem because the journal has always been for me.

I don't think I can toss this into the fireplace.

Not yet, anyway.

But I think I can be finished with writing in it.

We are done, aren't we, Emmy? I did all that I could to find you, all that I could to restore to you what I took from you.

Dr. Diamant assures me that with all that I have told her about you, you would have forgiven me. That you did forgive me.

I think maybe if we end it here, perhaps I can learn to believe it. Maybe not as quickly as Simon would like, but if I know anything about time, it is that it stretches to walk with you when you grieve. The rest of the world may zoom past at breakneck speed, but when you are learning to live with loss, time slows to the pace of your breathing.

I will never forget you, Emmy.

But I need to release you.

Your sister always,

Julia

ᴄℓ◦

August 15, 1958

Emmy,

I can hardly believe what has happened.

Gwen found the brides box.

She found it.

In Rose's old room.

She called me this morning as I was getting ready for work.

I am stunned beyond words.

She wants to meet me in Stow to give it to me. I don't even care that she doesn't want me to come back to Thistle House.

I have called in sick to work. I begged Simon to let me use his car.

He wants to come with me but I told him no. We can't both call in sick.

And I want to go alone.

Emmy, after all this time. I am bringing home your brides box.

❧

August 15, 1958

Evening

My dear Emmy,

As I write this, the brides box is just to the right of my bent elbow. I could reach out and run my fingers across it with my other hand if I wanted to.

There are signs of neglect on its top and the hinges have corroded to uselessness. The top doesn't stay on unless you bind it shut, which is how Gwen found it.

And Emmy, the drawings are inside. Just like you left them.

The paper has yellowed and the sketches have faded, but I can still make out nearly every feature you drew if I look close. The images are a bit ghostly, but not unpleasantly so. It's almost as if you have materialized from beyond the grave to return to me.

It's as if you have given the brides back to me, not I who have given them back to you.

How like you to look after me, even after all that I did to you.

Do you want to know how Gwen came to find them?

I was right about her not telling her mum that I had come by before. She didn't tell her. She was afraid her mother would get after her for letting me in. Her mother's overprotectiveness is apparently an enormous bone of contention between them.

And between you and me, I think she liked having a secret that she could keep from her mum. I don't approve of it; I'm just saying that's what I think.

Anyway, she said she couldn't stop thinking about me after I left. She felt bad for me, and she went back inside the crawl space in the yellow room twice, making sure the brides box hadn't fallen into a hollow of some kind in the framing.

She was in her bedroom, Rose's, thinking about it when it occurred to her that if our bedroom had a crawl space, maybe the one she was sleeping in did, too, and that I had just remembered the room wrong. In her bedroom, a cedar chest lines the far wall. Gwen didn't want to move it when her mother was home; otherwise she'd hear her pushing it across the floor. So she had to wait a couple of days until her mum had to go to Oxford on business. She emptied the chest and pushed it away from the wall. And found an identical crawl space door.

The brides box was inside, on the framing of the door, just like I had placed it in our bedroom. Rose had found it and put it in her room; I'm sure that was what happened. That wardrobe was on another wall when Rose had the room that Gwen is sleeping in now. Remember how Rose liked your drawings? She must have found the brides box after we ran away, took it, and put it in her own room. I know it was her because she wrote her name on the top of all the sketches, Emmy. She wanted the bridal gowns to be hers. So she made them hers in the only way she could. And she obviously never told Charlotte.

Gwen didn't want to tell her mum about the discovery because that would necessitate a conversation about why she went looking for it. And that was why she asked to meet me in the village to give me the box.

Oh, Emmy. She seemed so happy to be part of something wonderful that was just hers. Her mum wasn't privy to it, so she couldn't spoil it for her or take it from her. So like you, so like you.

I told her so.

I told Gwen she reminded me of you. And that I hoped she would change her mind and tell her mother about me and the brides box. It was our secrets that pulled our worlds apart, Emmy. First yours, and then mine.

But Gwen said her mother would have a conniption. They would have a huge fight over it, and, in the end, her mother would never leave her alone at the house again. Not at Thistle House and not in Saint Paul when they went back to the States.

I offered to come to Thistle House and explain things but Gwen told me not to. They only have a couple more weeks left before they head back to America. She doesn't want to spend them handcuffed to her mother.

I asked her why her mother worries about her so. Gwen said she's always been that way. She lost family members in the war, her father had told her, and it was too difficult for her to talk about it.

I feel for Gwen, poor thing.

And I feel for her mother.

Terrible things can happen to you that leave you unable to risk trusting the world with what you love; I know this better than anyone.

I don't want to live handcuffed to my regrets anymore, Emmy.

I hadn't really understood that was how I had been living until Gwen described it that way.

I tried one last time to convince her to let me go back to Thistle House and talk to her mum, but Gwen said her mother was in Oxford that day, apparently meeting with a long-lost half brother who had contacted her mother out of the blue.

I was jealous in an instant, Emmy, that Gwen's mother could have a long-lost half brother suddenly crawl out of the folds of the past and reconnect with her. I told her how wonderful that was.

But she just shrugged and said it would have been nice to know before now that her mother had a half brother.

I wished her safe travels back to America and a happy life.

She seemed sad to see me go.

I was strangely sad to leave her.

It was a little like saying good-bye to you all over again.

October 22, 1958

Dear Emmy,

I haven't had much luck finding any clothing designers or bridal shop owners interested in your sketches.

Make that, I haven't had any luck.

The ones I have spoken to have been quite taken by the story of the brides box, and especially moved by what happened to you and me. They've all found it intriguing that I want to see your sketches become real dresses at last, but the designs aren't in style, said one; the sketches are too faded to be of any use, said another; and they aren't mine to give away or sell, said several others. Technically they are still your property, Emmy.

I wish I knew the name of the person you were to meet the day of the bombing. I remember your telling me how this was your one chance to be discovered. If I knew who that person was and where to find him or her, I would waste no time in arranging a meeting.

I can't remember the name of the lady you worked for at the bridal shop, either. The shop is gone. Everything on the street near where the butcher shop was is gone; it's all new buildings now.

I will keep trying, Emmy. I haven't given up.

In the meantime, Simon and I have set a date and I am now wearing the engagement ring he tried to give me last spring.

Our wedding date is April 7.
Your birthday.

◦≪◦

November 1, 1958

Dear Emmy,

No news to report on the sketches.

I found a seamstress willing to make one of the drawings a reality—I've actually found several who make custom dresses all the time, for a pretty price—but the one I like best is not interested in being part of launching a line of wedding dresses with your name on them. She will make a dress for me from one of your designs, but it won't be to sell in a boutique somewhere. It will be for me to wear.

I am discovering that if I want your drawings to become real wedding gowns, I will need a treasure chest full of money to fund the project myself and then peddle them to bridal shops door-to-door.

I don't have a treasure chest full of money.

Gramps isn't a rich man, but he's done well. I can only hope I can convince him to help me do with your sketches what you would have done with them.

But first I will have to tell my grandparents about the brides box.

And what I did.

Julia

cⅅ

November 9, 1958

Dear Emmy,

Gramps said no.

Simon and I took the train to Woodstock and had tea at Granny and Gramps' house this afternoon. Gramps said he was sorry but neither he nor I know anything about the bridal gown business. We don't have the know-how, the instincts, the connections.

He said it would cost thousands of pounds to have your drawings made into dresses, provided I could find a suitable seamstress able to read the faded sketches, and then I would have to traipse around London on foot, carrying them from store to store, hoping some shop owner would want to buy a gown that was in style twenty years ago, designed by an unknown who has disappeared off the face of the earth.

Gramps can't see the value of plodding across London with an armload of wedding dresses no one to date has expressed any interest in.

He also commented that the designs aren't truly mine to do this with. They belong to you. I don't have your permission and I'm likely not going to get it.

Gramps and Granny were both appreciative of my desire to make things right between you and me, but they don't think I've anything to regret. You and I both made mistakes that day. Mine were less egregious, perhaps, but that's not the point, Gramps said. The point is, London was bombed a few hours after you and I arrived. The war is the true destroyer of your dreams, not I. So it's not up to me to restore what the war shattered.

Simon was sitting next to me the whole time, stroking my hand under the table and saying nothing. I wanted him to say, *But Emmy's designs are really good.* Or *I'll drive Julia around London so she won't have to tramp across the West End on foot with an armload of dresses.* Or even just, *Don't we owe it to Julia's sister to at least give her dresses a chance?*

He didn't. We left soon after that.

What was the good in finding Emmy's sketches if not to do something with them? I asked Simon on the way home.

He said maybe the finding was just for me. Maybe I was meant to find the brides box now because I happen to be in need of a wedding dress.

Pick the one you want for you, Simon said. *Wear one of your sister's designs to your own wedding. Wouldn't that be the good in finding them?*

I suppose he's right.

I laid out all the sketches on my kitchen table tonight after Simon dropped me off. The most faded ones I put back. A couple others just weren't right for my body shape.

Of the seven that were left, I picked the one I used to call the button dress. Remember it, Emmy? You had tiny pearl buttons going down the front, all the way to the floor. And a high, fitted waist. Lacy sleeves you can see through, a heart-shaped neckline, and a swishy skirt with a lace petticoat underneath.

I wonder if you ever imagined that someday your little sister would wear one of your dresses.

Perhaps Simon is right. Perhaps finding the brides box so I can wear one of your designs is what you would have wanted.

I am eager to take it to the seamstress who said she will make one of the dresses for me. I know what Gramps will say when I tell him my dress is to be custom made and might cost a little more than he thought he wanted to spend. He will say he doesn't care. The dress is for me, for my wedding.

It's for my happy ending.

One of us should have one.

I guess it will be me.

At least, as happy as I can make it.

Julia

November 19, 1958

Dear Emmy,

The seamstress who agreed to make the button dress for me told me she'd like to change the skirt to a tea length and drop the tops of the sleeves to off the shoulder. She said the style of the button dress is terribly outdated.

I wanted to throttle her.

Instead I told her I liked the original design just the way it was.

She said, *You do know no one is wearing this style of wedding dress anymore?*

And I said that wasn't true because I was wearing it.

But I know now why I can't seem to generate interest in your sketches, Emmy.

I'm too late.

I waited too long to look for the box.

Julia

❧

December 2, 1958

Dear Emmy,

I had my first fitting today. I nearly cried when I tried the dress on, even though it's only partially sewn.

It's so beautiful, Emmy. So incredibly beautiful. April seems like such a long way off.

Granny came with me to the fitting and she started to cry.

See how talented my sister was, I said to her as she blotted her tears away.

It's a wonderful dress, Granny said.

The seamstress just clucked something like *Every bride looks like a princess in a wedding gown that she loves.*

When I came home, I could feel the dress still on my skin. Your dress, Emmy. I still feel it on me, caressing me. Holding me.

I think I can be happy marrying Simon in the dress that came from the very heart of you. I think you would want me to be happy marrying him.

Snow is falling outside my window now, diamond white in the spreading dusk.

I feel you here with me, Emmy. It's as if you are looking down on me from heaven, for surely that is where you are, and the snow is a gift you've been allowed to give me so that I can mark this day.

The brides box is sitting on the table here next to me and it occurs to me that I shall marry only once.

I have no need of the other sketches in the box.

I have your forgiveness. I see it in the snow outside my window and I felt it earlier when your folds of white caressed my trembling body.

Across from me, my little coal fire is whispering condolences.

And something else.

I see it now, how I can hold you forever and also let you go.

The happy fire is sighing in agreement, the little beggar. It is eager to play its part for me.

The journal I will keep to remind me, should I ever need to be reminded, that you and I did indeed find each other again, within the seams of my wedding dress.

Good-bye, dear sister.

I will love you always.

Julia

Forty-one

KENDRA

WHEN I look up from Julia's journal, Isabel is asleep on the sofa. Her head is bent forward on her chest and a gentle wheeze floats across to me every time she exhales.

For several long minutes I am torn between waking her and letting her sleep.

I am dying to know how Isabel got her hands on the journal. She had to have been reunited with her sister. Had to have been. How else could she have come by it? I turn my head toward the window as the thought occurs to me that perhaps Julia is in the garden with the rest of the family.

As I ponder this, Isabel stirs awake, sees that I have closed the journal, and she sits up abruptly.

"Oh! I must have nodded off. What time is it?"

I glance at a clock on the wall behind her. "Just a bit after two thirty."

"Did you read it?"

"Yes."

She takes the journal gently from my outstretched hand. "You're the first to read it in many years."

"How did you get it?" I hear urgency in my voice.

She smiles knowingly. "Do you mean, did Julia herself give it to me?"

I nod, wanting very much to hear that this is exactly what happened.

Isabel runs her hand across the top of the journal. "She did."

Relief floods me. "Thank God," I whisper, and her smile widens.

"Yes, I've God to thank for refusing to let me continue with my stubbornness."

"How did you find each other?"

Isabel thinks about her answer for a moment. "Gwen brought us together, you might say."

"She finally told you about Julia coming to the house that day, didn't she?" I say, sure that this is what happened.

"I guess that is one way of looking at it. The short story is Julia handed the journal to me, from where you are sitting right now. The long story is a bit more complicated than that." She settles into the sofa cushions behind her and I settle into mine. "We'd been back in the UK for nearly a year, Mac, Gwen, and I. We decided to stay at Thistle House after Mac joined us that first summer. He and I needed a quiet place to rebuild our marriage, and since Gwen's best friend back in the States had recently moved to the West Coast, Gwen was amenable to staying and trying the high school here. I soon had other reasons for wanting to stay, which I will get to. But I still lived as though Emmeline Downtree had never existed. I still went by the name Isabel. I didn't see any great need to shatter the myth, and being back at Thistle House after so many years was rekindling old aches that I thought Isabel could handle better. The only person who deserved to know the truth was Gwen, and what was the point in finally confessing to her that not only was I living my life with a borrowed name, but I had also abandoned my seven-year-old half sister on the day the Germans bombed London and she was likely dead because of me? I was looking for ways to bond with Gwen rather than distance myself from her, and since Mac hadn't taken the news well when I finally told him the truth about who I was, it was easy to decide that nothing good would come from dredging it up for Gwen, either.

"So the three of us were in Oxford on a Sunday afternoon the following April for an art exhibition. Gwen and I had made some progress in our relationship, and she was fairly happy at Thistle House and with the new friends she had made. Things between Mac and me had improved, too, which was why the two of them had decided to come with me to this show. The Umbrella Girls had taken off, as the saying goes, and were selling well. The original was still hanging in Charlotte's old bedroom at Thistle House, and, strangely enough, it was the one daily reminder of Julia that didn't sting. It had quite the opposite effect, actually, which was why I was inspired to create more."

My eyes are naturally drawn to the Umbrella Girl painting hanging behind her. "Painting Julia over and over was like finding her?" I venture.

Isabel nods slowly. "Perhaps it was. Painting the Umbrella Girls was definitely therapeutic, and selling them made me feel that at last I had something to give back to the world." She draws a deep breath before continuing. "Anyway, Mac had bought a London newspaper to read over lunch that afternoon at the art show. When he was finished with it, Gwen began thumbing through the sections. She stopped at a page and said, 'Well, would you look at that,' and I asked her what she had seen. She folded the section over to isolate a picture. From upside down I could see that it was a wedding photo.

" 'I guess I can tell you this now,' Gwen said, 'if you promise not to go crazy,' and I said, 'Tell me what?' As she handed the paper to me, Gwen said that way back when we first came to Stow, the woman in the wedding photo had come to Thistle House on a day I had been out. But, Kendra, I heard nothing after those first few words. I was now looking at a photograph of a bridal gown I had only ever seen in my head. Buttons down the front, fitted bodice, sleeves of illusion. The dress was one of my gowns. And then I looked at the face of the happy bride. The woman was Julia."

"Oh my God," I murmur.

"Indeed," Isabel said. "You see, too, what lengths God had to go to reunite me with her. He had to practically move heaven and earth to undo all my mistakes."

"What did you do?" I ask.

"Well, I had to have Gwen repeat everything she'd said, because I had heard none of it, and I did go a little crazy, which she had asked me not to do. Mac, who was looking at someone else's paintings nearby, rushed over to see what I was fussing about. I thrust the paper toward him and through my sobs said who it was in the photo. I had not uttered Julia's name in a very long time.

"Mac kept saying, 'Are you sure?' but there was no mistaking that dress, and that face, even twenty years after I had last seen it. And, of course, the bride in the photo, the former Julia Waverly, had known about the brides box. This Julia was my Julia."

"So, you looked her up? You contacted her?" Stunned

at the play of events, I am already picturing the sisters in a tearful embrace.

Isabel pauses to inhale deeply, as if the memory of that day still took her breath away.

"I asked Mac to get in touch with her. I didn't know what Julia's feelings would be toward me, though I should have guessed that wearing one of my dresses at her wedding was evidence that she did not hate me. But I could not lift the phone to call her when Mac found out where she was. It wasn't difficult for him to locate her. The announcement in the newspaper said the couple both worked at the same mapmaking company in London. The hardest part was waiting for Monday to arrive so that Mac could ring up this place and ask for her.

"I didn't want to be in the house when he called her. I stood at the edge of the pond while he and she talked. When he joined me outside a few minutes later, he said Julia had wept with joy to hear that I was alive, and that she and her husband would be driving out to Thistle House the next day. I sank to my knees on the wet grass, as overcome with emotion as I had been the day I lost her. Gwen had come out with Mac, and she dropped beside me, begging me to forgive her for not telling me that Julia had been to the house nearly a year before.

"But I knew Gwen owed me no apology. Everything was suddenly bright as a July noon, even though rain clouds spanned the horizon that morning. It was as if a great curtain that had been strung above me had fallen into a heap on the ground, and the sky was aflame with light. I could clearly see that fear and regret had made me so protective of Gwen, she had felt as if she were suffocating. That she'd had no desire to tell me about a stranger who had been by inquiring about a box of sketches had been my fault, not hers. And my inability to forgive myself for what I had done had made Julia an anonymous shadow to Gwen, a ghost whose name I never said nor allowed Mac to say. Gwen owed me nothing."

Isabel pauses a moment, as though gathering strength from the seconds of silence.

"I couldn't sleep the night before Julia was to come, so I had plenty of quiet hours to ponder my new reality. I had been Isabel longer than I had been Emmy, you see. No one knew me by any other name. And I had my Umbrella Girls by then. Emmy was no one. When Mac had reached out to Julia for me, he had to tell her who I had become. Who I was. And who I wasn't."

I shake my head. "But it's not true that Emmy was no one. *You're* Emmy."

"Am I?" Isabel looks intently into my eyes, as if seeking affirmation of some kind.

"Of course you are. None of this would've mattered if underneath that name you stole, you weren't who you've always been."

Isabel breaks into a wide smile. She looks like a proud parent whose child has figured something out.

"Right you are, Kendra. Right you are. But you can already guess I have been slow to realize what should have been clear to me the second I saw Julia again." She cocks her head to one side and I can see that she is remembering the moment she saw her sister after nearly two decades. I wait for her to tell me what it was like. A few moments later, she does.

"Mac led her into this room. I was sitting right here where I am now. She was so tall and beautiful. Taller than me, and looking so much like Mum, so very much like Mum. She wore a dress of pink with a ruby pendant at her neck. Had I passed her in the street and not seen her face, I might not have known her. But her eyes were locked on mine, and they were Julia's eyes. She ran into my arms as though no time had passed, as though she were simply rising from the sofa where I had left her, and there had been no war, no slow waltz of time, no silent years of longing. She was a little girl inside a grown woman's body, putting her arms around my neck, and saying the name Mum had given me—Emmy—over and over."

Isabel is looking past me, into that long-ago moment. A tear is slipping down my cheek and I finger it away.

"That was the happiest day of my life, Kendra. I did not think I would ever live to see the heaviness of losing Julia lifted from me."

I wait for her to tell me more. Several seconds later she continues.

"I was Emmy to her, not Isabel, but I really didn't know how to be Emmy to anyone else. Julia seemed to understand that I became Isabel so that I might find her and I stayed Isabel so that I would be able to live with myself when finding her proved impossible. She told me she had her own ways of coping with her mistakes and then she handed me the journal she had written to me."

Isabel raises her gaze to meet mine. "The journal answered many questions for me, and yet it raised new ones. If only I had gone to Mrs. Billingsley for help or answered the door when her butler came to the flat, either one would have told me that Thea had taken Julia to Neville's parents, and wouldn't I have been able to find her from the start? Or, if I had remembered Mum had gotten that letter from Neville's parents, wouldn't I have thought to look for it in the flat after Julia disappeared? Would I have figured out that since the letter was missing, someone had taken it? Or if I had been honest with Gwen from the start about who I really was, wouldn't she have known that the woman who came to Thistle House inquiring about an old box of bridal sketches was the sister that I had lost? Or if I had never tried to sneak away with those sketches in the first place, wouldn't Mum have lived?"

I see her terrible logic, but I also see that a larger force had been at work. "There was a war," I venture.

She nods slowly. "Yes. Strangely enough, war has a way of absolving us of the mistakes we make while in its dreadful shadow, but it keeps this absolution a secret. I didn't realize I was playing my cards against a cruel opponent that had its own cards to play."

We are quiet for a moment "So you remained Isabel, then," I say. "Even after you and Julia were reunited."

Isabel nods. "To all but family, yes. What is a name, really, but letters on a page, or a sound on the tongue? To the rest of the world, I was Isabel MacFarland, wife of the American writer, painter of the Umbrella Girls, half sister to a woman named Julia Waverly Massey."

"Is Julia here today?" I finally ask, even though somehow I can already sense she is not.

"No."

The word has never sounded more final to me.

Isabel continues as she strokes the cover of the journal. "Her son and daughter-in-law are here from York, and their three adult children and a great-granddaughter. Simon passed away five years ago. He married a lovely woman from Leeds many years after Julia was taken from us, but we stayed close, he and I. Losing her was very hard on Simon. He knew that I understood more than anyone what that loss felt like."

A sliver of silence rests between us. At last I ask, "What happened to her?"

"Breast cancer."

"I am so sorry."

She nods once, accepting my meager condolences,

and then turns her gaze to the Umbrella Girl just to her right. "You know, I tossed away twenty years of Julia's life, but I was given them back—all of them. She died twenty years after we found each other again. They were very happy years, Kendra. Happier than I could have imagined. Much was restored to me."

I am suddenly reminded of the letter in the bedside table that Charlotte had mentioned. I ask her if she wants me to know what it said.

"It was from my half brother, Colin. He had traced me to Charlotte's in 1956 and written to her to see if I might possibly be willing to communicate with him. Start fresh. His mother had died and I was the only family he had. Imagine that."

"And did you?"

She smiles, sniffs the air, and points to the open window. "Tell me, do you see a stooped old man sitting by the hydrangeas, smoking a pipe?"

I rise from the sofa, cross to the window, and peer out. In addition to party streamers, children on the lawn, and rows of fruit trees, I see on the terrace an elderly man puffing on a pipe. I catch a whiff of fruity tobacco. "I see him."

"That's my brother, Colin Thorne. Half of the children on the lawn are his great-grandchildren, and their parents are my nieces and nephews."

"Was it hard to forgive Colin for what happened that day you were at your father's house?" I ask, and then I wish I hadn't. It was far too personal a question.

"Colin had done nothing that required my forgiveness. I'm the one who chose to believe he wanted me to be paid off so that I would leave the Thornes alone."

"And that's not what he wanted?"

"What he wanted was a relationship with his half

sister. He thought the inheritance that our father had left me would be the overture to begin having it. I never gave him a chance."

"But then you did."

"Again, I think Providence was prodding me to mend the brokenness where I could. When I arrived at Thistle House in 1958, the place was a tumbledown mess, slipping into ruin and in need of extensive repairs that I couldn't afford to make. Before I even contacted Colin, I was thinking I would have to sell the place. When I agreed to meet him in Oxford for tea—on the very day Julia came to the house, no less—he handed me the bankbook for what he had done with my original inheritance. It had more than quadrupled in value. And he insisted I take it. Not as payment for anything I had done or hadn't done, but because our father had given it to me.

"That money allowed me to make the needed repairs to Thistle House and, strangely enough, gave Mac and me a haven in which to reconnect with each other. Mac came to realize that part of the reason I wanted to remain Isabel to the outside world was because of him—because she was the woman he loved. He was also a forgiving man and always had been. So while he was ready to love me as Emmy, he saw how much a stranger Emmy was to me. And as I said a few moments ago, I saw no compelling reason to resurrect her. Graham Dabney had died some years earlier and his widow had remarried. They were the only family Eloise Crofton had and who could've possibly appeared out of the blue to challenge my maiden name, which I didn't even use anymore. Mac was able to write a whole new series of books here, and we ended up selling our house in Saint Paul and making Thistle House our permanent home. Mac and Colin became very good friends. I think each having the other to talk to was good for them. They both knew who I had been before and I think they found a kinship because of that."

Isabel smiles easily as a memory slips across her mind. "Reconnecting with my brother allowed me to learn who my father was. I knew his faults—who of us doesn't have those?—but I knew nothing of his merits, if I may call them that. I don't think he planned to seduce Mum when she was a young maid in his house. They were both starving for love and affirmation. When you are hungry for something, you often do not use your best judgment. I know that better than anyone. After Agnes died, Colin found personal papers that belonged to our father, which led him to believe Henry really did love Mum and perhaps, me, too. But Henry Thorne had been a slave to his position in society. He saw no other way to provide for me and Mum than by paying her rent, giving her money for food and clothes, and adding me to his will. Even when Mum was with Neville, my father still supported her. He wasn't a terrible person, nor was Mum. They made choices, some good, some bad. Just like I did. And then they had to live with those choices, just as I had to live with mine. And as you will have to live with yours."

At that moment my recorder clicks off. I've run the battery down to nothing. We both look at it.

"I suppose that means I've given you enough material for your essay," Isabel says.

It is a comment made to make us both laugh. We do. But it also calls to attention that just as I came to this house with a goal in mind, Isabel MacFarland surely agreed to this interview for a reason of her own.

"You want me to do something for you, don't you?"

I ask. "That's why you said yes to an interview about the war when you've never said yes before."

Her gaze is tight on mine. "I do."

A thin ribbon of silence stretches before us and then I ask her what she wants from me.

"I want you to secure one of those five spots in the London paper."

I laugh lightly. "But that's not up to me. I—"

"It most certainly is up to you. Write the essay as if your life depends on it. Stay up late writing and rewriting it. Make it the most compelling paper you have ever written. I very much want it in the newspaper."

"Isabel, I can't *make* my professor choose my paper. I can't—"

Again she cuts me off.

"I wouldn't have agreed to this chat if I didn't think you have the ability to secure one of those spots. You're not the only one who has been interviewing today. I have been listening to everything you say as intently as you've been listening to me. I have chosen you to write down my history. You are the one who will give me what I've wanted all my life now that I am at the end of it."

For a moment or two I can only stare at her in confusion. I can't resurrect her long-dead bridal gown career or her deceased sister. And I can't give her anything in a newspaper article except perhaps the return of her real name.

But that is not what she's wanted all her life.

She inclines her head toward me, coaxing me to remember all that she has told me from the history of her life in the short time I have spent with her. What did she always want? What did she want before she found Julia?

Before she lost Julia?

Before she sketched the first wedding gown?

Before she stood on a sunny beach with her toes in the sand and her mum at her side?

"You wanted your mother to be proud of you," I whisper.

Isabel nods once as tears rim her eyes.

"You can give Mum the honor of having flesh and blood and a name again. I want people to know the sacrifices she made for me and Julia. Anne Louise Downtree is a forgotten soul, Kendra. She is nothing but a three-word entry in the record of the war's dead, remembered by no one except me, her daughter, Emmeline. I don't know that she can see me from where she is, but if she can, I want her to view me as I stand at the end of my existence. I want her to see that I understand there are no secrets to a charmed life. There is just the simple truth that you must forgive yourself for only being able to make your own choices, and no one else's."

Astounded at what she is suggesting I am able to do for her, I hesitate a moment before responding. "If I'm going to write this paper the way you'd like, I need to know why you've waited until now. You've had more than fifty years to come clean about who you are."

"I'm not the historian you are. All these years I've failed to see what you historians already know. I'm an old woman and I have a grand opportunity with you, so I'd best take advantage of it."

"What do you mean, 'what historians already know'?"

"Surely you've not forgotten what you said about history when you first walked into this room, Kendra?" She is half grinning at me, half frowning.

I think back to when I had arrived a few hours ago and Isabel and I were talking about the value of recording the past. I had asked her what was the good in remembering an event if you didn't remember how it made you feel. How it impacted others. How it made them feel. You would learn nothing.

"You want to pass on what you have learned, don't you?" I say.

"Well, aside from the fact that it seems a good thing to do, I think Mum would want me to. I think she would be proud of me if I did."

I let her answer settle over me for a moment. "This is just one article in one newspaper. I'm afraid you will be disappointed."

"A great many movements have begun from one article in one newspaper. I am only responsible for my own choices. I am choosing to tell my story, Kendra. Who listens to it is not my burden. Telling it is."

We hear a knock at the door and then Beryl pokes her head inside. "Everyone's here. It's time for the party, Auntie."

"We'll be right out, Beryl." Isabel turns to me. "You will stay, won't you? There are people you need to meet."

"I would like that very much."

She rises a bit unsteadily and I move quickly to help her. Isabel thanks me when she is firm on her feet, and then draws a manicured hand gently across her brow to brush away a stray strand of hair. "How do I look for a ninety-three-year-old?"

"I'd say you don't look a day over ninety."

Isabel tips her head back and laughs. "Julia would have liked you, Kendra. Oh my. Yes, she would have."

"I would've liked her, too."

Her laugh ebbs away but her grin remains. "I've been a coward most of my life, you know."

At first I say nothing. Sages of the past would say we

are—all of us—just imperfect people on a flawed planet who are trying to hold on to what is good and lovely and right.

"On the contrary," I finally reply, "I think history will prove that Emmeline Downtree was actually very brave, considering all that she had to endure."

Isabel regards me thoughtfully, then crinkles an eyebrow in contemplation before reaching for my arm. "Shall we?"

We make our way down the hall, into the kitchen, and through the laundry room, where the garden door is ajar and sounds of celebration are skipping on the breeze. On the threshold, the eyes of those who have been waiting for the guest of honor turn expectantly toward us. Among the many faces, I see Professor Briswell, standing a few feet away from a woman who looks very much like a younger version of Isabel, as well as more than a dozen happy children who've not a clue what war is like.

As we pass the open door's window, a bit of lace curtain lifts on a ribbon of air, caresses the back of Isabel's neck, and then falls away like a discarded bridal veil.

We step out onto the terrace and the people, young and old, begin to sing.

ACKNOWLEDGMENTS

NO work of historical fiction can be written without the assistance and expertise of others, and this has never been truer for me than with this book.

Thank you, Tim and Joyce Norris of Stow-on-the-Wold, for your friendship, for arranging all those interviews at the British Legion, for the many e-mails sent and received, and for answering my relentless questions. Next time the tapas are on me.

Thank you, Tom and Judy Hyde, for your sweet hospitality: for the fish and chips; for letting me meet your mates, share a pint with them, play a game of dice, and talk about what it was like to be a child in a time of war. And, Penny Culliford, thank you for the many helps with this and that, and for the lovely cabaret show at Battersea.

Many thanks to my amazingly gifted editor, Ellen Edwards, for your insights into what affirms life and satisfies the soul, and for knowing when I needed to dig deeper into the hearts of these characters.

Thank you, Professor Margaret Dyson of the University of California, San Diego, for helping me understand the basics of child psychology in the early 1940s, and to British author and historian Julie Summers, thank you for sharing with me your expertise on the evacuation of London's children.

To my mother, friend, and proofreader extraordinaire, Judy Horning, thank you for accompanying me on an unforgettable research trip to Gloucestershire; for poring over the research materials at the Imperial War Museum in London; for trudging in the rain, cheerfully jumping onto countless trains, and, of course, reading the raw manuscript.

The following works opened to me the world of London at war and I am grateful: Amy Helen Bell's *London Was Ours*, Ben Wicks's *No Time to Wave Goodbye*, Julie Summers's *When the Children Came Home*, Lynne Olson's *Citizens of London*; Peter Stansky's *The First Day of the Blitz*, Mark Bernstein and Alex Lubertozzi's *World War II on the Air*, Philip Ziegler's *London at War*, Jessica Mann's *Out of Harm's Way*; Stanley Cloud and Lynne Olson's *The Murrow Boys: Pioneers on the Front Lines of Broadcast Journalism*.

And to those Britons who shared your war stories with me, I know how timeless some of those memories are to you, even all these many years later. I saw it in your eyes. Grateful thanks are extended especially to Jean Ashton, Eddie Warren, Ron Bockhart, Maj. Gen. Clive Beckett, Dorothy Donald, Faith Jaggard, Colin Mayes, and Roy Holloway.

SECRETS

of a

CHARMED LIFE

SUSAN MEISSNER

A CONVERSATION WITH SUSAN MEISSNER

Q. This novel is quite different from your previous book,
A Fall of Marigolds. *What inspired you to write it?*

A. I've long been intrigued by the evacuation of London's children into the English countryside at the start of World War Two. Many of these kids were separated from their parents and lived with foster families for the entire five years of the war. As a mother of four, I found that cut me to the core. I can't help but imagine how hard it must have been for those London mothers to relinquish their children even though to have them remain in the city was just as terrible an option. As I began to research the evacuation and then the Blitz that followed, and as I talked to people who were either evacuated or who had survived the bombings, I discovered how truly devastating the Blitz was, and yet how resilient Londoners were. This was a city of civilians, not of military troops, and the bombing of it was relentless. Every person that lived through this time had a story of survival. I wanted to imagine what one of those stories might have been like.

Q. *This story of two sisters becoming separated during the war depends on a complex series of events—any one of which could have gone the other way, and brought the sisters back together again. In your mind, does fate or providence determine the outcome?*

A. That is such a great question. If we say fate means a person can't change what will happen by what he or she does, then I'd have to say fate doesn't seem to be a player in this novel. Actually, I think any great story is peopled by characters who *do* have the power to effect change, and it's what they do with that power—or don't do—that keeps us turning the pages. I think that's true for everyone's life story. The way I see it, we play the cards we've been dealt—as Isabel in *Secrets of a Charmed Life* says—based on finite knowledge, and while being largely unaware that everyone around us is playing their own cards. Their cards mingle with ours, and the outcome of our played hand affects and is affected by their played hand. I believe we've been given free will to choose and that God in his providence sees all and knows all but doesn't do all. When Emmy ponders so many years later the owl that hoots outside her window and wakes her sister the night they steal away back to London, she sees it as the providential hand of God giving her an opportunity not to make a choice that would prove disastrous. God doesn't make the decision for her; she does. That is the terrifying beauty of free moral choice. Every choice Emmy, Julia, Annie, Gwen, and Isabel make is affected by all the other choices made around them.

Q. At only fifteen, Emmy is determined to become a designer of wedding dresses. She is so focused and talented, yet life takes her in a very different direction. So many of us share her experience in that the dreams we have for our lives during our formative years never come to fruition. Yet popular culture in this country tells us again and again that we can make all our dreams come true. Was it your intention to explore this contradiction in the novel?

A. I think one of the more overly simplistic and faulty mantras of our day and age is that if you just believe in your abilities, you can achieve anything you want. Emmy has a rather idealistic view of life when the novel opens, and those pristine images of the perfect dress for the perfect day for the beginning of the perfect life are emblematic of a dream that at face value is a bit self-centered, unrealistic, and nearsighted. That's one of the subtleties of following dreams when the life goal is solely based on you and what *you* want out of life. There is wisdom in the quote by Ralph Waldo Emerson that "Life is a journey, not a destination." It's easy to miss all the amazing things that come your way if you are chasing only the dream, and that's all you see or want. I think Emmy comes to realize this by the novel's end.

Q. I found Emmy's relationship with her mother particularly well-done, and heartbreaking. Can you tell us a little about how that relationship took shape?

A. When the novel was first evolving, and even in the completed first draft, Emmy's mother, Annie, was a throwaway character that I felt I didn't need to spend much time on; I didn't think she would advance the plot beyond the few scenes she was in, and I wrongly assumed it was more compelling to have Emmy not need or want her mother's approval than the other way around. But the more I probed into what Emmy really wants out of life, the more I saw that her relationship with her mum is the key to unlocking Emmy's deepest desire. I also saw that this profound need for her mother's affirmation is more universal than just the yearning to be a successful designer. I'm hoping it will resonate with many readers.

Q. On one level, the novel explores the very long-lasting trauma inflicted on two ordinary girls as a result of the war. In your research, did you get a sense of the many ways in which the war reverberated in the lives of ordinary Britons?

A. I interviewed more than a dozen Britons about their experiences during the war, and I was struck every time by how swiftly these survivors were transported back to those years, seven decades after they'd lived through them. I could see in their faces, in their eyes, in their voices, how impactful the war had been for them as young children. It was by no means an easy time, but they all seemed to recall the same spirit of resilience that I caught onto while reading the letters and memoirs of those who had been adults during the war, and who had already passed. The call to Keep Calm and Carry On was truly the rallying cry for these ordinary Britons. When I'd ask them how they'd managed to get through such a devastating time, more than one answered, "Well, you just had to. What was the alternative? When you are called upon to survive, that is what you do."

Q. *Your historical novels always include a section set in contemporary times that often frames the past story. Has that structure naturally evolved over your writing career, or was it an early deliberate choice? What does that structure in particular allow you to achieve?*

A. This kind of structure as a brand for me came about by accident. In 2008, I wrote *The Shape of Mercy*, not my first novel but the first to be constructed as a historical story framed by a contemporary tale. That book went on to be named one of *Publishers Weekly*'s top one hundred novels for 2008. I found I enjoyed having a contemporary story and a historical one collide in an interesting way so that the characters in the current day are changed by something they learn from past events. I think this is largely the reason why we, as a society, archive our history. We don't want to forget where we've been and what we've seen. The past informs us, and can easily transform us, if we choose to let it.

Q. *Despite the many novels I've read and films I've seen about England during World War Two, this book made me more keenly aware of how widespread the bombing was. Was that a surprise to you, too?*

A. In the early stages of plotting *Secrets of a Charmed Life*, I read Kate Atkinson's wonderful novel *Life After Life*, the first of many eye-opening books I read about the bombing of London. Yes, I was astonished at how little I had been aware of the extent of the attack on Britain, especially because I had lived in England in the late 1980s and early 1990s. My United States Air Force husband was stationed at an RAF base in Oxfordshire for three years and I had been to London and the Cotswolds many times, and yet I left England without having thoroughly understood the toll that the war had taken on its citizens so many years before. I think this is the danger we face whenever time passes and those who have suffered recover from what flattened them. The generation coming up behind might underestimate or miss completely all that the older generation survived.

Q. What would you especially like readers to take away from Secrets of a Charmed Life?

A. The title, which I love, is meant to cause the reader to wonder if there really are secrets to living a life that has happily-ever-after written all over it. The title seems to suggest there are hidden truths to being able to have everything you've always wanted. But in actuality, and what I hope readers will take away, is that a happy life is not made up of what you have dreamed of, chased after, and achieved, but rather whom you poured your life into, who poured their life into yours, and the difference you've made in the lives of others. Most of the dreams we pursue don't have intrinsic worth, but people always do. It's not a perfect world, and we can only play our own hand of cards—if you will—but if we play the hand as best we can, with love for others as the motivation, I think we can rest content.

Q. *Can you tell us about your next novel?*

A. My next novel is set primarily in Hollywood's golden age, specifically in 1939 when a treasure trove of timeless movies was released. *Gone With the Wind*, *The Wizard of Oz*, and *Wuthering Heights* are just three of them. I want to explore the idea that "the world is full of magic things, patiently waiting for our senses to grow sharper," a quote by W. B. Yeats that I love. Old Hollywood, with its beautifully contrived sets and back lots, excelled in catering to a sense of enchantment. No one knew that it was an era in its twilight years and that the advent of television would change everything. I envision two young women coming to Hollywood to seek purpose and notoriety— what they deem are the essentials of a fulfilling life. And both women gain what they seek, but in ways neither would have ever guessed. First, though, their senses must grow sharper. And when they do, the real transformation happens.

QUESTIONS FOR DISCUSSION

1. What did you enjoy most about *Secrets of a Charmed Life*? What do you think will stay with you?

2. Would you describe the novel as a story about sisters or a story about mothers and daughters?

3. Discuss the secrets that the characters keep from one another. What facts does Annie hide from her daughters? What do Emmy and Julia not tell the men they eventually marry? What does Charlotte keep to herself, and when does she finally reveal the truth? Can you think of even more secrets in the novel?

4. How is this book different from other books you've read about World War Two?

5. Describing Emmy, Susan Meissner writes in the novel, "She stood at a crossroads, half-aware that her choice would send her down a path from which there could be no turning back. But instead of two choices, she saw only

one—because it was all she really wanted to see. . . ." Has there ever been a time when you couldn't see the other choices open to you?

6. Later in her life Julia writes in her journal: "Fear does not start to fade until you take the step that you think you can't." Do you agree? What is Julia afraid of when she writes this?

7. How similar or dissimilar are Emmy and her mother? Does Emmy have an accurate view of the kind of person her mother is?

8. Isabel tells Kendra that there are no secrets to a charmed life. There is only the task of forgiving ourselves for being able to make only our own choices, and no one else's. What do you think she means by this?

9. What do the sketches of brides' dresses represent to Emmy?

10. What are Emmy's reasons for choosing to remain Isabel throughout her adult life? Would you have done the same?

11. Did you find the novel ultimately uplifting and inspiring? Why, or why not?

12. On one level, the novel is about losing something very precious. What's the most precious thing you've ever lost? What were the consequences?

13. Have you ever lived through a time of war, or of social chaos? It might have been a major life-threatening event, or merely an unsettling situation. Would you like to share your experience? How does it compare to what Emmy and Julia go through?

Photo by Amber Dawn

A native of San Diego, **Susan Meissner** is a former managing editor of a weekly newspaper and an award-winning columnist. She has published fifteen novels with New American Library, Harvest House, and WaterBook, divisions of Penguin Random House. She lives in San Diego with her husband and has four grown children.